Blood Wedding

*To the memory of
Dr Jacqueline Frances Roddick O'Brien,
an inspired writer, who, had she lived,
would have made a fine novelist.*

BLOOD WEDDING

P J Brooke

CONSTABLE • LONDON

The lines from 'Lord of the Dance' by Sydney Carter are reproduced by kind permission of Stainer and Bell Ltd, London, England. They were first published in *Greenprint for Song*, Stainer and Bell, 1974, and then in *Lord of the Dance, and other Songs and Poems*, Stainer and Bell, 2003.
Excerpts of Spanish-language works by Federico García Lorca © Herederos de Federico García Lorca from Obras Completas (Galaxia/Gutenberg, 1996 edition). English-language translations © Translators and Herederos de Federico García Lorca. All rights reserved. For information regarding rights and permissions, please contact lorca@artslaw.co.uk or William Peter Kosmas, 8 Franklin Square, London W14 9UU.

Constable & Robinson Ltd
3 The Lanchesters, 162 Fulham Palace Road, London W6 9ER
www.constablerobinson.com

First published in the UK by Constable, an imprint of Constable & Robinson, 2008

First US edition published by SohoConstable, an imprint of Soho Press, 2008

Soho Press, Inc., 853 Broadway, New York, NY 10003
www.sohopress.com

A copy of the British Library Cataloguing in Publication
Data is available from the British Library

UK ISBN: 978-1-84529-741-1
US ISBN: 978-1-56947-529-4
US Library of Congress number: 2008019894

Printed and bound in the EU
1 3 5 7 9 10 8 6 4 2

Chapter 1

It was Thursday, market day in Diva. A breeze from the Sierra Nevada tempered the burning Spanish sun. The town was hungry, rationing enforced. The people, silent, bought what they could afford. They looked at no one. Carmelo, the young herdsman, eyes alert for danger, crossed the street. No Guardias, Franco's fascist police. His buying done, he walked down the Río Sierra path, and turned right along the track towards El Fugón. He checked he was alone, hid his sack of food in the hollow trunk of an olive tree, looked around again, and continued down the track.

The guerrilla leader, Manuel Paz, El Gato, stepped lightly across the field of red poppies towards the olive tree. He sniffed the air: there was a faint smell of the harsh black-tobacco Gitanes. He reached for his gun.

'Fire,' shouted the officer. A volley rang out. The force knocked El Gato back. He fell among the flowers. Capitán Vicente González stepped up to the body, blood still seeping from the wounds, and kicked it hard.

'That's another Red bandit dead. Gracias a Dios.'

It was the feast of San Juan de Dios, 1947.

Leila smiled as she saved and closed the file on her computer. 'That's better. More fun than the thesis,' she said to herself.

It was Thursday, market day in Diva. A breeze from the Sierra Nevada tempered the burning Spanish sun. Leila quickly crossed the square in search of shade. She had arranged with Hassan to take the bus up the mountain. A

1

crowd, shopping bags full, lined the street outside the bus office. Hassan came round the corner. They smiled at each other. The bus from Granada pulled in and a mob of elderly ladies surged forward to grab the available seats. Leila and Hassan just managed to find two seats together. Crowded, noisy and overloaded, the bus took off up the steep, winding road.

'You're looking good,' he said.

'Thanks.'

'How's the thesis going?'

'Great. Some fantastic interviews. Loads of new material. Did you know, this place really was in the front line of resistance to Franco?'

'Really?'

'Absolutely. There were guerrillas holding out for ages . . . in the hills just over there.'

Tentatively she put her hand on his. He moved it away gently. She looked out of the window, across the valley, and then upward: scraps of snow still sparkled in the highest valleys.

'Will you be at the "Stop the War" demo next week?' he asked.

'Sure. Dad's on the platform again.'

They got off the bus, and took a path that climbed steeply. The old mule track crossed a few streams, winding its way round the mountain. The air was sweet with wild thyme and rosemary, cooking in the midday sun. Olive trees lined the path. They passed a mulberry tree.

'Hey, look what the Moors left us!'

'Huh?'

'They planted them to feed the silkworms – this was one of the world's most important silk-producing areas. The Granada weavers once exported to Damascus.'

'Yes, Leila . . . but that's ancient history. Muslims are suffering today. In Palestine. In Iraq.'

'But if you don't understand what's gone before, you won't get things right now. Will you?'

2

'Okay. Point taken.'

The mulberries were ripe. Hassan scrambled down the gorge to the mulberry tree.

'Careful. Don't fall.'

'Don't worry. I've been working out.'

He reached up to the lower branches, and began to gather the mulberries. The sun glinted on the hair of his forearms. 'Here.'Leila smiled. 'These are so good.'

The juice from the berries stained their hands purple. She glanced at Hassan's lips, smudged with rich juice.

'Hey, wait. Just like that,' said Hassan. He took out his camera, and photographed her laughing at her mulberry-stained hands.

'Let's eat.' Leila sat down, took off the small rucksack, pulled out a flask, unscrewed the top, poured mineral water into the cup, and handed it to Hassan.

'Go easy on the water. We may need it later on.'

She took out olives, cheese and bread. Silently they ate, looking across the valley to the mountains beyond. Leila stretched out on the bank, and gazed up at the silver leaves of the olive tree. Now and again a bird chirped. 'Cool, eh? A bit of paradise.'

She sat up and smiled at him. Hassan's gaze became more intense. Leila glanced at him again. The sun, filtered by the leaves of the olive tree, streaked across his face and lit up the mulberry juice around his mouth. All she could see were his eyes, luminous. She stroked his cheek. Her fingers ran round the outside of his eyes and along his lips. He froze.

'Leila, don't tease. You know I can't get involved – I've got really important things to do at the Centre.'

Leila laughed. 'More board reports to write then?'

'No, but it's important.'

'Oh? So what is it then?'

'It's . . .' Hassan faltered, and quickly added, 'We'd better go. I can't be late for my lift back.'

They set off down the path. She brushed his hand, but he pulled away.

3

'Will you be at prayers tomorrow?' she asked, more upset than she cared to admit.

'Maybe.'

They reached the Café Paraíso, its large 'Stop the War' banner covering half the front wall. Javeed was waiting. The car horn tooted.

'Need a lift?' Hassan asked.

'No, that's all right. It's not far. But thanks all the same.'

Javeed made Leila uncomfortable: there was something taut and hard about him.

She waved as Hassan got into the car, then she walked slowly back to her father's house.

'Dad, it's me.' She entered his study.

'Hello, dear. Had a good day?'

'So-so. Went for a walk with Hassan. He's really sweet. But . . . he does go on and on about how important his work is at the Centre. Then when I ask him about it, he just clams up.'

'Leila, I'm sure Javeed is doing excellent work. A European Training Centre for young Muslim entrepreneurs is quite a breakthrough.'

'Maybe.'

'Give him time. Zaida thinks he's really keen on you.'

'Hmm. Okay, dad. What are you doing?'

'Making a few notes for my talk tomorrow. The graffiti by the mosque has upset some of our people.'

'But we're okay here, aren't we? Remember when you came back from your first visit. You couldn't stop talking about this valley – a little bit of paradise, you said.'

'Maybe less so now. Sub-Inspector Max Romero wants to see me. He's coming on Saturday for a chat.'

'That's nice. He's cute.'

'Cute? Leila, he's a police officer. It's not respectful.'

'Dad, please! What time is he coming?'

'About five. He asked after you. He said his grandmother is enjoying your interviews.'

'Me too – she's a gold mine! She even knew Lorca.'

The next day, Friday, was prayer day. Just before one, the muezzin gave the traditional call: '*Allahu akbar*! *Allahu akbar*! God is great! God is great! Come to prayers. Come to prayers. I testify that God is the divinity. That there is no other God but God, and that Muhammad is his messenger. *La ilhaha illa Laah*! There is no God but God!'

Leila found the simplicity of the call comforting. She hurried to the mosque, slipped off her sandals, placed them in the rack, and padded into the small female washroom. It smelled of bleach and floor soap. At the one cold tap, she washed her hands three times, then face, mouth and nostrils. Feet last, according to ritual. Refreshed, she climbed the staircase to the women's balcony, overlooking the prayer hall. She used to resent this separation of male and female, but now accepted it. She looked down at the prayer hall with its plain, whitewashed walls and the arch facing Mecca, a small wooden platform and a plain chair placed within it. To the left was a framed print with the ninety-nine names of God written in classical Arabic, and to the right a row of brown pots on the shelf around the prayer niche. The hall was filling up now. But still no sign of Hassan.

Leila glanced down at her father, Ahmed. He stood up, and began the *khutabah*: 'We created human beings in order to test them with suffering. Do people think that no one has power over them? They boast, "We are so rich that we can afford to waste riches." Do they think that no one observes them?'

The door opened and Hassan slid in, late. He made no effort to glance up at the balcony. After prayers, Leila joined the women and children for their communal meal of rice, small fish and spiced lentils, while the men ate in the other dining room. She wanted to talk to Hassan, but couldn't go next door before the meal was over. The meal ended, she slipped next door. Hassan was alone in the corner.

'Hi.'

'Oh. Hi.'

'Good walk, wasn't it?'

'Yeah. It was good.'

'The mulberries were great. Thanks.'

'No problem.'

'The Abdel Karim band are in Granada next week. Some friends are trying to get tickets. Would you like to go?'

Hassan clenched his hands together. 'Look. Er . . . Javeed has talked to me. I've got important things to do. He says it's b—b—best if I don't go out with you again.'

'What! I thought you liked me! Can't you decide anything for yourself?'

'Leila. Please!'

Leila's voice rose angrily. 'Hassan, this is stupid. Sit there. I'll get some tea, and we'll talk this through.'

The whole room was looking at them. Leila ducked through the roses on the arch, and went into the kitchen. A few minutes later she returned with two cups of mint tea on a tray. Hassan had left. Leila banged the tray down on the table.

'Damn you. Damn you.' And then, caught in Zaida's stare, she flushed crimson, and muttered, 'Gotta go.'

Leila stomped up the hill to her father's house. He wasn't in. She went to her room, and opened her thesis notes. But she couldn't concentrate. She needed to get out. She walked down the hill and then up to El Gato, the foreign hippies' bar. She hadn't tasted alcohol for months. The barman gave her an inquisitive look.

'A Coke, please.'

She took the Coke, and retreated to the far corner. The bar filled up quickly. She recognized one of the men. He smiled at her, and she smiled back.

'Never expected to see you here.'

'Just Coke.' She lifted up her glass.

'You're looking a bit upset?'

'Not really. Just angry with someone who can't decide things for himself.'

6

'Can I join you?'

'Sure.'

'I'm Jim.'

'Leila. I'm Ahmed's daughter, over from Edinburgh.'

'Ahmed. Oh, sure. I like your dad. He spoke at the peace rally in Granada. He's good.'

Jim was a bit scruffy even by local standards, not what you would call good-looking. But okay. She had seen him with a wife or at least a regular. Never again a married man.

'We're having a gig, an Irish night, down at Felipe's. Fancy coming?'

'Yeah. Why not?'

'That's good. I said I'd be there before eleven. Another Coke?'

'Please. Without ice.'

Jim returned with the Coke, and a San Miguel beer. 'How long you here for?'

'Until the beginning of October. Have to be back in Edinburgh for the start of term to see my supervisor. Hey. Know why this bar is called El Gato?'

'The Cat?'

'El Gato was the nickname of the guerrilla leader here after the Civil War. He escaped to France towards the end of the Civil War, and then came back home to set up resistance to Franco. Got shot in 1947.'

Jim was a good listener. Within five minutes she was telling him everything about her thesis.

'Jesus! Look at the time – it's nearly eleven. We have to go.' He took her round the corner to his battered van. 'Sorry about the mess. The Ferrari's in the garage.'

Leila laughed. The van clattered down the road to Felipe's bar in the orange groves at the edge of town.

Inside Felipe's, Jim took out his bodhran, the Irish finger drum, and started to play . . . first a steady pulse, then faster and faster, driving the fiddles and flute on and on. Couples got up to dance, swirling round and round. Leila began clapping, shyly at first, then louder and louder, faster and faster. A guy asked her to dance. Soon the wooden floor was shaking. Another dance. Another partner. Leila sank breathlessly into her seat. And then got up to dance again and again.

'Let's see the dawn in, at El Fugón,' shouted Jim.

They all staggered into cars and vans, and then drove off through the town to the valley of El Fugón. In a few minutes a bonfire was blazing. The music started again, this time, plaintive, sad Irish tunes, Jim's voice drifting like smoke.

Everyone was silent, waiting for the sun's rays to crest the mountains and fill the valley. She hadn't seen Jim most of the night. He came over.

'I'm for my bed. Fancy joining me?'

Leila laughed, not offended. 'Thanks, but no.'

'Sure? You look like you could do with a good hug.'

'Maybe another time, Jim.'

'I've a spare bed. You can kip down there.'

The spare bed was a single mattress in the back of the van. In five minutes she was asleep, snoring heavily.

She slept until the early afternoon, woken by the stifling heat inside the van. Jim was up, brewing tea on a gas ring.

Leila looked at her watch. 'Help! It's nearly two. My dad will have a search party out for me in a minute. Oh no . . . I should have called back and said not to wait up for me. I didn't tell him I'd be staying over. I have to get back. I'll phone him now.'

'Don't worry. I'll give you a lift home. I'm off to the beach this afternoon. Fancy coming?' said Jim.

'Maybe some other time. But not now. Gotta make peace with dad.'

Jim drove slowly. The springs had nearly all gone. Leila held on to the van door handle to lessen the bumps.

She pointed: 'See that hollow olive tree over there . . . it's haunted. It's where they shot El Gato.'

Leila jumped out at the traffic lights. She failed to notice Zaida's black look. The women often disapproved. *Inmodestia* was just the polite term they used to describe her. When

8

she got home, her father was out. She called him on his mobile and left a message to confirm she was home, then went straight to her computer, her mind racing with ideas. She typed fast, and this time the El Gato story just seemed to flow.

She smiled. With luck she might finish early next year.

She clicked on Save, then Turn Off, waited a minute and then shutdown the computer.

After showering and washing her hair, she put on her new linen trousers, white silk tunic, flat gold sandals and her mother's turquoise earrings, carefully arranging her head-scarf so a few black curls framed her oval face. A breath of fresh air might help. She closed the door behind her and set off down the Jola road. There was a slight breeze. The green figs were out, hanging over the irrigation canals alongside the road. She passed a garden with a little girl on a swing. Back and forth. Back and forth. *De norte al sur de sur a norte.* A mother's voice called, 'Jane. Jane. Get off that swing, come and get ready. It's nearly five. We have to leave for the airport right now.'

Leila smiled and waved to the girl. 'Hello, Jane,' she called out. 'Got another silly rhyme for you!

> "My young friend Jane
> Is leaving Spain.
> We think that's an awful pain.
> But we're both sure you'll come again."'

Jane stopped, giggled, waved and then ran inside.

Leila walked on quickly. As she crossed the road bridge, the sky suddenly darkened. Leila looked up at the mountains. Dark, pregnant-bellied clouds were drifting down lower and lower. A colder breeze blew. The tops of the mountains disappeared. Rain. Sullenly, persistently the rain fell. Leila stopped, turned, and walked quickly back. A car stopped at the ravine bridge.

'Get in,' a voice called.

Leila approached the car. 'Oh, it's you.'

She got into the car. It was exactly five in the afternoon.

On the same day, Saturday, at exactly five in the afternoon, Sub-Inspector Max Romero arrived at the house of Ahmed Mahfouz.

Chapter 2

A cinco de la tarde.
Eran las cinco en punto de la tarde.

At five in the afternoon.
It was exactly five in the afternoon.

Frederico García Lorca, *La cogida y la muerte*
(*The Goring and the Death*)

Thank God it's Friday. Practically the whole weekend off, thought Max. He looked at his watch. It was time to leave. What to wear . . .? Meeting Ahmed tomorrow. Leila might be there. Okay, pack the light grey Paul Smith shirt, and the Pedro de Hierro charcoal jeans. He checked the mirror. Not bad. His mother's Scottish blue eyes, and his father's aquiline Spanish looks stared back at him. 'Not the face of a cop,' Davila had once said critically. Max regarded that as a compliment.

He picked up the briefing from his boss, Inspector Jefe Enrique Davila of el Grupo de Homicidios de Granada, from the table, and glanced at it again. 'Inspectora Jefe Linda Concha and Inspector Martín Sánchez from the Anti-Terrorist Group, el Comisario General de Información, (CGI), have confirmed they are due to arrive at Granada Airport, Thursday, 31st July 2003 at 14.00 hours. Be on time, and dress smartly. Remember, the Prime Minister himself has stated the fight against terrorism is top priority and surveillance of Muslims must be stepped up.'

Max sighed. Could be worse. Madrid was sending Linda. It would be nice to see her again. She'd been a good tutor. Her presentation on the new terrorist threats had been good – perceptive and funny. And she'd joined him for a beer and tapas most lunchtimes. But this 'increased surveillance of Muslims' was really going to change his liaison role with la Brigada de Participación Ciudadano. It had taken months to develop good relationships with the different Muslim groups, and it could all go down the pan.

As he shut the door of his flat he glanced up at the Alhambra, and the Sierra Nevada mountains behind the fortress walls. He walked down the street, la Calderería Nueva, then along crumbling Calle Elvira. He crossed Gran Vía, dodging traffic, roadworks and tour groups. The police car park was past the fountains of la Plaza Trinidad, just behind the Faculty of Law and the old Botanic Gardens.

It wasn't a good idea to walk so far in the heat. By the time he reached his old Peugeot he was really sweating. He got into the car: the seat was hot enough to fry an egg.

At least the new motorway cut the journey from Granada to Diva to less than an hour, and once out of Granada the air should freshen. Clear of the city, Max put on a CD by his mother's group, the Maxwell Consort. 'Time stands still, and gazes on her face,' sang the soprano soloist. He immediately felt calmer. The mountains in the late afternoon sun were sentinels to another world: one where police procedures and violence had no part. The comment from his boss, 'Are you sure you're in the right job?', still rankled. He had to be on his guard all the time in the police. The old guys dismissed the fast track graduate programme as liberal wankers who knew shit about real police work. Max's sharp tongue hadn't endeared him either.

Perhaps he would see Leila for a coffee again. She was a real beauty. Bright and funny as well. He wondered how her interviews were going. His family never talked about the Civil War, though the Romero clan had done well under Franco.

He passed the first houses in Diva and turned right, down the Río Sierra track towards his little summer cottage, *el cortijo*. He smiled as he remembered telling his Scottish friends that he, or rather, his grandmother, had bought a *cortijo*. They thought he had a mansion. No way. Just some old sheds slung together. Best ask Leila straight out whether she fancied a coffee in the evening. She must be dying to talk to someone about her thesis.

He parked the car outside the big metal gates of his cottage, unlocked the padlock, pushed the gates open, and breathed in deeply. There was a perfume from the summer lemons. As he walked under the trellis of jasmine, he breathed in even more deeply – it was like smelling a fine wine.

Max opened the front door, went to the fridge, and took out a San Miguel beer. He was just getting comfortable on his battered sofa when the phone rang.

'Max, how are you?'

'Fine, grandma. Just fine, *abuela*. How are the kids?'

'Both well, but Encarnita is turning into a real little madam – and Leonardo should spend less time playing football, and more on his homework.'

'So they're growing up fast?'

'Yes . . . but Isabel told Juan I was interfering with how she wanted to bring them up. And all because I said it was too late for Encarnación to stay up to watch a programme on television. I'm right, aren't I, Max?' Her voice broke. 'I would never have let my children sit all evening in front of the television. I'm sure it's not good for them.'

'*Abuela*, I'm sure Isabel didn't mean to be hurtful. How's the rest of the family?'

'Juan's very moody. I don't think he's spoken to Isabel for days – though I can't blame him. But could you have a drink with him, Max? He won't talk to me about his problems, of course.'

'Sure. I'll give him a ring. See you Sunday.'

Max phoned Juan. Ten o'clock in el Café Paraíso. Just

13

before ten, Max checked he had his torch, and then climbed up the goat track into town and on into the café. Juan was already there.

'Beer, Max?'

'*Sí*. How's business?'

'Huh. Could be better.'

'Problems?'

'The mill conversion in Recina – you know, the one that went really over budget – well, it came on the market just when the Brits stopped buying. So I still haven't sold one of the damn flats, and the bank's being a pain now.'

'You'll sell. It's another rotten summer in Britain. Another *cerveza*, Juan?'

'Why not? No point in spoiling Friday night.'

Max raised his glass. 'Here's to Barcelona. This season is going to be ours – I just know it.'

'No way. Real Madrid will sweep the board. We've made some really good signings. You just wait and see.'

'I'm not too sure. I doubt the Brits will fit in – not their style of play.'

More drinks, more football.

Juan looked at his watch, 'Better go. Isabel and Paula are scrapping again. Isabel's wanting to move into town. Difficult. It'd break Paula's heart to lose the kids.'

'*Sí*. And Paula couldn't stay in that big house on her own anyway. I'm sure it will all blow over again. *Chao*, Juan. See you Sunday.'

As Max left, he noticed Sargento León from Diva's Guardia Civil drinking alone in the corner. He smiled, and saluted him.

Saturday morning was hot and sticky. His neighbour, Alvaro, was already pulling up weeds when Max took his breakfast on to the terrace.

'*Hola, Max. Mucho calor*. This is going to be a real pig of a day . . . look at those clouds. Need some rain though. How long you staying?'

'Just the weekend.'

14

'Your land's a jungle. Mariana saw a tiger in it last week.'

'Okay, okay. Point taken. Never thought it would be so much work.'

'Just get on with it, city boy, before it's too hot.'

By one o'clock, Max had managed to clear the last major patch of weeds. He still had time to wash, get changed and drive up to the supermarket before it shut at two. Home again, he sat quietly under the old olive tree, waving his hands to keep the noisy flies away from his sandwich. The black clouds had come right down the valley. Rain would arrive soon. Max picked up his book – a new biography of Federico García Lorca. At the end of the third chapter, he glanced at his watch. 4.40 p.m. – time to go to Ahmed's. As he walked up the track to his parked car, the rain began to fall.

Saturday, at exactly five in the afternoon, Max arrived at Ahmed Mahfouz's house. Rain was falling heavily as he rang the bell. Ahmed opened the door.

'*Hola*, Max. Good to see you. *Wa' alaykum As-Salamu wa Rahmatullahi wa Barakatuk.* In the Name of Allah, Most Gracious, Most Merciful. All praise and thanks are due to Allah, and peace and blessings be upon his Messenger. Not too wet, I hope? Do you need a towel?

'*Wa' alaykum As-Salamu wa Rahmatullahi wa Barakatuk.* No, I'm fine, thanks.'

'Let's go to my study. It's more comfortable there. Leila's not back yet – looks like she's not gone far. So she shouldn't be long. Tea?'

'Thanks.'

Max looked round the neat study, lined with books, classical and Arabic music CDs, photographs of Leila graduating, Leila on her mother's knee, Leila on holiday. The photographs did not do her justice. He looked at the book lying on the table, *Islam: Art and Architecture*. He opened the pages at random: a photo of the Great Mosque of Cordoba. The alternating brick and cream stone columns always made him feel slightly dizzy.

'Good photo,' said Ahmed. 'An oasis in stone, quite mystical.'

He placed the tray on the table, and poured the jasmine tea into small elegant glasses.

'Yes,' replied Max. 'Here's to the Golden Age of Andalusia, the most tolerant and artistic place in the world.'

'I agree. So what's it about this time?'

'Well . . . I'm worried this war is going to put a real strain on inter-community relations. I was hoping you might have some ideas.'

'This invasion of Iraq is a terrible mistake. No Muslim can support it. It's only increasing support for the extremists. I was thinking . . . we need more popular education on Islam and the history of the Middle East. Perhaps an exhibition of modern Islamic culture would help, just to show we are not all fanatics. Maybe something on food and music.'

'That could be useful. If you could work up some ideas, I'll look into funding.'

'I'll talk to my colleagues . . . and Leila of course. I'll try to get you an outline next week.'

'Thanks.'

'It has always been good to work with you, Max.'

'That's the easy thing I wanted to talk to you about.'

'And the difficult thing?'

'We think there might be some terrorist cells here in Andalusia. We'd be grateful if you reported anything suspicious to us.'

'You mean act as a spy? You're crazy. Look, you know I have no sympathy with terrorism, but I can't go reporting every odd character I come across who happens to be a Muslim.'

'We're not asking you to do that. Just to report the real fanatics.'

'But who are they? Every Muslim sympathizes with the Palestinians, and hates this war. But I'm not going to write a dossier on everyone I know. How could you even think of it?'

'No. No. But Spain could be a target now.'

'But terrorists aren't going to tell me if they're planning to blow something up, are they?'

'Okay, okay. How's Leila? How's her thesis going?'

'She's fine. She was hoping to see you. I don't know what could have happened to her. I'll ask her to give you a ring when she gets back.'

'Sure. It would be nice if she phoned.'

Max stood up. He looked at Ahmed's lined, ascetic face. He liked him, and did not want to press him hard. But his superiors wanted information on terrorist sympathizers.

'How do you think this invasion in Iraq will end?' Max asked Ahmed.

'It will be a disaster. The American, British and Spanish governments have made a terrible mistake . . . they just don't realize it yet. There'll be resistance, fanatics flooding into Iraq, and probably civil war. The Yanks won't have the stomach to stay the course. And then, who knows?'

'I really don't understand why the British and Spanish governments are so keen to support the Yanks.'

'Me neither. You'd have thought, given our histories, we'd have known better.'

'Yes, but our leaders don't. Not much understanding of history.'

'More tea, Max?'

' No thanks. I really have to go now.'

Max drove back to his *cortijo*. He knew many Muslims regarded him as a police spy. But *simpatico*. A nice guy. And someone who actually knew something about Islam. Pity about Leila. He grimaced as he passed the skips with rubbish strewn all around them. Bloody hippies. He must complain to the council. The rubbish was becoming a health hazard as well as an eyesore. Now that he owned a *cortijo*, he did not want the value of his property falling because of a rubbish tip on the way to his home.

Once inside, Max took out a beer. He had looked forward to having a pleasant evening with Leila. She would probably call when she got home. He finished his beer and read his book for a while. The heat was oppressive – he needed a shower. He was getting out of the shower when the phone rang.

Leila, he thought. That's nice. *'Hola.'*

'Sub-Inspector Max Romero?' A woman's voice. But not Leila's.

'Sí.'

'Cabo Anita Guevarra. It's urgent. We've found a body. It's Teniente González' day off, and we can't get hold of him. Sargento León knew you were in Diva, and would very much like your assistance. I'll be at the station.'

'I'll be there as soon as I can.'

It took Max less than ten minutes to walk up the goat track to the Diva police station. Cabo Anita Guevarra was waiting for him at the door. Max glanced at her. She looked young enough to have come straight from a convent school. She was definitely pretty, very slim. Too slim . . . better to have something to grab. Shit, I'm beginning to sound like the other cops, thought Max.

'Thanks for coming so quickly. I'll drive you over, could be murder.' Anita had a pleasant, low voice.

'Do you have an ID for the body yet?'

'Not sure, but Sargento León thinks you probably knew her.'

Oh God. Isabel? Mariana? Macarena? Dolores?

They drove in silence. There was a police car stationed at the side of the Jola road, just before the road bridge over the ravine. Cabo Guevarra drew up beside the green tape that cordoned off the road. Sargento Mario León came over to greet him, chest puffed up with importance.

'Thanks for coming, Max. I think you might recognize the body.'

Max felt a flood of relief: at least it wasn't family.

'Where is she?'

'Under the bridge. We'll have to get down the ravine. But the path isn't too bad.'

They clambered down. The banks, usually bone dry at this time of year, were slippery with mud. The water was still ankle deep at the bottom. They scrambled along the riverbed and under the road bridge. The body of a young woman lay in the mud, crudely covered with a few branches of oleander, white flowers still gleaming.

'Recognize her?'

Oh sweet Jesus, he was never going to have that date with Leila. He reached for his inhaler and took a quick puff. Leila, Leila.

'What happened?'

'We don't know. Broken neck, we think. Jaime, the goatherd, had to scramble down after his dog, and found the body. Not well hidden, is it?'

'No. But then it might have taken days for someone to look under the bridge. She's Leila Mahfouz, the daughter of one of the British Muslims. God, I had tea with her father this afternoon. She was due home any minute . . . I'll tell him if you like.'

'Thanks. Definitely Muslim? Is that going to complicate things?'

'Yes, could do. We'll have to move fast. Muslims like to bury their dead within twenty-four hours.'

'Didn't know that. I'll tell Forensics. Can't be too politically correct these days. The duty *juez de instrucción* is arriving any minute.'

'Who is it?'

'Juez Falcón. He's fine – lets us get on with it. I'll tell him about the twenty-four hours. Thanks for the advice.'

Max bent over the body. 'Look, her watch is broken, stopped at five exactly. Could have broken when she fell over the ravine.'

'Maybe, but that's an old trick. Kill her, change the time on her watch, break the watch, and the killer, of course, has an alibi for that time.'

Max took another quick puff of his inhaler as they climbed up the bank.

'Okay, Max, we'll have to wait here for the *policía científica*, Forensics and the judge to arrive . . . Anita, you got hold of the boss yet?'

'Still no luck,' replied Anita.

León turned back to Max. 'Can't understand why he's not answering his mobile. He'll be annoyed he's missing the excitement. It's our first Muslim. Look, Max, I know you have a lot of experience with Muslims, and you're in Homicide. I'd be grateful if you could keep us straight on this one. We don't want any more complaints.'

'Mmm.'

'I know you and González don't get on too well. But we can't be too politically correct these days, you know, and . . . well . . . the Teniente has had some problems recently, and . . . you know what he's like, drowns his sorrows. He won't admit it of course, but I'm sure he would really appreciate any help you can give.'

'It's not my patch, Mario.'

'I know, but . . . you know how he is.'

'Mmm. Okay, I'll see what I can do.'

'Thanks. Cabo Guevarra will drive you back to town. Could you ask the father to ID the body?'

'Sure. I'll see what I can do to help.'

'Shall we go, sir?' said Guevarra.

Max got into the car beside her. He felt guilty that all he could think of was the waste of a lovely body.

Guevarra was very pale.

'Your first body?'

'*Sí*. I suppose you get used to it.'

'Not really.'

'You knew her then, sir?'

'Yes. I saw her father this afternoon.'

'A pretty girl. You couldn't miss her in a town like this.'

'*Sí*, very pretty.'

'The Teniente won't like it. He hates having to deal with the foreigners.'

They arrived in silence at Ahmed's house. Max rang the doorbell.

'Max what a surprise! I'm still waiting for Leila. I hope you haven't found a terrorist gang.'

'Nothing like that. Can I come in?'

'Certainly. The study again?'

This time Max preferred to stand . . . Ahmed looked at him, waiting.

'I've very bad news for you Ahmed.' It was somehow reassuring to use his first name. ' The police have just found Leila's body. She's—she's dead.'

'Dead? What do you mean? She can't be—no, can't be.' His voice started to break.

'It looks like murder.'

'Murder? I don't understand.'

'Neither do we. We suspect her neck was broken, and her body hidden in the Jola ravine.'

'My precious Leila, my precious Leila.' Ahmed tried to hold back the tears, but sobs came.

'I'm sorry. I'm so sorry.' Max put his arm around the crumpled shoulders. There was nothing he could say. 'I'm so sorry, Ahmed. When you feel up to it, we would like you to formally identify the body. You can do it now or later, whatever you prefer. If now, we can do it before she's taken away. Or we could go to the mortuary in Granada in a couple of hours.'

'Now . . . but . . . I must have a few minutes alone to pray.'

Ahmed stumbled from the room. There was a racking, retching sound. Ahmed was bent over double, vomit on the floor. Max gently helped him up. Ahmed muttered his thanks, closed his eyes, and in a whisper stammered out his prayer.

'In the name of Allah, the compassionate, the merciful. All praise belongs to Allah, the Lord of all being. He is compassionate and merciful. He is the master of the day of judgement. The day of judgement is certain to come; this is beyond doubt. Those who are in the grave, God will raise to life.'

Ahmed turned to Max, repeated his thanks, and staggered off to the bathroom. Max returned to the study, stood awkwardly, turning the pages of the book on the table, seeking comfort. There was none. Ahmed returned pale, but upright.

'Let's go. No . . . I need some white cloth to shroud her. Just wait a minute, please.'

Ahmed left and returned a few minutes later with two white sheets on his arm. Guevarra was waiting outside in the car. With quiet dignity, Ahmed thanked her for waiting. He asked no more questions. Only the shaking of his hands betrayed him. It was dark now. González had finally arrived, and was talking to Judge Falcón. An ambulance and the forensics van partially blocked the road. Leila's body was already in the ambulance, covered by a red blanket. A line of a Lorca poem went through Max's head: 'Everything else was death, only death.'

González came over to Max, sweating profusely and smelling of alcohol. 'I gather León asked you to come and help, Max. But we can manage. Bad news this. Always happens on the day off, doesn't it. Sod's law. I was working on my land, and the mobile reception is lousy. I barely had time for a wash and brush up, and get into uniform. Don't want Falcón to think we're a bunch of scruffs.'

He turned to Ahmed. 'Thanks for coming straight away. But we need a formal identification of the body. Are you okay to look?' González sounded surprisingly gentle.

'Is she—is she . . .?'

'It's okay, her face is fine.'

Ahmed and González entered the ambulance. Guevarra was crying. She fumbled in her pocket, and took out a pack of cigarettes. 'A cigarette, sir?'

'No thanks.'

A grim-faced González was the first to come out. '*Sí*. It's his daughter. He'll be out soon. He says he has to shroud the body.'

A few minutes later Ahmed scrambled out, his face like a death mask. He was stooping badly, and he stumbled as he walked. Max helped him upright.

'Is there someone to stay with you tonight? I could stay.'

'Thanks. Members of my community will help me. We will pray.'

'We'd like to ask you some questions. Could you manage Monday morning? About eleven?'

'Yes.'

The car with Guevarra and Ahmed sped away. Judge Falcón, González and León consulted, huddled. Judge Falcón turned to Max and the technicians.

'I've finished for now. This is a tough one. The rain seems to have wiped away all evidence. I'll sign the order, so the body can be taken to the Instituto Anatómico Forense. Sargento León tells me Sub-Inspector Romero says her community will want to bury her as soon as possible. I'll instruct the Médico Forense to be as quick as they can. Sargento León also says that Sub Inspector Romero may be willing to help with the case if Granada agrees.'

'I don't think that will be necessary, Judge. We can manage on our own,' interrupted González.

'This could be a sensitive and complicated case, Teniente. I think someone with excellent English and knowledge of the Muslim community could be invaluable.'

'Okay, if you insist, Judge,' muttered González.

'I do,' said Judge Falcón. 'We'll come back in the morning when it's light. You can all go now.'

'Okay,' said González, turning to Max. 'I'll get the results of the autopsy tomorrow. Left my car at Felipe's. León here is driving me over to pick it up. Can we give you a lift home?'

'*Gracias*. I'm down the Río Sierra track.'

González eased his overweight body into the back of the car. León got into the driver's seat. Max sat beside him. González was perspiring alcohol. He reached into his pocket, took out three mints, peeled the silver wrapping paper off two, and started crunching them vigorously.

'A mint, Max?'

'Thanks.'

González's hand shook as he handed a mint over to Max. 'I think we can manage okay on this one. Don't know why León asked for your help.'

'Sorry, sir,' said León. 'We tried and tried to get hold of you. And then I remembered that Max might have known her.'

'I was working on my land, can't get a signal there. Got the message on the landline when I got home. You should have waited for me, León.'

'Sorry, sir.'

'Well . . . my guess is it was an accident,' said González.

'Doesn't look like an accident to me,' said Max.

'I agree with that,' added León.

'Mustn't jump to conclusions,' said González. 'I think we could still be dealing with an accident here.'

'Maybe. But I doubt it,' said Max. 'I'm willing to help if you want. I did know her and her father. It's Judge Falcón's call really. If that's what he wants I'll have to get the okay from the boss first, and you'll then have to ask formally for assistance. Got to be back in Granada midweek. Babysitting two posh suits from Madrid.'

'Well, if the judge insists, then I suppose we must. But I'm sure we can manage. Mind you . . . that's some police job you've got. Don't know whether you're a tourist guide or a bloody social worker.'

'You mean you don't believe in good community relations?'

'Sure I do. But our job is to protect the Spanish public. Too many foreign Muslims. We should send them all back. If the buggers want to drown at sea then let them.'

'If we sent them all back, then we'd have nobody to pick

the olives and grapes. No Spaniard seems willing to do that these days.'

'Oh, you know what I mean. We could let some of the buggers in for the harvests. But don't let them stay. They're costing us too much in taxes.'

'But those who stay also pay taxes.'

'Bloody few. Hey, you're not going to become a fucking Muslim, are you, like some of those weirdo foreigners?'

'No. But it's not that different from Christianity. Same God, you know.'

'Maybe. But I don't trust the bastards. Never have done, never will.'

'Where to, Max?' called out León.

'Just turn left here. Let me off at the end of the field. It's easier for you to turn there.'

'Wasn't that Pepe's old place?'

'*Sí.* Nice location. The orchard's been well looked after, but *el cortijo* needs a hell of a lot of work.'

'At least you've got town water and electricity,' said González. ' I can't believe what some of these foreigners are paying. My uncle Gonzalo got twenty million pesetas from a German for a dump a pig wouldn't shit in. The German said he liked the view. My land will be worth a fortune when it gets rezoned.'

'Any chance of that?' asked Max. 'I thought the Junta was tightening up – been too many scandals in this town already.'

'I'm working on it,' replied González.

'If the boss is working on it, then there's a good chance it will happen,' interrupted León.

Max got out of the car. 'Okay. If Falcón wants me on the case, then so be it. I'll give Davila a bell for now, but you'll need to put in a formal request to Granada for cooperation. Assume I'll see you Monday.'

González scowled. 'Really, I don't think this is necessary, but if Falcón insists then—'

'Where's your car, sir?' asked León.

'Oh – at Felipe's,' replied González.

The car sped off, churning mud from the puddles on the track. Max glanced at his watch. It was exactly midnight. He stood quietly for a minute beneath the stars, before opening his gate.

Chapter 3

Tape Number 2

Leila: Tell me about the first time you met Lorca.

Paula: Oh, I'll never forget it. Of course I didn't know who he was. I was only six. He was staying with his family in Banjaron, you know. His mother was taking the waters at the spa. Antonio invited Lorca over for a day. Well . . . I was playing in the garden, and he was there on his own, talking to himself. I can't remember how now, but I must have fallen and scraped my knee, and started crying. Lorca came over, and picked me up. He recited what I thought were magic words – I've never forgotten them.

> The girl on the swing goes
> from north down to the south,
> from south up to the north,
> And on the parabola
> a red star is trembling
> beneath all the stars.

It must have worked because I stopped crying . . . and it was love at first sight – at least for me.

Leila: You met him again, didn't you?

Paula: Yes, the second time I met him I was so excited. I must have been about thirteen or fourteen.

Leila: So when was that?

Paula: It must have been 1931 or 1932. Yes it was 1932, the four hundredth anniversary of the foundation of the

University of Granada. Lorca's company were putting on a play in the old Isabel la Católica theatre.

Leila: What was the play?

Paula: I can still see the poster. La Barraca Presents – Life is a Dream, by the Spanish poet, Calderón de la Barca.

Leila: Why La Barraca? Does it mean anything?

Paula: Yes, very odd. I think he called it that because Lorca's company went round the poor villages and towns, and would perform in barns or whatever they could find. The right wing really hated La Barraca . . . and all it stood for.

Leila: Ah. La Barraca – The Barn. Of course. Sorry for interrupting. This is so good. Have you spoken to anyone else about this?

Paula: Not much. My children found it all . . . well, embarrassing. The grandsons . . . I've got two. There's Juan – he's not really interested either, but Max likes Lorca's poetry. He's a good boy, isn't he? I know he likes you. You are so pretty.

Leila: Doña Paula, thank you for the compliment. Can we get back to Lorca?

Paula: Well, in 1932, Antonio invited my mother and me to see the play. I was overjoyed. I must have spent a week deciding what to wear, and I think mother took longer. We both looked stunning. Mother wore a blue corded-silk dress from Madame du Maurier's with pearl and gold earrings and a wonderful bracelet. She had the smartest hat, a cloche, you should have seen it, and a coat trimmed with Arctic fox. I finally decided on my plum-coloured velvet dress with the fine lace collar. And mother bought me a new winter coat . . . and I had a fur muff.

Leila: Did Lorca act in the play?

Paula: Oh yes. I was too young to really understand the play, but it looked wonderful. Lorca played the part of La Sombra, The Shadow, and he was so dramatic in black veils and a horned headpiece. As he moved across the stage, he was lit up by a single beam of light. He was obsessed with the moon and death, you know. We cheered and cheered.

And he came on stage at the end, and spoke passionately about something or the other. It sounded marvellous. We went backstage afterwards, and Antonio introduced us to him. He still had make-up on, and his eyes were like black coals set in a white face. He kissed me on both cheeks, and then I began to recite: 'The girl on the swing goes . . .'

He looked at me with that strange smile of his. 'Ah,' he said, 'the little girl in the garden, crying. Let's recite it together: "*de norte a sur de sur a norte*".'

And he went across to a piano in the corner of the room, and started playing, he played the piano so well, you know, and we all started singing: '*de norte a sur de sur a norte* . . .'

I could have cried. In fact I did later on. I was so happy. It was a time of such hope and promise.

Leila: I know.

Paula: Yes. Did I tell you my parents took me to the first performance in Granada of Lorca's most famous play *Bodas de Sangre*? And we stayed the night in the Alhambra Palace Hotel. It was magical.

Leila: It must have been. Did you know that the English translation is *Blood Wedding*? The Spanish sounds so much better.

Paula: Did you know that little Juan and Max are arranging a treat for my birthday? We are all going to the new production of *Blood Wedding* in the outdoor theatre of the summer palace in the Alhambra, and then spending the night in the Alhambra Palace Hotel. Isn't that wonderful of them?

Leila: Yes indeed . . . and *Blood Wedding* is one of Lorca's best works. It should be quite a night.

Chapter 4

La piedra es una fuente donde los sueños gimen
Sin tener agua curva ni cipreses helados.
La piedra es una espalda para llevar tiempo
Con árboles de lagrimas y cintas y planetas.

Stone is a forehead where dreams groan
For lack of curving waters and frozen cypresses.
Stone is a shoulder for carrying away time
With trees made of tears and ribbons and planets

Frederico García Lorca, *Cuerpo presente* (*The Laid-Out Body*)

Max had been in the police for four years now, but had never seen the body of someone he knew before. Last year thirteen Moroccans had been washed ashore, and he had seen the bloated corpses: men, women and children. There was a little girl with a silver necklace, her name in Arabic, around her neck – Fatima. No one came to claim the bodies. He was shocked by that girl's tragedy. 'Let the buggers drown,' González had said. No, that was wrong. But Spaniards had to be seen as good Europeans, and the heat was on to act tough against illegal immigration. Hell! Most Spaniards wanted that.

Leila's death was different. She didn't just sparkle; she was radiant. He slept badly. A quiet Sunday would have been nice, but he had to go to the family barbecue. For the Romero family, Sunday lunch was sacred. But he would go to Leila's funeral afterwards.

The sun woke him far too early. The heavy rain had left

olive, orange and lemon tree branches strewn across the terraces. Most of the banana plants were down. He cleared the debris, carefully stacking it in the middle terrace. Hard work, but the air was fresh with the rain-washed scent of jasmine and roses, and the tops of the two mountain ranges shone in the morning sun.

The new gazebo had survived the rain and wind. Good. It had passed its first test. Juan had warned him that the thin metal poles would not withstand the first strong wind. Better to buy one with a solid frame, he had said. But Max couldn't afford that.

Eleven was his allotted hour for irrigation. At ten, he let the water out of the *alberca*. The earth had been soaked by yesterday's storms so he lifted the little metal shutters, which usually guided the water along the canals to feed his trees and plants. The water gurgled out, straight down to the river at the bottom of the valley. It was the water, flowing along the ancient Moorish canals, which made the land such a mosaic of colour and butterflies. Max refilled the *alberca* with water, cold from the Sierra Nevada.

He phoned the mosque: the funeral was at eight. At two he drove to the old family home at the end of the Jola road. Juan's wife came to greet him. 'Isabel la Católica', Paula had christened her, and the name had stuck. He pecked her on both cheeks. Christ, she was getting seriously fat.

'Good to see you Max. *Una cerveza*?'

'*Gracias.*'

'Juan's in the garden. Can you give him a hand?'

'Sure. Are you coming?'

'In a minute. Have to sort out the laundry mess the lord and master made yesterday. Put all his wet clothes in the washing machine together, so there's blue dye all over the good white shirt that my mother bought for his birthday. If she knew, we would never hear the end of it.'

Isabel's daughter, Encarnación, ran up to Max, and jumped straight into his arms.

'Uncle Max. *Tito* Max. Come and see. I've got a kitten.'

Max was dragged off into the kitchen. Encarnación slid under the table and reappeared with a tiny black kitten.

'He's called David.'

'How do you know it's a boy?'

'Course he is, silly.' And she tipped the kitten on to its back before skipping off to the garden.

'Max.'

Paula came into the kitchen, her white hair carefully dressed, her face lined like a relief map of the mountains. She looked even frailer and tinier than usual. Max bent down to give her a kiss on both cheeks. Paula hugged him tightly.

'Are you well, *abuela*?'

'I can't complain. Max. Did you speak to Juan?'

'Yes. As you thought – it's money problems.'

'That's not too bad. I thought it was bedroom problems. It would be better if la Católica spent less time in church, and more on her back.'

'*Abuela por Díos*! And you being a good Catholic and all.'

'You know what I mean. Isabel wants a modern house closer to town. The silly bitch. Here is ideal for the children.'

Max adored his grandmother. At eighty-three she felt she had the right to say exactly what she thought – and boy, did she take advantage. She picked up an antique glass vase.

'Max, would you like this? Isabel's been admiring it. What's bothering you, love? You didn't laugh. You can tell your *abuela*,' she said, putting her arms around him.

'I've got some bad news. I can't think of an easy way to break it to you.' Max took her hand in his. 'It's about Leila. She's been found dead. I'm afraid it might be murder.'

'Oh Sweet Mary! Murdered? No, she can't be. Can't be.'

Max put his arms around her. She cried in short, gasping sobs.

'She was so young. Such good company. I was hoping you and she, you know, might have gone out together. It's time you settled down.'

Max said nothing, just held her in his arms.

'Don't worry, *cariño*. I'll be all right. I'll miss our afternoons together. You know, she was really interested in the past, in our family. She loved all the stories.'

And she started crying again.

'A little glass of brandy?'

'No. *Anís dulce*, please.'

'Sit down here, *abuela*.'

Max went through to the living room, opened the old tiled inset cupboard, and poured a generous portion of the sweet liquor. 'Have this, it will do you good.'

Paula sipped the *anís dulce*. 'That's better. I'll be fine now. We'd better go and join the others.'

Arms linked, they went into the garden. The table under the old olive tree was covered with bottles of wine, water, a mountain of rough bread, bowls of olives, peaches and cherries. Sitting at the table were Isabel, her two children, Leonardo and Encarnación, and Isabel's parents, over from Granada for the day. Juan was at the barbecue, blowing the vine twigs under the big pan of paella. Juan always took charge of the barbecue.

'The *langostinos* are great,' he called out to no one in particular.

Paula sat at the head of the table. And she burst into tears again.

Isabel's mother rushed up, clean hankie in hand. 'What's wrong? What's wrong?'

Everyone came up to comfort Paula.

'It's Leila. She's gone . . . Max says she's been murdered.'

'Dead? Murdered?' exclaimed Isabel's mother.

'What happened, Max?' asked Isabel.

'We're still not sure. But it might have been an accident. Her body was found under the Jola road bridge last night.'

'Do you know who did it?' interrupted Isabel's father.

The questions billowed around like choking smoke. It was Paula who finally took charge.

'Isabel, please, say a prayer for her soul. Then, let's eat and enjoy our meal. Leila would have wanted that.'

Isabel bowed her head in prayer for the soul of a dearly departed friend. 'Hail Mary, Mother of God, Forgive us our sins. Look down upon us. We beseech you to intercede for the mercy of the soul of Leila, our dearly beloved friend. Hail Mary Full of Grace, the Lord is with thee . . .'

Everyone round the table joined in. As Isabel began the third Hail Mary, Paula intervened. 'Come. No need for the whole rosary. I'm not sure Leila would appreciate it.'

Juan, pale, stayed at the barbecue. Meals at Paula's were usually boisterous affairs with Max and Juan arguing continously: Barcelona or Real Madrid? Vote for the PP and get lower taxes or PSOE and social spending? Support the Yanks or not? But today everyone was subdued, apart from the protesting meow from David, allowed on to the table by Encarnación and then knocked away by Isabel. Max had to give all the details. He concluded: 'The funeral will be tonight, at eight.'

'I'm going,' announced Paula firmly.

'That's not a good idea,' said Juan. 'It will be Muslim.'

'That doesn't matter. I loved the girl, and I'm going anyway.'

When Paula had made her mind up, that was usually that. But this time Juan tried to argue; only to be told to shut up.

'I'm going myself,' said Max. 'I'll take you.'

Just before eight, Max and Paula arrived at the mosque. Paula in the suit and veil she had worn to her husband's funeral ten years ago. Max had explained to Paula that many Muslims did not allow women and non-Muslims into the mosque for a funeral. He had checked with the community, and they had no objections to non-Muslims attending, but would prefer it if women did not go to the burial.

'Paula, even in this mosque men and women will be separated by a screen, and you will have to stay behind at the mosque, while I go to the burial. The women will look after you and give you tea afterwards, while I am at the graveyard.'

34

'More rules than the Holy Mother Church then. I thought we were bad enough,' she replied. 'But I'm glad to be here.'

The service was simple. Leila's washed body lay on a plain wooden table, wrapped in five white shrouds. The mosque was full. Ahmed began the Salat-ul-Janazah, the funeral prayers. As he spoke, a plain wooden casket was placed in front of him. Ahmed finished the prayers, and Leila's body, still wrapped in the five shrouds, was placed in the casket. Four men lifted the coffin and carried it outside. Max and all the men silently filed out of the mosque and followed the coffin up the hill. The procession passed the little white round hermitage of San Joaquín, built on top of both a Visigoth chapel and then a mosque, and entered the small field where one plain headstone testified to an earlier death within the community. As the body was lowered gently into the grave, Ahmed, weeping silently, began to mutter the last prayer, joined in unison by all the Muslim men gathered round the grave, and then went through the rituals.

Each man stooped, took three handfuls of earth and threw them into the grave, repeating the same words: 'We created you from it, and return you into it, and from it we will raise you a second time.' Facing the grave, they offered a prayer, invoking Allah's mercy on Leila, and then turned from the grave, and facing the headstone in the bare field intoned: 'Greetings of peace to you all. Allah-willing, we will also join you. May Allah forgive you and all of us!'

When they had finished Max and three other non-Muslims went to Leila's grave, picked up three handfuls of earth and threw them on the burial spot. Max stood quietly, looking down at the grave. He did not believe in any God or life after death. Your body would be recycled back into life on earth, and that was it. But the quiet dignity of the ceremony, the loss of a life so full of promise, affected him. He said his farewells, a tear trickling down his cheek.

Max returned to pick up Paula. She was sitting in the

courtyard of the mosque, sipping mint tea, with Zaida, a handsome woman, her face framed by an elegant blue headscarf.

'Max, this is Zaida, a close friend of the family. We were talking about Leila. She has something to tell you which may be important.'

'Yes. I saw Leila on the Saturday. It must have been about two twenty in the afternoon. The shops had just shut. I was standing at the traffic lights, you know, by the church, when Leila got out of this really battered van. She looked a bit of a mess. I didn't really see the man she was with, scruffy type. He drove off immediately, and Leila headed for her home.'

'That's interesting. It makes you the last person we know to have seen Leila alive.'

'Oh dear, that's an awful thought.'

'Can you remember anything else about the man or the van?'

'Not really. I just remember the man looked a mess, long hair, unshaven. A traveller, I'd say. The van . . . well, I don't know one make from another.'

'Can you describe it?'

'It was really battered. A bluish colour, I think'

'Anything else?'

'It was rusty. And there were sunflowers painted on the side.'

'Zaida, that's really helpful. Did you speak to Leila?'

'No. She dashed off.'

'You said earlier she looked a mess. What did you mean by that?'

'Just that. Looked as if she had slept in her clothes.'

'Ah.'

'She's normally so careful about her appearance, a bit vain. Oh dear, the poor girl.'

'Thanks. We'll need a formal statement later, if you don't mind. I suppose you don't know where she was Friday night?'

'No. She's a bit wild sometimes. Ahmed gets worried about her, but really dotes on her. She needed a mother. She needed guidance, and in my view, he's too soft with her. I have spoken to him about this. But he won't face up to the problem. It's too late now. She was a lovely girl.'

'Problem?'

'You'll find out sooner or later, I suppose. Yes. Leila, was a bit, well . . . *inmodesta.*'

'Immodest?'

'With men. You know.'

'So you think she could have spent the night with the bloke in the van?'

'No. I'm not saying that. I just don't know.'

'Oh, come on,' interrupted Paula. 'Leila was a very pretty, lively girl. You don't expect a girl of twenty-three to be a virgin these days.'

'In our community we do.'

Max bit his lip.

'Sorry, I'm tired now,' said Paula. 'Max, take me home, please. Thanks, Zaida. You've been very kind. Look after the poor girl's father. It's been so nice talking to you. And thanks for the recipe. I'll try it. We must talk again soon.'

Paula limped out of the courtyard, into Max's car.

'Max, this is the first time I've ever been inside a mosque. They seem good people. Oh, why do we always emphasize our differences. So absurd.'

Max didn't reply. They drove silently back to the house.

'I'm glad you came, *abuela.*'

'Glad you took me, Max.'

Paula said goodnight and kissed Max affectionately. '*Buenas noches, cariño.*'

'*Buenas noches, abuela.*'

Max waited until she entered the house. His heart beat. Leila's death reminded him that even his beloved *abuela* could not live for ever. It would be hard to imagine life without her. He drove away slowly. The rain had cleared the sky. Bright stars and a full moon illuminated the black road. Max glanced at the moon, and murmured one of Lorca's invocations:

> '"Night here already
> Moon's rays been striking
> Evening like an anvil."'

Chapter 5

Los caballos negros son,
Las herraduras son negras.
Sobre las capas relaces
Manchas de tinta y de cera.

Black are the horses,
The horseshoes are black.
Glistening on their capes
Are stains of ink and of wax.

Frederico García Lorca, *Romance de la Guardia Civil Española*
(*Romance of the Spanish Civil Guard*)

Monday morning, the sun rose, an inflamed red, over the Sierra: another scorching day. Max drove to the police station, next to the town hall. Davila had agreed he should stay over in Diva to help. He regretted he did not have his uniform with him. It was the sort of thing González would note, and make remarks about. It was a little after nine. González looked pointedly at his watch.

'Seems like an accident. Don't understand what all the fuss is about, but Falcón wants you involved. Remember I'm in charge. León here wants a little operations room at the back, Operation Leila. He's been watching too many police movies.'

González' big belly looked even bigger; his bald head was sticky with sweat, and his breath even worse than usual . . . cheap brandy, mints and mouthwash.

Fuck it, Max thought. He's going to make a speech, a pompous one at that. Best be polite.

At last González came to a close. 'Right. Almost certainly an accident, but we need to move fast on this one. Don't want to waste Max's time, after all – he tells us he has important business in Granada.'

'Remember she's a Muslim,' said León. 'Max's experience with Muslims could be very helpful. And these days we've got to go careful with them. Why, I don't know. Don't trust any of the bastards. But we don't want any more complaints about religious or racial bias.'

'You're right, León. A lefty paper might create a fuss. And our General López would not like that. No siree. But as far as I'm concerned if it ain't an accident, then every goddam Muslim in our patch is a suspect until proved innocent.'

With that González moved to the stand, and dramatically flipped the cover over.

Oh my God, thought Max. A flip chart. It'll be a Power-Point presentation next.

'Perhaps Max would like to write up for us what we know. After all, he has been to university.'

'Certainly.'

Max went to the front, and waited, the felt tip pen poised.

González continued. 'The girl's name, Leila Mahfouz, a Muslim, the daughter of a British Muslim, resident here.'

Max interrupted. 'She's actually not resident here, but visiting from her university in Scotland to do research on Diva during the Spanish Civil War.'

'What for?' asked González. 'That's past history. Best forgotten.'

'That's what history is,' explained Max, 'a study of the past.'

'She's no right to go poking her nose into other people's business. We've learnt to live and forget.'

Max smiled. Everyone knew that González' family had been Franco supporters, and had made a tidy pile out of the Civil War.

40

'She's no right to do that. We don't go over to England and dig up dirt there. Okay. Let's get this show on the road. What else do we know about her?' asked González.

The two other police in the room, Anita Guevarra and Mario León, looked at each other, and shrugged their shoulders. '*Nada*,' they said in unison.

Max waited. It wasn't his job to conduct the investigation.

'I have a preliminary report from Forensics,' continued González. 'Time of death was Saturday afternoon, about five, with the usual fifteen minutes each way. And it started raining, León . . . at about four thirty, yes?'

'Her watch had stopped at five exactly, could be a trick to deceive us,' said León. 'But if Forensics say about five, then we can assume that's probably the time of her death.'

'Thanks, León. As I was saying . . . cause of death, broken neck. No sign of sexual assault. Nothing else suspicious. Healthy normal girl about twenty-three. Not a virgin though. Bruising consistent with having fallen down the ravine. Any footprints or whatever washed away by rain. No mobile on or near the body. Suicide or accident most likely. Any ideas?'

'What's the evidence for suicide?' asked Guevarra.

'Not likely,' chipped in León. 'Nobody in their right mind would want to top themselves at that ravine. You might mess it up, and then you're stuck at the bottom with flies and ants. Dead dogs too.'

'Could have been an accident though,' insisted González.

'I don't think so,' said Guevarra. 'She wasn't dressed for hiking, and there's no evidence of intoxication. Sober adults just don't go around falling off a road into a ravine.'

'I had a cousin once who did just that,' said León.

'Okay. Thank you, León. But maybe she had an accident up on the Capa road, and the body got swept down in the storm?' said González.

'No, there's the gorge between the Capa road and the Jola bridge. A body would probably get stuck in the narrows there,' commented Max.

'I don't know how us poor peasants could manage without you, Max.'

Max coughed. 'It's likely to be murder, isn't it? Her body was found under the road bridge, covered with oleander branches. There were still flowers on the oleander, and they didn't look to me as if they'd been swept downstream. So someone must have attempted to cover the body.'

'Teniente,' smiled León, 'I would like to suggest then that it is not feasible that she accidentally fell down the ravine, broke her neck, crawled under the bridge, and then covered herself with branches.'

'I was just about to point that out,' snarled González.

'Sorry, sir.'

'Right. Where did we get to before some fool interrupted? Murder. Murderer unknown. Reason for murder? Unknown. Murder weapon, probably hands, but unknown. In fact we know almost bloody nothing about her, except she is a fucking Muslim. Why a pretty girl would want to be a Muslim I don't know.'

'Muslim girls can be quite pretty, you know,' said Max.

'Fancy them, do you? I've always thought there was some reason for your job.'

The scientific, operational inquiry was clearly going nowhere. Best retreat.

'Her father will be here shortly. He'll fill us in on the background,' said Max.

'Coffee then. Remember the father's a suspect until we know otherwise. You never know what goes on in some of these odd sects.'

'Sufis are not an odd sect. They're an old and well-established group within Islam .'

'Fuck off!' shouted González. 'I need a coffee.'

'Best keep quiet,' whispered León as they walked along the corridor. 'The boss has a short fuse. And he can't stand liberal wankers.'

'You'd better do the interview,' muttered González. 'You

might as well do something useful for that fat salary of yours. If I had my way you wouldn't be here.'

Ahmed arrived precisely at eleven. He was still pale, but his shoulders were straight. Max greeted him warmly.

'How are you?'

'Bearing up.'

The interview was in the operations room. The flip chart had been removed.

'Make yourself comfortable.'

González switched on the tape recorder. Max began the interview.

'We know very little about your daughter. So we would be grateful if you would fill us in on her background. At this stage we have no clues as to why it happened. We are definitely treating it as murder. So if you could just begin by giving us as much information on her as possible.'

'Her name is Leila Mahfouz. My own parents were Egyptian. Came to Britain when Nasser took over. I was ten, I think, at the time. Leila's mother was Scottish . . . from Edinburgh. We met at university, and married when I finished my PhD. I taught History of Art at various universities. Leila was born on 18th August 1980 in York. I was working on Islamic art and architecture in Spain, so we used to come to Spain most holidays. Leila was our only child. Her mother died when she was sixteen.'

Ahmed's voice faltered. Sobs began, but he paused, took a deep breath, and continued.

'Shortly after, I rediscovered my faith. When Leila left for college, I moved permanently to Spain to help set up a Sufi community, first in Granada and then some two years ago here in Diva. Leila went on to do graduate work in History at Edinburgh. She chose to do her thesis on Diva during the Civil War, and was over here doing her fieldwork.'

The sobs could no longer be contained, and Ahmed's head collapsed into his hands. Anita Guevarra left the room, and returned with a glass of water. She placed it beside Ahmed, and put an arm around his shoulders. Ahmed sipped the water, straightened his shoulders, and wiped his eyes.

González glared at Guevarra. Max continued with the interview.

'We'll get all the documentation later, if we may. Have you any idea who might want to kill her?'

'None whatsoever. The thesis was going well. She seemed happy and contented. She spent some time in Granada, and was interviewing people there and here in Diva.'

'Did she have any particular friends in Granada and Diva?'

'She'd made a lot of friends locally – and there was a graduate student at Granada University with whom she would sometimes stay overnight. She knew nearly everyone in our small community. I can give you their names and phone numbers if you want.'

'That would be useful. Any boyfriends?'

'She was invited out to parties and such things. But nothing serious, I think. There's a boyfriend back in Scotland, but I had the impression that had cooled off.'

'Is there anything else you can think of that might be useful?'

'Not really. A young man in our community was fond of her. They'd gone for a walk last Thursday. And apparently quarrelled after prayers on Friday.'

'Do you know his name?'

'Hassan Khan. He's a British Muslim. He works at the Ibn Rush'd Centre.'

'What's that?'

'It's an adventure training centre up in the mountains. But where exactly it is I don't know. Leila and I were going to visit soon.' Ahmed's voice broke, but he managed to hold back the tears.

'Ah! A Muslim kid?' interjected González. He tried to make the 'Ah!' seem significant. 'We should interview this lad. When did you last see your daughter?'

'Friday at prayers. There was a message on the answer-

44

phone to say she was going to a party. Must have stayed over with friends – she didn't come back that night. And then she called me on my mobile on Saturday afternoon to say she was home.'

'Do you know where the party was?'

'No.'

'Isn't it unusual for a Muslim girl to stay out by herself overnight?' asked Max.

'Unusual? In some families, yes. But Leila's twenty-three. She'd spent all her life in Britain. My faith doesn't make me an authoritarian patriarch. My girl and I can work things out. Oh Allah be merciful. It's all lost now.'

'I think that will be all for now. We'll obviously want to talk to you again. Could León go back with you and look around Leila's room, collect anything that might be useful?' asked González.

'Yes, of course. But I'd prefer it if a woman touched Leila's things.'

'Okay. Guevarra then.'

'Ahmed, could you manage one more question?' asked Max. 'I have to ask . . . where were you between say four and six on Saturday afternoon?'

'I was having lunch with the new family over from Britain. They wanted to talk about the present difficult situation.'

'Difficult situation?'

'Yes. The war. The problems in Palestine. The problems here in Spain.'

'You have witnesses?'

'Yes. Of course. Would you like their names? Then I came home before five for the meeting with you, Max.'

Ahmed turned to Guevarra. 'We were expecting Leila, but she didn't turn up.'

'Could she have returned to the house while you were out?' Max asked.

'Yes, she did. There was a load of laundry on. And she must have had a sandwich. Am I a suspect?'

'No, of course not,' said Max.

45

González glared at Max, and then asked, 'How long were you in the house alone?'

'Oh, about twenty minutes.'

'So you could have gone out?'

'I could have, but I didn't.'

'Okay. We'll check up on the family.'

'Did Leila have a mobile?' asked Max.

'Yes, of course. She always had it with her. She called me on it on Friday and Saturday.'

'We haven't found it.'

'Maybe it's in her room. I don't know . . .'

Guevarra and Ahmed left the room together.

'It's that bloody British Muslim kid. I feel it in my bones,' said González.

'We've no evidence. It's not illegal to go for a walk in the hills,' said Max.

'Yes, but what's a bloody British Muslim doing up the mountains here? Doesn't sound right to me. Let's go and pick the bastard up.'

'We'll certainly want to question him. But don't jump to conclusions. Innocent until proven guilty, remember.'

'Fuck that. If you feel someone is guilty, you're usually right.'

'Do you want me to come?' asked Max.

'Sure. You're the expert. And you've been assigned. I don't want to be accused of bloody bias. Bite to eat first?'

Max did not fancy eating with González. The fat bastard probably had disgusting personal habits. 'I have to go to the bank and post office. So see you back here at four?'

'Agreed. Right – León, get a fix on this bloody Muslim adventure centre. Never heard such crap in my life.'

Max slipped away quickly. He could eat in el Paraíso. Alone.

'Terrible news about that British girl,' said the waiter as he took Max's order for garlic soup, the fish and half a bottle of the Márquez de Abaxurra. 'To think I served her and that young man on Thursday.'

'You did? What time?'

'Late afternoon. They sat outside there, quite friendly like, until a car came up. The young man left, and the girl set off on her own afterwards.'

'You don't know who was in the car?'

'I've seen him around. Foreign, very dark, grey hair. Runs some centre or other in the mountains.'

'That's interesting.'

'Any suspicions, Max?'

'Can't comment.'

Max had picked up the European edition of the *Guardian* on the way over. *El País* was good, but he still liked to read a British paper now and again. He glanced at the headlines: 'US Government Warns Terrorist Attack Likely'. Not again. They'd been saying that for over a year. Still no attack. Some balls-up about to hit the press. You always get terrorist warnings just before. Max turned to the inside pages: 'Intense International Pressure on Palestine to Sign Peace Deal'. He quickly skipped to the sports pages. Celtic beat Rangers. Great. He walked slowly back to the police station. The shops were all shut: siesta sacred.

González was waiting when he arrived.

'It's four twenty,' he announced 'León has a fix on that Centre – five kilometres north of Capa, off the old Sierra Nevada road.'

Max told him what he had learnt from his waiter.

'Could be two bastards involved,' grunted González.

The three of them got into the car, León in the back seat, González' face shiny with expectation. The road out of Diva wound its way up the mountain. They could soon see Capa, its white houses climbing on top of each other up the hillside.

'So, León, what do you know about this centre then?'

'It's an old farm – used to be called Los Moros, but they've changed the name.'

They passed another dirt track turn-off, and then entered Pampa. Max knew there was a good mountaineering centre

47

in the office of the Parque National de la Sierra Nevada, but González refused to stop to ask for directions. Next was Buba, busy with tourists, the local rugs outside the craft shops. Ten minutes later they entered Capa.

'Best ask the route,' said Max.

'No. Just keep going. There can't be many roads north of here,' said González.

But ten minutes beyond Capa, there were no roads, just dirt tracks to farms. The Centre could be along any of them. Something had upset González' stomach. A loud fart filled the car. Max and León hastily opened the windows. González pretended nothing had happened. He grumbled all the way back to Capa.

'What fucking bastards would want to live in such a remote place. They must be up to no good.'

'Adventure training centres usually are in remote places,' Max reminded him.

'Sure. But have you ever heard of a Muslim adventure centre?'

Max admitted he never had. They stopped at the Sierra Nevada bar. Max remembered a memorable tapa of aubergines in honey. He was with some girl at the time, but damned if he could remember who. The manager was helpful. Left, third left, and keep going. But which was third left? The track was bumpy, and tempers were beginning to fray.

Max noticed that León had picked up his trait of correcting González' more absurd pronouncements, making Gonzo more and more angry. Although he had lived all his life surrounded by mountains, González did not like them. 'Tracks all over the fucking place,' he kept repeating. And then shouted, 'Where the fuck is this bloody Centre?'

'I think it was the other track we passed,' said León.

González muttered all the way to the farmhouse. 'Any fucker living out here must be pretty dodgy.'

It was a two-storey farmhouse with low wings on each side. New buildings completed the square, with a small domed building a little way off. González tooted his horn angrily. Nobody came out.

'Let's have a look around. If necessary, kick the doors in,' said González.

'We don't have a warrant.'

'Fuck that. This is a murder case. We can do what we like.'

They approached the farmhouse. A man appeared.

'Bet they've hidden everything,' muttered González.

The man, tall, athletic, silver grey hair, dressed in a crisp shirt and pressed chinos, walked up to them. He bowed formally and greeted them in Arabic. 'Can I help you? This is the Ibn Rush'd Centre.'

'You sure can,' said González. He showed his identity card. 'We're police officers. We're looking for a young man called Hassan Khan.'

'Yes. He's here.'

'Good. We need to speak to him.'

'Is this about Leila?'

'Leila Mahfouz . . . yes.'

'Okay. Hassan was just about to phone you. He was her friend.'

'How did you know about the girl?'

'We were invited to the funeral. But come in. Follow me. I'll show you into the dining room, and then find Hassan.'

'Your name, please.'

'I am Dr Javeed Dharwish, Director of the centre.'

They entered a dining room, plain but comfortable with a long wooden table and ten wooden chairs, maps of Spain on the wall. There was a large kitchen, well equipped, off the dining room. Max noticed a mobile phone on the table: it had a booster antenna, which you had to buy in the States. Next to the phone was a small Moroccan dish filled with mints wrapped in silver paper. He also noticed a powerful radio. Come to think of it, the roof of the farmhouse had a large antenna on top of it, and a mass of solar panels.

'If you wait here, I will go and fetch Hassan,' said Javeed.

'Well,' said González. 'What do you think?'

'Not much here,' replied León, 'pretty sparse.'

'Of course it is. They'd have hidden everything. I smell a bunch of Muslim terrorists.' said González.

The thought had crossed Max's mind, but he wasn't going to admit that to González. 'No evidence of that. If it were a bunch of American Boy Scouts we'd have thought it was okay.'

'Sure. But what's a bunch of Muslim blokes doing living here except they're up to no good? Speaking of which, he's been gone a long time. He could have warned Hassan to do a runner.'

Javeed and Hassan entered the room. Hassan looked pale and worried. He introduced himself to the policemen. González glared threateningly at him.

Max asked him if he knew Leila. Hassan confirmed that he did, and muttered how shocked he was at what had happened. He volunteered he had been with her for most of Thursday afternoon, walking from Pampa to Diva.

'Just walking?' interrupted González.

'Just walking and talking. There's not much else to do between P—Pampa and Diva.'

Hassan's story tallied with everything they knew.

'Did you meet her on Friday?' asked González.

'Yes. We met after Friday p—prayers.'

'Oh. So you were in Diva on Friday. And on Saturday?'

'Yes. I went in with Javeed ... to the supermarket. We drove back up about seven in the evening. But I didn't see Leila.'

'How did you know something had happened to her?'

'Javeed told me. Zaida from the mosque phoned him. I still can't take it in.'

'Do you know what happened to her?'

' How would I know? Zaida just said she was dead.'

Tears welled up in his eyes, but he refrained from crying.

'When did you find out?' continued González.

'Sunday. Before the funeral. I wanted to go. But Javeed said I was too ill.'

'Why?'

Javeed butted in. 'He was very upset, and had a bad migraine. The others went, but I stayed with Hassan.'

Max turned to Hassan. 'Why were you upset?'

'We were close friends. I was very fond of her. Her death and . . . well, we had a row after p—prayers, a silly one . . . gave me migraine.'

'A quarrel? Over what?'

'Nothing really.'

Javeed came in again. 'I told Hassan he had to concentrate on his work and the course, and it was better not to get involved with Leila.'

'That's enough for me,' interrupted González. 'We'd like to take Hassan in for questioning.We can hold him for seventy-two hours if the judge consents, you know.'

Max was inclined to agree. He felt they would get a lot more out of young Hassan when Javeed wasn't present.

Javeed replied, 'Are you arresting him? If so I'd have to check with my lawyer first.'

'At this stage we are not formally arresting him. Just want to ask him some questions. But do check with your lawyer,' said González.

' Before you phone, could you tell us about the centre?' asked Max.

'Sure. The Ibn Rush'd Centre is named after the great Andalusian Islamic philosopher – Averroes, he's called in the West. It is an adventure training centre, set up less than a year ago, for young European Muslim entrepreneurs.'

'Muslim entrepreneurs?' interrupted González.

'Sure. What's odd about that? I'm a business consultant, specializing in training courses for businessmen. In Britain there's John Baltimore's place in Scotland, in France, Pierre Boulez has a centre in the Alps, and in Spain Javier Solaga has one in the Picos de Europa. We realized there wasn't a training place for up-and-coming young Muslims, and decided to make it a European centre. We got money from the EU. But most of our other funds come from

Muslim businessmen, based in Europe. Would you like a brochure?'

'Yes. And any other information you have,' said González.

Javeed left the room, returning after five minutes.

'The lawyer recommended we cooperate as we have nothing to hide. But he insists he has to be present before any questioning. And here are some leaflets, our brochure, even our business plan if you're interested. We also have a website.'

'But what do you do here? That looks like an assault course outside,' asked Max.

'Yes, it is. Our practice is partly based on Baltimore's course in Scotland. He used to be an SAS officer, and developed a course that tests people to their limits. It brings out leadership, resilience and innovation. You know what you're made of when you've finished here. We chose this area because of its Islamic past, with mosques not too far away, and because the mountains here are ideal for training. We've only just begun, but I think it will go well.'

González interrupted. 'Any weapons?'

'No. I've an old rifle for shooting rabbits and suchlike. They're tasty.'

'Do you mind if we look around?' asked Max.

'Not at all. Let me show you. We're quite proud of what we've done here in such a short time.'

Throughout the conversation, Hassan stood pale and frightened, anxiously looking from one policeman to another.

'León, you keep an eye on the young lad here,' ordered González.

'He won't cause any problems. He'll do all he can to help. He's very upset about the girl's death,' Javeed assured them. 'This is the dining room, sparse but well equipped. We do our own cooking and cleaning. Everything is run to schedule. It's certainly no holiday camp. I can give you some books on the theory and practice if you want. It's a well-established training technique now, though every director brings some-

52

thing of his own experience to it. Mine of course is unique as I bring an Islamic slant. Muslims make good businessmen, you know. Making money honestly and spending it wisely is not against Muhammad's teachings. All praise to Allah.'

They moved out of the dining room into the TV and living room. Comfortable but not luxurious. Next was a small library with five computers set up in it. Max glanced at the shelves. Books in Arabic, English, French and Spanish. Mostly management books. But there were also novels.

'Nice computers,' Max commented.

They moved on into a dormitory, clean, but spartan. Then into a bathroom, another dormitory and another bathroom.

'This is my office – there's a powerful computer here as well.' Javeed smiled as he emphasized 'powerful'. 'There's also a fax, telephone, everything. Next door is my bedroom.'

Max noticed it was impeccably organized, not a paper out of place. A complete contrast to his own office. There was a faded photo on the desk of a very beautiful, dark-haired woman.

'Your wife?'

'Was. She's dead.' He offered no other comment. Both Max and González said nothing.

'And this is my bedroom.'

They entered a small room off the office. Again, everything impeccably in order. Max walked over to the bedside table. A novel lay open on the top. Max looked at the cover: *The Flanders Panel* by Arturo Pérez-Reverte, with a picture of a white knight and a black bishop.

'I'm told that's good,' he said, turning to Javeed. 'I must read it sometime.'

'I'm enjoying it,' replied Javeed. 'The details on chess are good. He's really done his homework.'

'Yes?'

'I was a good player myself . . . once.'

They went back to the dining room, and then through a door into the open countryside.

'We have a large water tank up there,' said Javeed pointing upwards. 'Big enough to splash in after a hot day in the hills. And over here is a small prayer room. I'll show you around, but I'd be grateful if you would take your shoes off.'

Max and González followed Javeed, removed their shoes, and entered the small prayer room. González had clearly never been inside a Muslim prayer room before.

'Pretty bare.'

'You don't need ornaments to worship Allah.'

Max turned to Javeed. 'Thanks. We'd be grateful if you and the others here could come down to the Diva police station tomorrow with all your documentation. How many are you?'

'There's seven of us. Hassan is the Centre's administrative assistant, and is also doing the course part-time. The others are training up in the hills. There are not many trainees at the moment, but we have only just started.'

'That's enough. We'll take Hassan with us now,'said González.

'Okay. The lawyer agrees. But we must emphasize that Hassan is going with you voluntarily, and we are all keen to cooperate. My lawyer will be in Diva tomorrow at ten, and insists he is present during questioning. This is a goodwill gesture, to show we have nothing to hide.'

'Okay,' mumbled González.

They went back to the dining room, and ordered Hassan to follow them after he had packed a small case.

'You can drive, León,' said González. Once in the car, González took out his handcuffs, and snapped them on Hassan's wrists.

'Hey. There's no need to do that,' intervened Max.

'Yes there is. I'm not having the young bastard trying to escape. That Dr Dharwish was just too smooth to be true. Notice how he talked down to us – superior git. I just know there's something up.'

'I thought he was very polite and helpful. Quite an impressive set-up he's organized there. In any case, you don't think the EU would give money to the centre if it wasn't okay, do you?'

'That EU bureaucracy doesn't know its arse from its elbow. Look at the cock-ups it's made all over Andalusia. Mind you, we need the money. I'm not happy about letting in all those East Europeans – it will mean less money for us. Someone told me they're even thinking of letting in the bloody Turks. They're not European, not even Christian. Hey. You know what's odd about that place – they didn't even have a picture of a saint or anything, even in that prayer room of theirs.'

'Muslims don't. Haven't you been round the Alhambra?'

'No. Can't stand that arty stuff. I don't like all this Muslim baloney, Al Andaluz and all that shit. Don't like all that fuss over that poofter poet, what's his name, Lorca, either. You know . . . got shot in the Civil War for siding with the Red rebels.'

'They weren't rebels; they were the democratically elected government of Spain. It was Franco who was the rebel.'

'Not in my book. Franco saved us from the Commies, and kept our Christian traditions alive. I remember my dad telling me what those Red bastards did, raping nuns and all that. Franco kept good law and order. He wouldn't have allowed all these Muslim immigrants in, nor those hippy scruffs either.'

They were approaching Diva now. Hassan had not said a word.

'Out you get, lad,' said León as he stopped the car outside the police station.

González and Hassan went on ahead.

'Best keep off politics with the boss. He reckons he missed promotion for years because he supported Franco. Mind you, he's not wrong about a lot of things,' said León.

As González got to the door of the police station, Max called out, 'I'll help you question the young suspect tomorrow. But only until lunchtime. I have to be back in Granada for the afternoon. Remember to write officially to Granada so I can continue to help.'

González disappeared into the Guardia Civil building. There was a black horseshoe nailed on the outside wall.

Chapter 6

Jorobados y nocturnos,
Por donde animan ordenan,
Silencios de goma oscura
Y miedos de fina arena.

Hunchbacked and nocturnal,
They command where they appear,
The silence of dark rubber
And ears of fine sand.

Frederico García Lorca, *Romance de la Guardia Civil Española*

Max arrived before nine at the police station. He pointedly looked at his watch when González entered fifteen minutes late.

'Good morning. Shall we begin? Don't have much time.'

González grunted, and turned to Cabo Guevarra. 'Girlie, get us two coffees.'

Guevarra returned five minutes later.

'*Gracias*. Max, one for you. Okay. Let's get the show on the road. What we got? Bugger all. If we had any brains we'd have questioned the lad last night, and stopped poncing about. But Max here said we had to wait for his lawyer. The lad's our prime suspect. Probably got given the heave. She starts playing silly buggers, he swipes her, and she's down the ravine. Just got to get the bugger to confess.'

'But only in a legal way,' interrupted Max

'Sure, only legal. But there's legal and legal. No new

evidence. Still no mobile. Spoke to the doc. Says she could have been pushed, could have jumped, could have stumbled, could have been hit. Difficult to say with broken necks. Okay I'll kick off with questions to the lad. Then Max can take over. Try the bad cop, good cop routine. Any questions? Any opinions?'

Guevarra looked at Max in disbelief. 'I felt the father's grief was genuine. For me he's not in the frame.'

González guffawed. 'Two years in the force now, girlie? The grieving parent act is the oldest con in the book. But you're probably right for once. I reckon it's the boy. But best double check on the dad's story. Guevarra – you follow that one up. And get any gossip on that community. Always thought they were a little bit doolally. Bloody bunch of hippies playing at being Muslim.'

The heat was beginning to build up. The ends of González' droopy moustache were dripping water. González wiped his face and moustache with a handkerchief that had seen better days.

'León – you pop up to Capa, and sniff around. See what you can get on that lot in the hills.'

'Before you start questioning people, I have to declare an interest,' interrupted Max. 'I have met Leila's father on several occasions through my police liaison work with the Muslim communities. I met Leila at her father's house and . . . I invited her out two or three times for a cup of tea to talk about her doctoral thesis.'

'A cup of tea?' laughed León.

'Yes, a cup of tea.'

'Tea and sympathy, was it?' said León.

Max tried to maintain his dignity. 'It was more a case of tea and thesis.'

León could hardly speak with laughter. 'And she invited you up to see her thesis notes, I suppose. Tell me . . . do these Muslim girls have it in the shape of a crescent moon?'

It was González who pulled the meeting to order. 'There's a serious point here. Max has to be a suspect.'

58

'Yes,' interrupted León. ' He clearly hoped to have it off with her, but he implies he didn't . . . so it could be a case of sexual frustration and jealousy. I suggest, sir, we ask Max to give us notes on what was said and even happened at these tea meetings, and then if you like I'll interview him. He of course does have an alibi for the time of her death – he was with her father.'

'That's true,' said González, grinning.

'Very decent of you to notice my alibi, Teniente,'said Max. 'But you do need to know that I recommended Leila to interview my *abuela*, Paula, for her thesis. So she visited our place at the end of the Jola road pretty often, and got to know all the family there.'

'Hmm,' said González. 'That does further complicate things. Guevarra, you'd better interview Doña Paula, and that wife of Juan's, Isabel, isn't it? And León – you interview Juan. Anything else to tell us, Max?'

León giggled lasciviously. 'Perhaps we can get some interesting details when Guevarra isn't present?'

'It was only tea,' protested Max lamely.

There was a knock on the door, and the secretary entered. 'The lawyer from Granada has arrived, sir.'

'Okay, bring him in. Sure to be some posh git if he's working for that guy, what's his name?'

'Dr Javeed Dharwish,' offered Max.

'Yeah. Javeed. It gets my goat when them foreigners think they're superior to us poor Spaniards.'

A young lawyer, hair brushed back to silken perfection, pale grey suit, cream shirt with silver cuff links, came in. He looked round the room, placed an expensive leather briefcase on the table, and smiled.

'*Buenos dias.* Gabriel Martín Facarros.' He handed out a gold printed card to everyone. 'My client, Dr Javeed Dharwish, telephoned me last night. He explained what has happened. The suspect Hassan Khan, if he is a suspect, is entirely here of his own free will, and is willing to cooperate fully. But if there is any overstepping the legal boundaries, and I will be the judge of that, then cooperation will cease, and a formal complaint will be made. Is that clear?' And he smiled at everyone again.

González grunted. 'Bring the lad up.'

Hassan entered the room. He had not slept much.

'Sit down,' González said. 'Would you like a coffee?'

'No thanks. I had one not long ago.'

'We'd like to ask you a few questions. Standard procedure at this stage.'

'Am I a suspect?'

'No, no. We just want you to help us with our inquiries. Max here will ask you a few questions.'

'Okay. You told us yesterday a bit about your walk and tiff with Leila. But could you begin by telling us about yourself, and how you ended up as an assistant to Javeed and on this training course?' asked Max.

'Is this really relevant?' interrupted the lawyer.

'Just getting some background.'

'That's okay,' said Hassan. 'I'm British. Dad came over from P—Pakistan to work in Leeds, then moved to London where he married mum. She's a Londoner. I was six when she left us both, and I lived with my dad.'

Hassan shuffled awkwardly in the chair. Wiped his palms on his shirt. Scratched his ear.

'Sorry about the heat,' said Max. 'Water?'

'P—please.'

Guevarra left the room to fetch some water. Hassan slowly drank the whole glass. González raised his bushy eyebrows. 'Come on. Come on. We haven't got all bloody day.'

Hassan cleared his throat. 'There's not much to say. I was good at maths at school, good with computers, and then went to Brunel to study computing and electronics. I did a work placement with Dr Dharwish's consultancy firm. Then Javeed – Dr Dharwish – told me he had this job at the Ibn Rush'd Centre. I needed a break before p—postgrad, and was fortunate to be chosen.'

'Why a break?'

'Oh. Just needed to get my head around things. Find out who I really am, that sort of thing.'

'Religious?'

'Muslim of course, and I practise my religion as devoutly as I can. More so now.'

'Fanatical?' butted in González.

'What's that meant to mean?' asked Gabriel. 'Muslim and fanatical are not the same thing.'

'Okay,' said Hassan. 'Javeed said I'm to tell everything to show we have nothing to hide.'

'Why we?' continued González.

'Because we're Muslims. These days we're all suspects.'

González grunted.

'No. Not fanatical, but I am devout,' continued Hassan.

'Political?'

'Voted Labour last time. This time I'll probably vote Liberal. But I'm not in any group or party.'

Max decided to take over again. 'How did you get chosen for this job?'

'I first met Javeed at a Palestine Solidarity Meeting. I was pretty low, and he helped me out. We got to know each other, and I had a work placement in his office. I also used to help him with his charity work, collecting money for a hospital in Gaza.'

'But didn't you need references and some qualifications for the Ibn Rush'd job?'

'Yes. Three references. Also I'm good with IT, and Javeed needed someone to set up systems and help him with the administration. And I had a good project idea, it's—'

'Tell us about the girl,' González butted in.

'Leila. We met at p—prayers, talked a few times, and sometimes after p—prayers some of us would go to her father's place for tea. I went out with her a few times. Last Thursday I went for a walk with her, then met her after p—prayers on Friday, and had this silly quarrel.'

Hassan's voice began to croak.

'More water?' asked Guevarra.

61

'Please.'

'Oh bloody hell. Guevarra, get a bloody jug of the stuff,' interrupted González. 'We'll be here all night just to make sure he's comfortable.'

Max pointedly continued. 'Quarrelled? Over what?'

'My fault. I said I couldn't go out with her again.'

'Why?'

'Javeed advised me against it.'

'Do you do everything Javeed suggests?'

'No. But he's helped me a lot, and he said I should concentrate on the job and the course. It's tough, trying to do both, you know.'

'Back to the girl. Nothing else to tell us? Nothing happened?' said González, impatiently.

'What could happen? It was just a walk, and then a silly quarrel.'

'You didn't touch her or anything?'

Hassan blushed. 'Of course not. I respect her.' His voice broke, and tears clouded his eyes. 'I mean respected her.'

Gabriel interrupted. 'There's no need for that sort of questioning.'

Max felt the questioning was becoming insensitive, but let González continue.

'On Saturday you met up with her again?'

'No. I've already told you. I went into Diva with Javeed before five to get some things for the centre. I never saw her again after Friday.'

Hassan's hands shook, and his shoulders slumped.

'Come on. Expect us to believe that? You met up with her, didn't you? You grabbed her, and she fell over the ravine.'

'I told you I never saw her after Friday.'

'It'll be easier for you if you just admit it.'

Gabriel again interrupted. 'If you continue this way I will advise my client not to cooperate any further.'

Max came in again. 'Could you give us a detailed account of your movements, say between four and six, the evening of last Saturday?'

Hassan controlled his breathing a little. 'Well, Javeed and I set off for Diva at about three. We drove down the mountain, and got here a bit after four. We were early, so the shops were still all shut, so we went for tea and a game of chess in the Al Andaluz café. They can give you the exact time we got there. It was raining when the shops reopened, so we decided to stay in the café and finish our chess game.'

'Who won?'

'I did,' said Hassan smiling, faintly.

'What was your winning move?'

'Oh. Let me see.' Hassan closed his eyes. 'Yes. I remember now. Javeed had taken my second white knight, the one on B1. I then moved my bishop to D3 to put him in check, and that won the game because the black king had to move from A4 to B3 leaving the white bishop to take the black queen. Once that happened I was able to advance my pawn on D5 to become a queen.'

'Come on. Who cares how he fucking won a game of bloody chess?' interrupted González.

Max gave González a withering stare, and then turned back to Hassan. 'What did you do next?'

'It was still raining when we went to the supermarket where we stocked up, and then b—back up the mountain.'

The secretary knocked at the door. 'Those chaps from the Centre are here, sir.'

'Bugger,' said González. 'They're early. Take him away. We'll continue later.'

'Only if he agrees,' said Gabriel.

Hassan turned to Gabriel. 'It's fine. I know I'm a suspect, but as I keep saying I've nothing to hide.'

'If you agree, that's acceptable. But I am not happy with the tone and implications of many of the questions. With your permission, Teniente, I will speak to Dr Dharwish to let him know my doubts.'

'If you must. We will speak to them all after you've spoken with your Don Javeed.' González said, emphasizing the Don.

63

Gabriel and Hassan left together. When the cops were alone González exploded.

'Bloody smart story. Bloody chess game. Alibi all the fucking time. But each other. Just give me ten minutes alone with that young shit and I'll sort him out.'

'But sir,' said Guevarra, 'he's just a scared kid. We can check up on the alibi.'

'Telling me how to do my job now, girlie? Watch yourself.'

González turned to León. 'I'll give the Judge a bell, and ask him to question the boy. León, you get the papers ready requesting another forty-eight hours.'

Max butted in. 'Look, I don't think you have sufficient grounds at this stage to hold him for another forty-eight hours. He has a decent alibi, and there is nothing to link him to the crime scene. I suggest you leave the request to the judge for the moment.'

González paused and scowled. 'You're probably right. Okay, but I tell you he did it.'

The air conditioning hardly worked. They were all sweating.

Gabriel, Javeed and four other men knocked and entered. It was Javeed who spoke.

'I have all the documents here you asked for. Gabriel has complained to me about your questions. Note we are cooperating fully and voluntarily. But, believe me, if you overstep the mark I shall complain to the highest authorities.'

González said nothing. Javeed pulled out some neat plastic folders from his briefcase, and handed them to González who passed them over to Max.

'We'll keep these for a few days if you don't mind,' said Max, taking the folders.

'We're not going anywhere, so that's okay.'

'We'd like to ask you a few more questions,' said Max, after glancing at the file.

'Fine. Go ahead,' replied Javeed.

'Javeed Dharwish. British passport, I see.'

64

'Yes. Originally Palestinian. But I lived for fifteen years or more in London where I still have a flat and consultancy business.'

'Omar Rahmin? French passport.'

'*Oui*. Parisian. I was born there, but my parents came from Algeria.'

'Faslur Hashim? And you have a Spanish passport.'

'I came over from Morocco twelve years ago, and was given Spanish citizenship two years ago.'

'Rizwan Ahmet? A Belgian passport.'

'Yes. My father was Algerian, and he married a Belgian girl, my mother, and stayed in Belgium where I was born.'

'And finally, Hakim Lasnami with a German passport. Don't tell me your dad also married a local girl?'

'No, our family emigrated from Iraq. My father's a doctor, and after taking some exams in Germany he was allowed to stay and practise medicine there.'

'Quite a collection we have here,' said González.

'Yes,' replied Javeed. 'The Ibn Rush'd Centre is a European one. We intend to bring young Muslims from all over Europe, and help them become good European businessmen and leaders. We want to show that Muslims can be good Europeans, and also successful ones.'

'Hmm,' muttered González.

Max glanced at the Ibn Rush'd brochure, glossy with pictures of the mountains, the centre and the statue of Ibn Rush'd in Cordova. 'Quite a collection of sponsors you have here.'

'Yes. We did surprisingly well. Many of our successful Muslim businessmen have contributed, but also interfaith groups and others have agreed to sponsor us. I have here all the documentation on the purchase of the centre, planning permission for alterations, receipts for building work, the CVs of all our applicants, and a daily outline of the courses they follow. I keep a progress report, but that is confidential. I also have letters of support from the Spanish Ministry of Culture and of Foreign Affairs. The Management Centre at the University of Granada is also a co-sponsor, and we attend their lectures. And this is the application we sent to the EU for funding together with their positive response.'

'Could you leave these with us. We will return them in a few days.'

'Certainly. If you have any further questions I would be pleased to help. Can we take Hassan back with us?'

'Okay. Take the lad for now. But he'll be back.'

'In which case we will leave. Any further questions? Any way we can be of assistance?'

Max replied, 'I don't think so. No, just one thing.' He turned to Javeed. 'How do you select candidates?'

'We have a rigorous application form, three referees, one of whom has to be religious. The candidate presents an outline of his business proposals, and if possible two members of our Board of Management, plus myself of course, do an interview.'

'Did you interview Hassan?'

'Yes, in London. I knew him in London. He was on a placement with me and was also a volunteer for a charity I support, HosPal, which collects aid for a hospital in Gaza. I decided he would be a good administrative assistant for the centre. He also came highly recommended as a potential high-flyer, and his proposal of a quality software company writing in Urdu, Arabic and English appealed to me.'

'By the way, who won the chess game?'

'Chess game? Oh, Hassan did.'

'His final move?'

'Let me see now. I was attacking, and took his white knight, which left me open to check from his bishop, which eventually led me to losing my queen. It was a very good game.'

'What time did you leave?'

'There was very heavy rain. So we both left about six, Yasmin in Al Andaluz can confirm that. We stocked up in the supermarket. We must have left Diva a bit after seven. We filled up with gas so the station should be able to confirm the time. We wanted to get back before dark. Is that all?'

'For now, yes.'

They all left, together with the lawyer.

González snorted. 'Fuck it. The town would have been deserted with all that rain so the kid has the alibi of that smooth bastard, what's his name? Don Javeed. Convenient, eh? Okay, I'll check every home on the Jola road, somebody might have seen something.'

'All looks above board to me. They do have alibis, if only each other,' said Max, looking at his watch. 'Sorry. Have to go now, but if you need any further help, write in officially to request it, and we'll see if I can get time off. Let me take all that documentation, and I'll get Granada and Madrid to check it. We'll need to run the names through our computer files as well as other EU ones. And even ask the US if they have anything.'

'That would be good. You've got some uses after all.'

On his way back to Granada, Max passed the Boabdil restaurant, built on the site where Boabdil, the last Moorish Sultan of Granada, wept as he had his final glimpse of his beloved Granada, only to be rebuked by his mother with the famous words: 'You do well to weep like a woman for what you failed to defend like a man.' The restaurant stood next to a cement factory.

If Boabdil could see it now, thought Max, looking at the mess of new housing and industrial estates crawling across the rich farmland of the Vega, he'd do more than weep.

In midsummer, the heat turns Granada into a ghost town. The pigeons would go to the coast if they could. But the traffic is lighter, and journeys faster. Some consolation.

Max went straight to police headquarters, a dull, battered block in the San Jerónimo district. The *barrio's* glory days were over. The streets were a mess of ugly university buildings, cheap shops and run-down offices, the fine mansions converted into budget hostels or student flats. But rising above it all, the still magnificent Renaissance churches of

67

San Jerónimo and San Juan de Díos gleamed in the sun. Max slowly climbed the stairs, the clammy heat beginning to bother his asthma. He knocked on the door.

'Come in,' said Clara.

'Hi, Clara. How you coping with this heat? Boss free?'

'My, you look all hot and bothered. Have some water. I'll see if he's still here.'

'Thanks. I hate this weather.'

Max cleared his dry throat, sipped the water and took a quick puff of his inhaler.

'Yes, he's free. Can see you now.'

'Max, come in,' Davila called. 'Nice and cool in here. I keep the conditioning on full blast. Problems in Diva?'

'Could be a tricky one, sir. British Muslim girl found dead at the bottom of a ravine. We're pretty sure it's murder. Teniente González is in charge. Judge Falcón wants me to help, seeing she's both British and Muslim.'

'González? Reputation for being very solid.'

Max swallowed. Best keep the lip buttoned. 'If you say so, sir.'

Davila glanced sharply at Max. 'He may be a bit old-fashioned. The Mayor of Diva thinks highly of him.'

'I'll remember that, sir.'

'Yes, do. You should continue to help but he has to officially request it. If Falcón wants you then I'll get the permission for you to assist approved quickly. Keep me fully informed of all developments. But make sure this doesn't interfere with the briefing for the CGI meeting.'

'There's a complication. A potential suspect is a young British Muslim lad on some adventure training course above Capa. The Centre's documentation seems rock solid. Probably nothing, sir, but I think we should check up on it all.'

'That's wise of you, Max. Don't want to overlook anything. I'll send it all off to the appropriate bodies.'

Max handed over the Centre's documentation.

'I'll look into this. Give me a written note on the Diva case right away. Done the final draft of the briefing? It's got to be first rate. It's important we impress them. But make sure it's bland. We don't want them or us investigating this and that group. Might stir up the media. You know what they're like.'

Max smiled. 'Here's the disk, sir. Needs some final polishing. You'll have that first thing tomorrow morning.'

Inspector Jefe Davila had built his career on four golden rules: nothing in the media, keep any potential difficulties low key, never offend those in authority or with influence, and always maintain the appearance of a safe pair of hands. The rules had served him well.

Max returned to his flat, put on his noisy and inefficient air conditioning, stripped off his sweaty clothes, and ran the shower as cold as he could before standing under it for ten minutes. Even then the water was tepid rather than cold. But it helped.

After tidying up the report, and checking it was suitably bland, Max went to bed early, and lay naked on top of the sheets. He slept restlessly. In the early hours of the morning, the air conditioning packed in, and Max woke in a pool of sweat. He changed the sheet, but found it difficult to get back to sleep. Leila's death was a real puzzle: no suspects except Hassan, who really didn't look the part, and nothing to go on from Forensics. He awoke groggy and tired. A cold shower revived him.

Max drove slowly to the police station, and handed his final report in, as promised. Davila was in one of his petty, officious moods.

'I'll make the final corrections. Your grammar, Max, is still not as it should be. Too much foreign education. Can't understand how you got through your entrance exams. Off to the airport tomorrow then. Remember we want all this to go well. Top priority in fact.'

'Certainly, sir.'

Max went to his office. Piles of unopened correspondence and files lay in his in-tray. Best get it cleared: it would be a busy few days. Must be getting popular with some Muslim groups: he'd go to 'The Chants Mystiques des Femmes du Maghreb', and the French film on the Sufis of Afghanistan if he could. Max looked at the files and groaned: reports, performance indicators, more reports, Spanish legislation, EU legislation. It would take all day.

Chapter 7

Dale limosna, mujer,
que no hay en la vida nada
Como la pena de ser
Ciego en Granada.

Give him alms, woman,
for there is nothing in life
So cruel as being blind
In Granada.

Francisco de Icaza, popular refrain

The next day Max arrived at the airport more than thirty minutes before the plane from Madrid was due to land; Davila had been losing sleep over this visit, so it was a belt and braces job.

Bang on schedule, Linda and a stranger came through Domestic Arrivals.

'Max! How are you?'

'Fine, Linda. I mean . . . fine, Inspectora Jefe Concha.'

'No need to be so formal, Max.' She turned to her companion. 'May I present Inspector Martín Sánchez from CGI. He's here to keep an eye on me. He thinks I have a tendency to overstep the rules.'

'You two know each other then?' asked Inspector Sánchez.

Max shook hands, 'The Inspectora Jefe was lead tutor on my promotion course. Her lectures were very good.'

71

'I'm sure they were,' Martín replied. 'The Inspectora Jefe likes to lecture.'

Max turned back to Linda. 'It's a long time since you were in Granada.'

'Yes, on a school trip.'

Linda was looking good. Slim as ever. Blonde hair expensively cut. The shoes alone would have set most people back a week's wages. Lively blue eyes quickly reappraised him. He was pleased he still passed the test.

Martín seemed as comfortable as a sausage on a barbecue.

'Shall we go? I've booked you into the Alhambra Palace Hotel. It's nice. Pure Moorish fantasy. And a great view over the city.'

The official car was waiting outside the airport terminal. They took the ring road towards the Sierra Nevada before turning off to the Alhambra, and through the grounds to the hotel, spotlit by the evening sun. Martín did not look too pleased.

'Bit remote.'

'Martín – it's class.'

'It's quite a way from town. We'd have to get a taxi if we wanted to go anywhere.'

Max was bewildered: most people coming to Granada would be thrilled to be staying there.

'We've got to consider security,' Martín added. 'With all these trees and everything we'd be sitting ducks.'

' Martín, who the hell knows we're here? Do you think terrorists have been following us?'

'It's no joke, Linda. Sub-Inspector Romero, can you get us a modern hotel in the town centre?'

'Leave it with me,' Max said. 'I'll make a few phone calls and see what I can do.'

He was back in a few minutes. 'Okay. You're in the Hotel Santa Paula, a five star on Gran Vía.'

'Sorry about that. You can't be too careful. Women only see the romantic side of things. I'm trained to be practical.'

Linda sniffed. This was not going well. They got back into the car, and drove through Plaza Nueva and along Gran Vía.

'Here we are, the hotel.'

'That's better. Looks like there are some good bars down that street.'

So much for security, thought Max. 'I'll leave you to settle in. The restaurant is good. Everything is on us, so order what you like.'

'That's generous of you,' said Martín.

'The meeting tomorrow is at five. When do you want to be picked up? I can show you around Granada after your meeting with the Mayor if you like.'

'Well, I don't know. I've got papers to work on. I'm not one for all that tourist stuff,' said Martín.

'Don't be such a bore, Martín. The more we know about the city, the better. I think we would be free from about eleven.'

'Eleven o'clock then?' said Max.

'Great.' Linda flashed a smile. Martín grunted assent.

'Have a good evening. See you tomorrow,' said Max, saluting.

Max returned to the Albayzín in his own car, wondering how deep the obvious conflict between Linda and Martín was. He parked three blocks below his flat. Parking in the Albayzín was a nightmare. There was building work everywhere, and a faint smell of ancient drains, which didn't appreciate the disturbance.

Next morning, Max reported to Davila.

'I've had to correct your grammar again, Max. Your presentation is still a bit long, but it should do. I've asked Clara to email it to you. Just don't make any anti-American jokes. What's your impression of the . . . um . . . Madrid team so far?'

'Inspectora Jefe Concha seems very positive. Inspector Sánchez is hard to please, and I don't think they're singing from the same hymn sheet at all. The politics is probably a lot more complicated than we thought.'

'Hmm. I'm told she's one of the PM's girls. You know she's General Concha's daughter, don't you? She didn't get any favours though, and none of this positive discrimination crap either. Comisario Bonila told me that the Socialists are considering positive discrimination for Muslims. I'll fight that one. So will the PM.'

'More Muslims in the force here in Granada would be handy. Help us with our work.'

'Maybe. But only on merit. The PM. thinks we've got too many Muslims in Spain as it is. So he's recruiting all these Argentinians.'

'You mean men like Navarro. Had to get out of Argentina before he got picked up for torturing some kids, wasn't it?'

'Max, I've told you before to keep your politics out of this office. Navarro was only defending his country. He's a good cop.'

'Shall I go now, sir?'

'Yes. And watch that tongue of yours. It could get you into serious trouble. The meeting will be at 5 p.m. prompt. We don't want them to think we take long siestas.'

'Don't worry, sir. They want the Tour, so I'm picking them up at eleven. I'll be here at four for the final run-through.'

At eleven, Linda was waiting alone in the lobby. She smiled when Max entered.

'*Hola.* Just us, I'm afraid. Dear Martín went off drinking alone last night. Must have eaten some rubbish, and now he has to sit by the toilet. It's no loss.'

'So you had to do the Mayor's office on your own?'

'No problem. The usual bullshit.' She stood up, smoothed her white linen dress. 'Won't be a minute. Forgotten my fan.'

'I'll wait here.' Max took out his mobile, and made a quick phone call.

Linda returned, fan in hand. 'So what's the programme, Max?'

'Well, I thought we'd start at the Alhambra. We won't have time to go in. We'd need half a day for that. You can do the evening tour later when it's cooler. I'll point out the cathedral and all that, but I get pretty bored with the insides of churches.'

'Me too.'

'Then we'll drive through Sacromonte to the Abadía to meet a friend of mine. A little time there, then I know this great tapas bar, where we can have lunch and relax, and still give you plenty of time to rest before five.'

'Sounds great. Let's go.'

As they got into the pool car, Linda turned to him. 'Just got a new BMW. Lovely car, quiet as a sleeping kitten, marvellous air conditioning. You should get one, I strongly recommend them.'

'On my salary?' scoffed Max. 'You must be joking.'

'You never know. If you play your cards right I might be able to help. By the way, when we're on our own, you can call me Linda.'

The car nosed its way down Gran Vía.

'This is Gran Vía de Colón, usually just called Gran Vía, one of Granada's main streets. Enlightened Granada Council knocked down half the medieval city to build it, and the sugar merchants built these god-awful mansions to their greater glory.'

'When was that?'

'Late nineteenth century, I think.'

'They're not that bad. Some really fine buildings. Need doing up, and then they'll be splendid.'

'The cathedral is on your right. The Royal Chapel is worth a visit. Bit gloomy. But the sculptor had a bit of fun. Isabel's head sinks lower in her cushion than Ferdinand's to show she was the brains.'

Max turned past Plaza Isabel la Católica into Plaza Nueva.

'Up there on your left is Felipe Segundo's Audiencia, well worth a visit, and a bit further on are the remains of Arab baths dating back to the eleventh century. This is the Cuesta de Gomerez. God, I remember when all the tour buses to the Alhambra had to come up here. The exhaust fumes nearly killed you. Okay, this is Puerto de los Granados of the Renaissance Palace of Charles V, and here . . . we enter the grounds of the Alhambra. Yesterday, we came in from the ring road so you didn't see it at its best.'

'Oh! This is pretty. I never thought the woods in summer would be so fresh and green.'

'Some books claim the Duke of Wellington planted the elms, but he didn't. Whenever I feel a bit down I come and sit here. Haven't done that for a while. So maybe the job's picking up.'

'You mean you don't like the police job?'

'It has its ups and downs.'

'What job doesn't?'

They drove slowly up to the Puerta de Justicia, and the Alhambra ticket office. There was a queue. A Japanese group, laden down with cameras, waiting patiently; a family who could only be British, red-faced, red-kneed, guidebooks in hand; an impeccably dressed French couple; giggling Spanish schoolgirls in pleated tartan skirts; and official guides herding their sheep of all nationalities.

'Not worth going in. You need a good half-day to do it justice, and the evening tour is much cooler, of course. How about I park here, and we walk down to the Parador San Francisco for a drink?'

'Okay.'

Max parked the car. 'Don't forget your fan. You'll need it.'

They strolled down to the Parador through the gardens.

'This used to be a convent. I think Isabel la Católica once stayed here. We can sit in the garden, if you like.'

'It's lovely. Fresh orange juice and a nice cake for me.'

They sat quietly, sipping the fresh juices and eating the cakes. Once finished, they walked to the parapet of the garden and, leaning on the mossy wall, Max pointed upwards.

'Over there is the Torre de las Infantas – if you're romantic . . . That's where the sultans' daughters lived. Over there,

76

that's the Torre de la Cautiva, where the Sultan Muley Hacén kept his Christian mistress, Isabel de Solís. He dumped his wife for her. And that started the civil war which led to the fall of Granada.'

'Yes. I remember the TV series.'

'There are lots of copies of the painting of the handover of the keys of Granada to Isabel and Ferdinand around the city. And right over there, the Generalife, the finest garden in the whole of Spain. The orange-red colour of the buildings, *al hamra*, gave us the name, Alhambra.'

Max paused, and pointed up to the mountains. 'I was brought up over there, on the other side of those mountains, a little town called Diva.'

'You didn't stay in Spain, did you?'

'Went to Glasgow for final school years and university. Why I drifted into the cops I'm still not sure. A long story – I'll tell you sometime. But you get used to the life.'

'Me, I was born into it. Couldn't do anything else. I married a cop; my grandfather was a cop, and my dad. It's difficult at times. I've one kid, she's ten now. Don't care what she does as long as it's not the cops.'

'Better go,' said Max.

The waiter handed Max the bill, carefully folded inside a small leather case. Max winced as he paid a ridiculous amount for what they had eaten. Old Skinflint in Expenses would be bound to tell him he should have gone somewhere cheaper. They walked slowly up the hill to the car. It was now even hotter. They drove back down the Cuesta de Gomerez, turned right at Plaza Nueva to enter Plaza Santa Ana. A traffic cop stopped them. No Entry. Max showed his police ID.

'Showing an important visitor from Madrid around.'

'Okay, sir.'

They crawled along the Paseo de los Tristes, the Alhambra towers and walls smouldering above them, then found themselves behind the little Albayzín bus, chugging up the Cuesta del Chapiz.

'That's the Casa del Chapiz, one of the few Moorish houses to survive. It's now a centre for Arabic studies. I was there for almost a year.'

'How's your Arabic?'

'Not great. It's a difficult language.'

Only when they turned right into Sacromonte could they pick up speed.

'There are some of the famous Sacromonte caves. Tourist traps mostly, but some have good flamenco.'

'Oh, I'd love to go.'

'Well, you've come to the right man.'

'You're on.'

Max stopped the car on a passing place. 'This is one of the best views of the Alhambra. You can also see most of the Darro valley from here. "As one should remember a sweetheart who has died."'

'That's lovely, Max. Who said that?'

'It's Lorca – about Granada.'

'Lorca. I love his stuff. Pity he was on the wrong side.'

Max gulped. He didn't expect Linda to say something like that.

They drove along the Darro valley road. 'Doesn't take long to get right out into the countryside,' said Linda.

'No. We're close to the Abadía. The abbot's a friend. He's offered to show us around.'

Max pulled the string of the ancient bell outside the large, carved chestnut door. The door creaked open. A bear of a man, in blue jeans, sandals and a white smock shirt hauled the door open. Fuzzy white beard, round face and twinkling eyes greeted them.

'Max, great to see you. And this is the young lady. High up in something mysterious. Not bad.' And he stepped forward, gave Linda a bear hug, almost lifting her off the ground, and smacked two kisses on each cheek.

'Jorge, you rogue. Getting more like Friar Tuck every day.'

'Friar Tuck?'

'You know Robin Hood and his band of Merry Men?'

'No. You forget I didn't have your English education.'

'Scottish, Scottish education. How many times have I told you we Scots ain't English.'

'Judging from your football team, you'd be better off if you were.'

'Okay. Okay. Peace.'

Linda looked bewildered. Max suspected all her clergy were grave, solemn and formal. Jorge offered his arm.

'Come on, my dear, just ignore him, and let me show you around my little home.'

And he strode off with Linda, leaving Max trailing behind.

'The abbey stands on the top of Mount Valparaíso, the Paradise Valley. Lead tablets with Arabic inscriptions on them were found here, describing the martyrdoms of three saints. An oven with ashes was also found. This was handy.'

'Yes?'

'If you have saints you need an abbey and an abbot. So here we are. The Star of Solomon, see here, became the symbol of the abbey. We keep the ashes of the martyred saints here below their statues. Here we are now at the catacombs, my dear. Mind your head. Over there we have a cross carried by San Juan de Dios. And this large stone here has real magical powers – if you kiss it you will find a husband within a year.'

'That's the last thing I need.'

'In which case Jorge's law says you have to kiss the abbot to ensure that fate does not befall you.'

Linda laughed, stood on her tiptoes, and kissed Jorge fully on the mouth. 'My. I'm not sure I agree with this celibacy lark.'

Max interrupted testily. 'Linda, this is really interesting. See this grille here – behind that is the oven where the martyrs were burned.'

Linda shivered. 'Let's go, father. Why do all religions put so much emphasis on suffering?'

'Because it makes our own real suffering easier to bear.'

They came up into the bright sun, and moved quickly into the shade of the cloisters.

'I was going to show you a genuine document written by our great Conquistador, Pizarro. If he were alive today he'd be tried for genocide. But you look as if you need a small refreshment. We've prepared something special, Tortilla Sacromonte. Goes well with a really dry sherry. Some for you, Max?'

'Just the sherry for me. I'm not sure Linda will like the tortilla.'

'Come on, Max. Don't be rude,' said Linda.

'Okay. If you insist. Don't say I didn't warn you.'

Jorge gave Max a schoolboy grin. They walked down steps to an ancient cellar. On the plain wooden table stood a bottle of sherry and three glasses.

'María. We're ready for the tortilla.' Jorge turned to Linda. 'Max said I'm not to ask what you do. High up and top secret.'

'That's okay. I'm a cop working in the Anti-Terrorist Unit.'

'Anti-Terrorist Unit? My. You're just a slip of a girl. Could be dangerous, no?'

'Could be. But most of my work is gathering intelligence.'

'Well, make sure you don't slide from anti-terrorist to anti-Muslim. Fine group of people, the Muslims. We owe them a lot here. They're a bit puritanical for my taste . . . like your dreadful Scottish man, Max, what's he called? Yes. John Knox. Anyone who doesn't enjoy a good glass of wine is missing out on one of God's great gifts. Good. The tortilla. Sure you won't have some, Max?'

'Absolutely sure.'

'If you ate this, instead of hamburgers, you English would be healthier.'

'Scottish, Jorge. Scottish.'

'How do you find it, my dear?'

'Er, tasty. Unusual.'

'Let me tell you a story about it. This is served every year on the day of San Cecilio. One year our cook here was ill, and we had to call in the chef from the Parador, and he served us ham, peas and kidneys in the tortilla. The abbot, not me at the time, sent it back. So the cook said, "What's wrong, father? I've made thousands of Sacromonte tortillas." "Ah," replied the abbot. "You've missed the main ingredients of the true Sacromonte tortilla." Know what they are?'

'No,' replied Linda.

The abbot bellowed with laughter. 'Lamb's brains and testicles'.

Linda turned pale. 'It's great. Can you give me the recipe?'

'Recipe? Sure. Well done, girl. You cook the brains and testicles in salted water, drain and brown in olive oil. Then you mash them to a paste. Got that?'

'Mmm.'

'Beat the eggs, fry one layer of the eggs, add the paste, another layer of eggs, and when set, turn the tortilla. Eat. Enjoy. Extra dry sherry is essential.'

'We'd better go,' said Max. 'You can never be sure what Jorge will get up to next.'

'Max, come and see me soon for a good drink. Just got in some wonderful Malaga wine.'

'Will do.'

Linda was still a little pale. But General Concha's daughter would not admit defeat. It was she who gave the abbot a big hug, and two loud kisses on each cheek.

Once in the car, Max laughed. 'I did warn you. You handled it well though. Congratulations. We'll go to a great bar where the food is much safer. I'll park the car in the police car park, and we can walk from there.'

'Not that pious, is he?'

'Oh, don't be taken in by that act. He just believes we should enjoy all the things God has given us. But underneath it all he's a bit of a saint really. The gypsies adore him, made him an honorary gypsy. You should see him when their procession arrives back at the Abadía during Holy Week. He's in his element during the Flamenco Mass . . . then dances and drinks until dawn.'

Max swore as a group of motorcyclists sped past him.

'Where was I? Oh, yes, Jorge. He spends most of his time helping illegal immigrants and rough sleepers. Started a campaign against under-age prostitution, and rescues a lot of the poor kids. When he takes on something he just won't give up.' Max smiled admiringly. 'He's never afraid to take on the rich and powerful. I reckon there are quite a few would like to see him out of the way. Did you know that of all the men in Europe, we Spanish men are the ones who most visit prostitutes?'

'Doesn't surprise me, one bit.'

Max parked the car. Linda had recovered her colour. They entered the Bodega La Castañeda. A waiter came up.

'Max, I've kept a table in the window for you.'

'Thanks, Ramón. The Castañeda special, and a bottle of your best white Rioja, very cold.'

'Okay, Max.'

Max turned to Linda. 'Ramón plays flamenco guitar when he's not a waiter. Maybe not the best, but very good. We could go sometime when he plays in La Platería.'

'Love to.'

Ramón brought a wooden platter of smoked *bacalao* and tuna, fresh white anchovies, cheeses, olives, tomatoes, asparagus and artichokes. He returned a few minutes later with a bottle of Faustino V and two glasses. He poured a drop into Max's glass. Max swirled it round, sniffed it, and sipped it slowly.

'Great. What year is it? '92. Good year.'

Ramón smiled. 'So how you doing, Max? Are you going to introduce me to your pretty companion?'

'Linda, this is Ramón. Ramón, Linda.'

Ramón lent over the table, and kissed her on both cheeks. 'You're welcome.'

'*Gracias*. Max says you play the guitar. Hope I can come and hear you sometime.'

'I'm playing at the weekend, come along. Not an Andalusian accent?'

'No, from Madrid.'

'Well, no one's perfect.'

'How do you like the wine?'

'Mainly peach aroma, I'd say. I find the Riojas a bit insipid, but this is quite a good one. Myself, I prefer Ribera del Duera.'

Okay, you win, thought Max. No more trying to impress.

'These cheeses are interesting.'

'All from Andalusia. This one is Pedroches, a sheep's cheese from Cordova. That over there, moulded in esparto, is from Malaga, a white goat's cheese. That's Grazalema, from the mountains south of Cadiz. And that's another goat's cheese from Las Alpujarras.'

'You were going to tell me how you ended up in the cops?'

'To be honest I'm still not really sure. But you can probably blame Jorge. It had never crossed my mind. I was at a really low ebb with parents finally divorcing . . . and I'd split with girlfriend. Life going nowhere, and not even knowing where it should be going. Couldn't decide if I wanted to be in Spain or Britain, be British or Spanish. Drinking much too much, and to be honest, smoking too much pot.'

Linda sniffed disapprovingly.

'Well, to cut a long story short I was really depressed, and decided to take a walk in the hills behind the Abadía, and as I was walking back Jorge stopped to give me a lift. One thing led to another. He talked me out of depression, and we became friends. It was Jorge who suggested the police. Said he'd seen a police advert for university graduates.' Max laughed. 'He kept going on to me about the importance of having sensitive, progressive police now that Spain was a democracy, and how it would be a good thing all round. Well, nothing else came up, and I thought, why not, give it a try, and I just drifted into it. Still not sure I made the right decision.'

'So different to me. Never even thought about anything else. So apart from looking after Martín and me, and writing a report on the Muslims here, what else are you doing?'

'I'm in Homicide, but I do a bit of community liaison work with the Muslims. Right now I'm involved in a really sad case. Pretty Muslim girl, Edinburgh University history student, found dead in Diva. Body under a bridge at the bottom of a ravine. I've been asked to help out. I knew her, and her family. It's the first time I've actually known the victim – before, they were simply victims. It's hard to stay detached.'

'Bit unusual, straying from your patch?'

'Yes. But a tricky one for the local police. She was British and Muslim. So it makes sense to ask me to help.'

Max glanced at her finger. 'Still wearing your ring?'

Linda laughed. 'Yes. I decided to keep the ring. Keeps randy cops at bay. If I ever remarried, I don't think I'd marry another cop again. It's funny how cops keep everything in the family. Must be because we think differently to ordinary folk, always asking questions. Suppose we need someone who knows how we think.'

She looked sad, sighed, and then smiled. 'You, you don't seem a cop. Too open.'

'No? My family's not exactly standard. Mum's a musician, and Dad now runs a wine business in Barcelona.'

Linda glanced at her watch. 'Oops. Better go. Getting on, and I've got to look my best for the meeting.'

'I'll show you back to your hotel.'

'Thanks. But I'll be okay. It's just a bit further along Gran Vía on the other side, isn't it? A lovely morning. You're sweet – but don't try so hard to impress. Doesn't work.'

Max watched her leave. As she left, she turned and saluted, a reminder of her superior rank. Nice bottom.

Chapter 8

Max walked slowly back to his flat, thinking about Linda. That was an odd comment on Lorca. Maybe he'd misheard. The only Franco supporters these days were like the old man in the open air market in Plaza Larga, selling key rings with a portrait of Franco. But she definitely flirted with him . . . and progress might be possible if he played his cards right. There was just time for a quick shower, pack the computer and get back to the office.

Max arrived at the conference room at exactly four. Davila was already there.

'Everything go to plan, Max?'

'Yes, but Inspector Sánchez didn't come on the tour. Upset stomach . . . and he may not make it to the meeting.'

'No matter. I'm told she's the one who makes the decisions. I'm going for a coffee. Let me know if you need anything.'

Max went to the front and set up the computer. He tested PowerPoint, and ran through his notes. Max disliked the conference room: it was all air conditioning, AV equipment and artificial light. The long mahogany table had been moved to the side, and the coffee urns, cups, water jugs and glasses placed upon it. There was a portrait of the King and Queen and the Spanish flag behind the podium. He began to feel nervous. It was his first big presentation. He patted his pocket to check his inhaler was there. It was. He had better go to the toilet, straighten the tie, comb the hair. A splash of cold water on the face would help. A black coffee would also help.

Max returned at quarter to five. The Jefe Superior de Andalucía Oriental, Pedro Cifuentes, and the head of the Policía Nacional of Granada, Comisario Bonila, had arrived together, their medals glistening on their crisply pressed uniforms. General López from the Guardia Civil was easing his way towards the great ones, followed by Teniente González up from Diva. All the other officers began to drift in, anxious to impress. The mutual admiration society was in session.

At exactly five, Linda and Martín arrived. Martín sat down heavily and began writing. Linda carefully did the rounds, beginning with the top rank and working down. She ignored Max until Davila introduced him.

'You two of course met earlier.'

Max bent over, and shook hands. An expensive perfume.

'Yes. It was most gracious of the Sub-Inspector to meet us at the airport. And I appreciated his tour of Granada. Most informative.'

And with that she moved on.

Cifuentes opened the proceedings, welcoming all those present and especially the guests from the CGI, the Anti-Terrorist Operations Group. He turned to Linda.

'I knew your father well, served under him briefly. A most distinguished officer. We are honoured to have you here with us. Our anti-terrorist unit here is busy, and we like to think they and we keep on top of the brief. We already have monthly coordinating meetings of all units. But we look forward to hearing your advice on how we might improve our coordination, intelligence gathering, and cooperation with the CGI.'

He was followed by General López, then Comisario Bonila, and then the heads of all the police divisions had their three minutes. Then it was Linda's turn. She stood up, went to the front. Her voice, though soft and low, projected clearly.

'Gentlemen. Thank you all for coming.'

Max noticed she spoke without notes.

'General Martínez, our head of CGI, ordered both Inspector Sánchez and myself to visit all the police zones to personally assess the effectiveness of counter-terrorist activities. General Martínez will be reporting back to the PM. As you know, the PM regards the anti-terrorist fight as top priority. Spanish support for the war in Iraq has increased the possibility of a terrorist attack on Spanish soil, and all the branches of the security forces have to be on full alert.'

She smiled at General López, and continued.

'The PM, the Ministerio del Interior and the CGI are concerned that anti-terrorist coordination is perhaps not all it should be. Traffic police, for example, could be crucial, and it is vital they report any suspicious vehicles immediately. Instant sharing of information and full cooperation is essential. My task, with help from Inspector Sánchez, is to ensure that all the units and all the regions are up to scratch.'

Linda paused, and waited.

'Granada is our first visit because we see it as key. We have intelligence from the Americans that a major terrorist operation is being planned right here in Andalusia. Where, when, what, how, we don't know. But the intelligence is reliable. So we are concentrating on preparations in Andalusia and Granada in particular.'

As reliable as the claim of weapons of mass destruction, thought Max.

'We also have intelligence that Islamist terrorists have made contact with ETA and a joint action by them may be possible.'

How convenient, thought Max. But not bloody likely. Why would a bunch of Basque separatists chum up with Al-Qaeda – more likely to shoot each other than cooperate.

'So I'm here to learn what you are doing, what you are planning to do, and to ensure that all the mechanisms for cooperation are in place. We also want increased surveillance of all the local Muslim groups, and reports on their activities. We are looking forward to hearing your preliminary report and assessment of the dangers of Islamist terrorists obtaining a foothold here in Granada.'

She smiled at the assembled audience, saluted the top brass, and walked briskly to her seat in the front row.

'Inspector Jefe Davila,' called Comisario Bonila, now chairing.

Davila stood up, his bald head glistening in the artificial light, his moustache newly trimmed, the ruddy colour of his face betraying a fondness for brandy and cigars.

'Um. Well, yes. Oh, *perdóname*, Comisario.'

And he turned, and saluted.

'*Bienvenidos Generales y todos*. It fell to my department to prepare this report. We had not been given much warning so I apologize for it being rough and ready. We are very over-stretched at the moment, and um, well, yes, we will need extra resources if we are to combat these new threats.'

Davila stopped, took out his handkerchief, and wiped his brow.

'We are however pleased that we did manage to have a young officer appointed some time back to our Homicide Division who is also helping us with our relations with the Muslim communities. He is an officer who studied at the famous Centre for Arabic Studies here in Granada as well as, um, at a university in Britain. And Sub-Inspector Romero kindly agreed to prepare the report on the various Islamic groups here in Granada. *Muchas gracias.*'

Max walked smartly to the podium, and placed his notes on the lectern. As he cleared his throat, he checked his pocket. The inhaler was still there.

'Gentlemen, Inspectora Jefe Concha, I would first like to thank Inspector Jefe Enrique Davila for all the help and advice he has given in the compilation of this report.'

Davila's advice was to keep it bland, non-political and not disturb anybody, particularly anybody important. The real help for the report had come from the librarian at the Centre for Arabic Studies.

'Granada is known as the Islamic capital of Europe, a not

inaccurate description. Here we have not only a large concentration of Muslims, but also some of the most important centres of Islamic learning in Europe.'

Max paused, and pressed the Remote. He turned, and with his laser-pointer highlighted the first paragraph.

'The divisions in the Muslim world are as complicated and at times as bitter as those in Christianity. It is easy to become a Muslim. All a person needs to do is make a declaration, freely and sincerely, a *Shahadah*, literally bearing witness, that "I testify that there is no deity worthy of worship but God and I testify that Muhammad is the messenger of God."'

Max smiled. 'In Christianity, we have Catholics and Protestants. In Islam, the two great divisions are between the Sunni and the Shi'a. The Shi'a are very much the minority, concentrated in Iran, southern Iraq and Lebanon. Most Muslims in Granada are Sunni, but we do have Shi'a. There seems to be no enmity between the two groups here, but that could change as tensions increase in the Middle East. It is mainly Sunni Muslims who take part in the protests against the war. However, opinion polls show that over ninety per cent of Granadinos are opposed to the Iraq war, so being anti-war does not tell us much about the politics of the protestors.'

Linda and Davila looked disapproving.

'The Shi'a, as we know from Iran, can be very hardline and have a more centralized religious authority. And although the Shi'a were the first to use suicide bombers – both in the Iran/Iraq war and in Lebanon – my personal assessment is that the Shi'a community here in Granada is very unlikely to become involved in any acts of violence, although that could change depending on political developments in the Middle East.

'The Sunni community here is more complicated. Internal divisions within them are intense.'

Max turned and highlighted a text. 'One of the most important divisions is between the more rigid, puritanical, fundamentalist sects such as Wahhabism, the sole creed in

Saudi Arabia, and those advocating *ijtihad*, a rethinking of Islam for modern times. But for the majority of Muslims, Islam is a road map for life-community, ritual and rules around which to structure daily life. In that respect, it very much resembles Catholicism, but they have no Pope, no bishops.'

There was a slight murmur.

'Because there is no central religious authority among the Sunni, each learned scholar can claim he alone interprets the Qur'an correctly. There are thus many Mullahs, Imans, Sheikhs and Ayatollahs with their own followers. This makes it difficult for us to pinpoint who might become terrorists. Religion and politics are much more interwoven than in modern-day Christianity. Advocates of political violence are usually fundamentalists, but not necessarily so. Political objectives are crucial.'

Max paused. Linda looked bored.

'We have legal and illegal immigrants from nearly all the Islamic countries, especially Morocco, Tunisia and Algeria. Granada is also a magnet for students from Islamic countries. We have evidence that some radical Islamic groups have a presence on our campuses.'

Max paused, turned, and highlighted a list of organizations. 'These groups are dangerous. They can and do cooperate. It is unlikely that they will attack Spain – their objectives are very much related to their own countries. However, we maintain a careful watch over all members of these groups.'

Max noticed Linda shake her head. He paused, moved to the side table, filled his glass and took a swig of water.

'Islam is the fastest-growing religion in Andalusia, through migration and also European converts to Islam who see Granada as a special place. There are conflicts between the Islamic immigrants and converts, each tending for example to worship in different mosques. It is mainly the converts who form some of the more exotic Islamic sects. And the most violent conflicts are often between these groups.'

A chair scraped. Max stopped. Inspector Martín Sánchez stood up, his face a pale green in the artificial light. 'Sorry. Stomach bug. Have to go. Be back.'

He clambered across various bodies, and almost ran out of the room.

'I didn't realize our tapas were that bad,' said Max.

There was laughter round the room.

'Well. We have a group calling for the restoration of the Caliphate of Cordova, another for the creation of an independent Islamic state of Al Andaluz. Some groups claim to be following the Sufi tradition – a mystical tradition within Islam. We suspect, but as of now have no definitive evidence, that some groups may even be involved in the hashish trade. There is a small Muslim, largely Sufi group, in Diva, in the Alpujarras. From my knowledge of this group they are colourful but peaceful, though the leader of the group, Ahmed Mahfouz, a powerful orator, is prominent in the anti-war movement. These groups may seem outlandish, but our assessment is that they are not involved with any terrorist group nor are they likely to be.'

Max stopped again. Inspector Sánchez returned, and fell over an outstretched leg as he scrambled back to his seat.

'As I was saying, rivalries between groups and even between mosques can be strong. We even had the bizarre case of our courts having to adjudicate the ownership of a mosque after one group seized it from another. The building of the mosque, opposite the Alhambra, next to the Mirador de San Nicolás, did create problems. A Christian group, calling itself Covadonga, after the battle in 722 when Christians defeated the Moors, mounted a vociferous and at times violent campaign against the mosque. But that seems to have quietened down now. And we in Granada now see that mosque as a positive asset to the city – though they did have a quite notorious call to prayer when the attack on Iraq began.'

Max remembered that moment well. As dawn broke over the city, a powerful loudspeaker summoned all Muslims to the mosques to pray and campaign against the war.

'Our assessment is that there are no terrorist cells oper-ating in or around Granada, but of course we must not be complacent. As the US President recently said, complacency will bring us what we thought we knew was coming but didn't know it was coming until it actually came, and when it came we knew what we should have done but didn't because we didn't know it was coming.'

Max stopped. He hoped his joke had gone down okay. There was a polite round of applause, and even a little laugh-ter. Davila, chairing the meeting, frowned, and then thanked Max for a most efficient and comprehensive survey.

'Would anyone like to ask a question?'

Everyone waited for Jefe Superior Cifuentes to ask the first question. He cleared his throat.

'Yes. Thank you, Sub-Inspector Romero. That was a very comprehensive report. You said you believe we have no Al-Qaeda or similar cells operating here in Granada. Can you be sure of that?'

'No. I cannot be absolutely sure, but I do have my ear very close to the ground, and there isn't even a whisper that they are here in Granada.'

Cifuentes was followed by Comisario Bonila, then General Lopez who emphasized the importance of the Guardia Civil in watching out for potential terrorists in the rural areas. Both congratulated Max. The Inspectores Jefes, all making various minor points and all congratulating Max, followed Lopez. Max felt himself relaxing. It was going fine.

Finally Inspectora Jefe Linda Concha stood up, and walked to the front. She began without the usual polite preliminaries.

'I would like to make a number of comments on Sub-Inspector Romero's analysis. It might do as an academic exercise. But it is not serious police investigation. I have not come all the way from the CGI headquarters to be told everything is fine. The days when we might have regarded some of the groups he mentioned as no more than eccentric oddities have passed. Also there is no doubt that extremist

Islamic groups have been recruiting among immigrants and students.'

She paused, and moved forward to increase the dramatic effect.

'Sub-Inspector Romero made no mention of links between the Basque terrorist group, ETA, and extremist Islamic groups. We have good evidence that such links exist, and that ETA have probably acquired missiles from them. The Prime Minister is very concerned about these links. The analysis is complacent and wrong-headed. The threat is serious.'

She dropped her voice lower, and spoke slowly.

'The likelihood of a terrorist attack here in Andalusia is high. We have to get serious, and change our intelligence gathering and our way of working. All of these groups advocating the establishment of Al Andaluz are potential breeding grounds for terrorists. The radical Islamic groups in the communities, and those around the University of Granada, are very dangerous. Some of the mosques have Imans who have never criticized Al-Qaeda or the call to jihad, and there are quite a few pamphlets circulating here in Granada defending jihad. There is, I repeat, no room for complacency. You have given me no evidence that Granada is taking the threat seriously, and I must have an action plan to show that you are. We have a lot to learn from the Americans in this.'

'You are quite right, Inspectora Jefe,' interrupted Davila. 'We are taking the threat seriously, and I did ask Sub-Inspector Romero not to be bland. But we have to be careful not to antagonize the Muslim population, and to work cautiously.'

'Inspector Jefe, I am more concerned that we don't antagonize our Spanish population by failing to prevent a terrorist attack. That is why surveillance has to be stepped up. Having cups of tea with friendly Muslims is just not good enough.'

Max flushed. 'The Inspectora Jefe forgets that I was giving an overview of the make-up of the Muslims here in Granada.

There may be a serious threat. And I certainly would not like to question American intelligence – though so far they have not found any weapons of mass destruction in Iraq. We should not be complacent, but we should not exaggerate either. In my experience the Muslims here are not involved in any terrorist threat. They are opposed to the Spanish government's foreign policy in support of the war. And having tea with friendly Muslims, as you put it, is important as a way of both obtaining information and building goodwill. If we are to win the so-called war on terrorism, then we need the support and trust of our Muslim population.'

'Sub-Inspector, may I remind you it is not our job to agree or not with our government's policies. Our job is to support those policies. And the so-called war on terrorism, as you put it, is a real war. There is no harm in having friendly cups of tea, but that can be no substitute for serious police work.'

'I think Inspectora Jefe Concha is correct,' interrupted Comisario Bonila. 'Sub-Inspector Romero's survey is but the first step. We need a top level planning team to develop a strategic and tactical plan which can be implemented almost immediately.'

Linda smiled, 'Thank you, Comisario. That is what I wanted to hear. Both Inspector Sánchez and myself will be here over the coming week to help you set up such a plan. We are pleased that Granada sees the importance of the threat we are facing and is willing to take the necessary action.'

'Inspectora Jefe,' said Davila, 'I do apologize for the inadequate presentation. The Sub-Inspector is young and relatively inexperienced. I had advised him to be less bland, and give more emphasis to the real dangers we are facing.'

Max managed to hold his tongue.

'Inspector Jefe, I am not making any personal criticisms. The Sub-Inspector does have a good knowledge of the Islamic groups, and he could be useful to our planning exercise. I suggest he participates in our planning group. What do you think, Martín?'

Martín, though now looking less green around the gills, had still not said a word. 'Yes, he could be useful.'

'I was about to suggest that myself,' said Davila. 'I will arrange for Sub-Inspector Romero to be free whenever he is required.'

'Thank you,' replied Linda. 'The Sub-Inspector is fortunate in having you as his commanding officer.'

'Thank you all for coming,' said Davila. 'I will arrange a planning meeting as a matter of urgency.'

They filed out, Comisario Bonila rushing to reassure Linda about how seriously they were all taking the threats, and reminding her of the last time he had met her father.

'Max, stay behind a minute, will you,' said Davila.

'Yes, sir,' replied Max, collecting his materials and returning them to his briefcase.

When everyone had left, Davila turned to Max.

'Romero, that was a complete and utter balls-up. You made me look stupid. If Inspectora Jefe Concha hadn't asked for you on the team, you'd be on a disciplinary. Okay. You can go now. But watch your step.'

'Yes, sir,' said Max. 'I will certainly do my best to follow your advice and orders.'

He saluted, and left.

Linda was waiting outside on the steps. As he attempted to pass, she moved to stand in front of him.

'Max. Sorry about that. Trust me, it wasn't personal. I had to get real action. Look – the PM's Anti-Terrorist Coordinating Committee is monitoring all the forces, and Granada got flagged up for a kick in the balls. No hard feelings.'

She smiled, a little girl's *please forgive me* smile.

'Max, stick with me and you'll do well. Let's have a drink. You can tell me what really goes on in these famous monthly coordinating meetings.'

'I don't know that much about them. I just prepare the odd briefing memo now and again.'

'As I thought. An excuse for a coffee morning. A drink then?'

'Inspectora Jefe, I'm very busy. I have a lot to do.'

'Oh, it's not personal. I can help you. I've already got your pompous fool of a boss, what's he called, Davila, eating out of my hand.'

In spite of himself, Max smiled. 'I really am busy. Still have that murder case in Diva to see to. Leila – remember, the girl who was killed – is the daughter of Ahmed Mahfouz, the anti-war campaigner.'

'Now that is interesting. There might be some leads there. Come on. You look as if you need a drink.'

'Well . . .'

'I remember the first time I had to do something like this. My dad was there, and he really put me down. It was all I could do to stop myself from crying.'

'Oh, okay. One drink then. The Aben Humeya is on my way home.'

'This one's on me. I wouldn't want you to have problems with expenses. But I must get out of this uniform first. It's stifling me. Give me a minute to change in the hotel.'

The Santa Paula was cool. The fountain in the middle of the foyer splashed gently. Fifteen minutes went by. Max felt awkward in his uniform. He amused himself guessing which of the couples coming in and out were married or not. He thought you would be able to tell: a glance, a smile, the way an arm or hand was held, a stray hand brushing a bottom. But in the end he gave up: there were no obvious clues.

Linda appeared in a blue silk dress, so plain it must have cost a fortune.

A taxi was waiting outside.

'The Aben Humeya please,' said Max.

The taxi passed underneath the mosque overlooking the Alhambra. 'That's the mosque I mentioned in my presentation.'

'Impressive. But I wouldn't have given permission for it on that site. It would only encourage the radicals.'

As Max and Linda walked down three flights of steps to

the bottom terrace of the restaurant, the sun began to set behind the Alhambra and the Sierra Nevada beyond.

'You're right, Max. This is delightful.'

Max took off his jacket and tie, and placed them on a spare chair.

'You look better already. No hard feelings now, I hope. Your presentation wasn't that bad, Max. Too much of the bleeding heart liberal and it wouldn't have shaken up the departments, would it? And I'm here to get results. A bottle of really cold, white wine, no? Don Darías be okay?'

'Don Darías would be fine.'

The owner arrived with a bottle, and poured them each a glass. Linda swirled the wine around in her glass, and sniffed it appreciatively.

'Fine. A touch of peach, wouldn't you say?'

Max laughed. He was being teased.

'Okay, give me the low-down on who's who, and what's going on.'

So Max told the story of the day when Comisario Bonila's mistress ran off with a flamenco dancer.

'. . . then Bonila wanted to haul in the Drug Squad and get the guy's flat raided. It took his deputy hours to talk him out of it. But not before everyone in the force knew about the mistress – and of course one of the secretaries knew his wife's cousin, so it all got back to Bonila's wife and she wasn't best pleased.'

'Another bottle, Max? And a bite to eat?'

'Why not?'

'I meant to go back to Madrid this weekend. But my daughter's fine, and wants to stay on with her grandparents. I've some reports to finish, and Bonila has invited me to a barbecue on Sunday. Terrified I might give a damning report. I won't be able to look at him with a straight face now. So, Max, what does a girl like me do on her own in Granada on a Saturday night?'

Chapter 9

Tape Number 4

Leila: Paula, you said at the end of my last interview that your family suffered a lot because of the Civil War. Would it be too painful to tell me what happened?

Paula: Oh, dear. I haven't talked about this for a long time. I think a lot about it. My last wish is to bury my brother, Antonio, before I die. I . . . I . . .

Leila: Here, take this tissue.

Paula: *Gracías*, Leila. Silly old woman, aren't I? I'm okay now.

Leila: Are you sure you want to talk about it?

Paula: *Sí, sí. Está bien.* I'm sure. If you could help me find his body, I could go to my grave at peace.

Leila: Oh, Paula, I'll do what I can. I've permission to go through the archives of the Guardia Civil – there might be something there.

Paula: Where shall we start?

Leila: Why don't you start with your family?

Paula. *Sí*. My parents were quite wealthy, good Catholics, conservatives, very respectable, you know. We had servants, and an old town house in Granada as well as this farmhouse. The Granada house was lovely. There was a pond in the patio, with a goldfish I called Cleopatra. I went to a convent school of course. I would have liked to have gone to university like my brothers, but in those days girls just didn't. I do envy you your education – you know so much more about the world than I did at your age.

Leila: Your life sounds just like a novel.

Paula: It was a different world; you can't imagine how things have changed. Where was I?

Leila: You were telling me about your family.

Paula: *Sí*. Well . . . my two elder brothers went to university, Antonio to study Law, and Carlos, Literature. Odd, it turned out to be Antonio who went on to become a writer. Antonio met Lorca at the Faculty of Law . They became good friends; part of what Lorca called 'the magic circle'. I wish I had been older. Everything was so exciting.

Leila: Did you know much about Antonio's political involvement?

Paula: At the time, not much – I was very young. But I've read a lot since then. I think neither Lorca nor Antonio was really political – always talking about the noble peasant and the honest worker. In real politics they were babes. But Carlos joined the Communist Party at university, and lived and breathed politics; demonstrations, propaganda. I think he even received some military training. I don't know what he was in the Communist Party , but I understand he was quite senior .

Leila: Do you know why he joined?

Paula: Not really. It seemed like a religious conversion: it changed him. He started off as idealistic as Antonio, but then he became much tougher. I was too young at the time to know what was going on. But I've read some books on the Civil War – the best are the French and British ones. Max gets them for me when they come out in Spanish. I just cannot believe how all the Republican groups fought each other, even with Franco's troops on their doorstep.

Leila: Can you tell me a bit more about Antonio and Lorca?

Paula: Well, as I said, Antonio became part of the Lorca circle. He had a fine singing voice, you know, and Lorca would often accompany him at the piano. He helped out with Lorca's theatre group, and even went on one tour with them. Like everyone, he was bewitched by Lorca. It was Lorca who encouraged him to write. Some of Antonio's poems were really good, but . . . but he took his notebook with him when he left us, and told us to burn anything of his in the house. So it's all lost. Lost. Oh dear.

Leila: It's all right Paula. Have another tissue. Can I get you a drink or something?

Paula: No, no. I just worshipped my brothers. But once Carlos got involved in politics, he didn't have time any more for his silly little sister. Though Antonio would always tell me things.

Leila: If you want to stop now, we can always continue another time.

Paula: No, it's good for me to talk about the past. It makes me even more determined to find out what happened to Antonio. You will help me, won't you?

Leila: Yes, of course I will. But don't overdo it just now.

Paula: I haven't much time left.

Leila: No, *Doña Paula*, don't say that. You've got years ahead of you.

Paula: I'm eighty-three . . . I know I haven't got much time.

Leila: I'll do everything I can.

Paula: Thanks. You are very sweet.

Leila: It's funny you haven't asked Max to help – he's in the police.

Paula: I've talked to Max a lot. He likes Lorca's poetry and plays. So he knows all about how I met Lorca. But I've never really talked about such family matters. He's a good boy; so he might help us.

Leila: Why didn't you talk to him?

Paula: Nobody wanted to talk about the Civil War when Franco was alive, even within families – too frightened. You never knew who might learn something. And after Franco died . . . well, there was this understanding that people would still keep quiet about the Civil War when we moved to a democracy. So many bad memories. Older people just wanted to forget and get on with life . . . and younger people were so fascinated by this new world of sex and money that they didn't want to dig up what had

100

happened to their grandparents. It's only now that we are beginning to discover the truth. People are beginning to open up the mass graves. They're all over Spain. There's one here, you know – down by El Fugón. Oh, I do so want Antonio to have a proper burial. After all these years, he must be dead . . . but no one knows where he is. I'm not very Catholic, but I want him laid to rest in a Christian grave.

Leila: We'll find him, Paula. I promise you. I think we should stop now. You're looking tired.

Tape Number 5

Leila: Can you tell me about the last time you saw Antonio?

Paula: It's as if it was yesterday. It was when Antonio escaped from Granada, and hid with us for a few days. That was about a year after Lorca was executed. And about two years after my father died. So Antonio was head of the family. The Falange were rounding up Republicans, and taking them off to be shot. My mother was frantic, both for Antonio and for Carlos. We got word that Carlos had joined the Communist militia, and had managed to escape north after the fall of Granada. But we had heard nothing from Antonio for nearly a year.

Leila: Why was that? He was only in Granada.

Paula: In those days it was too dangerous for him to contact us. The army was in control of the city. Travel was very difficult, and you couldn't trust anybody . . . not the telephone operator, not the nice young man who delivered the post. Civil war's like that.

Leila: I just can't imagine it.

Paula: You are lucky to have been born in Britain.

Leila: Yes, I suppose so. You were telling me about Antonio.

Paula: I remember my mother saying Antonio was so naive he had probably handed himself in. People just disappeared. Then one night, at three in the morning, we were woken by the dogs barking. It was Antonio. He had walked for three nights from Granada over the mountains. You can imagine how dangerous that was. He was half dead from exhaustion. We hid him in our cellar to recover, and hoped no one had heard the dogs. There were always bad neighbours who would denounce you to buy your land dirt-cheap. Civil war's like that. You can't trust anybody. Mother and I talked until morning trying to work out what to do. Carlos had already got out of Granada, and gone north to join the battle around Toledo.

Leila: Couldn't Antonio go and join him?

Paula: No. Carlos had the Communists to support him. They had safe houses along the route north. But Antonio didn't have connections. In the end we agreed Antonio should stay with us as long as possible to rest and recover. And then set off again walking at night along the Sierra Contraviesa, down into Almeria, which was still in government hands. And from there he could take a boat to Morocco or somewhere. It would be dangerous. But he couldn't stay for long in Diva. Already houses were being searched . . . I think I will take that drink now, Leila, if you don't mind.

Leila: Sure, here. My goodnes, I hadn't realized how much danger you had lived through.

Paula: Danger? Yes. But you learnt to survive.

Leila: What did you do?

Paula: I had a young admirer at the time, Pablo. He was on the fringes of Lorca's circle. He was right wing, but Lorca was more interested in people's talents than their politics.

Leila: Yes – I read that after the fall of Granada Lorca actually hid in the house of Falangist supporters, and it was from that house he was taken to be shot.

Paula: Yes, that's true.

Leila: But back to Pablo.

Paula: Well, Pablo was a Franco supporter, and had relatives high up in Acción Popular, a small fascist group. Antonio had introduced me to Pablo well before all the trouble started. He used to visit the house a lot. He was a good-looking young man, from a respectable family, and my mother took a real liking to him. I suppose there was an understanding between our families that Pablo and I would naturally become engaged when I was old enough. Then for some reason, just after Lorca's death, Antonio wrote to say that Pablo was no longer welcome in our house, and I should break off any contact with him.

Leila: My goodness. Do you know why?

Paula: No. Antonio never explained.

Leila: How did you feel about that?

Paula: I was upset, but not devastated. I was young, and not too sure I wanted to get married, settle down and have babies. I wanted to see more of the world. There was so much I wanted to do.

Leila: I know just how you felt. To be honest I still feel that way.

Paula: But for you it's so much easier. You can get jobs, can travel on your own . . . that would have been my dream.

Leila: But why did you think Antonio had fallen out so badly with Pablo?

Paula: I don't know. I spoke later to Pablo about it. He said he didn't know either.

Leila: Any ideas?

Paula: If it had been Carlos, it would have been because he considered Pablo a fascist. But Antonio had many right-wing friends. And he had once said Pablo wasn't really political – he just had fascist family connections.

Leila: What happened to Carlos?

Paula: He was lucky . . . ended up in Chile. Married a nice young woman, and had four children. He visited me after Franco died. It was lovely. Max has been out to see his cousins too.

Leila: So what happened to Antonio?

Paula: I don't know. One day Pablo turned up at our house, wearing the Falange uniform. We were frightened. The Civil War did such strange things to people. Friends were denouncing friends, neighbours denouncing neighbours.

Even families were divided. I was very nervous, as we still had Antonio hidden in the cellar. But mother welcomed him into the house as if nothing had happened. Thank God for that. Pablo had come to warn us that our house was on a list to be raided. It was obvious Pablo was still keen on me, and we desperately needed a protector. So I let Pablo know I was still interested in him. Of course we didn't tell him about Antonio. That night we helped Antonio leave for a little shepherd's hut up in the hills above Banjaron, which we owned. He could hide and rest there for a few days, and then make his way to Almeria.

Leila: And did he?

Paula: We don't know. He just disappeared. We don't know whether he got to the coast . . . whether he was shot, and dumped in a ravine in the hills . . . we simply don't know.

Leila: Oh, how awful. I can't imagine it.

Paula: It's not just losing him, it's not knowing what happened that's so bad. Mother never got over it. She died soon after I got married. I remember her as always being such a busy, happy woman. I still lie awake at night, just wondering.

Leila: But what happened to you?

Paula: Well, Pablo was right. We were raided late the next night. It was dreadful. Pablo was with them. They dragged mother and me out of our beds, and made us stand in our nightdresses in the middle of the dining room. I noticed the young lad guarding us kept eyeing me up and down. I was so frightened that I peed on the floor. They searched the house from the attic to the cellar. Fortunately we'd removed any sign that Antonio had been there. They found nothing. Even though I was standing in a pool of pee, this young lad kept eyeing me. El Capitán and Pablo came back up, and el Capitán started questioning us: when had we last seen Antonio and Carlos, had they been in touch, had any Republican scum been in touch? Fortunately my mother was a good liar. I was just too nervous

– if he'd concentrated on me I'm sure I would have blurted out something. El Capitán finally decided we knew nothing. I remember vividly every word that was said at the end.

Leila: Oh, my goodness, this is so dramatic.

Paula: El Capitán said, 'Okay let's go. They know nothing. But ladies, we'll be back. If you hear anything let us know, if you know what's good for you.'

Leila: What a threat!

Paula: Then the young boy guarding us, piped up: 'Capitán, how about a bit of fun? The young one looks like she could do with a tumble.'

Leila: What? I don't believe this.

Paula: And the boy stepped forward, and yanked my night-dress at the shoulder. It tore, and one of my breasts became uncovered. '*Virgen santo*,' he said. 'Look at that! Let's see what else you're hiding.' El Capitán just laughed. But Pablo stepped forward, knocked the lad to the ground, and said, 'Touch her again, and I'll kill you.'

Leila: Gosh. That was brave of him.

Paula: Yes. But el Capitán just put his arm around Pablo's shoulders, and said, 'Come on, Pablo. The lad here meant no harm, just a bit of fun. Surprised you're defending the sister of a fucking Red.' He saluted, and they all left. I was so terrified I peed myself again.

Leila: Oh, Paula. That's terrible.

Paula: After that, I became Pablo's *novia*, and after the Civil War we married.

Leila: So that's how you married Pablo.

Paula: Mother and I were pretty much on our own, and it looked like the new government might confiscate the family's property because of Carlos and Antonio, so it was the only sensible thing I could do.

Leila: Were you happy?

Paula: Yes. Pablo wasn't a bad husband. And he was a really good grandfather to Max and Juan. They loved it here when they were young. But Pablo had terrible, black days.

105

When we were first married, I kept asking him to find out what had happened to Antonio, but he would just get angry. Once he got drunk, and hit me hard and ordered me never to mention Antonio's name again.

Leila: Why do you think he did that?

Paula: Terrible things happened in the Civil War. He said it was best to forget, and not keep harping back, and that with no news for so long Antonio would certainly be dead. He kept saying nothing would be gained by digging up the past.

Leila: Oh, dear me. You look really tired now. That's more than enough for today. Can I get you something to drink?

Paula: That's kind of you, Leila. A cup of coffee would be nice. You will help me, won't you?

Leila: Of course. I'm starting work on the Guardia Civil archives this week.

Paula: I'll come with you into the kitchen. I need to stretch my legs. I get so stiff if I don't move around. Can you fetch me my stick over there?

Leila: Here. Let me help you up.

Paula: Thanks, my dear. There really are no benefits to old age, you know.

Chapter 10

Venus del mantón de Manila que sabe
Del vino de Málaga y de guitarra.

Venus is an embroidered shawl who knows
The guitar and sweet Malaga wine.

Frederico García Lorca, *Elegía, Diciembre de 1918, Granada*
(Elegy, December 1918, Granada)

Max woke with a hangover. Three bottles of wine was one too many. But it had been a good evening. Linda had a wicked sense of humour, and she had kept him laughing with her tales of the follies of the great and the good in Madrid. The venality, in-fighting and pomposity were much worse than even he had imagined. Flamenco tonight. Max looked round his flat: what a tip! No way could he invite Linda back for coffee. He had really let the place go. He hadn't even done the washing up for three days. No choice but to get on with it. Strong, black coffee first. Max opened all the windows to let in some fresh air. He needed a quick shower to cool down. *Madre mía*, the shower looked as if it hadn't been cleaned in months! It would take a good ten minutes to make any dent on the grime. Once he got going, Max enjoyed housework. It was one of the few things that gave instant results.

By noon, the flat was beginning to look habitable. Max looked around him with satisfaction. Textiles and pictures from his trip to Latin America, ancient Moorish tiles picked up in Morocco, traditional Alpujarran rugs bought in Diva scattered on the terracotta floor tiles, made it bright, but connected to his past. In pride of place, a framed John Houston poster of the countryside south of Edinburgh – a field of corn flowing down to a blue sea with a blue sky above. More like Spain, but it reminded him of the rare sunny days he had enjoyed in Scotland. His flat, on the top floor of a nineteenth-century block, had a tiny terrace looking out over the Alhambra. The terrace could only hold a small table and chair. But hibiscus, scented geraniums, a small lemon tree and jasmines growing along the low terrace wall made it his private sanctuary, a place to breathe in the magic of the Alhambra.

It was time for a break. Max went to the fridge. He opened the door, and was hit by a dubious smell. Something nasty. Hell . . . he had forgotten to chuck away the remains from last week: a spaghetti marinera. Best chuck everything, and scrub it clean. Max disinfected the fridge. By the time he finished it was after two thirty. He changed into clean clothes, walked down the hill, crossed Plaza Nueva, and entered El Taberna.

'Hola, Max. ¿Tubo y tapas? How's it going? Haven't seen you for days.'

'Sí, really busy. Murder case up in Diva on top of the usual stuff.'

'Is that the one where a pretty British Muslim girl got dumped under a bridge? All over the papers.'

'That's the one.'

Max retreated to his favourite corner, sat on a tall stool, and placed his *tubo* of beer on the sherry cask. Felipe arrived shortly with the tapas: a slice of good tortilla with bread.

'Another *tubo*, Max?'

'Sí. Por favor.'

Max went to the counter, and picked up *El País* from the stack of newspapers. The election campaign was hotting up – 'Prime Minister Accuses Socialists of Being Soft on Terrorism'. Max skimmed the article – 'the PM also accuses the Socialists of opening secret contacts with ETA'. He glanced at the international news page – 'USA Begins Nego-tiations with Israel and Palestine to Broker a Final Peace Settlement'.

The *tubo y tapa* finished, Max walked to the Carrera del Genil, down to the Corte Inglés. Best get in some good wine and food just in case Linda agreed to come back. Max went down the stairs to the food section. The fish counter was like a Dutch still-life painting. Max chose prawns. Big meaty ones, wee tiny ones to eat whole. And some lemons, garlic, fresh bread, an expensive Don Darío and a couple of Rioja whites, oh . . . and some extra virgin olive oil. That should keep them both going if needed. With luck she might stay over for breakfast, so best get some fresh orange juice, croissants, and a box of the best Costa Rican coffee beans. The mixed carnations looked pretty – they would help to brighten and freshen the flat up. Max took a taxi back to the flat, put the food away in the newly cleaned fridge, cut the stems of the carnations and arranged them into his only vase – a gift from his mother. He then settled down to fin-ish yet another silly job evaluation form for Davila before beginning his report on Leila's murder. At times, it was just like being back in university, having to write essays every fortnight. He began reading the thick form, and felt his eye-lids droop. It had been a late night. If he didn't have a siesta now, he would fall asleep over it.

After a longer than intended siesta Max finished the form, made the final touches to the flat to ensure it looked fresh and inviting, and then at 9.45 p.m. took the tiny Albayzín bus. The bus, scraping between churches, convents and cafés, wound its way through the Placeta de San Miguel Bajo, down the Cuesta de la Loma, and stopped almost right outside Linda's hotel. The receptionist phoned her room to let her know he was waiting. Ten minutes later she appeared in an elegant black dress with an embroidered shawl.

'Max. *Muy elegante*. God . . . do I hate these reports. I promised to show it to Comisario Bonila tomorrow. But

Bonila should be pleased. I've said how well the meeting went, and how cooperative Granada has agreed to be. That way he can't refuse any requests I make. He wouldn't want to weaken the close, friendly relations we have now, would he?'

Max laughed, 'As long as he's praised he'll be happy. I suggest we go and enjoy some flamenco in La Platería. Ramón, the waiter in Castaneda, may be playing . . . and there's a good, young crowd there who really know their stuff. The Sacromonte caves can be a bit touristy.'

Max had booked a quiet corner table. He ordered two glasses of sweet Malaga wine. Ramón wasn't playing. But if the evening went well, once the formal performance had ended and most of the tourists had left, the aficionados might get a spontaneous performance. He was right. The performers returned, dressed in their street clothes. Members of the audience ordered bottles of wine for them. They drank slowly, but thirstily. Then someone shouted, 'Come on, Pepe. Let's have some real flamenco this time.'

The guitarist, his long hair curling down to the nape of his neck, smiled, finished his glass of wine, took the guitar back out of its case, and started tuning. Halfway through, Ramón and a friend arrived. Ramón waved to Max and Linda, took out his guitar, his friend a drum, and together they joined the first guitarist in a favourite piece by the God of Flamenco, Camarón de la Isla. Immediately the audience joined in, marking the rhythm with tocando palmas – which made a counterpoint to the percussion. Two gypsy girls got up, and curling their hands in slow, sensual movements began stamping the floor in ever more complex rhythms. Max looked at Linda – she was absorbed in the music, joining in the ever faster clapping. Her blue eyes flashed at Max as she smiled, and he felt a spark of fire pass through him. He smiled back at her, and thought, maybe, just maybe. The Don Darío, the best one, was chilling in the fridge, and that and prawns on the terrace looking up at the floodlit Alhambra might do the trick. When the music stopped for a short break, Linda put one hand on the table. Max cautiously placed his hand over hers. She didn't move her hand away. Then Ramón came over, and the moment passed.

'Enjoying it?' he asked Linda.

'Very much,' she replied. Ramón pulled up a chair, and sat beside them.

'Hey,' he said to Max, 'what does your pretty companion do?'

'Oh, something in the police.'

'Something in the police? That reminds me of the time I got pulled in by the cops in Madrid. False arrest it was. It must have been four in the morning . . .'

And with that Ramón launched into a long, complicated tale of his false arrest. Linda and Max looked at each other, and smiled sheepishly.

It was four in the morning before they stumbled out into the dark, narrow streets of the Albayzín. A crescent-shaped moon illuminated the Alhambra towers.

'My flat is not far,' said Max. 'If you want a coffee. And I've some nice prawns and a bottle of Don Darío in the fridge.'

'Thanks. Don't tempt me. Have to be good. Have to revise the report before I show it to bloody Bonila at his damn barbecue.' Linda took hold of Max's arm to steady herself. 'I must be getting old, Max. Once . . . you know . . . I could dance all night, change into uniform and go straight into the station.'

Max laughed. 'You could still do that. You can come back to my flat and borrow my uniform.'

'Oh Max, it'd drown me .'

'It'd be fun trying it on though.'

'You are a silly, sweet boy.' Linda giggled, and then burped. She swayed unsteadily, and pressed closer to Max. 'There is something you could do for me.'

'For you, Linda, anything.'

'Well, if you do discover something, make sure you tell me before Martín.'

Linda stumbled. Max put his arm around her, pretending

it was just to steady her. She clung tighter to him. 'Those prawns do sound nice. But I have to be good. So much to do. And we're off to Malaga on Monday for more meetings. Can I get a taxi?'

Max was tempted to say there were no taxis this time of the morning, but decided against it. 'Yes. Down at Plaza Nueva. I'll walk you down there.'

'*Gracias*. Whoops. Little tiddled, no? Wouldn't do to have a senior anti-terrorist officer arrested on drunk and disorderly, would it?'

Max had carefully not said yes or no to her request about Martín. Best assume it was a slightly drunken request, and wait and see if she brought it up again.

The fresh air seemed to sober Linda up quickly, and she disentangled herself from Max's arm. Plaza Nueva was still buzzing, la Heladería still doing a roaring trade in ice creams, and clusters of young people singing and dancing in the street. Unfortunately, the taxi queue was short. Max helped Linda into the taxi. He kissed her on both cheeks; she likewise. So much for his night of passion.

He walked briskly back to the flat, the cool night air clearing his head. At least she had made him clean the flat. He opened the fridge to get a glass of cold water. Bloody prawns. He took them out, and shoved them into the freezer compartment. He sipped the water. He would have to phone Paula in the morning, and make some excuse. It would be too much to drive over to Diva, and then back to Granada after such a late night.

Max slept till noon. Hell, he'd better phone Paula immediately: she fussed so if he didn't make it to the Sunday lunch.

'*Abuela*, how are you?'

'*Muy bien*. Is anything the matter ?'

'No, nothing wrong. Just have too much work on, a report to get in by first thing Monday. So, I'm really sorry but I won't be able to make it for lunch. Any news?'

'Oh, Max. *Por favor*, I am so disappointed that you're not

coming for lunch. Max . . . I was interviewed by the police, a nice lady police officer. She asked me lots of questions. She wanted to know exactly what Leila and I talked about. Am I a suspect?'

'No, of course you're not. We're just desperate for clues. Anything might help.'

'Do think there might be any connection between Leila's death and her research?'

'Not likely, *abuela*. I don't think so.'

'Did you know what a terrible time that nice young lady – Anita, she's called – is having with the local police officers? Your Teniente González sounds as bad as his *abuelo*.'

'I'm not surprised.'

'So what are you going to do about it?'

'It's nothing really to do with me.'

'Maximiliano! Of course it's something to do with you.'

'Okay. I'll do what I can to help. But if you tried to sack all the police who behave like that, you wouldn't have much of a police force left.'

'She is a very sweet girl.'

'*Abuela*, I'm not keen on her, and I don't need a wife to look after me. I can manage perfectly fine.'

'Did you know they've interviewed Juan? Do they think he's a suspect?'

'No, of course not. We have to interview everyone who knew her, including Juan and Isabel.'

'But you're getting nowhere?'

'Come on, *abuela*. I'm doing my best. It really is very complicated. I'll tell you all about it next Sunday.'

'Promise?'

'Honest. I promise. *Chao, abuela*.'

Help, thought Max. Paula's got her teeth into the Leila case. He groaned aloud at the thought of the phone calls he was going to receive. He'd better see Anita Guevarra or he would never hear the end of this.

An hour later the phone rang.

'Mother, what a surprise! How was the concert?

'It went well, Max, really well. The *Herald* gave us a good review. Are you okay?'

'Yes. Fine.'

'Paula just phoned to say you were a bit grumpy and that you refused to talk to her. So she's convinced herself something is wrong.'

'Mum, you know what Paula's like – I could hardly get a word in edgeways.'

'Paula told me all about this murder case you're working on. She said you'd been out with the poor girl. A very pretty Muslim girl from Edinburgh, Paula said.'

'That's right. But how's Scotland?'

'Raining of course. Has been all week. But what's new? '

'It's brilliant sunshine over here. Bit hot. How's the family?'

'They're all well. Aunt Jessie and Uncle Bob are going on a cruise to the Canaries from Greenock. I have no idea how they are paying for it. Doing it just to show off, if you ask me.'

'Oh, I don't know. They probably needed a rest. What with family, and both working, they deserve a break.'

'Are you saying my music job isn't tiring?'

'Of course not. I'm sure you could do with a rest. When I win the lottery, I'll treat you.'

'Are you sure you're fine? You should settle down, you know. Paula worries about you. And she thinks you're too sensitive for that job in the police.'

'I sometimes wonder as well, mum, what I'm doing in the police. Nice to know you all think I'm too sensitive for the job. But I can cope.'

'Okay. Speak to you next week. Love you lots.'

'Love you too, mum.'

Max put the phone down, and went to the fridge, pulled out the bottle of wine, and poured himself a generous glass. It would be dad next. It might have been easier to have lunch with Paula. Two hours later the phone rang.

'Dad. How are you?

'Max, I just had a phone call from the *abuela* – she was telling me all about the murder in Diva. Said she's very worried about you. I know what she's like, Max, she's my mother, but she just wouldn't stop. Apparently, you're very depressed about the girl's death, the heat's bad for your asthma, and you're coming down with something serious.'

'That's impressive, but I'm perfectly okay. Just have a lot of work. You know how Paula exaggerates – and for the record I wasn't deeply in love with her, and her death hasn't left me in a state of bad shock. Changing the subject, how's the wine business?'

'Good. It's picking up. The northern Europeans are really developing a taste for Spanish wine and the order book is full.'

'That's excellent . . . so did you get the flat?'

'Yes, a bit expensive, but the Barrio Gótico can only go up in value – and I've got a spare room now.'

'Dad, you know I'd love to come and see you in Barcelona. Soon as I get some time off, I'll be up.'

'We could go to a match.'

'That would be fantastic.'

'*Hasta la vista*, my son.'

'Give my best to Montserrat. See you.'

One more of the family to go. And just as Max was finally concentrating on his report, the phone rang.

'*Hola*, Juan, I'm fine. A hangover, that's all – a night out in the Platería. You know . . .'

'So who's the lucky girl?'

'You don't know her, Juan, fortunately.'

'So . . .?'

'No, I didn't get my leg over, if that's what you're thinking. But as the whole family would like to see me married with three children and a nice safe job like teaching – well, a guy's got to start somewhere.'

'I suppose you could put it like that but Paula—'

'Juan, I love Paula dearly, but I want to go to Hannigan's to watch the football! I just wish you'd all give me a break. If

I don't go now it will be Susanna next, and you know what my sister's like.'

'Okay, have a Guinness on me. You sound as if you need it.'

Max was just about to leave when the phone rang again!

'*Abuela*! *Sí*, Mum, dad and Juan have all phoned . . . I know you are worried about me. *Sí, sí*, they phoned – all is well. Stop worrying. You do a great job keeping the family together. But I've got to rush now – the football is just about to start.'

'But Maximiliano . . . Why is football so much more important than family?'

'Don't know, *abuela*. I *promise* you that I won't miss lunch next Sunday. *Buenas noches*. Sleep well.'

Max put the phone down, and almost ran out of the flat. Hannigan's was full when he got there. He joined the queue for the Guinness, grabbed his pint, and managed to find a space from where he could view the screen, a friendly: Spain v. Austria. It was a source of great disappointment to all Spaniards that the national Spanish football team never lived up to expectations. Tonight was no exception: a draw, two each. Didn't augur well for the European cup.

Chapter 11

Monday morning, another scorcher. Max went straight to Davila's office with his report on the murder case.

'This is getting a lot of press coverage,' commented Davila. 'Pretty girl, Muslim and British. The left-wing papers are saying could be a racially motivated murder. What do you think?'

'Not likely, sir. For a start, she was definitely not a poor, downtrodden immigrant. There was some anti-Muslim graffiti near the Diva mosque, but that seems to have been a one-off. As you will see from my report, sir, the main suspect at the moment is a young British Muslim.'

'Hmm. See if you can move on this one. With all the press coverage, it would be good for us to solve the case quickly. The foreign press are getting interested as well. So a bit of glory could come our way. Help me in the staffing review. You're not needed until the Friday afternoon strategy meeting, so spend all your time on this. Oh, don't forget – you can claim full mileage.'

'Shall do, sir. I'll go over straight away.' Max turned to leave.

'One more thing,' said Davila. Max turned round. 'You're late with your job evaluation form. This is not the first time. I will have to mention this in my staff assessment and development report on you.'

'Sorry, sir. I have finished it. Just have to run it through the spellchecker. You'll have it as soon as I'm back from Diva.'

Max saluted again, went to the car park and set off for Diva, a route he felt he could do blindfolded. Just past the Bobadil restaurant his mobile rang.

'*Dígame. Sí*, Ahmed. What can I do for you?'

'Hassan Khan was arrested last night, and taken to the Diva police station!'

'Oh.'

'He's been beaten up by the police!'

'I'm on my way to Diva now.'

'I've contacted Javeed, and his lawyer.'

'Okay. I'll be with you in about half an hour. Thanks for phoning.'

Fuck! This could make the front pages – and the TV. Davila wouldn't be pleased.

Max arrived at the Diva police station to find a small group of men outside. He recognized some of them from Leila's funeral. Ahmed was inside, waiting for him.

'He's got cuts and bruises all over his face, and possibly a broken rib as well. Javeed and his lawyer are with him now.'

'Where's González?' asked Max.

'In his office, I think.'

Max went straight in without knocking.

'What the fuck do you think you're doing? We'll have the press all over us, and once this gets out there'll be protests across the province.'

González, surprisingly calm, looked straight at Max. 'No need to worry. Picked him up yesterday – a witness claims he saw him on the Jola road just before the time of the murder. This morning the kid tried to do a runner. Then he attacked us, and we had to defend ourselves.'

'Defend yourselves? How come there's not a mark on you?'

'Not so. León there has a cut lip, and I've got a nasty bruise on my leg. We're compiling a report to send to Judge Falcón at the moment. The fact he made a bolt for it makes him all the more guilty, doesn't it?'

'Maybe. If he did try and make a bolt for it?'

'Calling me a liar then?'

Max bit his lip. 'No. Of course not.'

'What's happening now?'

'That Javeed whatever his name is and that smart-arse lawyer of his are with the kid. I hope they see sense. Won't do them any good otherwise. You should use your influence. They're in the interview room.'

'Okay. I'll go and talk to them.'

Max walked along the corridor, knocked on the door, and entered. Hassan was slumped on a chair, holding his side, his face bruised and cut. He had been crying. Javeed and Gabriel the lawyer were conferring in a corner.

'Sub-Inspector Romero,' he announced.

Javeed turned to him. 'Oh, yes, the officer from Granada. This is disgraceful. I trust you'll throw the book at these officers. We will, of course, press charges.'

Max looked at Hassan again. 'I think the first thing we should do is have the young man examined by a doctor. Has anyone called an ambulance?'

'Yes. Teniente González has called for one. It should be here any minute. In my opinion, a clear case of police brutality, probably racially and religiously motivated,' said the lawyer.

'There's no evidence of that,' said Max. 'I've been told that the young man was trying to escape, attacked two police officers, and they responded in self-defence.'

Max looked at Hassan's hands: no signs of resistance there.

'You don't expect us to believe that, do you?'

Max didn't believe it either. But any doubts were to be pursued within the police, not outside.

There was a knock on the door. It was Anita Guevarra.

'The ambulance has arrived.'

Javeed and Gabriel helped Hassan into the ambulance, then got in after him with León. Javeed turned to Max. 'We'll go to the hospital in Motril with Hassan Khan. Then we'll be back. At this point we won't be making any statements to the press. That can come later.'

Max and Guevarra stood watching the ambulance disappear.

'Can we talk alone later?' asked Max quietly. Paula was right – Anita was pretty, though she'd look better without the uniform.

'Sure. Where?'

'Lunch at the Camping at two. González and León would never go there.'

'Sí.'

They entered the room where González and León were waiting for them.

'I've persuaded Señor Khan's friends not to make a press statement now.' Not quite true, but might as well get credit for something. 'They say they want to press charges – police brutality, racism, religious bias.'

'What for? Defending ourselves? They don't have a leg to stand on.'

'You'd better go to the health centre, and let the doc look at these famous wounds. Get a report and some photos of your injuries while you're at it.' Max looked González straight in the eye. 'This ain't the old days, you know.'

'More the worse for that. But I'm glad you see how right we are.'

Max snorted. He noticed a smudge of blood on the ring on González' finger. 'Better clean your ring. Be unfortunate if it were León's blood.'

He had the satisfaction of seeing González blush.

'I'll deal with the crowd outside. Then I'm going for lunch. Can we have a meeting at four?'

'Four should be okay.'

Max went outside. Ahmed was with the men. Max went up to them. There was a hostile murmur as he approached.

'Okay. It seems there was a scuffle when Hassan Khan tried to escape. In that scuffle, two police officers received minor injuries, as did Hassan Khan. Hassan Khan has been taken to the hospital in Motril for a check-up. We will be making a formal statement later.'

There was a hiss of disbelief. There were shouts: 'Liar!' 'Cover up!'

Ahmed came up to Max. 'I don't believe this. I don't believe you believe it. It's just not credible Hassan would try to escape, and assault two police officers.'

'Ahmed, there will be a thorough police investigation.'

'A whitewash?'

'You know that's not true. I will do my best, but it won't help anyone, especially Hassan, if this goes all over the press.'

The men around Ahmed began to press forward. Ahmed held up his arms.

'Calm,' he said. 'Aggression won't get us anywhere. Go home.' He turned to Max. 'You will keep me informed?'

'Sure.'

Max waited until all the men had left, and then went back inside the police station. The black horseshoe on the door shone in the noonday sun. Anita Guevarra was waiting inside.

'I'd better phone Granada. I could do with a cup of coffee first.'

'I'll get you one, sir.'

'*Gracías.*'

The coffee was welcome. He finished it slowly before phoning Davila. The response from Davila was as expected.

'Look, Max, this could be awkward. Keep as much from the press as possible. Back González to the hilt. Judge

Falcón, I'm sure, will back him. Try and see if some deal can be made with the lawyer. We don't want a lawsuit, do we? But let me know as soon as possible what really happened.'

'I will do my best, sir,' replied Max.

'By the way, Max, you've done well so far. Keep it up. It's all good experience. I could modify my staff assessment report, you know.'

'Thank you, sir. I'll do what I can.'

Would Jorge approve? Probably. He was a realist, had always advised Max to fit in on the minor issues, and only break ranks on really important problems. The question now was, is this a minor or major issue?

Max sought out Guevarra.

'Let's go for lunch now. I think we should take our own cars in case González sees us.'

They arrived at the Camping car park within five minutes of each other. The terrace of the Camping overlooked the Diva valley, green and fertile, and the rounded hills of the Sierra Contraviesa, its benign goddess. They settled for a shady corner. Max decided to go for the *menú del día*. Guevarra asked for an avocado salad. She looked shy and timid. A bottle of wine would cheer her up.

Max called the waiter over. '*Una botella de vino blanco, por favor. Vino de las Alpujarras.*'

Max smiled at Guevarra. '*Salud*, Anita.' He raised his glass to her. 'Señora Romero, my grandmother, phoned me to say you had interviewed her. She told me that it was a long interview, but that you were very nice and sympathetic.'

'It was good to meet her. She gave me a lot of information, but I ended up being interviewed myself.'

'*Sí*, that's my *abuela*. She still treats me like a kid, phones me twice a day to make sure I'm eating properly and keeping my flat clean.'

Guevarra laughed, and relaxed.

'So what happened back in there?'

'Don't honestly know, sir.'

'Call me Max, everyone else does.'

'Well, sir – Max, what I understand is that Teniente González got a call from Granada, emphasizing the press interest in the case, and saying it would be good for all concerned if there were a quick result.' Guevarra ran her hand through her jet-black hair, almost the colour of her eyes. 'González and León found someone who thought he had seen someone who looked like Hassan Khan on the Jola road just before Leila's death. They took Hassan Khan in yesterday, and then decided to interview the boy late last night. I heard him crying.'

'Oh.'

'León came out, said they had got nothing, but they were sure he was guilty and would try again in the morning before Judge Falcón had to become involved. González ordered the lights in his cell to be turned off. He said something like . . . a night in darkness would help him reflect.'

She paused, and smiled at Max. 'Nice wine. But I'd better not drink too much or else I'll fall asleep in the afternoon.'

'So what happened then?'

'Well, I came in the next morning. They were both in early. González was in a foul mood.'

'The González we know and love.'

'Absolutely. He was swearing like a devil, saying how he was going to beat the truth out of the little Muslim shit.'

'Really?'

'They sent me on a daft errand to Banjaron. When I returned . . . well, you know the rest.'

'Did you see or hear anything? Did he try to escape?'

'I didn't. I doubt it, sir. Can't see how he could have.'

'So it's his word against theirs.'

'I can't speak out, sir. I have enough problems in the police as it is. And I really need to keep the job. What are you going to do?'

'Do? Defend the upright police of course. Only pursuing their duty. I don't know how you put up with González.'

'Oh, he's not really that bad. He seems worse when you're around. It's almost as if he's trying to prove something,

123

show you up. He can be quite kind. Sympathetic when my mother died.'

'Your mother? *Mi abuela* said your parents were Argentinian refugees.'

'That's right. They came over after the military coup. Father was arrested, and disappeared. Ended up in the Naval Training School, where he was tortured. He was lucky to escape with his life.'

'So what happened?'

'He had been a teacher of one of the guards. They were shooting prisoners, but this guard let him escape. Father's grandmother was Spanish, so he managed to get into the Spanish embassy, and got asylum in Spain. The family joined him here later.'

'You must have been born over here then?'

'I was. It was tough for us at first. Dad couldn't settle down. Never did. We had a flat in Güejar Sierra.'

'Pretty place.'

'Yes, it is. But we never had any money. Getting this job in the police was a real break for me. But then mum got cancer. It was a horrible death.'

Tears came to her eyes. She took out a tissue, wiped her eyes, then ran her hand through her hair.

'Dad, he's gone back to Argentina, and I've got to get my younger sister through college.'

'Things can't be easy for you.'

'It could be a lot worse. I've got a salary and a decent flat in Diva. Oops – it's three thirty. I mustn't be late.'

'You go first. I'll keep your name out of any report.'

Max watched her leave. Nice swing of the hips. He ordered another coffee. Fifteen minutes later he was back at the police station. González and León had returned.

'You don't look much the worse for wear after such a savage assault. How did he do it?'

'We had to restrain him when he tried to escape. He just lashed out at us.'

'Hmm. How come he was able to attempt an escape?'

124

'We'd let him out to have a coffee.'

'Okay. Do we really have anything on him for the murder?'

González and León looked at each other.

'Not yet,' said González. ' Our witness wasn't sure she could identify him. The kid sticks like a leech to the same story. But I just know it's not true.'

'True or not, do we have any grounds for asking Judge Falcón to question him, and keep him in for a further forty-eight hours?'

León and González looked at each other again.

'He had a very public dust-up with Leila on the Friday night. He was definitely in Diva around the time of death, and his only alibi is Javeed Dharwish, who swears that they were both in the Café Al Andaluz until after six o'clock and then went straight back to that centre of theirs. But there's no corroboration for the time they say they were in the café, so he could have left the café, nipped along the Jola road . . . maybe to apologize after the row . . . met the girl while she was out for a walk . . . they have another fight and she ends up down the ravine with a broken neck.'

'You mean you can't come up with anything else? Wouldn't persuade the judge, would it? Where's the motive? Where's the evidence he was at the scene of the crime? Did he call the girl to say he wanted to see her? Where's the statement that suggests he could be capable of violence against a young woman? It doesn't stack up.'

'Hmm.'

'Look, I'll try and make a deal with the lawyer. We'll let the young man go right now in return for bland statements from him and us. We ask the judge to let us hang on to his passport. And he has to sign in regularly.'

'But I know he's hiding something,' said González. 'With more time, we should get somewhere.'

'But tough questioning hasn't produced any results, has it? And from what you say, it isn't likely to either.'

'Okay. But mark my words, it'll be him.'

'Maybe. Let's review what we've got tomorrow morning. Davila said you want me to go through Leila's computer. If it's okay with you I'll sign out for it, and take it with me back to Granada.'

'I've tried to get into the computer, sir,' said Guevarra. 'No joy.'

'The tech boys in Granada should be able to solve that one.'

There was a knock at the door. The secretary entered. 'The lawyer and the other gentlemen are back from Motril.'

'Okay.' Max looked at González. 'I'll deal with this one. It requires some diplomatic skills.'

González snorted. Max left the room. He returned in fifteen minutes.

'It's a deal. The lawyer's no fool, and he knows the score. But it took a lot of persuasion. There will be two press statements, one from us and one from them, pretty much saying the lad panicked, tried to run, and that the two police officers attempted to restrain him. He lashed out, they defended themselves, and in the scrum both Hassan and the officers suffered minor injuries But there was no malice intended on either side. The young man by the way does have a broken rib. So the hospital will keep him overnight for routine check-ups. There will be no charges in return for Hassan's release on the terms as agreed.You'd better get your report in to Judge Falcón immediately. He'll have to approve it.'

González and León smiled at each other.

'See you all tomorrow at ten.'

'*Sí*. And thanks, Max,' smirked González.

Max just hoped he had done the right thing.

The next morning at ten, they all assembled in the interview room. González made a point of being in charge. He didn't want his lost authority of yesterday becoming the norm.

'Okay. What have we got? The Muslim kid's the guilty one, but there's no proof. I've interviewed every house on the Jola road. The one person who thought he might have seen someone like Hassan Khan failed to identify the kid. Can't find any other bugger who wasn't at the beach or asleep. Some are away. One family left for England round about the time of the incident, but I doubt they saw anything. Phew. Still no mobile. It's hot.'

González paused, and mopped the sweat off his face with a dirty handkerchief.

'Where was I? Yes, the girl in the Café Al Andaluz confirmed that snooty Arab's story. And the petrol station confirmed their times. But, apart from that hippy guy the victim seems to have spent the Friday night with, there ain't no one else in the frame. Me, I think there's something sexual. Young Hassan didn't get his rocks off, and lost his cool. León, you've been snooping around Capa. Anything?'

'Absolutely nothing. The locals have noticed the group. But they keep very much to themselves. There are all sorts of rumours of course. It's a Spanish army camp, training secret agents of Middle Eastern origin to infiltrate the terrorists. Or they are a bunch of terrorists. Or orgies. All very colourful.'

'Guevarra, you were looking into that doolally community?'

'Not much, sir. I've talked around. There's a lot of gossip about the girl. A couple of older women felt her father, Ahmed, was too soft with her. Gave her too much freedom. Got a whiff of a scandal – a hint she might have got off with one of the married men in the community. But there's no definite evidence. And if you push too hard they clam up. They're all very upset. I actually found most of them very sweet and gentle.'

'Sweet and gentle? What sort of crap is that? Push this married man lead. Try befriending one of the women, and see if you can get anything.'

'Yes, sir. But it may be difficult.'

'Max, anything at the Granada end?'

'Nothing yet. I've handed over all the documents from the guys in Capa, and they're being checked.'

'Hmm.'

It soon became obvious González was going to enjoy the next question.

'I have to ask you this one, Max. Did you screw the girl or did you attempt to?'

'The answer to both is definitely no.'

'Okay. This will all have to go on the record of course. Judge Falcón may want to question you.'

'I have no objections that it's known I went out with Leila a couple of times.'

'Right. Anything from the interviews with Max's family?'

'I spoke with Don Juan Romero and his wife, Doña Isabel,' said León. 'Don Juan is a most respectable man. He had met the girl on various occasions when she came to interview his *abuela*. He fetched her from Diva a couple of times, and gave her lifts back. He met her again when Doña Paula invited her over for a meal. He answered the phone two or three times when she had phoned. Yes, and ran into her in a restaurant in Granada one lunchtime when Leila was there doing her research. There's nothing whatsoever of interest from Doña Isabel. She was around sometimes when Leila was interviewing Doña Paula, but didn't get involved in conversations and didn't give lifts.'

Max blinked. Juan had never mentioned a lunch in Granada.

'Seems clean as a whistle,' commented González. 'But just check on that lunch.'

'Anything from Doña Paula?' said González turning to Guevarra.

'I've a massive amount of information, sir. Nearly all of it related to Leila's research. Leila had offered to look into the disappearance of Antonio Vargas, Doña Paula's elder brother, in 1937. Doña Paula thinks there may be some connection between the research and her murder. I've got all the details on Antonio Vargas' disappearance. Doña Paula says there are also tapes of conversations between herself and Leila on this and her memories of Diva in the Civil War.'

'I don't see how this could be relevant to the investigation.

128

Everybody local already knows what happened here. What do you think, Max?'

'I haven't heard that Leila had found out anything new. Even if she had, it's unlikely to be connected to her death. When I go through her materials, I'll see if anything is there.'

'Don't waste too much time on it. Unlikely to be relevant.'

'One other thing, sir,' said Guevarra. 'Leila had visited the website on 'the Disappeared', you know, those who just disappeared in the Civil War. Doña Paula says she is still hoping she might find out something through the web about her brother, Antonio.'

'Again fail to see the relevance. My grandpa used tell me how he shot El Gato. That's *mi abuelo's* lucky horseshoe on the door outside. Had it with him when he shot the bastard.'

Max interrupted. 'If that's all, I'd better be getting back to Granada. I'll go through all the material, and let you know if there is anything of use.'

'Fine. I'll want written reports from you all. Judge Falcón needs regular reports for his Auto, his formal record of the case. And with all the press interest, we have to have everything really well documented. Oh, hang on . . . there's one more thing I was chasing up. It's the guy she was with the night before she died. I've been checking up on the hippies. They had a fiesta down at Felipe's. Went on to the early hours of the morning. I'll have to get that bastard's licence revoked. Leila was there, then went with the hippies to *El Fugón* for a party. Sure to have been lots of drugs. So that's a lead we'll explore. Bound to be some Muslims using the Morocco connection to smuggle in drugs. Well, apparently she left with this bloke, Jim. Don't know if he screwed her or not. He's gone off on holiday somewhere.'

González paused and guffawed. 'Holiday! As if all their fucking life wasn't one long holiday, on someone else's money. Well, no one seems to know where this bloody Jim is. But I'm told he'll be back shortly – key player at some fiesta or the other. We'll take him in for questioning as soon as we have him.'

'Make sure he doesn't try to escape,' said Max drily.

González glowered at him. 'Time you went.'

As Max left the police station, he stopped and looked at the horseshoe nailed to the door.

Chapter 12

A la memoria de
Federico García Lorca
Y todos las victimas
De la Guerra Civil
1936–1939

To the memory of
Federico García Lorca
and all the victims
of the Civil War 1936–1939

Memorial plaque, *Fuente Grande; Ainadamar*
(*The Fountain of Tears*)

The following day Max spellchecked his form, and walked upstairs to Davila's office to hand it in.

'Good, Max. So what happened in Diva?'

Max summarized the events.

'Very good, Max. That was handled well. I suppose this makes up for the late submission of your performance report.'

'Thank you, sir.'

'At times, Max, I've been worried about you – but you've come through this well. I think you're finally getting the idea of teamwork. Always keep everything within the force, and deal with any problems through the . . . um . . . proper channels.'

'Yes, sir.'

'Give me a written report on the Diva incident. Make sure you file everything in duplicate. You may be right about what happened. But support González' story.'

'What are you going to do about González, sir?'

'I'll speak to—have a word with him. He has to be more careful in future. By the way, I had a phone call from him. Have to ask you this, Max. Did you or did you not . . . um . . . sleep with that girl?'

'I did not, sir.'

Davila's eyes twinkled.

Bloody González. He might as well have sent out an 'all-user' email. With cartoons. The lads are really going to have fun.

'If it's okay, sir, I'll go through the murdered girl's materials in my flat. I find it easier to work there.'

'Okay. Just make sure we can get in touch.'

Max saluted, and left. Praise the Lord. Max walked down the stairs to the basement of the police building. He handed Leila's computer to one of the technical staff.

'Can you get into this? It's quite urgent.'

'No problem. Give us half an hour.'

His coffee finished, Max returned within the half-hour and collected Leila's computer.

He followed the little Albayzín bus below the Alhambra viewpoint, El Mirador de San Nicolás, down to the Cuesta de María de la Miel, and found a parking spot close to the chemist. The bougainvillea, purple and red, was still in flower, tumbling over the ancient walls of the houses. He sniffed the air, a mixture of sweet scented flowers and urine, a smell peculiar to the Albayzín. He climbed the narrow stairs slowly to the fourth floor, his flat. He put the bag with the computer, disks, tapes and exercise books on the tiled floor, unlocked the double lock, entered, deposited the bag on the desk, and went straight to the shuttered french doors. He opened the shutters. The Alhambra burst into view, the early evening sun lighting up the blotting paper pink walls. No Sierra Nevada behind it, too cloudy.

132

He stepped outside on to his small terrace. The geraniums were wilting, in need of water.

Max breathed quietly for a minute, then returned to his desk, set up the computer quickly, removed jacket and tie, and then paused. He remembered a quotation from John Ruskin, 'Books are the souls of the dead, bound in calfskin.' Going through Leila's laptop felt like an invasion of privacy, a lack of respect for the dead. He went to the fridge, took out an open bottle of the Sierra Contraviesa white, poured the cold wine into a glass, sniffed appreciatively at the citrus aroma, took a sip, and returned to his desk and Leila's computer. This had to be a private conversation.

He started the computer, and then flicked through My Documents, scribbling the contents down on a notepad. Most were thesis-related: thesis notes, thesis chapters, thesis outline, thesis references, thesis supervisor. But there was also a folder marked Poems; another, Novel; and some personal files – finance, jobs, CV. Max turned to the emails. It looked like there were hundreds. He would have to go through every one; any clue would help. He felt sad. What an awful way to get to know Leila.

There were a lot of emails to a Paul Drake, boyfriend probably; yes, definitely boyfriend. The emails started off long and detailed, almost a diary of daily events. But then she launched into her thesis. Boy, did she have the thesis syndrome. Poor sod: he was going to get every detail whether he liked it or not.

Leila went to Granada regularly; the university librarian was very helpful. Most of the historians she wanted to speak to were on holiday, so she would have to wait until they got back. She liked Granada a lot. She had done a tour of Lorca's last days with an English guide who turned out to be a real expert.

Something I've never done, thought Max.

Leila suggested that Paul came over to Spain, though her dad would not approve if they shared a bedroom. She was also having problems with some people in the local Muslim community. Dad had called her in to advise that her behaviour was causing comment. Leila regretted quarrelling with her father.

'But I'm a free spirit and I'm not going to accept the petty, narrow views of some ignorant Muslims. There is nothing in the Qur'an to say women shouldn't enjoy life.'

Paul immediately became very sympathetic and sent an email back.

'Absolutely, honey, absolutely. But I've never understood why you became a Muslim in the first place. I understand the family solidarity thing, but it's not a good time to be Muslim. It could harm your career prospects.'

That was a mistake. Leila's reply was acid.

'It was my decision to become a Muslim. I may have become interested in Islam because of my dad's rediscovery of his faith and my mother's death. But I need a spiritual life, and for me Islam is the correct path.'

Paul made no response. Leila returned to her thesis descriptions. She had discovered the librarian of Diva's little library.

'Ricardo, the librarian in Diva, has a lot of information on Diva during the Civil War. People are still reluctant to talk about that period. Spanish governments ignore the mass graves all over Spain. But people, people who I've met, are still looking for relatives who 'disappeared'. And Ricardo confirmed what I had heard from others; that there is a mass grave somewhere outside Diva. It's beginning to be like a detective novel, trying to find out what happened here.'

Max looked at the list of names and email addresses he had noted down. Most seemed to be connected to her thesis: librarians in Granada and Diva; people who she had interviewed in Diva and Granada. The other names were probably members of the Muslim community and her boyfriend.

Max stood up and stretched his legs. He went to the fridge, and took out a small bowl of olives. Enough for today: amazing how much time it takes to go through material on a computer. He needed a break; maybe some of the usual gang were in La Taberna.

The next day, Max continued with the emails. There were emails to her thesis supervisor. Then a lot of emails to a Shona Monroe, clearly a close friend. These were more revealing.

'I think Paul's more of a conformist than I realized, and he's probably worried a Muslim girl would do his career no good.'

And they were gossipy.

'After Friday prayers the men eat together in one room, and the women in another. I bet the men have interesting political discussions or deep theological disputes. With us women, it's babies and recipes. Boring! I mentioned my thesis once, and was told that's most interesting, but a bit controversial. Controversial! I ask you!'

Yet again, Max warmed to Leila.

There were descriptions of the various men she had met. She found handsome Spaniards very appealing. The librarian at the University of Granada was cute, as well as helpful. Hell, Max Romero was on her list!

'He's a nice cop – interested in my thesis. Did his degree at Glasgow Uni. What a small world! Been for a coffee with him twice. He put me in touch with his grandmother, Paula. It's great to have someone in Diva who understands what I'm trying to do in my thesis . . . AND he's really flirtatious, and that's quite fun.'

The next emails concerned Paula. 'She's fantastic. We really have a good laugh though some of the things she tells me about are so sad.'

And then finally, there was something significant.

'The cute cop is still interested. But I'm keen on someone else now. Tell you all about it later.'

Well, thought Max sadly, I wouldn't have got anywhere. He felt a stab of pain. Murder, even more than accidents, leaves a strong sense of a vacuum, of what might have been.

135

But, as he was nearing the end of the emails, Max at last found a clue. Leila returned to the person she was keen on.

'He's tall, dark and handsome. How conventional can I get? But married with children. Typical!'

Can't be Hassan then, thought Max.

Shona's reply was sensible, warning Leila to steer clear of married men with children. 'All they want is a bit on the side.'

And then Shona was leaving. Bother.

'Off to Nepal tomorrow. I'll email when I hit civilization. Take care, and don't do anything I wouldn't do.'

Leila's final email to Shona: 'Have a great trip. See you when I get back. Be good, if that's possible. I think I'm really in love this time. Tell you all about it when you get back. Love Leila.'

Blast. Absolutely nothing. No mention of Hassan or the guys up the hill. Hassan couldn't be the dreamboat with wife and kids. What was it that Guevarra had said: there was gossip about Leila and a married man in the community. That's the only real clue so far. Better phone Guevarra to ensure she really did chase up that gossip. He took a sip of wine, and paused.

Okay. He needed to contact just about everyone Leila sent emails to, and check with Shona Monroe when she got back.

The more he got to know Leila, the more he liked her. He looked at the row of tapes. He needed some fresh air before tackling them.

Back in the flat Max switched on the tape recorder, and played the first of Paula's tapes. He laughed aloud. Paula was . . . well, so Paula. Paula interviewed Leila as much as the other way round. Leila told Paula all about her family. Her mother had committed suicide when the cancer became too much to bear. Her father was seeing another woman at the time, and he thought it might have been that which pushed her mum over the edge. But it wasn't. Her mother had even left a note, telling Ahmed to remarry soon. He didn't, became grief-stricken, and rediscovered his Muslim faith. He later decided to help set up a Muslim community in Spain. Leila was a bit vague on her own faith.

'Paula, I suppose it is partly out of sympathy with my father. But it wasn't just that. Mum's death sort of pushed me to ask what really matters in life; who am I, that sort of thing. I had never felt Scottish, and even less Christian. Becoming a Muslim was part of discovering myself. Can't say I'm there yet.'

'Leila, I'm eighty-three. I'm not sure you ever get there.'

Tape 2 was all about Paula's meeting Lorca. Invariably Paula did a bit of matchmaking. Blast Paula's keen eyes: how did she know he was keen on Leila? Tape 3 dealt with Diva on the eve of Civil War. Tapes 4 and 5 were the family. Max was shocked at how close she'd been to getting raped by the soldiers who came looking for her brother. She had never talked about it. He couldn't bring up the subject now: she'd be embarrassed. The tapes confirmed what he had suspected: that grandpa had been a strong Franco supporter. *Mi abuelo*! Max had such happy memories of grandpa teaching him how to ride a bike . . . and going with Juan to catch fish in the river. Leila had given Paula the website address of 'The Spanish Civil War Disappeared', and other websites on the period.

So that's why Paula insisted on getting a computer, thought Max. He smiled: Paula had never given up learning, she was always trying out something new. He hoped he would be like her if he ever reached her age. But there was nothing in the tapes relevant to Leila's death. Although Leila had promised to investigate the circumstances surrounding Antonio's disappearance, there was nothing on what she had found – if she had found anything. Maybe Paula knew more?

The tape of Leila's interview with Ricardo, the librarian, was interesting. Diva had really been on the front line of the Civil War. And yes, it had been González' grandfather who had shot Manuel Paz, El Gato. So it wasn't all bullshit. Amazing. El Gato had returned from France after the Civil War to establish a guerrilla resistance in the hills around Diva. The guerrillas were convinced that Britain and the USA would help them to overthrow Franco. Max knew this part of the history.

Leila: So what happened then?

Ricardo: Apparently the Americans were quite keen. But the British had persuaded them that this would destabilize Spain, and might bring back the Communists.

Leila: Gosh. I never knew this. So what finally happened?

Ricardo: Well, with the Cold War hotting up, Eisenhower eventually cut a deal with Franco in 1956, and got the huge American base at Rota as a reward. And after that . . . well, there was no international pressure on Spain to move towards democracy.

What's new, thought Max. So much for bringing democracy to the poor, benighted world.

Alfredo, the librarian in Granada, likewise offered nothing that might throw any light on Leila's death. In his second interview, Leila asked lots of questions about Lorca's death. The librarian felt that this had been thoroughly covered, by British, French and American historians, as well as Spanish, and had given her a reading list.

Alfredo: There's been a lot of speculation. There was a view that Lorca had been murdered by a homosexual lover, another, that he was killed by the Reds because he was about to come out in support of Franco.

Leila: But recent research has shown this was just black propaganda.

Alfredo: Absolutely. Lorca almost certainly was arrested by a group of members of Acción Popular, out to make a name for themselves. He was then shot on the orders of Comandante Valdés on 18th or 19th August 1936. It was one of the hottest days in an unusually hot August.

Leila: Yeah, that's Ian Gibson. Great book, don't you think?

Alfredo: Interesting, but it has its weaknesses. My reading is that Lorca was actually well hidden and protected in the house of the Rosales family. Somebody must have betrayed Lorca's hiding place to political fanatics of Acción Popular. There's still a mystery to solve. You know, there just might be more in the Guardia Civil archives. They weren't open at the time Gibson was carrying out his research.

Leila: Betrayal? That's interesting. I've been working on that hypothesis.

Alfredo: If you do find anything, come and see me. It would be quite a coup.

Max grinned: cunning bastard. That's a nifty chat-up line.

But he was still puzzled. There was the family connection through Paula to Lorca, but why did Leila have such an interest in Lorca's death? It wasn't part of her thesis topic. Maybe Leila wanted to make a name for herself . . . discover something new about Lorca. Maybe she was just fascinated by the thought of conspiracy or cover-up. Who knows?

Max looked at his watch.

'*Díos*, it's late. Must stop now.'

Chapter 13

Muerto se quedo en la calle
Con un puñal en el pecho.
No lo conocía nadie.

They left him dead in the street
With a dagger in his breast.
No one knew him.

Frederico García Lorca, *Surpresa* (*Surprise*)

God, time flies. It had taken Max almost two days to go through the first box of Leila's materials. But no leads except the 'married man with children'. He still had to start the poems and stories. There was the thesis itself, and then another three notebooks. Did she ever throw anything away?

Max opened one of the notebooks: philosophical musings, notes, observations and descriptions. Max suddenly remembered his tutor, on a creative writing course, advising them to carry a notebook to jot down anything which struck them. 'Even the most seemingly trivial thing could be transformed into good material,' he had said. These were Leila's observations for a novel. Max sighed; he remembered only too well how all his great thoughts, his dreams of the great Anglo-Spanish novel, had come to naught. He had a couple of chapters in a drawer somewhere. Maybe Leila would have had better luck.

At lunchtime Max walked down to La Taberna, and sat at

his usual sherry barrel. He was lucky: didn't have to share it with anyone. He fetched the papers. 'Government Warns ETA Has Acquired Missiles from Al-Qaeda.' Hmm. Maybe. 'Pressure Mounts on Palestinians to Make a Deal.' That's for sure.

Max finished his tapas and beer, walked out into the stifling heat of Plaza Nueva, strolled down to the back of the cathedral in search of shade, and then to his office. At least the air conditioning was working. No urgent messages. He was about to leave for the strategy meeting when his phone rang.

'*Hola. Ah. Hola Don Gabriel. Sí*, I understand. *Sí. Sí.* I will phone Teniente González right away, and then phone you back. No, I will do what I can.'

Max dialled the Diva police station and got through to González.

'How's it going, Max?'

'*Bien, gracias, bien.* Don Gabriel Martín Facarros, the lawyer, called me. The hospital in Motril are wanting to release Hassan Khan. However, they insist he needs rest. Don Gabriel thinks going up and down the mountain from Capa to Diva every day would be bad for him.'

'So?'

'Don Gabriel asked if Hassan Khan could be allowed a week's recuperation before he starts officially signing in.'

'Cheeky bastard. This is a murder investigation, not a bloody holiday camp.'

'Teniente, given the circumstances . . . You could always go up there to check on him.'

'Okay then . . . but if this goes wrong, it's your problem! I'll ask Judge Falcón to agree.'

'I'll emphasize that you agree reluctantly, and that the lawyer should note the police willingness to cooperate.'

'Anything from the stuff you took back with you?'

'Not much. There's a slight suggestion that she was interested in a married man with children, but she doesn't name the guy.'

'I'll get Guevarra on to this.'

'Any joy with the hippy in the van?'

'Ah, yes. Picked him up. He's in the cells. Leila's mobile was in his van. I've asked León to look at it.'

'Do you want me to come over to help interview him?'

'No. That's okay. He speaks good Spanish.'

Max quickly phoned the lawyer to confirm the agreement, then left his office to go to the strategy meeting.

'Sub-Inspector Romero, I've just had you paged,' said the desk Officer, Bardon, as he passed reception. 'There seems to have been some sort of breakthrough.'

'Breakthrough?'

Max pushed through the heavy doors of the conference room. Linda was seated at the head of the table. Davila, Bonila, López and others were there.

'Max, we've struck gold. Just had a fax from London about the Ibn Rush'd guys. I can read it out to you. Madrid translated it quickly.' Linda cleared her throat, and read at a deliberately slow pace.

'Heading – Hassan Khan. Passport number: 451455904. National Insurance number: YA 501977F. Occupation: student at the University of Brunel, studying Computer Sciences and Electronics. Marital status: single. Mother: Elizabeth Wilding. Father: Omar Khan. Parents separated. Lived with father after separation. Last known address: 169, Finchley Road West, Finchley, London.'

Linda paused, took a sip of water, and then continued.

'This is the good stuff. "In relation to the above. The Anti-Terrorist Group has had the above on their list as a potential terrorist suspect for some time. The above is thought to be a member of, or at least to have close connections with, Hisb ut-Tahr which although not a terrorist organization as such is suspected as acting as a forum for ideological indoctrination, and as a potential recruiter for terrorist organizations.

'"The above has taken part in frequent demonstrations against both the war in Afghanistan and the war in Iraq, and has handed out leaflets justifying armed resistance. He is a known supporter of Palestinian independence, and has had contact with Hamas, an extremist Palestinian group. He has demonstrated against the government of Pakistan. He has attended the Finchley Road Mosque, again thought to be terrorist recruiting ground.

'"He is known to have visited northern Pakistan, ostensibly to see relatives. The last known visit was July and August 2000. We have requested information from the government of Pakistan regarding the above.

'"Although there is no definite evidence linking the above to terrorist support or action, we are of the opinion that the above has the potential to either support or become involved in possible terrorist actions. He moves within circles of known supporters of terrorism. We suggest close surveillance. Please keep us informed of actions and movements of the above, and of any further information you may require."

'There you are,' said Linda triumphantly. 'There you have it. The terrorist connection we have been looking for.'

She looked round the table. 'And there is more. Heading – Javeed Dharwish. The usual stuff from his passport. Other details. This is what matters.'

She paused again, and sipped at her water.

'"Occupation: business training consultant. Education: degree in Business Studies, University College, London. Master in Business Training, University of Colorado, USA. PhD, London School of Economics.

'"Marital status: Widower. Wife killed in Chatila massacre, on 18th September 1982. No known children. Known to have lived for a while with Fatima Khalid, a Palestinian militant thought to be a member of the Hamas organization. She returned to Palestine three years ago. No definite record of her whereabouts since.

'"The following information is from the government of Israel: Javeed Dharwish was a known militant of Al Fatah. He is believed to have been involved in a number of attacks against Israeli property and personnel. He was an important

143

organizer within the Chatila refugee camp where he helped organize young militants. He escaped from Chatila, and ended up in London. He worked for a number of years in a variety of jobs: waiter, construction worker and hospital porter. He studied at night classes and extra-mural classes before being admitted to University College, London. Active in student groups supporting armed struggle for Palestinian independence. He obtained a Master's degree in the USA, and then a PhD from the London School of Economics. Since then he seems to have dropped out of political extremism, and has been running a business consultancy firm. Obtained European Union money to help set up business training courses in the West Bank. Some students on the courses were known Al Fatah and Hamas militants.

'"We have nothing to connect him to terrorists at present. But we suspect he has retained his political sympathies for Palestinian independence. He has donated to the so-called Palestinian Charity, HosPal, which was declared illegal by the government of Israel as a front for Hamas. He is probably one of a number of Palestinian businessmen outside the Territories who channel money to militant Palestinian groups."

'There, becoming more and more obvious,' said Linda. 'The British have been efficient. Nothing back yet from the French, Germans and Belgians. The Spanish, I'm sure, will be the last to respond.'

She took a sip of water. 'Gentlemen, we should move fast on this one. I don't think we can afford to wait for information requested from other countries. We should pick them up without delay.'

'On what charge?' asked Max.

'On what charge? Planning acts of terrorism, of course. We need to take that training place of theirs in the hills apart.'

'But should we not wait for more evidence?' persisted Max.

Surprisingly Davila came in to support him. 'Yes. I think we need clearer evidence. The Centre is legitimate – went

144

through all the correct procedures. Hassan Khan seems to have kept some odd company. But he's very young. And perhaps a bit stupid. Javeed Dharwish has been a . . . um . . . legitimate businessman for many years We don't want to get it wrong, and make a laughing stock of ourselves. If we mess this one up, we could even have questions in the European Parliament.'

Linda turned to Bonila. 'Comisario, what do you think? After all, we have just agreed how well Granada is cooperating in the anti-terrorist fight.'

'*Sí*. And we will continue to cooperate of course. But I wonder whether we should not be just a little bit cautious. Maybe we can take another angle. Sub-Inspector Romero, Davila told me that one of the group, this Hassan Khan, is also a suspect on a murder charge. Maybe there is something there we can use.'

Max came in. 'He's just been released on grounds of insufficient evidence. He was also injured whilst trying a so-called escape from the Diva police.'

'*Dios*,' shouted Linda. 'Do we know where he is now?'

'*Sí*. He's recovering in the Ibn Rush'd Centre. But he has to report regularly to the police.'

'Are you stupid or just bloody naive? He could have killed the girl because she knew too much.'

Max was speechless. He could hardly say that the attempted escape was trumped up. After all, his official report had backed up González' story. Linda glared at Martín.

'Inspector Sánchez?'

Martín paused. 'Well, the Centre could be a front. But there's been nothing on him for years, and he's now a successful British businessman. We can put aside the Israeli comment. They would say that, wouldn't they?' He took out a large handkerchief and wiped the sweat from his face.

'How about the Palestinian girlfriend?' asked Linda.

'Could mean something, could mean nothing.'

'And the boy, Hassan Khan?'

'I'd ignore the anti-war activities. But I agree – the mosque connection is worrying, and I don't like the company he keeps.'

'Your conclusion?'

'I still think we should wait. See what we get on the others, keep them all under surveillance. If we're wrong, it could backfire.'

Martín took out his handkerchief, wiped his face again and turned to Max.

'Max, you've been up there. What do you think?'

'I agree, sir. It could be a perfect cover. But everything is in order. And they've got EU money, so either they're clean, or very, very smart.'

'And the girl?'

' You want my honest assessment? I reckon the evidence against Hassan Khan's weak, but Teniente González in Diva disagrees.'

Linda snorted. 'So I'm alone on this? I don't think so. But I'll give it the weekend to see if anything else turns up. Meet Monday morning, 10 a.m. Send secure emails to all the anti-terrorist units in Europe and the USA again, and say it's urgent. Meanwhile Inspector Sánchez and I will fly to Madrid, and give our report there. They may have more information.'

With that she left the room.

Max turned to Martín. 'Could I have a word with you, sir?'

'Sure. A coffee? Let's go outside. Your coffee here is foul.'

As they were leaving, Davila called out to him. 'Max, can I have a word with you in an hour's time?'

'Certainly, sir.'

Martín and Max sat down in a quiet corner of the Bar Alonzo.

'*Dos cafes, por favor.*'

'Well, I see the spider hasn't quite got you in her web yet,' joked Martín.

'I have the greatest respect for Inspectora Jefe Concha,'

146

said Max, 'but maybe she's a bit hasty. Also, I'm sure Hassan Khan didn't try to escape. Maybe the police were hoping for a quick confession.'

'Oh. Wouldn't be the first time. You still sure there are no terrorist cells here?'

'No. I wouldn't go as far as that. Just seems unlikely.'

'We have to check everything thoroughly. These guys are serious. But there's also serious politics behind this. The Partido Popular really needs a terrorist threat to win the elections. We have to be careful how to play it. Inspectora Jefe Concha is a very determined and ambitious woman, PP to the core. And always needing to prove she's a tough guy.'

Max smiled. Should he tell him about Linda's request to report only to her? Better not, that would be going too far. 'Have to go now, sir. Need to see my boss.'

'Sure. I'll have another coffee. Keep in touch if you need to talk. And let me know if you discover anything, preferably before *la Inspectora*.'

'Thank you, sir. Will do.'

Max glanced back as he left. Martín gave him a broad conspiratorial smile.

Back at HQ, Davila was going through a report. He looked up. 'I didn't know about the release of Hassan Khan. Could have been awkward. Best clear such things with me first.'

'Sorry, sir. I had checked with Teniente González first. Could have created problems, and I had to think on my feet.'

'I'm worried about launching a full-scale raid on this Ibn Rush'd place. If we don't find anything, the papers will hang us out to dry. Any insights?'

'The Centre's very high tech, sir. No sign of weapons when I checked up on them, but it would be easy to hide if they have any. The other thing is that the Director, Javeed Dharwish, seems to have friends in Brussels.'

'That's what worries me. Be hellish embarrassing if we don't find anything. Okay. Keep me posted. Let me be the first to know. Don't want any more surprises.'

'Sir, now that I remember – the hippy guy, his name's Jim

Cavendish, has turned up, The Diva police have got him in for questioning. Leila Mahfouz seems to have spent most of the night before she died with him. Teniente González thinks there might be a drug connection. Do you want me to go over to Diva?'

'What does González say?'

'He reckons they can manage with the interviews. Cavendish speaks good Spanish.'

'Okay, leave it then. We need you here Monday. That Inspector Sánchez speaks good sense, doesn't he?'

'Yes, sir. He seems very balanced.'

Max smiled as he left. He was meant to be keeping Linda, Martín and Davila, all fully informed, separately, and all first.

The weekend was hot and sticky. The air conditioning in Max's car failed. And the chocolate cake he bought in Granada for the family lunch melted into a gooey mess. He arrived in a bad mood. Then Paula, upset with the lack of progress on the Leila case, kept repeating, 'The police are doing nothing. Deliberately nothing.' Until Max snapped, 'Paula, believe me, we are doing our best. Just give me a break.'

Juan hardly said a word, and avoided Isabel. Isabel, her eyes puffy from crying, fussed around. Only Encarnita was pleased to see him. She loved sticky chocolate. So when Paula declared the heat was too much for her, and she had to go and lie down, Max made his excuses and returned to Granada. In this heat everything that could go wrong does go wrong.

Monday came too soon. Max arrived promptly at 10 a.m. for the Strategy Group's reconvened meeting and Linda again took the chair. She began the proceedings quietly.

'Are there any developments?'

Davila spoke first. 'Sí. The murder case in Diva. The hippy the girl spent her last night with has been found and taken in for questioning. I phoned Teniente González just now. No confession or anything. But there was a stack of hashish in his van, and more in his shack. The Teniente thinks there may be a drug connection. He is keeping me briefed.'

'Drugs? Any sign of drugs from the autopsy?'

'None . But the Teniente thinks there's a Moroccan connection. The Muslims go there quite often, and Diva's on the drug route.'

'Yes,' interrupted Max, 'but the hippies also go over to Morocco. They're more likely to bring back hashish than the Muslims.'

'Thank you, Sub-Inspector,' said Linda. 'I suspect the drug connection is a false lead. But everything should be pursued.' She paused for dramatic effect. 'Well, I've now received information on most of the other guys in the Centre. I will summarize it for you. The German citizen, Hakim Lasnami, is the son of a prominent member of the Iraqi Communist Party, and is an active member of the Party in exile. The French citizen, Omar Rahmin, is the son of an Algerian member of the Armed Islamic Group, GIA, who fled to France during the conflict in Algeria. He has been active in anti-war activities, has handed out leaflets supporting armed resistance, and is on the French list of people to be monitored.'

Bonila looked impressed.

'I even have information from our Spanish authorities. Faslur Hashim is a Moroccan immigrant. He has been arrested for drug trafficking and possession of a false passport. He spent two years in jail in Madrid. After release there have been no charges against him. But he has been seen in the company of members of the Moroccan Groupe Islamique Combattant Marocain, the GICM. I have no information from Belgium on Rizwan Ahmet as of now. But I suspect there will be a connection to militants there.'

Linda paused and took a sip of water. 'Gentlemen, the evidence is overwhelming. We should go in tonight. I have cleared it with Madrid. Do you agree?'

Comisario Bonila frowned. 'This is a tough one. It needs careful consideration. What do the others think?'

Coronel Ramirez from the Guardia Civil immediately said, 'I agree with the *Inspectora*. We should go in now.'

There was silence around the table. Max felt he had to object. 'Yes, but . . .'

Linda scowled. 'Yes, but? Sub-Inspector, you always have doubts. What is it this time?'

'Well, for a start, being a member of the Iraqi Communist Party puts him in opposition to Saddam. Saddam massacred the Party which is partly why the Americans supported him for so long . . . along with his war with Iran of course.'

'I agree,' added Martín. 'I also think terrorists would not risk having a drug runner on board. The Algerian . . . . well, the Islamic Party had won the election fair and square, but the army didn't accept it. Nothing really against the son apart from leafleting.'

'Get real,' snapped Linda. 'Is it just a coincidence that every single one of our trainee businessmen comes from a background of political militancy?'

She looked round the table. 'I formally propose we go in tonight.'

Comisario Bonila, still with a worried frown on his face, finally uttered his judgement. 'I suppose so.'

Max knew Davila would follow.

'Yes, if the Comisario agrees.'

'Martín?' questioned Linda.

'I still have doubts, but we can't risk not going in.'

'And our yes but Sub-Inspector?'

Max knew he was clutching at straws. 'The evidence does not seem convincing to me –we're almost condemning people just because they are involved in politics. But . . . yes.'

'Ah. A shift from yes but to but yes. The rest of you?'

There was never any doubt they would agree.

'Sub-Inspector Romero knows exactly where the Centre is. I suggest he goes with the advance group,' said Linda.

'Full equipment, flak jackets, the lot. They may be armed,' added Martín.

'Should we inform the Diva police?' asked Comisario Bonila. Then remembering his rank, he added, 'I shall inform General Lopez immediately, and also inform Teniente González with an order to him to keep this top secret.'

'How quickly can we go?' asked Linda.

'3 a.m. is the best time to catch everyone off guard,' replied Martín

'Okay,' said Comisario Bonila. 'Assemble here 10 p.m. for full briefing. I will order maps and everything else. A helicopter will be based in Diva. In case the press get nosy, we are having a farewell bash for one of our officers. Top secret.'

Max felt a thrill of excitement.

At 10 p.m. everyone reassembled in the conference room.

'Everything is in order,' reported Comisario Bonila, striking a pose of the competent commander-in-chief. 'I will now hand over to General Miguel Ponte from the CGI. He has flown in specially from Madrid, and will be in charge of the operation.'

A tall, fit man with greying temples stepped forward.

'Right. We strike exactly at 3 a.m. That gives us plenty of time to assemble in the hills outside the Centre. A helicopter will support us. It's already on the Diva pad. The second car will pick up Teniente González and, and . . .' He paused, and looked at his notes. 'Ah, yes, Sargento Mario León. That means we will have three people present who have been round the Centre before. We go straight to the bedroom and dormitory as Sub-Inspector Max Romero has described. We depart with twenty-minute intervals between us, and assemble in the car park outside Capa for final instructions. Okay, men. Only shoot if you have to. But if necessary . . . shoot to kill. Any questions?'

There were none. At 1.30 a.m. all assembled in the car park.

'Everyone here?' asked Bonila.

Max looked around. 'We're still waiting for the car with González and León.'

'Hell. Where can they be? Better wait a few minutes.'

151

Ten minutes later a car drew up. González, León and the driver got out.

'Sorry, sir,' said González. 'This fool of a driver went to the wrong bridge.'

'No matter. Two CGI men have gone on ahead to spy out the place. We wait here until they report back.'

Everyone paced up and down, most smoking. There was no moon, just myriads of bright stars, the black silhouette of the mountains etched against the dark sky.

Finally the reconnaissance group returned.

'No sign of life. Assume they're all asleep. We can drive to half a mile of the place, then go on foot until the Centre's fully surrounded. We go in first.'

They drove in complete silence. Max, González and León circled the Centre, and waited on the far side in the hill. Max looked at his watch. 3 a.m. precisely. He could just make out shadowy figures running into the building. He turned to González and León.

'Go.'

They scrambled down to the back of the house, and waited, guns ready, blocking escape. There was a loud bang, the smell of gas, shouts, and a single shot from inside the building. Max checked his pistol, breath bated. Three minutes later General Ponte appeared.

'It's all over,' he shouted. 'Got them all. One wounded. The chopper'll get him to hospital.'

Max put his pistol back in its holster, and together with González and León entered the building. There was an acrid smell of tear gas. Five men in underpants lay spread-eagled on the floor of the dormitory; one lay on his bed, the sheet bloody, his arm dangling towards the floor, towards his spectacles.

'Okay,' said General Ponte. 'You can get dressed. We are taking you into custody under the anti-terrorism law of Spain.'

'The chopper's landed, sir.'

'Right. Carefully now. We don't want a fatality.'

152

'What shall we do with the others, sir?'

'Cuffs and hoods. Take them outside, and wait for the van.'

'Yes, sir.'

'Take the pictures outside. Make sure there's a good shot, but nothing which identifies them or this place.'

General Ponte turned to the assembled officers. 'Right. Tear this place apart. Photograph everything first. Anything of interest: computers, disks, mobiles, diaries, into the bags. Anything suspicious, call me, Inspectora or Inspector Sánchez. Remember, anything could be booby-trapped.'

Linda stepped forward. 'Let's divide this up. Two to a room. Teniente González and Sargento León – you do that little prayer room outside. Sub-Inspector Romero and Coronel Ramirez – you take the kitchen. Be careful, could be ricin or other toxics hidden there. You others split into pairs and cover every room. And congratulations, men. I'm sure the Prime Minister will be pleased.'

Max and Coronel Ramirez went to the kitchen. Ramirez turned to Max.

'Okay. I'll do the food cupboards. You do the fridge and rubbish. Careful. Anything suspicious, call me over.'

Max went to the fridge, and systematically took out everything, checked it, then placed it into the bags. Nothing. He then began on the rubbish. His plastic gloves were now sticky with sweat. Nothing. He felt anxious about the wounded man. What if they had got it wrong? There was no gun by the man's bed, only his glasses.

'Could be something here,' said Coronel Ramirez. 'Looks like they've hidden this jar at the back.' He gingerly took out an unlabelled jar, half full of white powder, and carefully put it aside. He noticed Max looking at it. 'Could be something nasty here. Ricin or whatever.'

They worked in silence. Soon there was nothing further left to examine and they returned to the dormitory. Everyone had finished. Dawn was breaking.

'Anything?' asked General Ponte.

153

'Could be something here, sir,' said Ramirez. 'White powder in an unlabelled jar.'

'Okay. Take all the files, computer stuff etc. We'll go through it all thoroughly.'

After all the excitement, Max felt a sense of let-down, a sense of foreboding growing. They drove back in silence. Once in the conference room, General Ponte addressed them.

'Well done, men. I have to return to Madrid immediately to brief the Minister. Inspectora Jefe Concha will organize the interrogation of the suspects. Meanwhile, you all get a good rest. I'll put out a press statement.'

Linda broke in: 'Make sure it leads with the suspected ricin. We want the front page.'

Martín interrupted: 'No. That's not the way to do it. Never put it in writing. Let the media know that it's from official, but off-the-record, sources.'

'Agreed,' said Linda. 'And the same source can say the police believe there is an ETA connection.'

Max sighed. They all broke up, and he returned to his flat. The danger had been exciting, but now he felt like a burst balloon.

Chapter 14

The moon leaves a knife
Hanging in the sky
An ambush of lead
That lies in wait
For the agony of blood.

Frederico García Lorca, *Bodas de Sangre* (*Blood Wedding*)
in a version by Ted Hughes

Any excitement, any sense of achievement, had passed,
and the image fixed in his mind was that of the man lying
on a bloody bed, one arm outstretched to reach for the
glasses on the floor. Max had helped carry him, wrapped
in the bloody sheet, to the helicopter. The medical orderly
had done his best to stem the flow of blood, had assured
everyone present that the young man would live. But Max
felt he was carrying a dead man. He slept badly. That
image of the hand dangling above the glasses recurred as
he tossed and turned. The air conditioning, now repaired,
was on full, losing another battle against the heavy, stifling
heat. Max got up in the middle of the night and took a puff
of his inhaler, and drank a full glass of water. When he
awoke his head throbbed, his mouth was parched, his eyes
red and itchy. He took a cold shower. For ten minutes he
felt cool and alert. But then the heat, heavy and oppressive,
returned.

He took the bus down to Gran Vía. A heat haze lay over
the city, guarding the pollution. Granada lay entombed in

dirty, streaky smog. The Granadinos who had not escaped to the beach were in a foul mood, blaring their horns at the least provocation. Max got off before the bus even reached Gran Vía, and willed his legs to walk into the police station. He climbed the stairs to report to Davila. He knocked and entered.

'Max, how are you? You look as if you've come from the night of the living dead. Join the club. Bugger all to report. The bastards keep banging on about their innocence. We got their CVs right, so that's something. But they say all they were doing was opposing an illegal invasion, and there's no law against that. The Inspectora has been asking for you. She thinks you might have some bright ideas on how to break them down.'

'Not really, sir. My job's about maintaining good relations with our Muslim community.'

'Okay then. They're in the basement. Get down there and make yourself useful.'

Max's legs felt heavier and heavier as he took the stairs down to the basement. He needed another coffee. He heard voices, angry voices. Linda sounding tired, frustrated, insistent. He knocked. Linda came out.

'Max. Thanks for coming.'

'You okay? How's it going?'

'Shitty. Getting nowhere. I need a coffee. Come and join me. See if you have any ideas.'

They sat in a corner of the police canteen. In the bright morning light, Linda had aged ten years.

'Max. I'm half dead. Have to get some sleep.'

'Any progress?'

'No. None. Found nothing so far in all that stuff we took. These guys are tough bastards. We're getting zilch out of any of them. Nothing on the ETA connection. Some of the bastards say they've never heard of ETA. Can you believe it?'

'That's not surprising – most of them are foreigners. Why should they know about Basque terrorists?'

'I don't get it. It's like they'd rehearsed what to say. They

156

admitted the lot: the shit their dads got up to, the anti-war stuff, the works.'

'Why wouldn't they? Maybe they've got nothing to hide.'

'Are you a fool or just bloody naive? Of course they're hiding something. I don't buy their line, too many bloody coincidences. I could swallow one or two of them being involved in stuff. But all of them? No way. Peace and justice types? You must be joking.'

'Maybe. But it could be. What do you make of Javeed Dharwish?'

'Gives nothing away. Doesn't seem to need sleep. So damn polite and reasonable it turns my stomach. Says his financial contributions to HosPal are just for medical aid for the suffering poor of Palestine. What a load of crap. Did you know, he was in the Chatila refugee camp, but only doing youth work. What a saint!'

'What happened there? The massacre was really terrible.'

'Huh. Oh, Max – did you see the press this morning?'

'No. I haven't seen a newspaper or watched the TV.'

'You should. We're front-page news. They're all running the ricin connection.'

'Any reports back on that?'

Linda looked away, her shoulders sagging. 'No. Nothing definitive yet.'

'Hmm.'

'Some of the hacks are talking up an ETA link.'

'Can't imagine where they got that from, can you?'

'So we've got to get something out of them. Any bright ideas, Max? '

'Not really my scene.'

Linda managed a smile. 'Oh. *Sí*, I forgot. *Señor* yes but, and but yes. Really have to get some sleep. Can hardly stand. Over to you. Maybe a friendly smile will get a result. Find their weak spots, Max. We'll take it from there. I'll be in first thing tomorrow. Let me have your report then.'

'I'll try. But have you considered they might be telling the truth? That we made a mistake?'

157

Linda stood up, and looked Max firmly in the eye. 'I haven't made a mistake. They're guilty as hell. They're involved somehow. So is ETA. We just have to get it out of them. It's your job now. That's an order.'

She walked slowly out of the door. Max had to admire her tenacity, her drive. But her refusal to even consider that she might be wrong was worrying. He finished his coffee slowly, and then poured another. He could do with fresh air, but an order was an order. Best begin with Javeed Dharwish. If he cracked then all the others would.

Javeed had not slept much either. But he was still in control. Hardly a crease on his well-cut suit. He turned towards Max.

'Ah. Sub-Inspector Romero. Any news of Rizwan Ahmet, the man you shot?'

'I phoned this morning. They've removed the bullet. He's lost a lot of blood, but the medics think he's stabilizing.' Max thought it best not to add he was still in a critical condition.

'I hope so. Any chance you're here to sort out this mess? No. So it's the bad cop, good cop routine. And which will you be this time?'

'I am here solely to get the truth.'

'What is truth, said jesting Pilate, and would not stay for an answer. I know your Christian literature. But do you know ours?'

'"*Ana al haqq*,"' replied Max. '"Truth is me" to quote Al Hallaj. And he was beheaded for his claim.'

'Indeed he was. For only Allah can claim that.'

Both men relaxed a little.

'I've told your ill-educated police here everything there is to know. You have made an embarrassing mistake, and when it all comes out I hope heads will roll.'

'They never do. At least not at the top.'

'That's true.'

Max smiled. 'Okay. Can we start from the beginning?'

'You seem to have a full file on me. The Israelis, I suppose. What is it you want to know?'

158

'Start with the Ibn Rush'd Centre. How it was set up, how you chose the applicants for your course . . .'

Javeed went over all the details. Like Linda, Max thought there was something odd about the young entrepreneurs on the course. How could a convicted drug dealer have got on to it?

'Did you know Faslur Hashim had been in jail for drugs?'

'Yes, we did. But he's a reformed character. As with many Muslims he rediscovered his religion in jail. The EU funders were keen we had a social inclusion element in our programme. I was also keen on the idea.'

'What was his proposed business plan?'

'He had a detailed proposal to set up a business importing traditional pottery from Morocco. He has good contacts in Fez.'

'What! You must be joking! Spain's full of trinkets from Morocco.'

'Yes. But much of it is of poor quality. So he was planning to get the best from Fez, and work with local craftsmen to improve the quality and variety of products as the business developed.'

'And go bankrupt in a week?'

'Well, he might modify his plan. It was not fully developed as he was accepted late in the day.'

'Why was that?'

'Three of our original group unfortunately had to drop out at the last minute, and most of the waiting list had got fixed up.'

'And who was the other last-minute candidate?'

'That's Omar Rahmin.'

'He's the French Algerian, isn't he?'

'Yes.'

'And what was his great business plan?'

'He wanted to set up a construction firm with immigrant workers.'

'What? That's got even less chance of success than importing Moroccan rubbish.'

159

'It's not rubbish. That's just your prejudice.'

'Go on. Tell me about the others.'

'Hakim Lasnami had an excellent proposal to buy second-hand medical equipment in Europe, and then sell it to the Middle Eastern countries. Thanks to Western and Israeli policies, there is an enormous demand for artificial limbs . . . and any equipment to treat the wounded.'

'And the others would make good businessmen as well, you think?'

'Yes. Their proposals were well thought through. Rizwan Ahmet, the man you shot, is very competent. Just needs more confidence. He thinks there is a niche for the Muslim equivalent of the Body Shop. After all it was we Muslims who invented soap, cleanliness, natural perfumes and body products.'

'And Hassan Khan's plan?'

'It needs more work. But he's a natural with computers. And I also needed an administrative assistant. He had worked with me in London so I knew I could rely on him. But he's less robust than the others. I wasn't too sure he could take the hard physical training, so he only does part of the course.'

'Useful to have a hacker on-site if you are planning something, isn't it?'

'Back to that again. We weren't planning anything.'

'Hassan Khan looks up to you, doesn't he?'

'Yes. He's had a difficult family life . . . and I never had kids. I'm fond of him.'

'How does Leila Mahfouz fit into all of this?'

'Leila Mahfouz? She doesn't fit in at all. Just saw young Hassan a couple of times. Nothing to do with us.'

'But you knew her though?'

'Only to nod to.'

'Then how come she went out with Hassan Khan? How come she ended up at the bottom of a ravine?'

'Look, I don't know anything about that. Sure, I initially agreed Hassan could go out with her. But he was finding the work and the course tough. So I advised him to end the relationship before it started to interfere with his work. We've cooperated fully with you on this. I even let you take in Hassan for questioning. And then look what you did. Beat him up.'

'He tried to escape, and had to be restrained.'

'Who are you kidding? We both know what really happened. But are you really suggesting any of us had anything to do with her death?'

'Could be. Hassan had been out with her. He had a fight with her. You and he were both in the vicinity. Maybe she had learnt something. Something you're planning. You had to shut her up.'

'Don't be absurd. You've seen too many American films. This famous terrorist plot is just a figment of your imaginations. I've been over everything with your bosses, and they've got nothing because there's nothing to find.'

'Okay. Let's begin again at the beginning, shall we?'

Max began at the beginning. Date of birth, place of birth, parents, education, political involvement. The Israeli file was accurate. Nothing new to add.

'Can you tell me about your time in the Chatila refugee camp?'

'What more do you want to know? Look, I was a youth organizer for Al Fatah in the camp. You must have read about conditions there. They were atrocious. No sanitation, shortage of clean water, families in temporary shacks for years, no jobs, no hope. We had to keep some sort of order otherwise our people would kill each other over a loaf of bread. We needed to give a focus to the anger and the resentment. Yes, against the Israelis. They were responsible for our suffering. And yes, we fought back. I don't apologize for that. The right to resist tyranny and oppression. Isn't that part of the great British tradition – John Locke, I believe?'

'But where do you draw the line? A suicide bomber in a crowded restaurant?'

'The weapons of the weak are never sanitized. A suicide

161

bomber kills five, and there's body parts all over the front pages. A guided missile kills fifty at a wedding party, but that's a surgical strike with collateral damage, and your public never see the dead. A blown-up child is a blown-up child regardless of how you do it.'

'So you do defend the suicide bombers?'

'I know what you are trying to say. But I won't condemn them, if that is what you mean. I will criticize them for not being politically effective. And it's stupid to target civilians.'

'Were you planning a terrorist attack here?'

'What the hell are you talking about? Don't be childish. I've spent too long trying to do something useful with European Muslims. Of course not. It would be great if the oppressed didn't have to use violence. But recognizing that right doesn't mean I would be involved in terrorism, which is what you think, isn't it? '

'Okay. So you organized youth into militias to attack Israeli targets and presumably Israeli allies in Lebanon.'

'Your words, not mine.'

Max remembered the photograph of the beautiful woman on Javeed's bedside table in the Ibn Rush'd Centre. 'You were married, but then left the camp. But without your wife?'

Javeed visibly stiffened. Max had found a raw nerve. 'Yes. Without my wife.'

'Were you in love?'

For the first time Javeed's shoulders sank. There's something here, thought Max. Have to push it hard. 'So you were in love. But you left her and never went back?'

'No, I never went back. I have never been back.'

'An odd sort of love, isn't it?'

Javeed stood up, put his hands on the table, and shouted at Max: 'You, you understand nothing. You sit in your comfortable, secure homes here in Europe, and do nothing to stop what happens to my people. Okay, do you want to know what happened? Do you want to know what life was really like for us? I wanted to stay. I was desperate to stay.

The Israeli army had surrounded the camp. I knew I was on their list. My wife, six months pregnant, knew I was on their list. She begged me to leave.'

Javeed pressed his hand against his mouth. 'She cried, she pleaded. She said they would not harm a pregnant woman. She wanted me alive, she wanted me to come back for her and our baby. In the end I agreed. It was risky. But with two companions I got out. The next night, the Israeli army let the Lebanese Christian militia into the camp. The Israelis laughed as they let them in, some hanging around to watch the fun. Do you know what happened next? Killing, raping, burning, and all the while the Israelis stood by, laughing.'

Javeed stopped, his voice choking. 'My wife, my wife. They raped her, they cut off her breast, they then sliced open her belly, and took out the baby with a knife, and showed it to her, before they slit her throat.'

Javeed clenched his fist, shook it at Max, and moved towards him as if to hit him. 'And you, you have the nerve to ask me what I think about suicide bombers.'

He sank back into his chair, put his head in his hands, and sobbed. Max froze, unsure of how to respond, wanting to comfort the man, but knowing any real sign of sympathy would be against interrogation rules. All he could do was get up, leave and order a cup of coffee for Javeed.

Max needed another coffee. He sat alone in the canteen. His hand shook. This was not a friendly cup of tea with an Iman. Javeed? There was black hatred and anger there. But could he be capable of a terrorist act? Had he the motive and discipline to plan a spectacular? Yes, if he thought it politically effective. But where was the evidence? None. But there was something odd about the guys on the course. He'd better tell Linda about Javeed's outburst. She'd probably interpret it as proof he was hiding something. What would Linda do next? If there was nothing, that was her promotion down the pan.

Max went down the stairs for the next interview. He

163

would have to go back and continue with Javeed, but best not now. The other interviews produced nothing new. They all had sound alibis at the time of Leila's death. None of them had even spoken to her. Max had strong doubts about Faslur Hashim, the Spanish Moroccan. An ex-drug runner, a slippery character, evasive. Not the sort of person you'd like to meet on a dark night. Admitted he'd hung around with members of the GICM, but only because they were Moroccans and enjoyed a game of backgammon. Max disliked him, tired of his constant refrains to Allah, his born-again fundamentalism. But there was no evidence to link him to any potential terrorist act, though he was probably capable of violence. And when Max asked him about his famous business plan, he was so vague as to be laughable.

Omar Rahmin, the French Algerian, also seemed capable of violence: a fundamentalist, full of resentment, so convinced that the day of judgement was coming and that Allah was on their side, that he could easily do something to hasten that day. His business plan was definitely a joke. But nothing concrete. Hakim Lasnami, the German citizen, son of the Iraqi doctor, was a well-educated middle-class youth, bitterly opposed to Saddam, but against the invasion of Iraq, carried out, he thought, to give the Americans a new military base in the Middle East and thus increase their control of the oil market. Max found it hard to disagree with that assessment. His bitterness at the Allies' conduct came through strongly. The political motivation was there, but was he a likely terrorist? His business plan seemed thoroughly researched and well thought out.

Nevertheless, the more Max interviewed them, the more something just didn't seem right. Individually there was nothing. But there was something odd about the group, something smelled fishy . They didn't feel like a bunch of guys on a business training course. Max had always distrusted intuition, gut feelings, but this time? Who knows? Or was he just being prejudiced? Would he feel the same if they were a bunch of white Europeans? Only the murder suspect, Hassan Khan, was left to interview. It was getting late now, but better get it done.

Hassan was lying on a bench, asleep, when he entered. Max signalled to the guard to wake him up. The guard roughly shook him until he sat up like a startled rabbit. Max noticed the pained expression . . . the broken rib? Hassan rubbed his eyes, barely able to keep them open.

'Hassan Khan?' Max said.

Hassan looked round, puzzled, then remembering who Max was, said, 'Allah. Peace be upon him. You're the man who got me out of prison after they beat me. Have you come to release me again? Is Rizwan Ahmet okay?'

'We don't know yet. He's still in intensive care. Let's sit at the table, shall we? And talk.'

'Another interrogation? But I've told the others over and over again, everything.'

'Maybe. But I need to know everything again now.'

Hassan sighed, put his hand on his side, and shuffled over to the table. Max sat down opposite him. There were grimy, smudged tears on his face, a ghost of stubble, his eyes weary with pain and tiredness. He looked weak and vulnerable. If anyone were to break, it would be Hassan. How should he do it? Where was his weak spot? Max started his questions with Leila's death.

'You tried to impress her, didn't you? You said you were involved in something dangerous. Then realized you'd said too much. Panicked and killed her. You didn't mean to kill her. But you pushed her, and she fell down the ravine. That was it, wasn't it?'

'No. Where did you get this terrorism stuff? You're mistaken.'

'We'll see. Okay.'

Max went over the details of Hassan's relationship with Leila, his whereabouts, and his alibi. There was nothing new.

'Let's go back to the beginning.' Max steered the questions to Hassan's childhood. 'Your mother was English, wasn't she?'

'Yes.'

'She left you and your father when you were eight, I believe. Bit cruel to just abandon you, wasn't it?'

'Sh—she had to leave.'

Max noticed that Hassan's slight stammer had suddenly emerged. Emotionally this might be his weak spot. Best push hard. 'Ran off with another bloke, you mean?'

'No. Nothing like that. She had b—become a Muslim. But she had p—problems at the mosque. Nobody accepted her. She questioned things.'

'Questioned things?'

'The role of women. Things like that. Dad started hitting her.'

'Hitting her?' Max felt like a cad, but he knew he had to press deeper on this. 'You mean your dad beat her up? Frequently?'

'T—towards the end. Yes.' Hassan lowered his head, the pain obvious.

Max persisted, a hard, cutting edge to his voice now. 'So she just ran away? Just left you behind?'

'Sh—she had to.' Angrily, Hassan lifted his head, and looked straight at Max. The stammer for a minute disappeared. 'She loved me, you see. She left to save me.'

'Funny sort of love?'

'You don't understand. She told me she had to leave. She wanted to, but couldn't take me with her. Dad would come after us. He threatened to harm us both if she tried to take me.'

Hassan stopped, and looked Max full in the face. 'You know what her last words to me were? "I love you."'

'Loved you?' Max knew he had to be cruel. 'Loved you? You never saw her again, did you? She never got in touch again, did she? And you? What happened to you? That father of yours. Beat you up regularly, didn't he?'

Hassan was crying now. 'He knew no better. He was b—bitter, confused. Lost in a hostile land. All he had left was his faith.'

166

'How did you get away?' Max asked more gently.

'My local Iman. Discovered I was really good at maths. Encouraged me to study. My dad could not refuse the Iman. So I got out to university.'

'And it was there you became a member of Hisb ut-Tahir, wasn't it?'

'No. I never joined them. I went to a few meetings, that's all.'

'You were a member, weren't you? They told you it was a religious duty to defend your fellow Muslims by attacking those countries killing Muslims. Didn't they?'

'No. You've got it all wrong.'

'Come on. We've got photographs of you with them. We know what they say. We know what they preach. Just admit it all. It'll be easier for you.'

'I've t—told you the t—truth.'

'The truth? You went to the mosque in Finchley Road, didn't you?'

'Yes. It was my local mosque.'

'Tell me about the Iman?'

'He's famous. He doesn't hide his views. He tells us what is happening to our b—brothers round the world.'

'Doesn't just tell you, does he? He says it's your religious duty to fight back. Kill or harm anyone whom he sees as an enemy of Islam. Kafirs, unbelievers, were legitimate targets. That's right, isn't it?'

'He sometimes went too far. But he also collected money to help the refugees in Chechnya and P—Palestine. He helped our b—brothers when they arrived in London with nowhere to stay, with no money.'

'You mean extremists, don't you? Were you one of those pledging allegiance to Al-Qaeda?'

'I never heard of that. Sounds like one of those stories in the *Sun*.'

'Did you ever meet Shagufta Hanif? Were you ever instructed on how to make ricin?'

'No. No. Why all these questions about ricin? I was never

167

very involved in the mosque. Went there for p—prayers, that's all.'

'You went to Northern Pakistan in the summer of 2000?'

'Yes. I went with my father. His b—brother was dying.'

'How long were you there?'

'About three months.'

'Three months? A long time, isn't it?'

'I hadn't been b—back to Pakistan since I was a child. My last visit was with my mother.'

'Your mother?'

'She wanted to meet my dad's family.'

'Okay. Back to this visit in 2000. You crossed over into Afghanistan, didn't you?'

'No. I've told the others hundreds of times. I didn't leave Pakistan. I was with family the whole time.'

'How about a madrasah? Attend one of them?'

'I've told you, yes. My dad wanted me to renew my faith. After a difficult period, I too wanted that.'

'Difficult period?'

'With my dad and all. I hated him for what he did to my mother. She loved me, you see.'

'Don't give me that crap again. Loved you, my arse! She just got off with another bloke. Better in bed probably.'

'It wasn't like that. It wasn't.' Hassan started sobbing again.

'Come on, pull yourself together. An extremist madrasah, yes?'

'No. It helped me and my dad come together. We sort of made up. He died soon after we got back to the UK.'

'So you've got no one? Easy bait for extremists then.'

'No. I've told you. I did not get involved in anything at that mosque. Nor was I involved with any extremists.'

'Yet the London Iman gave you a recommendation for your course?'

'Yes. We were asked to have a recommendation from our mosque.'

'But you hardly knew him, you claim?'

'No, of course I knew him. He was a p—powerful p—preacher. I didn't agree with everything he said. He showed us some videos on what was happening in Chechnya. It's unbelievable.'

'And then he encouraged you to go and fight, carry out jihad.'

'No. Yes. He said we should support our b—brothers, that was the duty of all true Muslims. I heard that some did volunteer to go to Chechnya. But I just wanted to get on with my life.'

'Nice and quiet like?'

'You know all about my anti-war work. I've told you everything. Yes, I demonstrated, I handed out p—pamphlets. I collected money. Yes, I was angry. But how often do I have to repeat that was all?'

'Come on. Just tell us what you were planning to do here in Spain. What was the target? You can then wash, rest. You'll feel better just admitting what you were planning.'

'Nothing. Nothing.'

'It's quite a set-up you have at this Ibn Rush'd Centre, isn't it?'

'Yes. Javeed has put a lot of work into it.'

'You look up to Javeed, don't you?'

'Yes. He's been good to me.'

'How did you meet?'

'At a P—Palestine Solidarity Meeting. He had started this charity, HosPal, to collect money and medicines for a hospital in Gaza. I got involved in that . . . and then he offered me a work experience p—placement in his London office . . . and that led to the job with the Centre.'

'And you're the computer whizz-kid for it all?'

'Well, I'm in charge of the computers. I also do the accounts and things like that.'

'There seems very little on the hard disks?'

'Why should there be a lot of stuff?'

'Well, websites, emails to your Islamic brothers for example?'

'We keep in touch with what goes on. But I use the *Guardian* and *BBC* sites a lot.'

There was a knock on the door. An officer entered.

'Urgent message for Sub-Inspector Romero.'

Max turned to Hassan. 'Okay, I'll be back. Just think. Tell us the truth. Tell us what you were planning to do here. In the end it will be better for you. You wouldn't want to end up in Guantanamo, would you? You might even be sent to Bagram, might be somebody there who recognizes you. You know what happens to you there, don't you?'

Max left the room. It was bad news. Rizwan Ahmet had died in the hospital. Linda, General Ponte and Bonila would be even more worried, even more determined to get results. Max had had enough. He had got nothing. But he now felt there might be something. Their stories just didn't convince. There was something odd about the group. He returned to Hassan.

'Okay. That's it for now. I'll be back. We'll be back. Remember – I'm the nice one. Easier for you just to tell me the truth, just confess to it all – Leila's death, what you were planning. If not, the others may be less kind. Remember Bagram. Oh. And your mother can't help you. She never has, has she?'

Max left the room. It is surprisingly easy to be cruel, he thought. But was there something? Yes, there probably was.

Chapter 15

Tonight there'll be blood
To warm my cheeks.

Frederico García Lorca, *Bodas de Sangre* (*Blood Wedding*)
in a version by Ted Hughes

Max reported to Linda first thing the next morning. She had recovered her poise after a good night's sleep. However she still looked worried.

'Max, I'm sorry about Rizwan Ahmet. There will be a full inquiry, of course.'

'Do you know what happened?'

'Of course – you weren't there when it happened. I came in after the elite squad. Apparently they rushed in, saw Rizwan Ahmet reach down for something on the floor. One of the squad thought he was going for a gun, and opened fire. The officer couldn't take risks. I know we did everything by the book. So I'm not expecting any negative consequences.'

'But a man's dead.'

'I know. The war on terrorism is not pretty. Shit happens, and it's our job to deal with it. So, what did you find out?'

'It's all here.'

Linda skimmed the report.

'That's interesting what you say about Javeed Dharwish. That's the first crack in his self-control. He hadn't lost his cool once with us. Well done. We'll have to push him hard and see if we can get any more. Okay – the consensus is that

Hassan Khan is the weak link. We'll concentrate on him. That stuff on their business plans is very useful. I hadn't thought of that. I agree it doesn't add up. I'm glad you've seen the light. There's something heavy going on. My money's on a terrorist attack. But where, Max, where? Malaga Airport? Here in Granada, the Alhambra? The Rota base would be a real spectacular – but that's too well guarded. It would have to be a soft target? We don't have much time. I had the PM's special adviser on national security on the phone to congratulate me. He's really piling on the pressure – wants a result before the election.'

Max bit his tongue. What did an election have to do with whether someone was guilty or not?

'I've called a review and planning meeting in an hour's time. Take a break Max, and have a coffee. You've done well. It won't go unnoticed.'

Max went up to the canteen. He looked at the papers. They'd all run the story on the front page. The pro-government press led with the ricin and the ETA connection. The opposition papers were speculating why no evidence had been produced. The opinion polls showed the election would be close, but with the PP still just in the lead.

After coffee Max went into his office to check his mail and emails. There was a testy email from Davila. Max was late with his input to the Service Plan Performance Indicators, and could he give it top priority. Great. A man was dead. The media were gorging on the terrorist plot, but the wheels of bureaucracy ground on regardless. Max filled in the Performance Indicator form and emailed it to Davila. He was tempted to add a sarcastic comment, but decided it was best to refrain. Davila took all these forms very seriously.

Where do we go from here? he thought as he walked down the stairs to the review meeting. There's not much more we can do except go over the questions again and again. I doubt if Hassan and Javeed will react so emotionally the next time.

He entered the meeting room. Linda, as always, sat at

the head of the table, laptop ready. There were no signs of tiredness now. She summarized the evidence, praised Max for finding a few vulnerable points among the suspects, and emphasized the importance of what they were doing. The PM personally wanted to be kept informed of any developments.

'So what we have to do is keep pounding away at the weak link. We keep questioning all the others, but we concentrate on Hassan Khan. We have to toughen up our act with him. I've consulted the senior officers here, and they have agreed we should call in this Argentinian on your force, a . . .' Linda consulted her notes. '*Sí*. Inspector Ernesto Navarro . . . I'm told he had experience of tough questioning and getting information when he was in Argentina.'

Max exploded. 'Tough questioning? Torture, you mean. Human rights groups in Argentina are trying to get him extradited back to Argentina to stand trial over the disappearance of a couple of school kids.'

'There's no proof,' interrupted Davila. 'It was a difficult period for the police with Communist guerrillas and all. Navarro says the accusations are false, and the Human rights groups in Argentina are Communist fronts.'

'He would say that, wouldn't he?'

'Sub-Inspector Romero, I've told you before to keep your politics out of the police force. Navarro has experience of getting information out of suspects. And that is what we need now.'

'I will not sit by and allow any physical abuse of the suspects,' interjected Max angrily.

Linda, her voice steady and calm, came in. 'Who said anything about physical abuse? This is democratic Spain, and not Argentina under the military. We will abide by our rules. But we need someone who can scare Hassan Khan into confessing what was planned. Max – you now agree something was being planned, don't you?'

'I'm uneasy about them,' muttered Max. 'There could be something there. I just don't know.'

'Which is why we need Navarro to help us find out. I've asked him to organize the questioning routine. Inspector Sánchez and I have to return to Madrid for some top-level consultations. Comisario Bonila has agreed we let Inspector Navarro take charge of interrogations.'

She turned to Max. 'Inspector Jefe Davila has had a request from Teniente González for you to help him with his inquiries in Diva. You are needed there.'

'*Sí*, Max,' came in Davila. 'There may something with this English hippy, and you, speaking English, are needed. That's an order. Report back to me in two days' time. Is that understood?'

How convenient, thought Max. They want me out of the way. He gritted his teeth. 'Yes, sir.'

Linda took over again. 'Good. We all know where we stand. Inspector Sánchez and I will be back in two days. Good luck to you all. Remember if we get results I'm sure the PM can help with extra resources. And who knows – there might be some promotions.'

With that she stood up, saluted, and left.

'Max, I suggest you leave straight away,' said Davila. 'Teniente González is expecting you.'

'Yes, sir.' Max looked at Martín, who nodded. Max saluted, and left the office. He went straight to the Bar Alonzo, ordered a coffee, and waited for Martín to come. Twenty minutes later Martín entered, and came over to Max.

'What's going on?' said Max. 'Navarro is bad news. What's planned?'

'I don't know,' replied Martín. 'I'm out of the loop. I'm being hauled back to Madrid tomorrow. It's all highly political. That bastard, Miguel Allende, the PM's personal National Security adviser, is behind this. He's a real poison dwarf. But Miguel and Linda go back years. They need something positive from all this. A little bird told me the Socialists have opened a line with ETA to discuss a ceasefire if the Socialists win. So the PP need to show the Socialists are weak on terrorism. The stakes are really high. Be careful,

Max. I'll tell you if I find out anything. I really must go now. We mustn't be seen together.'

'What are they planning to do with Hassan?'

'I don't know. They can't be too crude – it could backfire on them. I've warned Bonila that a scandal would blow up in their faces. But it sure as hell won't be a friendly conversation with coffee and cakes. I'm worried about that kid: too much pressure and he might crack totally. And that won't do anyone any good. Let me know if you hear anything. I'll see some of my political contacts back in Madrid. Right. Have to go. Take care.'

Max finished his coffee, a worried frown creasing his forehead. He took out his mobile and made a quick call. He had to see Jorge. Max walked back to the police car park, got into his car, and drove along the Sacromonte road to the Abadía. Jorge was waiting for him, outside the huge, ancient door.

'Let's go into the garden,' he said. 'It's quiet and peaceful there. Sounds like you need both. I know it's early, but I've got that bottle of Cartojal straight from Malaga I promised.'

'Thanks. I could do with a small glass.'

They sat by the fountain, its water spouting out of the mouth of San Miguel. Max sipped his wine slowly and appreciatively. The gentle splashing of the fountain, and the wine, calmed him down. He turned to Jorge and told him the whole story, beginning with the death of Leila.

'I'm really worried. One man is already dead. And what will happen to Hassan Khan I don't know.'

'It's a nasty business,' commented Jorge. 'The terrorist threat is real, and we've brought it home to Spain. It makes no sense. The Brits are determined to play Robin to the USA's Batman, but you'd have thought we would know better. But here we are – part of the invasion – so we've made our country a target. You said you have doubts about the innocence of these men?'

'No evidence. Just a feeling that something isn't right. I didn't think so at first. But now I've interviewed them all, there's something really fishy.'

'That's a worry. But torture won't help anyone find the truth.'

'Absolutely. So what can I do?

'You have to go to Diva. I'll call the Association for Muslim Rights and the human rights groups in Granada. With the Anti-Terrorism Law there's not much we can do. But a few questions, leaked to the press of course, will do no harm. I'll make sure nothing can get back to you. Best you left now. Thanks for coming to me. Keep me informed.'

Max got up, embraced Jorge and left. At least he had done something. And he felt the better for having done so. He drove straight to the police station in Diva. González was in his office.

'Come in, Max. Thank you for coming over immediately.' González gave a wolfish smile as he spoke.

The fat bastard's in the know, thought Max. He's in the loop.

'No problem, sir. What can I do to help?'

'We interviewed this hippy guy, Jim Cavendish. Says he met Leila at the bar El Gato, and then they went to Felipe's bar for a gig, and then saw the sun rise at El Fugón. Very romantic. He says he didn't fuck her, but believe that if you like. He claims at about two in the afternoon he drove her back to Diva and dropped her off at the church. Says she must have left her mobile in his van then.'

'That squares with everything we know,' said Max. 'So what's the problem?'

'No real problem. But he's a lying bastard. We found a stack of hashish in his van, and more in his shack. So there could be a drug connection. We'd like you to interview him to see if you can get any more.'

'But you said his Spanish is good, so I'm unlikely to find out anything new.'

'Maybe. But it's a cultural thing. We might have missed something.'

'Where is he?'

'Down in the cell. We had to let him go. But we've

176

arrested him again on drug charges.' González looked at his watch. 'It's a bit late now. You can interview him first thing tomorrow.'

'I'd prefer to do it now so I can get back to Granada as soon as possible.'

'Not possible. He's asked for his lawyer to be present. So we arranged it for tomorrow morning.'

Max flushed with anger. They were determined to keep him in Diva, come what may.

'Okay. I hope he doesn't have a broken rib,' he said testily.

'Now why would he have that?' replied González calmly. 'He hasn't tried to escape, has he?'

Max glowered at González, and left the office. He had the whole evening with nothing to do. He went to the bar, El Paraíso , and ordered a brandy and coffee.

'Unlike you,' commented the waiter. 'Something wrong?'

'No. Nothing.'

Max looked at his watch. Should he visit Paula? Good idea. A visit now, and maybe she wouldn't make such a fuss if he couldn't get over on Sunday.

Max drove along the Jola road. He slowed as he passed the ravine where Leila's body had been found. He stopped the car and walked back to the low concrete parapet. The forensics guys had already had a good root round, so he would be unlikely to find anything – but a second look wouldn't cost anything. He clambered down the bank and went under the bridge, looking around carefully. Nothing. As he scrambled back up, the evening sun glinted on something silver. Max stopped and leaned over to pick it up with a handkerchief. It was a sweet wrapper. Max dropped it in an evidence bag and stowed it in his pocket.

When he arrived at Paula's, he rang the bell, and waited. Nobody came. He rang again. Nobody. Most odd. Paula seldom went out. After the third ring, he heard footsteps. Paula opened the door.

'Max! What a surprise! I wasn't expecting you until Sunday.'

'Can't make it this Sunday. Police duties. As I was in Diva I thought I'd come round to see you. Hope you're not going deaf, *abuela*. I rang three times.'

'I was absorbed in my computer. Did you know – I can play music on it? It's amazing. Max, I think I've made contact with someone who was with Antonio. Leila will be so thrilled. Oh!' She dabbed her eyes with her apron. 'I still think it could be her when the phone rings. Who killed her, Max, who killed her?'

'I wish I knew, *abuela*. Still got nowhere. It's a real mystery. I've been through her computer. There are a couple of things we're chasing up. But nothing definite.'

Max followed Paula into the kitchen. He offered to make the coffee, but Paula refused. She still believed men should have nothing to do inside a kitchen.

'*Querido*, you're looking tired,' she said as she handed over his *cafe con leche*.

'I'm fine. Too much work, that's all. So what is it you've found?'

'You remember that website Leila found for me, the one run by La Asociación para la Recuperación de la Memoria Histórica? Well, they have something called a Notice Board. People were putting up messages – does anyone know anything about my *abuelo* who disappeared in Toledo on such and such a date . . . that sort of thing. I thought I would do the same. So I put a notice on it. Does anyone have any information on Antonio Vargas, last seen in Diva, Andalusia, on 17th August 1937? He is believed to have gone to hide in a shepherd's hut above Banjaron. But nothing more has ever been heard of him.'

Paula paused, her hand shaking with excitement. 'I didn't expect a reply. Then today I heard from Beatrice, a lady in Ceret, in France. She said she is the daughter of a Spaniard, Manuel Paz, though most people used his nickname – El Gato.'

'Wow.'

'Her father escaped to France with his young brother during the Civil War. He married her mother, but couldn't settle.'

'Could he be Diva's El Gato?'

'It's possible . . . can you imagine it?'

'So what did she say?'

'Her uncle is still alive – a bit younger than me.'

'Can he help you?'

'He told her that he and his brother had been hiding just outside Banjaron. She thinks he may have known Antonio.'

'That's amazing.'

'Max – my heart's on fire. I need to send a photo of Antonio. Have you heard about scanning? Could you do it for me? I'd ask Juan, but he gets grumpy whenever I mention what I'm doing. He's got a lot of his *abuelo* in him. I've a lovely photo of Antonio – you know, the one with Lorca. And I've also got one of Antonio and me together.'

'I can do that.'

'Don't tell Juan about any of this.'

'Course not.'

'It would have been so nice if Leila could have seen this. She would have been thrilled. What happened here was so real for her. As if we were family.'

Max stood up, and put his arms round Paula, and gave her a big hug. 'Of course, *abuela*. But don't raise your hopes too much. After all these years . . . well.'

'I know. But I feel I'm close to something.'

The front door opened and shut. Juan appeared at the kitchen door.

'Max! What a surprise! Didn't expect you till Sunday.'

'I know. Can't make it Sunday. As I had to be in Diva, thought I'd come over. How are the kids?'

'Fine. Well, not really. Usual scrapes and scraps. Isabel's fine. They're at the coast for a few days. I heard they had arrested someone over Leila's death.'

'Not really. The guy who might have been the last person

179

to see her alive has turned up. I'm to interview him tomorrow, but I think there's nothing on him. Oops. Shouldn't have said that.'

'That's okay. You'll stay for a meal? Be like old times, *abuela*. You, me and Max in the kitchen.'

Juan looked around the old kitchen and smiled. The mark from Max's football was still on the ceiling. 'God . . . I remember the tales you used to tell us here. You could terrify us when we were little.'

He smiled affectionately at Paula. 'You got any of the nice *cocido* left? Poor old Max looks as if he hasn't eaten properly for days.'

Paula laughed. 'Sit down, boys. Sorry about the *cocido*. But I've got your favourite white anchovies for you to nibble on. Then I'll see what else I can find. There's still some of your wild boar in the freezer. Juan, open a bottle of the best Rioja. I feel like a small glass myself.'

Juan tried to steer the conversation to the latest news on the terrorists, but Max gave nothing away that wasn't already in the papers. It was a happy evening, one of the best for quite a while. Paula fussed and mothered, convinced they weren't being fed properly, probing to see if Max had invited that nice policewoman out yet. Disappointed that he hadn't. Was that because he had another girl? Max tried to explain that he was too busy, but Paula wouldn't believe that. Another bottle of wine appeared. Juan slowly became his old, animated self, full of opinions and bad jokes. Soon he and Max were skirmishing like old times, each trying to cut through the defences of the other, hoping to score the final thrust. As always it ended in a honourable draw. Finally Paula, in tears of laughter, called it to a halt.

'*Chicos, chicos*. I'm exhausted. I have to go to bed. You two can carry on if you want.'

Max looked at his watch. '*Dios*! Is it that late? No, I have to go. A lot to do tomorrow.' He stood up, his legs a little wobbly.

'I'll get some strong black coffee,' said Juan. 'Still seeing that bird you went to the flamenco with the other night?'

'Oh, that. No, came to nothing.'

'If you want any advice, come to me.'

'You'd be the last person I'd ask,' said Max laughing, and punched Juan gently in the ribs. Soon they were scuffling round the kitchen.

'Boys, boys,' yelled Paula from the landing. 'Grow up. You'll knock something over. Max, I'll get you the envelope.'

Juan raised an inquisitive eyebrow. 'Nothing to do with this Antonio nonsense, I hope?'

'No. Nothing like that. Just a little errand Max has promised to do for me in Granada.'

'Yah, boo. *Abuela's* little favourite,' grinned Juan. 'Here. Have a mint, Max. Clean your mouth.' Juan reached into his pocket, and gave Max a mint, wrapped in a silver paper.

'*Gracias,*' said Max, and put it in his pocket. 'Must go now.'

A drop of rain fell in the night, not enough for the parched earth, but enough to create the illusion of a sparkling, fresh morning. The bougainvillea glistened with dew and the few raindrops. Max awoke with a slight headache. He took a paracetamol, and made some filter coffee. There was no bread in the *cortijo*, but he had some oatcakes and a jar of Paula's home-made jam. He felt anxious to get back to Granada, so best start early. González was already in his office when he arrived.

'*Hola*, Max. You're early. The lawyer phoned. Won't be here until noon. I've called a review meeting for five. Hope that's okay with you?'

So . . . a conspiracy to keep him away from Granada.

'I'll go and have some breakfast, then. If you need me I'll be at Pepe's having a coffee. Oh – do you have a scanner here?'

'Sure. In the secretary's office.'

Max called in at the newsagent's, full of magazines and

porno DVDs, but with all the English papers, more even than in Granada, reflecting the flood of English incomers, looking for who knew what in Diva. Diva was not exactly a picture postcard village. Max looked at the headlines, and decided to buy the *Indie*. Bit didactic, but it took a firm anti-war stance. More than you could say for the *Guardian*. The *Independent* had a little piece on the terrorist plot in Granada. Even they were reporting the 'official leaks' as if they were proven facts.

After a lengthy breakfast, Max returned to the police station. He scanned the two photos, saved them on the computer and emailed them to Paula. She had been a pretty girl. That done, he walked along the corridor to Anita Guevarra's office, knocked and waited.

'Come in,' she called out in a low and pleasant voice. She smiled as Max entered. 'You seem to be having lots of adventures. Is it all true, what the press are saying?'

'We don't know yet. Could be,' was his non-committal reply.

Anita had nothing new to report on the Leila case. 'There seems to be a lot of jealousy among the women in the community, hints of this and that, but no real leads,' she said.

Max smiled at her as he left. Should he invite her out? No rumours of any boyfriend, so she might be available. Another time maybe.

The lawyer arrived at twelve. He had come up from the coast. Max was surprised a scruff like Jim could afford him. Rich relatives somewhere in the background. He was proved right the minute Jim opened his mouth – public school, an expensive one. After two hours, Max was convinced Jim was as baffled about Leila's death as he was. No, he hadn't screwed her. Offered to, but she had refused. He had seen her around, and fancied her of course. What guy didn't? That evening was the first time he had talked to her. She was easy to talk to, clearly needed cheering up, seemed a bit down at first, but then really livened up. They had talked about this and that: the war, her thesis, her dad, his music. Then the next day he had driven her back to Diva, dropped her off, saw friends at Figorrones, then went along the coast road to Almeria and on to the beaches at El Cabo del Gato to chill out. Just like that.

Nice life, thought Max. Take off when you feel like it. Just disappear for days when you feel like it, stretch out in a cove and watch the waves break over the rocks. Beach almost to yourself, naked nymphs dancing in the waves. Lucky sod.

'Any evidence to prove where you were?' he finally asked.

'Shedloads. As I told that charmingly polite police officer, González, from about three to five – I was with Nick and Emily in Figorrones and we had a few beers in the Bar Río Tinto. There's a whole bar that can vouch for that. I stopped at the Cadiar petrol station to fill up at about seven – and I paid by credit card there. Then I drove down to Cabo, and stayed around there in the van. I managed to get the phone number of this chick from Barcelona. Always useful to have a floor to crash out on – and with luck even a bed.'

'Did González check up on this?'

' Yes. I gave him my friends' details so he could get statements. Never heard any more about it.'

'How did Leila's mobile end up in your van?'

'She must have dropped it. She slept the night in the van – alone – and then I gave her a lift back into Diva. It had fallen between the seat and the door so I never saw it. To be honest, given the state of the van I wouldn't see anything in it.'

'Hmm. Anything else you can remember about Leila?'

'Not really. The only strange thing,' Jim replied, 'was she pointed out a hollow olive tree as I drove her back to Diva. Said that was where El Gato was shot in 1947. Something to do with her thesis, I think.'

'El Gato?'

Max pushed the drug link. Familiar tale. Jim would drive over now and again to Morocco, spend a week or two in the Rif Mountains, and then drive back. Okay . . . just small-time smuggling. And with a good lawyer, Jim would get away with a fine and an admonishment. Case closed.

'Well, what do you think?' said González when the Diva team reassembled at five.

'Did you check up on his alibi?' asked Max.

'We did. Seems to be as he claims.'

'Then probably nothing to do with him,' snapped Max. 'Probably didn't even screw her.'

They went through the evidence carefully.

'Okay,' concluded González. 'Must be the Paki kid then. But we'll press for drugs charges on the hippy. Get his daddy to pay the fine, and let him cool his heels in prison for a few days. Spoilt brat. If I had my way I'd make him do five years' hard labour. Probably never worked in his fucking life.'

'Was there anything on Leila's mobile – the one found in his van?'

'León went through it. He made a note of the numbers she had phoned. But nobody and nothing important.'

It was exactly ten at night when Max got back to his flat in Granada. A sliver of pale moon hung over the Alhambra. It was exactly ten at night when the police dragged Hassan Khan into the cellblock. Moonlight filtered into his cell.

Chapter 16

Yo era.
Yo fui.
Pero no soy.
Yo era . . .

I was.
I had been.
But not I am.
I was . . .

Frederico García Lorca, *Lunes, miercoles viernes*
(*Monday, Wednesday, Friday*)

Hassan shivered. He felt the panic begin to crush him like a boa constrictor. The panic rose, subsided, rose, subsided. Sleep, above all sleep. For almost two days they had pounded him: voices harsh, relentless, accusing, merciless.

'What are you planning? Where are you putting the bomb? Were you going to blow yourself up? Where did you meet your ETA contacts? Give me names.'

The questions ebbed and flowed, but never ended. Whenever his eyelids began to shut they threw buckets of cold water over him. And the questions began again.

Hassan remembered one man in particular: tall, swarthy, a pencil moustache, his big belly protruding over his belt. He reminded Hassan of a butcher back in Leeds. It was this man who kept referring to his mother.

'Do you know where she is? I can help you contact her. Would you like me to contact her? All you need to do, Hassan, is tell me what was planned. Just whisper it to me if you want. Your friends will never know. You love your mother, don't you? You can see her again soon if you just tell me what you were planning. You love your mother, don't you? Soon she could be hugging you, just like she did when you were a child. You'd like that, wouldn't you?'

Hassan stammered, 'I don't know what you're t—talking about. I really don't know. There's no b—bomb. Nothing is p—planned. I don't know what you're t—talking about. Why am I being p—punished?'

The butcher's tone would then change.

'Your mother is nothing but a whore. She left for another man. She's never made contact since because she doesn't give a fuck about you. Just tell me what you were planning, then you can sleep.'

Then back again to the questions. On and on went the questions. When they left the cell, the lights were turned on full, Bruce Springsteen's 'Born in the USA', playing at full blast. Hassan eventually fell to the floor in sheer exhaustion. Then the butcher returned, kicking him on his cracked rib, laughing.

'Nobody will know. Just some problems with its healing, that's all.'

A couple of times Hassan passed out with the pain. More cold water. And then again the questions, again and again.

Eventually there was a pause. Nobody came. The lights were turned off. The music stopped. Nothing. The silence was as bad as the endless questions. He sat in the empty cell, waiting, fearful. Nothing happened. It was so quiet. He could hear the beating of his heart. The silence became more and more oppressive. The waves of silence echoed in his head. It was then that he began to panic again. Hour after hour he could feel the panic. The silence grew louder.

'Allah be praised. Allah the merciful. What have I done to deserve this?'

Hassan crawled to the corner of the room, and curled,

foetus-like, into a ball. Finally they came. The butcher entered first, alone.

'This is your last chance, Hassan. Tell me what was planned, and you can go and wash. You want to wash, don't you? There's a bed waiting. You want to sleep, don't you? You can phone your mother. You want to speak to her, don't you? Just tell me. Whisper it to the walls. Allah will understand.'

Hassan cried, 'I don't know.'

'If you don't whisper it now, I can no longer protect you. You will go somewhere where Allah can't protect you. You will wish you had never been born. Do you know what that means, Hassan? Just whisper the truth to the walls, Hassan. Then this can all be over. Just whisper, Hassan. Just whisper.'

'B—but there's nothing t—to whisper. Nothing.'

'Then nothing you will be.'

The butcher left, and returned with three men. The butcher stood over the cowering Hassan. He kicked him in the ribs again.

'To make sure you don't forget me.'

Two of the men lifted Hassan to his feet, and the third snapped handcuffs over his wrists. They dragged him out of the cell, and along the corridor to a car park, and into a waiting car. It was dark outside with a pale sliver of moon hovering over the heated darkness. Panic rose, subsided, rose, subsided. Welts swelled up under the cuffs. The car stopped. Hassan was dragged out, through a door, along a corridor, down steps, and into a bright, flickering light. Figures in uniform appeared. Hassan shuffled after them. Unable to focus, all he could see was the uniform. He needed to wash, wash away all the dirt, all these hands.

'Allah. Allah,' he intoned.

Then the uniform suddenly stopped.

'This is your cell, pretty boy. We'll see how a pretty boy like you gets on here. A pretty boy like this should get on just fine, shouldn't he, Jesús?'

'Just fine,' laughed Jesús.

The laugh pierced Hassan's eyes. He hardly noticed when they took off the handcuffs. He hardly felt being pushed into the cell.

Jesús laughed again.

'No need to lock the cell door here, you know. You're going nowhere. The Qur'an won't help you in here. Nobody can help you in here. Call if you want to confess.'

Hassan started to sob. He needed to wash away the hands. All those hands constantly touching him. He crawled to the corner, drew his knees up to his chin, and tried to melt into the wall.

'Just whisper it to the wall, Hassan. Whisper it to the wall.'

There was no light in the cell, only a flicker of the pale moon. All around him were noises: rough voices, loud farts, shouts, moaning.

'Check the cells,' a loud voice commanded. Batons rang against steel along the corridor.

'You have a new guest, a real pretty Muslim boy. He'll need a proper welcome. You should introduce yourselves. We've no need to lock his door. He's going nowhere. You have my permission to give him a welcome worthy of a king.'

Again the harsh laugh.

For the first time Hassan noticed the smell of urine, sweet and pungent. His eyes began to focus. The bucket in the corner, the wooden bed, the dark grey blanket, the Formica-top table. The shivering wouldn't stop. Cold. Cold. Wash. Wash. Pray. Pray.

'Only Allah can save me from the infidels. I must pray.'

His mother's face appeared. 'Hassan, I have to leave you now. Always remember, I always loved you, and always will.'

'Just whisper it to the wall, Hassan. Whisper it to the wall.'

There was silence. Then a voice called out.

'Hey. Pretty boy. I bet you've got a nice little arse. You a *maricón*? No matter. That little arse of yours needs a real welcome. Doesn't it, lads.'

There was laughter. 'A real welcome,' echoed round the corridor.

Hassan, whisper it to the wall. Melt into the wall. Hassan curled into the wall. Exhaustion. Sleep.

At exactly two in the morning they came. There was no noise. They entered the cell silently. Dark presences. Breathing.

Hassan woke. They lifted him to his feet. They dragged him to the bed. They stripped him naked. Hassan screamed with the first penetration. Whisper it to the wall, Hassan.

'I knew he'd be a right pretty boy. Your turn, José.'

'I love you, Hassan. I love you.' His mother's voice echoed in his head.

'Your turn, Pedro.'

Whisper it to the wall, Hassan. Whisper it.

'Hey. Where's that fucking Felipe? Go get the bastard. Tell him he's missing the fun.'

Whisper it, Hassan. Whisper it. Darkness.

They left as silently as they had entered.

The guards entered the cell at dawn.

'*Mierda*! We'd better get a doctor. They've overdone it. Get that doctor quick.'

'Oh Christ . . . Break the lock. Make it look as if they broke in.'

'They'll be no confession from him for a while,' said Jesús, looking at the still body.

Whisper it to the wall, Hassan. Whisper it.

Yo era.

Chapter17

Max awoke with a start. He reached for his watch. There was enough pale moonlight to make out the dials. *Mierda*. Two thirty. The heat was still oppressive, his T-shirt sticky with sweat. He stumbled out of the bed, and foraged in his cupboard for a fresh one. Not finding any, he crawled back to bed naked. He shifted around on the crumpled sheet, trying to find a cool, comfortable spot: his memory playing on like the radio. 'This is democratic Spain, not Argentina under the military . . . Hassan, I love you . . . What is truth, said jesting Pilate, and would not stay for an answer.'

He finally fell asleep, but at dawn a gang of noisy tourists decided to serenade the neighbourhood. There was no going back to sleep now. His head throbbed. He felt depressed. Had he done enough to help Hassan? Martín's warning to Bonila should have an impact. Hell. Max sat naked in the tiny kitchen, sipping a glass of cold water. It helped cool him down, but didn't lift his spirits. He felt tense, edgy and reluctant to go into the police headquarters, fearful of what he might find. His head continued to throb. He put on a Monteverdi disc, but for once that did nothing to help.

I must do something, he thought. I can't just sit here.

Happy thought . . . the little stub of kef, left over from a Moroccan trip, inside the silver inkwell on the desk. Would help him calm down and relax. He hadn't smoked for a long time. But boy – could he do with a drag right now. Max got the stub and skinned up a joint. He went on to the tiny terrace, and inhaled slowly, twice. The morning sun was now hitting the perfect geometric shapes of the Alhambra. Whether it was the *baraka* of the Alhambra or the dope, he slowly relaxed.

If Linda could see me now . . . Linda? What the hell. I still fancy her. Weird. She's impressive. Got that god-awful bunch of cops licked into shape before they knew what had hit them. Even Gonzo's eating out of her pretty little hand. But she's going to stick to the script on the ETA/Islamist link-up whether or not there's evidence, and I haven't a clue what's really going on.

Max paused in his thoughts, and breathed in the morning air deeply. He went to the end of his terrace, and looked down on to the narrow street. A pretty girl in a Muslim headscarf was walking up the road. He felt like waving to her. Perhaps she'd like a cup of mint tea.

Mierda. I'm bollock naked.

He stepped back sharply.

Dios. What a bloody mess with the Muslims. But some of the Christians in the USA are almost as bad. God save us from religions.

He looked at his watch. Stop faffing about, get into work . . . check the damage.

The shower, the fresh morning air or maybe the two puffs had revived him, and he jumped on the Albayzín bus almost with joy. But the minute he entered police headquarters he knew something was wrong, badly wrong.

'Urgent meeting up there. It's just the top brass,' said Bardon, on the desk as usual. 'They haven't asked for you. But Navarro's with them. Davila looks like he's lost a pound and found a penny. Whole load of shit must have hit the fan.'

Max went to his office and waited for the call.

There was an email from Davila saying he had filled in his performance indicators wrongly. And his time sheet didn't add up either – he was working more hours than there were in the day.

Still nobody phoned. The whole building knew something was wrong, but nobody on the outside knew what. Max decided to go for a coffee. Bardon was very good at getting information. Max paused at his desk on the way out.

'Just going for a coffee, Franciso. Any news?'

'Nothing. They've called in three rounds of coffee already. Head honcho of the press office is in now. It's not as if we're going on strike or anything. Nothing on the radio. Bugger all going on anywhere, except the Barcelona manager's resigned.'

Max smiled.

'That chap from Madrid, Martín's here. In the canteen.'

Martín, his body filling the whole seat, was working his way through a plate of doughnuts.

'Max. Come and join me. Doughnut?'

'Thanks . . . too sweet for me. And I'm trying to keep my figure.'

'Stopped worrying about that years ago,' smiled Martín. 'Any idea what's going on?'

'No idea, sir.'

'I'm told Linda's in a meeting with Bonila and the others. But I'm not invited. Doesn't look good. What's your guess?'

'Not sure. But if Navarro's in . . . must be the interrogations.'

They looked at each other. Had someone gone too far? Max finally broke the silence.

'How was Madrid?'

'Fine. Full of rumours. The election's going to be very close. Both parties spinning like mad. If the economy's the big issue for the public, then the Partido Popular wins. But the war's not popular, and that favours the Socialists. But they're a bit too liberal for a lot of folk to stomach – what with gay marriages and all that, plus they're negotiating secretly with ETA. And that's a really awkward one. I'm expecting some dirty tricks from that bastard Allende. You know . . . a decent scandal here could swing the election.'

'Hmm.' Max sipped his coffee.

'And you? Found out who killed that Muslim girl?'

'No. I think they just wanted me out of the way.'

Bardon came into the canteen. 'Thought I might find you here. The meeting's over. Bonila wants a word with you . . . both.'

They knocked on the door, and entered Bonila's office. He was sitting behind his big mahogany desk. Linda was sitting in the corner of the room, looking out of the window.

'Sit down. I thought I should inform you both personally that there has been . . . well . . . a slight mishap. As you know, we left Inspector Navarro in charge of the interrogations. He made the decision – and I'm sure he had good reasons – to soften that kid up, and . . . well, put him overnight in D Section. Apparently there was an unfortunate incident, and Hassan was injured by some of the inmates. And he is now in hospital. Most unfortunate. Not predictable of course. We're asking everyone not to say a word about this, particularly to the media. We don't want bad publicity. Delicate timing and all that.'

Linda continued to stare out of the window. Max waited for Martín to speak first. Martín paused.

'Injured? Seriously?'

'We don't know yet. We are waiting for the hospital's report.'

'Do we know what happened?'

'We've had a report from Inspector Navarro. Apparently some of the prisoners broke the lock on Hassan's cell door and, well, sort of injured him.'

Max could keep silent no longer. 'Beat the shit out of him,

193

you mean? Buggered the kid? Stinks, doesn't it? Pure accident of course—'

'Sub-Inspector Romero, that's enough. Any repetition and I will have to discipline you. Is that understood?'

'Yes, sir,' mumbled Max.

'We are continuing to make inquiries,' continued Bonila. 'There'll be a thorough internal police investigation of course. Most unfortunate. But meanwhile we want no mention of any of this outside this room. Is that clear?'

Max did not reply. Martín frowned. 'I take it we are no further forward with getting any evidence? It will be difficult to hold the suspects for much longer after this.'

On impulse, Max suddenly said, 'Can I see Hassan Khan?'

Linda finally spoke. 'No. I've asked the hospital to keep him isolated in a private room. We've put a guard on the door, just in case.'

'Just in case of what? He dies? Like the other one. And we hush it up? Just more collateral damage in the war on terrorism?'

Bonila cleared his throat, and in his top-brass voice said, 'Sub-Inspector, that's enough. There's no danger of him dying. That man in the Centre was an unfortunate accident.'

'But this isn't. It looks deliberate to me. Why put him in prison and fail to provide basic safety?' butted in Martín.

'Well, apparently he kicked Inspector Navarro. He's done this before. Sub-Inspector Romero has already recorded the attack on Teniente González.'

Max flushed in anger and embarrassment. That bloody lying report of his was coming back to haunt him.

'In any case,' Bonila went on, 'this is all for the police investigation to establish, not for you or us to guess. Well, I think it is time you left now.'

Max, Martín and Linda left together.

'You two seem to have come all matey,' she said. 'Can I join the club?'

Neither Max nor Martín replied. Max looked at Martín,

194

who nodded. Twenty minutes later the two were at a quiet table in the Bar Alonzo.

'What do you make of that?' asked Max.

'Don't know. Doubt it's the whole story. Navarro will get a slap on the wrist. The guards will get a fine – and they won't even have to pay it out of their pockets. We don't know what state Hassan's in. Could be serious.'

'Do we go public?' asked Max.

'Difficult. We'd be in the frame. Traffic duties for you . . . and "suspected terrorist sustains injuries" ain't going to stir the public up. No. We just sit tight. See what happens. Okay . . . we leave separately. I'll go first.'

Max waited until he left, and then took out his mobile.

'Jorge. How are you? There's been – as the boss puts it – an unfortunate mishap here. I think it's quite serious.' He gave Jorge the details. 'I don't know what hospital Hassan is in. But shouldn't be too difficult for the human rights groups to find out. Some medic will talk. *Chao.*'

Best get back and redo those bloody performance indicators.

It did not take long for the Granada Human Rights Association to find out which hospital Hassan was in. It did not take them long to find a medic to explain the nature of Hassan's injuries. It took them longer to decide which paper to leak the details to. In the end they decided on *Ideal*, not the most progressive of papers but, given the shortage of news in Granada in August, *Ideal* would run the story

Jorge had also called the Muslim Associations. It was agreed to call for a demonstration in two days' time. It took hours of negotiations to agree where. In the end they agreed to meet in Plaza Nueva, and march along Gran Vía to the police station. The *Ideal* story was picked up in other Spanish papers, and even got noticed abroad.

Max kept a low profile, staying in his office. It was a noisy, angry march, but passed without incident.

Jorge reported back later.

'Hassan's cracked rib is in a bad way. Probably been

195

kicked on it more than once. His anal injuries are severe. Gang-raped. But it's his mental state that's the real worry. He makes no sense. Keeps muttering, "Whisper it to the wall, Hassan. Whisper it to the wall." He then talks of djins coming out of walls in the darkness to humiliate him, torture him. But Allah and he will have their revenge. A day of reckoning is coming. And then he starts chanting 'Hassan Khan MA . . . MA.' The doctors are really worried. Any idea what it can mean?'

'None. MA? Might be the English for Master of Arts – a university degree title in Britain. But I don't see the significance of that. Probably isn't any.'

'Hmm.'

'I should have put up more of a fight,' said Max. 'Jorge, I'm thinking of resigning.'

'Why? You did what you could.'

'It wasn't enough.'

'Look, if every decent cop resigned when something went wrong we'd be back to the Franco years. You have to stick in there.'

'But—'

'I'm not going to let you pass by on the other side. Max . . . I know you're a good cop. You can be an even better one.'

'Okay, Jorge. What do we do?'

'There's the election coming. Calm it down. We'll keep the pressure up to get the Centre chaps released. Don't oppose any suggestion from the police to keep an eye on them. If you have doubts, then I do too. Just keep a low profile, Max. We've still got that bottle of Cartojal to finish. Give me a call sometime.'

Bonila did summon Max. But Max had no idea where the information in *Ideal* came from.

'Probably someone in the hospital, sir.'

'Yes. Hadn't thought of that. I can't imagine anyone on the force doing it.'

He looked at Max hard as he said it. But Max knew he

was happy with the idea it was someone in the hospital. It made his life easier.

Linda and Martín had returned to Madrid before the demonstration. Martín phoned a few days later.

'And as far as Partido Popular goes, the head honchos are fuming. Allende was so furious he threatened to cut Linda's balls off. Mind you, figuratively speaking, she needed them squeezed. She's still adamant something was being planned. Have you seen today's papers?'

'No. I haven't had time.'

'You should read them. There's an official statement that the Centre guys will be released after further questioning. The statement also says they have agreed to leave the country, and in return no charges will be made following the discovery of pornography on one of their computers.'

'Pornography?'

'Quite. These things happen.'

'But we must do something about it.'

'What? It's the easiest thing in the world to plant porn on a hard disk, and nobody can prove one way or another who put it there. So the guys from the Centre will be leaving quietly, except Hassan who has to stay until his doctor says he's fit to travel. We've asked their respective countries to keep them under surveillance.'

'Hell,' said Max. 'That's not going to do much good.'

'Hmm . . . The Ibn Rush'd Centre's an odd set-up. I need to do more homework. Any news on Hassan Khan?' asked Martín.

'Not good. Ahmed Mahfouz saw him in hospital, and he wants him back in the Muslim community. A friend, Zaida Alhuecema, offered to take him in to help him recover.'

'Okay. Keep me informed. That bastard Allende may try to pull another fast one.'

'So, it's stalemate.'

' Looks like the only thing we can do is keep checking on the Ibn Rush'd Centre. What are you going to do now?'

197

'Granada in August is just too much. I've a long weekend booked, so I'll go down to the coast. Maybe I should invite Linda?'

'You'd have more chance with López,' said Martín, laughing.

Just lazing on the beach for a few days did Max a world of good. He tried chatting up a few girls. There were some real beauties on the beach. But they only hunted in packs, and on his own . . . well, he got nowhere. Was he getting too old? Definitely putting on weight. At least he had a good book, *The Flanders Panel* by Arturo Pérez-Reverte. So he just lay on the beach, dozing, girl-watching, and reading. He remembered the book was the one Javeed had been reading when they first visited his centre. As he got towards the end of the book, Max realized something was wrong. Very odd . . . Hassan's account of the chess game with Javeed seemed remarkably similar to the one in the book. Have to check his notes on that. It was all too pat. Jorge was bound to be a good chess player – he'd better ask him about those final moves in the book.

Max returned to Granada with an all-over tan. The city was still sweltering, the main streets protected from the fierce sun by white canvas shades. Without them even the tourists would be too hot to shop. Davila and Bonila were on holiday. Navarro was nowhere to be seen. The incident with Hassan was all but forgotten. Old news. But some damage had been done to the Partido Popular. The full police investigation was scheduled for October.

Max phoned the hospital. Hassan had been released into the care of Zaida Alhuecema.

'Physically he should recover,' the doctor said. 'But mentally, although I'm not an expert, I think he may be suffering from post-traumatic stress disorder. In this case, he can't stand being touched by strangers. If touched, he has a compulsion to wash. The trauma seems to have left him with delusional problems relating to Islam. But he could get worse. Might even turn violent or attempt to commit self-harm. And then we'd have to take him back in. I've asked one of the Diva doctors to visit him daily, but unfortunately, as you know, the local clinic doesn't have a mental health unit. I've sent my report to Comisario Bonila, if you want full details.'

'And the others?' asked Max.

'I've examined them all. Can't say they're in great shape. Sleep deprivation, bruising, but nothing serious. Nothing to worry about.'

Max phoned Inspector Jefe Rodrigo Dacosta, in charge during Bonila's absence. He confirmed what the doctor had said.

'My advice, Max, is for you and everyone who inter-viewed that lad to stay away from him. The doctors say it could trigger something if he sees you. We've released the others, but we'll keep an eye on them all until they return to their own countries. For what it's worth we've asked these countries to maintain surveillance on them all. There's EU money in that Centre, and some bloody Green MEP is sure to get on to it. Also some posh lawyer here from God knows where has pitched up threatening to sue us for compensa-tion. Bad precedent if we allow that. Our tactic is to get them out of the country as soon as possible.'

'Thanks, sir, I'll take your advice. But there's still the mur-der investigation into the Muslim girl in Diva . . . and we haven't ruled out Hassan Khan there. Do you want me to continue to help on that?'

'Continue to help where you can. But do it carefully. You might want to visit the Ibn Rush'd Centre before they leave, and see if you can find out anything more. You never know.'

'I'll do that, sir.'

Chapter 18

Tis all a Chequer-board of Nights and Days
Where Destiny with men for Pieces plays:

Edward FitzGerald, *The Rubáiyat of Omar Khayyám*

The next morning Max arose early, made a cup of mint tea, and drank it on his terrace. He stared up at the Alhambra, hoping for inspiration. Without outside pressure, the official police inquiry would be fudged, and someone – Navarro? – gets a slap on the wrist. Max sat and thought. Then he remembered a murder five years go. Paco had stabbed his girlfriend in a flamenco club, then got religion in jail. Decent guy once you got to know him . . . and Paco just might know what had really happened to Hassan. Paco was one of Jorge's parishioners: nobody would be surprised if Jorge made a pastoral visit. Max picked up the phone and called him.

'Max, what's up? It's not even eight.'

'I know, Jorge. But I'm worried the police inquiry will do its usual, hum, haw, but, under the exceptional circumstances, unfortunate incident . . . and clear that bastard Navarro. I was wondering – could you talk to Paco and find out what really happened?'

'That's a good idea. I've already got a prison visit booked for this afternoon.'

'We have to make sure nothing can get back to Paco. You know what could happen to him if it does.'

'No problem. It's just a routine pastoral visit. I'll be seeing other prisoners as well. Leave it to me.'

'Great.'

'Just thought of something. The Archbishop. He's a right-wing son of a bitch on most issues.'

'That's true.'

'But he's very keen to maintain good relations with the Muslims . . . and he's worried about the impact of the Hassan Khan case.'

'So what's the plan?'

'I'll get the Muslim leaders to visit the Archbishop . . . to ask that justice is seen to be done, and that there is no whitewash . . . something like that. Then if Paco tells me what happened, I'll pass it on to the Muslim Association, and they can inform the Archbishop. That way there will be no names mentioned, and everything will be completely confidential.'

'That sounds neat.'

'The Archbishop, I'm sure, will write to Comisario Bonila emphasizing the importance of an open and thorough investigation, and explaining that he, the Archbishop, has received reliable evidence of Navarro's involvement. That'll worry Bonila, and whether he likes it or not he'll have to be seen to be doing something.'

'That will be great, Jorge. Can you do it as soon as possible?'

Max drove down to his office. There was a pile of papers to clear, a mountain of forms to fill in. It was so hot that even Davila's shirt had lost its starch.

At the end of the day, Max went home to his flat, took a shower, and lay on his bed listening to Handel's *Theodora* on the BBC World Service. The death duet moved him to tears. At the end of the broadcast, he dressed and walked down to the Sacromonte road. He sat outside at Pibe's, ordered a *tubo* of beer, and began to catch up on his copies of *El País*. The news was dominated by the Palestinian/Israeli negotiations. The USA was on a roll, and determined to push through a peace deal. It looked as if all the concessions were to come

201

from the Palestinian side. Max wondered what Javeed would think of all this.

The next day at noon he received a call from Jorge.

'You were right, Max. Paco and I did a deal. His girl-friend's mother won't let his little girl visit him, and he's desperate to see the kid. So the deal is . . . I persuade the *abuela* to let the girl see her dad, and Paco tells me what happened. I know the *abuela*, and she won't say no to me . . . so he told me the story.'

'Okay.'

'It's exactly as you thought. According to Paco, one of the inmates got the whisper that Inspector Navarro had arranged for the boy to be placed overnight in D Section. He thinks it was probably agreed high up.'

'This is getting interesting.'

'The cell door was left unlocked. The guards let the guys in the prison know they had a free hand – something about softening the lad up before further questioning. Paco claims he had nothing to do with what happened next. But those involved overdid it, and the boy was carted off to hospital next morning.'

'Right.'

'But there's more. The story is that Inspector Navarro is a real bad one, that he's part of an underage prostitute ring – some place in the Albayzín.'

'Christ!'

'Doesn't surprise me. I'd heard a whisper last year. I'll work on that one.'

'Take care, Jorge. That Navarro is a ruthless bastard.'

'Don't worry. The Blessed Virgin will protect me. And I've already advised the Muslim leaders about Hassan Khan. They have an interview with His Grace tomorrow.'

'Jorge!'

'It's okay. I'm seeing His Right Holiness this evening. We don't get on. He thinks I'm a troublemaker, and I think he's a pompous reactionary. But he's a shrewd operator. The Pope has ordered the Church to maintain good relations

202

with the Muslims, so a few well-planted words followed by a delegation from the Muslims and then a strong letter from the Archbishop to Bonila should do the trick.'

'Thanks, Jorge. I feel better already.'

'Now you can do me a favour. I promised Paco I would get a present for his little girl. No idea what little girls like these days. So could you get me something, and I'll pass it on?'

'Sure, but . . .'

'Just ask Encarnación. I think they're the same age.'

'You might be embarrassed by what little girls like these days, something to do with some bloody pop star or footballer.'

'Me, nothing can embarrass me any more. You should eavesdrop on what I hear in confession sometime.'

'I'll pass on that one.'

Two days later Max set out for Capa. The long winding road up the mountain reminded him of the raid. He had to admit he still didn't know for sure. The evidence against them was weak, circumstantial at the best. But something was not quite right. They could still be plotting something, and here he was going out on a limb to help them. He just hoped he hadn't got it wrong. Max sympathized with the Palestinian cause: their treatment by the USA and Israel was appalling . . . but this suicide bombing . . . he couldn't agree with that.

Max stopped for a beer at a roadside bar before Diva. The constant curves required concentration, and with the heat he felt tired and thirsty. He needed a break before the steep, twisting climb up to Capa. The bar usually had a copy of *El País*. He went into the bar, ordered a beer, and looked around. Someone else was reading it, so he had to make do with yesterday's *Granada Hoy*. A 'traffic chaos' front page again. Max agreed: getting round the city was hell these days. But the roadworks had to be done – increasing prosperity meant more cars, and cars needed roads. Finally, the person reading *El País* left. Max grabbed it, and settled down with another beer in the corner of the pub. 'USA and EU Pressure on Palestine Negotiators to Sign Intense.' *El País* predicted that in a week or so the Palestinians would give in, and sign. As always it was the fine detail which mattered: in return for international and Israeli recognition of a Palestinian state, Palestine would have to recognize Israel, crack down on any terrorist attacks on Israel, recognize the new boundaries, and give up any claims to the right of the Palestinian exiles to return to any part of Israel. And yes, of course the EU would help Palestine with finance. Max looked at the proposed boundary lines. Hell . . . they can't possibly sign that. The Palestine state would not be viable, and would be subject to total economic and political domination by Israel. The USA was apparently threatening that if they didn't sign they would give Israel carte blanche to invade to take out any so-called terrorist cells.

Shit, what am I doing, trying to solve the world's problems, Max thought. I've got a murder case, and a possible terrorist case, on my hands – that's more than enough. He felt reluctant to move. He had no real excuse for visiting the Centre; he was just fishing for more information, some clue or other. He should probably apologize for what had happened, and let them know that this time there would be a thorough investigation. 'Never apologize unless you really have to or else we will spend half our lives apologizing,' one of his police training teachers had advised. Best go.

Max arrived at the Centre just as the sun began to dip below the mountain top. He drove his car as close to the main entrance as he could. As he stopped the engine, a bearded man appeared, dressed in a djellaba, a loose white robe. It was the Algerian, Omar. Shit, thought Max. He'd been hoping to see Javeed first.

Max got out of the car as Omar approached.

'What the . . .' said Omar, and he bent down, and picked up a rock, closing in on Max.

Max raised his hands in a peace gesture. 'I've come to talk to Javeed,' he pleaded.

Omar stopped, the rock raised above his head. 'You . . . you filthy, murdering bastard!'

And he threw the rock at Max. Max stepped back, the rock hitting him hard on his ribs. He yelled in pain, fell backwards, and blacked out briefly as his head hit a boulder. Omar picked up another rock, and raised it above his head.

'Omar, stop,' a sharp voice rang out.

Omar paused. Javeed walked towards Max.

'Sub-Inspector Romero? Are you brave, or just stupid?' he said.

Max, his head splitting, his ribs throbbing with pain, struggled up. He rubbed the back of his head: blood stained his fingers. He looked down at his torn shirt, blood oozing from the cut on his ribs. He winced. 'I've just come to talk.'

'Talk? What's there to talk about? Your police killed my friend, let scum rape Hassan, and then planted pornography on one of our hard disks. And you just want to talk?'

Javeed glanced at Max's side, blood seeping through and staining his shirt. 'You'd better come inside.'

Max followed Javeed into the house. Omar came too, the rock still in his hand.

'Take your shirt off,' said Javeed. 'Omar, fetch the first aid box. And get rid of that rock.'

Omar scowled. In a few minutes he returned with the first aid box. Javeed took out some iodine.

'This should be sufficient for now, but you need to get it checked out.'

Max grimaced as Javeed applied the iodine. Javeed laughed. 'You wouldn't make much of a soldier.'

'Some people say I don't make much of a cop.'

'Here, turn round and let me look at your head.'

Max winced again as Javeed dabbed on some drops of iodine.

'Get them both looked at as soon as you can. Okay. You want to apologize . . . ease your good liberal conscience . . . but you're also checking up on us? Right?'

205

Max blinked. 'I am personally sorry for what happened, particularly to Hassan. Believe me, I had nothing to do with that.'

' I believe you. You are too subtle for such crudities.'

'Thanks. How is Hassan?'

'What do you expect? He's been tortured. I want an inquiry into police use of torture and compensation for Hassan, of course, but your friends threatened to push the pornography charge if we didn't agree to leave the country.'

'I can't believe they tried that old trick,' said Max.

'They did, and it worked. We have no comeback, except to deny it. They have our hard disk with the incriminating evidence, don't they? So we're the bad guys now.'

Max knew he was right.

'So we don't have much choice, except to leave to avoid charges. I've asked my lawyer to push for compensation. But I don't hold out much hope. What do you think?'

'There will be an honest and thorough investigation,' Max replied.

Javeed glanced at Max. 'You hope so.'

'No. This time I can guarantee it.'

'Maybe,' said Javeed.

'But forget any hopes for compensation. I don't see that being likely,'said Max.

'I don't think it's likely either.' Javeed turned to Omar. 'Don't just stand there. Go and get our guest some tea. You are lucky the Sub-Inspector won't press charges for assault. You won't, will you?' Javeed added, looking hard at Max.

'No, I won't.'

Javeed smiled. 'Then perhaps we can continue our previous conversation in more propitious circumstances. This time it can be you on the defensive. For indeed what is truth?'

Omar returned with two mint teas.

'Truth?' said Max. 'I believe you can approximate to it or else I wouldn't be a cop. You look at the evidence, weigh

206

it up, and then decide if it more or less fits the facts. But motives . . . intentions . . . you can never be certain.'

'Ah. The human heart. Only Allah, peace be upon him, knows that. You could say that we Muslims are a very fatalistic people.'

'Why?'

' On one level, we don't really believe in cause and effect. *You* are brought up looking for explanations, a 'because' for everything. *We* see the world as a series of events, like a story, 'and then this happened, and then that.' It all being Allah's will. You see, we don't believe it is Allah's will that the Jews should dominate Palestine for ever. So it is Allah's will that we should fight, and in that fight many will die. Allah leaves it up to us how we fight, but fight we must. Bin Laden understands that well . . . which is why he is so popular in the Arab world.'

'But what if the means he uses are counter-productive?'

'Maybe he's part of the problem too. But do you think if we pleaded with the American President to put right all the injustices he has supported, it would have any impact? I may disagree with Bin Laden's tactics, but his essential message that we will achieve nothing without fighting is true. I regret the deaths, but Allah's will is for an Islamic Palestine, and an independent Middle East. For that we have to fight. But our fight has to be like a chess game, sometimes you have to sacrifice a piece to achieve the final checkmate. We are at the sacrifice stage.'

'So you don't support the present peace offer?'

'Peace offer? That's not peace. It's not even peace without honour. That's giving us a piece of dirt in return for giving up everything we have fought for. And Al Fatah have become so corrupt . . . well, they might sign. I'm told the Americans have offered them large sums of money.'

'I thought you'd been an Al Fatah organizer in . . .?'

'Years ago. But now they are corrupt, and may sign. So these present negotiations are very dangerous. We may gain a pawn or two, but in doing so, sacrifice our queen, and without her we cannot win. Our queen . . . is our belief that one day we will reoccupy enough of our lands to have a viable state. So a bad peace in which we lose that hope is worse than no peace at all. Without that belief, we will start killing each other. And then we will have lost everything.'

'I'm not sure I understand.'

'No. I'm not surprised. You haven't lived our lives.'

'No.'

'One learns through sacrifice. The Zionists understand that – which is why they are so ruthless. The Americans are ruthless as long as it causes them no pain. But cause them pain and they look eventually for compromises. Pawns, you know, are there to be sacrificed. But yes, I love chess.'

'I noticed that the winning move was similar to the one in *The Flanders Panel.*'

'Back to that again. Yes. I had to manoeuvre Hassan into a position through sacrificing pieces where I could take his white knight to eventually win the game. In chess, as in war, sacrifices are necessary to win in the long run.'

Max grimaced, his ribs and head aching. 'I'm not one for sacrifices. My ribs are really beginning to hurt. I'd better go now.'

'Can you drive down the mountain okay?'

'Sure. No problem.'

'We leave at the end of the week. So you and I probably won't meet again. Or maybe we will, *inshallah.*'

'Maybe we will, Allah willing,' Max replied.

'I hope so. You are the only one of them who tries to understand.'

Max and Javeed shook hands. Javeed walked with Max to his car.

'Remember, what is truth?'

Max laughed. 'Only Allah knows that.'

He drove down the mountain, his ribs throbbing, his head aching. I must check up on the police notes on that chess game, he thought.

When he reached the turn-off to Diva he decided to take it, and spend the night at Paula's. She would fuss over him, but then he felt in need of a bit of fussing.

As he turned on to the Jola road, the pain in his ribs and head got worse. He began to feel faint. Best stop the car. Max pulled up near the bridge where Leila's body had been found. He got out of the car, and breathed in deeply. It was not far to go. He had better warn Paula he was coming, and that he was not feeling too well. He fished in his jacket for his mobile, and phoned Paula.

'*Abuela. Hola.* I'll be arriving in ten minutes or so. I'm not feeling too well. No, I'll be okay. Yes. I can make it on my own.'

The pain in his ribs was becoming unbearable. He felt nauseous. Best get there quick. Max looked around him. It was here that Leila had died. And he was still no further as to the reason for her death or the identity of her killer. There must be something out there that could give him a clue or maybe he already had a clue but had just failed to notice it.

Max got back into the car. His head was throbbing with pain. He reached to start the car, and gritted his teeth so as not to scream from the sharp pain in his ribs. The engine finally kicked in, and he eased the car forward. The pain made driving hazardous. He slowed down to a crawl, unsure that he could make it to Paula's. After what seemed like an eternity, he glimpsed lights in the distance, welcoming, beckoning lights. He could just make out Juan, waiting at the beginning of the driveway. Max felt sick, then suddenly he vomited over the steering wheel. He managed to stop the car before he passed out.

He awoke to the pleasant smell of fresh lavender. He opened his eyes to see two worried faces staring down at him.

'*Santo cielo,*' said Paula. 'Are you all right? Juan had to carry you in from your car. Mother of God, you could have killed yourself.'

209

'No. I'm okay. Just fell and hurt my ribs and head, that's all.'

'We've called the doctor. You could have broken ribs, and that head wound could be serious,' said Juan. 'What happened?'

'Slipped and fell, that's all. I'll be all right.' Max grimaced as he tried to move.

'Here. Let me help you,' said Juan. He put his hand on Max's back as he struggled to sit up. 'We've wiped the sick off you. You vomited all over the steering wheel, you know.'

'Thanks,' said Max as Juan straightened his pillows. Max smiled faintly. 'I'd love a strong cup of English tea, plenty of sugar.'

'I'm not sure we've got any,' said Juan.

'Yes, we do,' said Paula. 'The box Max brought back from his last trip to Scotland. You'll have a drop of brandy too?'

'Okay. What really happened?' said Juan, once Paula had left the room.

'Somebody threw a rock at me, a big one. Got knocked over, and hit my head on a boulder. I can't really blame the guy – he's got enough reasons to hate the police.'

'Anything to do with Leila's death?'

'No. It's these Muslims we arrested.'

'Nothing to do with Leila.' Juan licked his lips. 'Max . . .' he began. Then Paula returned, and he stopped.

'Here you are, *cariño*. A nice cup of tea just like your mother showed me how to make it. But first have this drop of brandy. Juan, help me get him out of these bloodstained clothes before the doctor comes. We can't have him looking such a mess,' and she started undoing Max's trousers.

'*Abuela*, for heaven's sake! Let me do that.'

'Don't be silly. It's not that long ago I wiped your bottom.'

'But I'm grown up now.'

'That's what you think. And there isn't anything I haven't seen before.'

'Juan . . . ask her to leave, and give me a hand getting out of these,' pleaded Max.

'Juan, get Max a pair of your clean pyjamas.'

For the next half-hour until the doctor came Paula fussed over him. Paula was good at fussing, better than mother. Max leaned back into the pillow, and started to relax.

The doctor confirmed it was quite serious: probably two broken ribs and a minor concussion. He patched Max up as best he could, and put a small bottle of painkillers on the bedside table.

'Take two of these every two to four hours. They will help you sleep. If we were closer to the city, I'd send you I for an X-ray now, but I think it can wait till tomorrow. I'll make an appointment for you.'

'I'll drive you over,' offered Juan.

'Thanks. Juan . . . Could you get my uniform jacket – I left it on the back seat, and it's got my mobile in it.'

'Max, call me if you get any new symptoms.'

'Okay, Dr Muro. My *abuela*'s a good nurse.'

Paula came in. 'Max, how about some nice chicken broth with a raw egg in it?'

'Thanks, *abuela*. But all I want to do now is sleep.'

Juan returned with Max's jacket.

'Thanks,' said Max. 'Hell. I should have asked you to get the charger. It's in the front compartment of the car.'

'Okay, okay. But remember I'm not your nursemaid.'

'I know. Remember the time I fell out of that tree, and all you could do was laugh.'

Juan laughed, and left. Max reached into his jacket pocket to take out the mobile. With the mobile came a mint, and the plastic evidence bag with the scrap of sweet wrapper. He placed them in the drawer of the bedside table. Juan returned with the charger.

'Shall I plug it in for you?' he asked.

'Please.'

'Anything else, sir?' joked Juan. 'Tuck you in? Wipe your brow? Hold your hand?'

211

'Oh, fuck off, and let me sleep.'

'I don't know how the police let in such a softie,' laughed Juan as he left.

Max took the painkillers, and was settling down when Paula entered.

'Max, would you like me to stay and make sure you're all right?'

'No, I'll be okay now, *abuela*.'

'Here, let me tuck you in nice and comfy. And I'll just wipe some of that perspiration away.'

She took Max's hand. 'You had us really worried, you know. I don't like all this dangerous work you've got yourself into. Something really nasty could happen to you.'

'I know, *abuela*, but it has to be done.'

'Sleep tight, *mi amor*,' said Paula, bending over to give Max a kiss on his cheek. 'I'll pop in later to see how you are.'

Better get the mobile out . . . you never know, Max thought. He gazed at the scrap of paper in the evidence bag, and the mint sweet. He began to drift in and out of sleep. There was something odd. Something odd. The mint . . . was that one Juan had given him when he was last at Paula's? Juan? Juan? He could hardly keep awake now. Why did that matter? And he then fell into a deep sleep.

Max awoke in the middle of the night, his throat dry. Paula had been in, and had left a glass of fresh water on his bedside table. She had left the night light on. His ribs were really sore. Max painfully sat up, and reached for the water. He took another two painkillers. As he did so, he looked at the mint and the torn sweet wrapper in the evidence bag. He felt sick again.

Chapter 19

No quise.
No quise decirte nada.

I was not willing.
Not willing to tell you a thing.

Frederico García Lorca, *Al oído de una muchacha*
(Whispered to a Girl)

The journey to the hospital was painful. Max wanted to talk to Juan, but not now. They arrived at the hospital, having spoken scarcely one word. Juan gently helped Max into Casualty. The Casualty doctor examined him thoroughly, ordered X-rays, and returned in half an hour.

'As I thought,' he said, 'two broken ribs and concussion. You've been lucky . . . could have been a lot worse. Not much we can do except give you painkillers. All you can do is go home, rest, and just take it easy. Assume you'll be off work for at least a week.'

Juan helped him back into the car.

'Max, come back with me to Paula's,' he said. 'At least you know you'll be well looked after.'

'No, I'd be so fussed over, I'd get no rest,' insisted Max. 'I've got my air conditioning fixed, so I'll be fine in Granada. If you could do a bit of shopping for me, I'll manage. If I need anything more, my neighbours won't let me starve.'

'Okay. If that's what you want. But let me talk to one of the neighbours so they can pop in to check up on you.'

'Thanks. But could you first go by police headquarters? I'd better tell Davila.'

'Why not phone?'

'No, I want to see him myself. I need to keep busy while I'm off sick.'

Juan parked the car in the police car park, walked through the public entrance, and returned shortly with Davila trailing behind.

'My God, Max. What happened to you?' Davila said.

'Slipped and fell when I was out walking, and brained myself on a rock, sir. Broke a couple of ribs too. Sorry.'

'How long's the sick line for?'

'Just out of Casualty, so I haven't got the line yet, but the doc at the hospital said I should take a week off . . . maybe more.'

'Pity. We really can't afford to lose you. Navarro's been suspended.'

'Oh? What happened?'

'Bonila says some evidence turned up suggesting Navarro gave the wink and nod to the prisoners to rape the boy.'

'Heavens.'

'I can't believe it's true either. But top brass are bringing in some tough nut from Murcia to do the investigation.'

'It sounds a difficult time for the force, sir.'

'It certainly is. Bonila's not a happy bunny. It's bloody bad timing to have you off sick.'

'I know, sir. I was wondering, sir – seeing I'm quite capable of doing something useful at home – whether I shouldn't go over the Leila Mahfouz case materials again.'

'Hmm. I can see the value in that.'

'Perhaps, sir, you could phone Teniente González and see if Cabo Guevarra might come and help me. She could bring over all the material, and if anything needs chasing up, she could do it.'

'Be a long drive for her to come over every day though.'

'Not really, sir. There's a family flat in Granada.'

'I'll see what I can do. Bit unorthodox, mind you. But we

do need some progress on this case, and it is connected to that bunch of Muslims at the Centre. Be useful to us if it turned out to be one of them. Yes, I'll put that to Bonila and see what he thinks. Certainly help us if we can link them to the murder.'

'I wouldn't want to jump to any conclusions, sir.'

'No, no, of course not. They've all left the country now except for Hassan Khan. He still has to wait for a medical okay. Certainly be useful, Max, if you unearthed something involving him. Make the force look a lot better. We've had a bad press recently.'

'I'd better go now, sir.'

'Yes, of course. Certainly be useful. Good idea of yours, Max. By the way, Navarro is . . . um . . . thinks you might have had something to do with his suspension.'

'Me, sir? What could I have done?'

'Max – if you don't know, how can I? But Bonila's been asking me about you. Had to tell him the truth, and say you're not a great team player – too fond of your own opinions. But cracking the Leila Mahfouz case could do you a bit of good, and if you can pin it on one of those Muslim guys . . . well . . .'

'I'll do my best, sir, to find the truth.'

'The truth? Hmm. Off you go now. Find us something on those guys.'

Juan drove off. 'Back to the Leila case then? I—shit,' he said, as a motorbike swerved in front of him.

'Sorry, Juan. My head's aching. I really need a lie-down. Can you drop me at my flat, and then pick up a bit of food?'

'Sure.'

Once inside his flat, Max took another painkiller, lay down on his bed and dozed off. When he awoke he found a note from Juan.

'Max. Didn't want to wake you. I've put all the food and drink away. I've spoken to your neighbour, María. She'll call in to see if you need anything. I've put her phone number by your phone. She said make sure to phone her if you need anything or feel a little strange. Have to be back in Diva for an appointment. I'll phone this evening. Paula's sure to phone every five minutes. I'll tell her you need to rest so at least she'll only phone every hour. *Chao*. Juan.'

Max smiled. Juan really was one of the good guys.

He slept soundly until the next morning. The pain had lessened. There was a knock at the door that Juan had left unlocked, and María bustled in.

'Max, how are you? Your cousin Juan came to see me. He's charming. He told me what happened. Let me get you some breakfast.'

'Thanks, María. But I'm sure I can manage.'

'It's no problem. What are neighbours for if they can't help out in an emergency? I had a phone call from your *abuela*, asking after you. We had quite a gossip. I feel I know all your family. I know what happened when you fell out of that tree. Could have been really nasty. She said I'm to make sure you are fine, and that you quite like a bit of fussing over.'

Max sighed, no point in protesting. Blast Juan. What on earth made him give María's number to Paula?

'Thanks, María. Orange juice, toast and coffee would be just fine. And if you could get me an *El País* later, that would be great.'

'No problems. As I always say, there are no problems, only solutions.'

Max was halfway through the second slice of toast when the phone rang.

'*Diga.*'

'Max, Davila here. I've spoken to Bonila. He's already phoned González, and he's agreed. Cabo Guevarra will be over later today. Bonila says if you find anything, let him know immediately.'

'Will do, sir. *Vale.*'

It would be nice to see Guevarra, a pretty girl. Max looked round his flat – in a mess again.

'María, you couldn't straighten up the flat for me, could

you? I've got a young colleague coming to see me this afternoon. Can't have it looking such a mess, can I?'

María laughed. 'Young and pretty, I bet. It'll only take me twenty minutes to straighten this. It would help if you put things away.'

Cabo Anita Guevarra did not arrive until five in the afternoon. She entered with a box full of files.

'How are you feeling, sir? What happened?'

'Fine. Just slipped, one of those things.'

'González says you were chasing a pretty sheep.'

'He would, wouldn't he?'

'Here's everything on the Leila Mahfouz case, sir.'

'Thanks . . . and just call me Max.'

She smiled.

'There's some cold beer in the fridge. Grab a couple of cans, and let's sit out on the terrace.'

Max put the cold can of beer to his forehead. 'That's better,' he said. 'Got a huge bruise at the back of my head, gives me a headache all the time.'

'I won't stay long, sir . . . I mean Max. You look tired. Lovely view you have from here. Must be nice to live in the Albayzín itself.'

'It has its advantages. Parking's a bit of a pain. But you always have these great views. And in ten minutes from here you can be right out into the countryside. You can walk to the top of Mulhacén without touching a road.'

'That would be some walk. A guy I know does the old track from Güejar into Granada most Sundays. Takes him nearly all day.'

'Must do that sometime. I like to get out into the hills. Clears away the police blues.'

Cabo Guevarra laughed. 'Well, you won't be in the hills next week. So what's the job you have for me, sir? Max?'

'I want us to go over all the materials we have on the Mahfouz case again . . . thoroughly. Check all the statements, notes. See if we can spot any inconsistencies, chase up any loose ends. You'll have to do any legwork.'

217

'But we've been through everything pretty thoroughly.'

'I know. But there's no harm in doing it again. Teniente González tends to jump to conclusions. So he may have missed something.'

'That's true, sir . . . Max. He has his prejudices.'

Max smiled. She was still a bit shy and stiff, but they should get on. 'I also want you to chase up Leila's research. I have a feeling there might be something there.'

'But she was doing historical research. I can't see the relevance of that.'

'Yes, I know. But there might be something we've overlooked. We don't have much to go on.'

Max moved to reach for his can of beer. 'Ouch,' he gasped. 'I never knew you used ribs so much.'

'Here. Let me get it for you.'

She handed him the beer. 'You don't look too well. I think I should go now.' She put a cool hand on Max's forehead. 'Perhaps you should lie down.'

'You're right. Could you get me my painkillers? They're by the bed. I'll take a couple of those.'

She returned with the bottle of pills. Max gulped down two.

'Can I help you get into bed, sir?'

You sure could, thought Max. 'No. I'll be all right.'

'Is there anything you need? Food? Drink?'

'No, my cousin Juan did a load of shopping.'

She looked round the flat, and commented, 'Very tidy for a single man. What time would you like me to come tomorrow?'

'With all the roadworks, it'll take you the best part of an hour to get in from Churriana. Let's make it about ten.'

She looked at him closely, and said, 'I could stay longer now, sir, and see you're okay, if you want.'

'No. I'll be fine. I just need to sleep now.'

'Okay. I'll go now, sir . . . Max.'

She smiled sweetly, turned and left. She really had a nice swing of the hips. Max limped into his bed, made sure he

218

had plenty of water by the bedside table, and curled up as best he could.

He woke with a start the next morning. There was a noise in the kitchen. He got out of bed cautiously. Hell. He had sweated like a pig in the night – his pyjamas were soaked. He looked round for some weapon. That bloody Navarro might be after him. The only possible weapon was a glazed Moroccan jug. That would have to do. He quietly tiptoed towards the kitchen, opened the door, jug in hand.

'María. Oh. It's you.'

María turned. 'What are you doing with that jug?'

'Just moving it to the . . . kitchen window sill.'

'That's not a sensible place. You'd be sure to break it there. My. You're wringing with sweat. I'll get you a towel and mop you down.'

'No. Thanks. I'll take a shower.'

'Okay. Breakfast will be ready by the time you've finished.'

Max slunk into the bathroom, Moroccan jug still in hand. As he stepped out of the shower he heard two women's voices, Anita and María. He looked round for his clothes. Blast. They were in the bedroom, and he'd have to cross the living room to enter his bedroom. The two women were still in the living room, having a good natter. He'd hung his pyjamas on the nail of the bathroom door, but, still soaked with sweat, they were even wetter now from the steam of the shower. Blast. The big towels were in the drawer of the bedroom cupboard . . . and all he had was a small towel. He put his ear to the door. They were still jabbering away. Nothing for it, except the small towel. Max opened the bathroom door, and put his head round.

'Excuse me, ladies. I have to get to my clothes in the bedroom. Could you turn round while I slip past you.'

There was laughter. María replied, 'We were just saying that as cops go, you're not too ugly. I was telling Anita here that the seriously handsome one is your cousin, Juan. And he is so charming as well. But go on, we promise not to look.'

219

They both turned away, giggling like a pair of schoolgirls. Max slipped past them, and shut the bedroom door firmly. There was more laughter.

'That was a small towel you had, Max,' said María.

Max began to wonder if that bloody cousin of his had set him up. María was recently divorced, forty-something. Might have been okay if she hadn't gone and dyed her hair blonde, and taken to putting on red lipstick. She also smoked, and Max had never gone out with a woman who smoked since the time he kissed a girl who tasted like an ashtray.

Once dressed, he returned to the living room with as much dignity as possible. María had left. Guevarra was still standing.

'Come and join me for a coffee and something to eat,' said Max.

'Just a coffee, thanks. Had breakfast not that long ago. María is a nice neighbour. You're lucky to have someone like her around. We were laughing about Paula. She had phoned María again this morning, and before she knew it María was telling her all about her divorce.'

'Hmm.' Max tried to sound as neutral as possible. He looked at Anita, and noticed that she did not wear lipstick nor did she dye her hair. Perhaps she'd stopped smoking.

After breakfast, Anita said, 'Well, Max, where should we begin?'

'Let's classify what we've got. Once in order . . . I read it, you read it, and then we discuss it. That way we should miss nothing.'

It took them all morning just to get everything in order. At two Anita stopped, looked at her watch, and said, '*Mira* . . . it's two. Can I get you some lunch?'

'That would be nice. It's too hot to eat on the terrace. Juan did the shopping. I'm not sure what he bought.'

'Let me look. Then I'll rustle something up.'

She returned in. a minute. 'That was some shop your cousin did. Looks as if he raided the delicatessen in El Corte

220

Inglés. There are a lot of juices and healthy stuff, and some really good wine. How about white anchovies, tuna and salad and a glass of white wine?'

Max smiled, one of his favourites – in spite of all his banter, Juan was really fond of him.

After the meal the headache started: the wine hadn't helped. Anita glanced at him, and must have noticed the pain etched in his face.

'You'd better lie down. I'll finish the classifying. What's the password for your computer? I'll set up a system for cross-referencing on it.'

Max looked round the room: papers lying all over the floor.

'Password – pilgrim204 – no capitals. We'd also better get some filing folders. If you go down to headquarters and ask for Cristina Boyas, she'll be able to supply you with some. In fact, can you stock up with stationery in general? We could do with some coloured felt tips.'

'Okay. I'll do that. I need a breath of air. But you'd better write me a request of what we need.'

Max did so, and handed the note to Anita. 'I'll sleep whilst you're away.'

It was comforting to know Anita was in his flat. She really was most attractive . . . and it looked like she'd stopped smoking. Max slept soundly. He awoke to find his fresh pyjamas sticky with sweat again. At this rate he'd run out of pyjamas. Better have another shower, and this time take a bathrobe. He looked at his watch. Jesus. Almost six o'clock. Then he remembered he only had two pairs of pyjamas. Max carefully tied his bathrobe.

Anita was in the living room, back to him, on the floor putting papers into folders and carefully sticking labels on the folders.

He coughed, and she turned.

'Didn't want to wake you, you were so sound asleep. You looked as peaceful as a baby. So I decided to just get on with this task while you slept. Almost finished.'

'Thanks. I need another shower.'

'I have to go soon, Max. I'm meeting my sister after her class finishes. She has some crisis or other – boyfriend problems probably.'

'Okay. But you must stay for a meal sometime. I'm quite a good cook.'

'That would be nice. I've left some pasta for you. All you have to do is heat it up.' Anita stood up, pulled her skirt down, and straightened her blouse.

'Well thanks, Anita,' said Max shyly. 'It's nice working with you.'

'You too, sir . . . Max. Certainly a pleasant change from that pig, González.'

Max laughed, 'He's a real swine in every sense of the word, isn't he?'

Anita smiled back at him, 'Better go now. Same time tomorrow morning?'

'Yes. Oh – there's one thing you could do for me. I've run out of pyjamas. You couldn't pick me up a pair, light cotton?'

Anita eyed him carefully. 'Medium, I'd say. I think blue would suit you.'

'Okay. Blue it is.'

Anita giggled. 'If you have no pyjamas, better be careful – that María will be back to make your breakfast tomorrow morning.'

Max watched her leave. It hadn't taken her long to get over her shyness. The pasta she had made, chicken with a cream sauce, was delicious. He enjoyed a quiet evening, listening to a birthday present from his mother, a boxed set of Handel's Oratorios. He remembered to put his bathrobe on before going to bed. It would be too hot to sleep under the sheet. He hoped María had not misinterpreted Paula's advice that he liked being fussed over.

When he awoke, Max noticed that someone had put a glass of fresh water by his bed. It was needed: his throat was parched. He wrapped his bathrobe carefully around him, and ventured out. María was in the kitchen, preparing his breakfast.

'I checked up on you,' she said. 'My, you do sleep peacefully, like a baby. I thought you might be thirsty, so I put some water by the bed.'

'Thanks,' said Max. Forget privacy – he clearly had been taken over.

'I'm off to the coast tomorrow. I've spoken to Anita, such a nice girl, and she says she'll get you breakfast from tomorrow when she comes at ten, and get you anything you need. She phoned me to remind you she'll be late today. Getting the pyjamas,' and with that she looked Max over. 'I agree, I think blue would suit you.'

Is nothing sacred? thought Max. 'María, you've been wonderful. I couldn't have managed without you,' he lied.

'Not a problem. I like to be a solution.'

Anita arrived at eleven.

'I had to look all over. I couldn't find the right shade of blue. I showed them to María, and she said they were just right, the colour of your eyes.' Anita looked at Max closely. 'Do you want to try them on now? The shop assistant said they would change them if they are not right.'

'No. No, they're perfect,' said Max taking them out of their wrapping. 'I'm sure they'll fit just right.' Max hastened to change the subject. 'Have we got everything in order now?'

'Not quite. But shouldn't take too long.'

They classified everything, side by side. It took longer than they thought. They were interrupted by phone calls from both Bonila and Davila, stressing the importance that something should be found. Over the next two days, they went through everything, sitting at Max's table. Anita built up a cross-referencing database. They listened to all the transcripts again. They discussed the tones of voices, the hesitations, any doubts. They listened together to Leila's interview tapes. They read her emails. They read her poems, the bits and pieces of her novel. Max translated all the English into Spanish. They noted down everything that needed

223

to be rechecked. They noted down everything they agreed might be dubious.

'Well, where are we?'asked Max.

Anita consulted her notes. 'There's no real alibi for Hassan Khan or Javeed Dharwish except each other. We should recheck with the waitress at Al Andaluz, and go over their times again. I've agreed to do that.'

'Fine.'

'You've said you're unhappy with the chess game, and you will give more thought to it.'

'Yes – I'll ask Jorge's opinion.'

'Nobody followed up on that English family who left the day Leila died. We both agreed they could be involved or could have seen something. You'll need to do that.'

'Yes, but you need to get on to the land registry or the electricity board – find their Spanish bank and get UK contact details for them.'

'I can do that next week.'

'Fine . . . then I will phone them. What else?'

'We know from her emails to Shona Monroe that Leila had fallen in love with some handsome, married man. I drew a blank with the hint of scandal concerning Leila and a married man in the local Muslim community, so it could still be one of them – or anybody for that matter. So I'd better pursue that one further.'

'Okay. Sounds good.'

'Um . . . sir . . . I noticed that nobody checked up on the lunch your cousin Juan had with Leila in Granada or indeed his statement on his whereabouts at the time of Leila's death. We all seemed sure he's not in the frame . . . sir . . . but . . .? And González did say we should check with the restaurant.'

'Yes. I agree we should check everything.'

'Your cousin did volunteer the information about that lunch with Leila. And it tallied with the statement we have from the librarian in Diva.'

'Statement? Don't remember that. Remind me.'

Anita consulted her file. 'Here it is. It's León's notes, so the grammar's not great. León asks Ricardo, the Diva librarian, when did he last see Leila. Ricardo replies, 'Let me see now. Didn't see her again for some time after she interviewed me. Yes, I remember now. Thought it a bit odd at the time. I was in Granada, and gone to *La Posada Duende* for lunch, and who should I see there but Leila having lunch with Juan? So I went over, got an update from Leila on the thesis, and asked Juan to give my respects to Doña Paula.'

'Hmm. Juan's coming here for an evening meal. It would be nice if you could come as well. We could sort of ask him, informally, then,' interrupted Max.

'Thanks. That would be nice.'

'What else?'

'There's Leila's mobile which turned up in that hippy guy's van.'

'Jim Cavendish?'

'Yes. León was meant to check out the numbers on it. I'd better go and dig up his report . . . if he's done one.'

' Could be important.'

'I agree. I think González and León are so sure it's Hassan Khan they've ignored other things.'

'They certainly have. They're in charge, but it could look bad for them if they've been inefficient. That only really leaves her thesis notes and thesis material. I'll have to go through that, and you can then chase up anything I might come across. See the librarians again, things like that.'

'There's also Jim Cavendish. His Spanish is good, so I could try and talk to him again. He says Leila talked to him about her thesis so he might remember something.'

'I should also track down Shona Monroe just in case Leila mentioned something else to her,' said Max. 'Nothing for it, I suppose, but for me to plough through her thesis stuff. At least it's on an interesting topic.'

'I can't really help you on that, Max. But if you give me a list of queries then I could follow them up.'

Max noticed Anita had relaxed sufficiently to call him

225

Max without stammering over the sir first. They were getting on fine. But he decided not to tell Anita about the sweet wrapper, the one matching Juan's mint. That was something he wanted to pursue on his own.

Juan called to say he could come over on Friday, and Max invited him and Anita for an evening meal. He would cook, Anita would do the shopping and Juan would bring the wine.

Max got up early on Friday to prepare the stock for the *zarzuela*. Anita arrived at nine in the evening, bang on time, wearing a long, simple white dress with a copper and lapis lazuli necklace around her throat. The white of the dress and the blue of the necklace set off the olive sheen of her skin and her jet-black hair. It was the first time Max had seen her out of her uniform. She looked stunning. There was a faint touch of lipstick. Pity, thought Max. But nobody's perfect.

'That's a lovely necklace,' said Max.

'Yes, it was my mother's. Dad had got it for her in Chile.'

Juan arrived late as always. 'I went up to La Bodega Valdivieso to get half a dozen of his best. These are really special.' He opened the wine, sniffed appreciatively, poured three glasses, took his own and swirled it around gently, then took a sip.

'Divine,' he said. 'Right temperature, right taste, right perfume, right everything. So, Max, what's the surprise you've cooked up for us? This invalid dodge seems okay, especially if you can get someone so pretty to look after you.'

Anita laughed. 'We've been working really hard, and fortunately no need for much nursing – he's recovering well. But he really likes it when someone makes his breakfast.'

'He always did. I remember when we went camping. It was always me who had to make the coffee in the morning, and get the breakfast ready.'

'I can't imagine you both camping.'

'We did it quite often. We even did Mulhacén from the Güejar side, and then across to Capa. That was some trip. Started off on a bright sunny day, and then got caught in a

226

blizzard. Fortunately we had all the gear and we were on the path down . . . but the family went frantic. Paula got a helicopter out to look for us.'

'That's dangerous. Some tourists died last year up there.'

'Yes. But they didn't have the right gear. Mind you, Max here got so exhausted I ended up having to drag him down the mountain.'

Anita and Juan chatted happily, nibbling the tapas of salted almonds, olives with coriander and fennel seeds, and marinated *manchego* cheese. Max stayed in the kitchen, preparing one of his specials. He kept having to call Anita for help. He found himself doing that even when he could have managed. Juan would be putting on the charm, and Anita seemed so innocent. Finally the meal was ready.

'Put the candles on, and the lights out. Then you two had better carry it all through,' Max called out.

'Oh, Max. This looks marvellous,' said Anita.

'Looks are only part of it,' said Juan. 'The taste is what really matters.'

They sat down, and looked expectantly at the *zarzuela*, a fine reddish gold colour from the saffron and tomato.

'Anita managed to get me the best fish from the market,' said Max. 'There's monkfish, small squid, gurnard, a flounder, lobster, mussels, king prawns and scampi. And a good slug of *anís* liquor.'

They tucked in with vigour.

'Don't pig yourself totally,' said Max. 'I've made some honey baked figs to go with that nice hazelnut ice cream.'

At the end of the meal, Anita went into the kitchen to prepare Max's best Costa Rican coffee, bought for another occasion. Juan took out two cigars.

'Managed to find these in that little place on la Calle Elvira,' he said. 'Good quality Cuban. Probably smuggled.' He took out a cigar cutter, carefully cut the ends off, lit one, puffed, and passed it to Max, and then repeated the task with his own. They both drew in slowly, and released the smoke together.

227

'Don't tell me,' said Max. 'It reminds you of the time you were in that brothel in Havana. Remember, I've heard all your tales.'

Juan laughed. 'No. I was going to say she's quite a girl, this Anita of yours. I think she quite fancies you.'

'We're just colleagues, that's all,' responded Max.

'More fool you.'

Anita, who had been a surprisingly long time, entered with the coffee. 'Done most of the dishes, Max. I'll finish what's left after the coffee. I noticed some good port, sweet wine, and *anís* in the kitchen. Fancy something with your coffee?'

'That's a white port I bought,' said Juan. 'For me, a white port.'

'For me as well,' added Max.

Anita returned with three white ports.

'Well . . . are you getting anywhere?' asked Juan, sipping his port.

'The Leila case, you mean? Not really. What do you think, Anita?'

'We've been so thorough, it's getting boring. We've a list of things to chase up. By the way, Juan, one of them is the name of the restaurant in Granada where you and Leila had lunch.'

'The restaurant? I don't see the relevance of that.'

'Neither do we. But we made a list of everything that should be checked.'

'Yes,' added Max. 'I didn't know you had lunch with her in Granada until León mentioned it.'

Juan looked at them both carefully, paused as if considering his words. 'No? It was nothing important. I just happened to be in Granada and bumped into Leila. So I suggested we meet for lunch in El Duende, you know, grandpa's favourite restaurant, Max. If I remember rightly all . . . all . . . she talked about was her thesis.'

'Did she say anything that struck you?'

'About her thesis, you mean? No, nothing I can remember.

We bumped into the librarian from Diva there. What a coincidence. But what's all this? I'm not a suspect, am I?'

'Of course not,' said Anita. 'Max and I agreed we had to chase up everything, however irrelevant it might seem. These are the questions we had to ask.'

'You had me worried for a minute,' joked Juan. 'Did I ever tell you the time I got arrested in Chile when I was visiting our cousins?'

'Yes, frequently,' said Max.

'But I've never heard that tale,' said Anita.

Juan didn't need another excuse, and launched into his epic. Max kept interrupting with jokes of a dubious taste. Anita kept laughing.

'Sorry, folks,' Max finally interrupted. 'A lovely evening, but my head's going again. Better not overdo it.'

'You two get on really well, don't you,' commented Anita.

'I had to,' said Max. 'He was an awful bossy elder cousin. Always sure he was right. My mother called him Don Juan of Austria.'

And he and Juan chanted together.

> 'Love-light of Spain – hurrah!
> Death light of Africa!
> Don Juan of Austria
> Is riding to the sea.'

They paused and then in unison yelled:

> 'Don Juan of Austria is going to the war.'

'And what were you called?' said Anita, turning to Max.

'Me? I was Maximiliano of Mexico.'

'On account of his incompetence,' interrupted Juan.

'That's not fair!'

'That's life, kid.'

As Anita left she kissed Max on both cheeks. Max returned the kisses.

Chapter 20

Sin memoria histórica, no puede construirse una sociedad totalmente libre

Without the memory of history, it is impossible to build a free society

> Inscription on a memorial near Granada
> to workers shot during the Civil War

It was a lonely weekend. Max had become used to Anita's company, and had to admit that he missed her. Paula phoned on Saturday to suggest Juan could drive down and take him back to Jola for Sunday lunch. But Max pleaded that he needed to rest. Paula phoned again on Sunday to check he was okay. It was a good opportunity to sit comfortably in his little armchair, and go through the rest of Leila's thesis material. He made notes as he went. She'd been working hard. And had found loads of stuff he didn't know – or perhaps knew, but hadn't put two and two together.

On Sunday evening, he reviewed his notes. Okay . . . she'd found proof that after the Civil War, the Socialist mayor who had saved Diva's beautiful church from being burnt down by the anarchists had been shot by Franco's goons.

What a bunch of idiots, thought Max. I'd have thought they might have shown him a bit of respect when he'd lost an arm to save that church . . . but no such luck.

She'd put together a list of local people shot after the Civil War: more had been executed than had died during the fighting. Another source claimed that most of the bodies had been dumped in *la fosa común,* the communal grave, outside Diva. Leila was pretty sure where the mass grave was located – a ravine off the track to El Fugón.

'So Paula's hunch was right – perhaps Uncle Antonio is there,' Max said aloud.

Leila had been very thorough: she had gone through the land registry to note the changes in titles . . . and boy, oh boy, property in Diva had changed hands rapidly after Franco's victory. Max knew that Republican supporters had sold for whatever they could get before their property was confiscated, but the extent to which a small group of Franco supporters had consolidated their wealth and taken control of local government in the town was a bit of a shocker. And there was his grandfather – right in there. Paula had kept her properties in spite of having two brothers fighting on the Republican side, and grandpa had picked up loads more land on the cheap. So that's where the family money came from, thought Max. Should have realized. How naive can you get? Wonder how much Juan knows?

But there was nothing so far to explain or understand why Leila was killed. Max reread her story on El Gato. She wrote well, he thought, she might have made a good novelist. There was a surprising amount on his family, but then Paula had asked Leila to find out what had happened to Antonio. Towards the end of her notebook, her writing became less legible. It was as if she thought she might be on to something significant, and had to note it all down quickly while it was fresh in her mind. She'd got sidetracked. There were pages on the death of Federico García Lorca. She had made a summary of the facts surrounding his last days where there was agreement between different authors.

1. The exact date Lorca returns from Madrid to Granada is uncertain. But three Granada newspapers announce he is in Granada on 15th, 16th and 17th July 1936. So it's logical to assume he arrived at the

family home, La Huerta de San Vicente, around 14th July. So lots of people knew Lorca had returned to Granada.

2. 17th July, military rebellion begins under General Franco.

3. 20th July, military seize Granada and, with the surrender of el Albayzín on 23rd July, control all of Granada. Arrests and executions of Republicans and Republican sympathizers begin immediately.

4. 6th August, Falangist squad arrive at La Huerta de San Vicente and search the house. Note – but not looking specifically for Federico.

5. 9th August, Falangists arrive again at the house. Mistreat family, beat up caretaker, Gabriel Pérez Ruíz, and take him away for questioning.

6. 10th August probably, Lorca phones the poet Luis Rosales, whose family were prominent members of the pro-Franco Falange, and asks for help. Rosales offers to hide Lorca in his house in Granada, in la Calle Angulo.

Max swallowed. The Rosales house was just round the corner from his office. He had passed it so many times without realizing.

7. Rosales orders the Lorca family *not* to reveal where Federico was hiding. Note – is there confusion over dates? Luis Rosales later claims it was 5th August. But can't be, was probably 10th August.

8. 11th August? Militia arrive at La Huerta de San Vicente, under the command of Ruíz Alonso?? looking for Federico. Luis Rosales claims that Lorca's sister, Concha, had inadvertently blurted out that Federico was hiding in the Rosales' house, and that was how Ruíz Alonso knew where to go to arrest Lorca.

9. 16th August, Lorca is arrested by Ramón Ruiz Alonso, and is taken to the Civil Government in la Calle Duquesa, and handed over to the Civil Gover-

nor. The same day Lorca's brother-in-law, Concha's husband, the Mayor of Granada, Manuel Fernández Montesinos, is shot.

10. 18th or 19th August, Lorca taken to the area of Víznar and shot alongside a lame schoolteacher and two bullfighters.

Max found himself drawn like a fly into the web of uncertainty surrounding Lorca's death. What was Leila going to come up with next?

She had drawn up a number of lists and a diagram.

List One. Who Knew Where Lorca Was Hiding?
1. The Lorca family.
2. The Rosales family.
3. The chauffeur who drove Lorca and Luis Rosales to Calle Angulo.
4. Possibly the caretaker, and the nursemaid, Angelina.
5. Perhaps some close, trusted friends of the Rosales family – but unlikely.

Leila then wrote: 'IT HAS BEEN ASSUMED THAT LORCA'S HIDING PLACE WAS COMMONLY KNOWN, BUT IT WASN'T. The assumption that Lorca's sister had blurted out to Ruiz Alonso or whoever on or around 11th August where Lorca was hiding CANNOT be true. Concha had returned to her Granada flat in la Calle San Antón on the same day Lorca left La Huerta San Vicente on 10th August.'

There was a gap, and Leila had scribbled: 'Recheck dates. Also if Ruiz Alonso knew where Lorca was hiding on 11th August why did he not arrest him earlier? ANSWER – BECAUSE HE DID NOT KNOW. WHO THEN REVEALED LORCA'S HIDING PLACE???'

Max paused. This was all very interesting, but did it have anything to do with her death? Unlikely. Leila was an ambitious PhD student, hoping to prove something other historians had overlooked. So what next? Max turned the page of her notebook. At the top she had written: 'SUM-MARY.WHAT DO WE KNOW?'

Max noticed Leila switched her list notation from numbers to letters. It was the sort of thing he did. He could never explain why:

a. Lorca was arrested by members or ex-members of Acción Popular.

'Acción Popular . . . that was one of the small fascist parties supporting the Franco rebellion,' thought Max.

b. Paula said that Antonio had forbidden her to ever speak to Pablo again because he may have betrayed a friend, and he could no longer be trusted.
c. Paula said that both Antonio and Lorca had friends across the political spectrum. If they were involved in the arts, their politics did not matter.
d. Paula said that Pablo, her husband, had been a member of Acción Popular, and then later had joined La Falange.
e. It looks like the only friend of both Lorca and Antonio who was a member of Acción Popular is Pablo Romero.

Shit, thought Max. I never knew grandpa was in that lot. Oh Sweet Jesus . . . Leila's been shifting stones. This is getting a bit too close to home.

What next? Leila had drawn a diagram of Lorca's friends in Granada with arrows linking connections between them. Antonio knew Luis Rosales; Antonio knew Pablo Romero who also knew Lorca. And then in red ink in a circle next to Pablo Romero's name, Leila had written, 'Acción Popular.'

Max's head had begun hurting again, and the asthma was going to kick in any minute. He took a quick puff of his inhaler. Why had he never tried to talk to his grandparents about the Civil War? Why had it taken a complete stranger to discover things about his own family? Okay . . . . it had all happened more than thirty years before he was born. But you can't decide to forget things like this. Sooner or later history comes back to haunt you. There are always those with a plan to destroy the past. It may even work for a generation or two if they all agree it's best to forget the past. Too inconvenient, too many harsh truths, so best forgotten. But the past never forgets you.

Max took more painkillers and went to bed. Next morning he felt a lot better, more willing to face the truth. In the end, the truth was concrete. He smiled: it was not just Allah's will. There had to be an explanation of what happened to Leila, and why.

Chapter 21

Red wool, red wool,
What are you saying?
Red wool, red wool,
What would you like
To tell us?

Frederico García Lorca, *Bodas de Sangre* (*Blood Wedding*)
in a version by Ted Hughes

Anita phoned early to say she would be staying in Diva to chase up some loose ends. 'I've just got León's report about Leila's mobile,' she said. 'Talk about sloppy work. I don't think he checked anything. There's a couple of things which I need to discuss with you when I'm back in Granada.'

'When will you be over?' Max asked.

'Should be tomorrow. But I'll ring and let you know.'

'Fine. I've got a feeling there's a lead in Leila's thesis notes.'

'Okay. See you tomorrow.'

Max decided he needed some air: he'd been cooped up in his flat for days now. He got a walking pole and gingerly descended the stairs. It was painful, but not too bad.

It was great to be out. A walk down to Plaza Nueva would do him good. The Albayzín, however, is not the easiest place for a man with broken ribs: the steps and cobbled pavements which gave the place so much of its character and beauty now made progress difficult.

Max walked slowly down la Cuesta de María de la Miel to

el Aljibe del Gato, then down la Cuesta de Granados into la Calle del Aljibe de Trillo, and then zigzagged through tiny narrow cobblestoned streets into la Calle de San Juan de los Reyes, and then finally down la Calle del Bañuelo to el Paseo de los Tristes.

The names are pure poetry, he thought. The hill of Mary of the Honey, the Well of the Cat, the Pomegranate Hill, the Street of the Threshing Well, the Street of St John of the Kings, the Street of the Bath, the Path of Sorrows.

He came out on el Paseo de los Tristes at the Arab baths. The restoration work was still going on. Max asked a workman when he thought it might be finished.

'Another six months,' the man replied. 'Every time we move a stone, some expert gets excited . . . and then another expert turns up to examine it. And then they have a fight. It's all over the papers, and we're off site for another month!'

Max laughed: typical Granada. Once you start digging, you hit an eighteenth-century wall. There's something Renaissance under that, then Moorish, and you end up with some Roman temple, which is when the quarrels really start.

Max paused at the bridge, el Puente de Espinosa. Espinosa, he thought. Thorny, prickly, difficult. He looked over the bridge, the ducks below squawking with indignation – not enough water in the river, el Río Darro. It was a sunny morning, surprisingly quiet for an August day. You could usually hardly walk along el Paseo de Los Tristes for the tourists taking photographs of the Alhambra, photographs of each other sitting on la Puente de Cabrera, photographs of each other in front of the view of the Alhambra. And every five minutes, the photographers all had to scuttle to the pavement, then breathe in deeply to let a taxi or a little bus squeeze past. It was a miracle nobody got squashed.

Max crossed into la Plaza de Santa Ana. There was a morning wedding in the church. He smiled. The ladies of Granada did love to dress up. There were some fine dresses on show, shimmering red silk, gold lace, and black linen

237

cutwork. The traditional rose-embroidered shawls were still popular. Lorca would have approved. He paused to admire the smiling bride and groom: he, a little embarrassed, she, proudly showing the wedding ring.

Maybe the family were right. Maybe he should get married and settle down.

Max entered Plaza Nueva, heading for la Gran Taberna. A familiar figure emerged from a bar. Blast, it's Navarro, thought Max, gripping his walking pole tight.

Navarro came up to him, big fist clenched in anger. 'You fucking bastard. I know it was you. Got me suspended. If you think you're going to get away with it, you're fucking mistaken. I've got friends in this city who owe me favours. Watch your fucking back. There'll be an accident one day, a nasty accident. Won't be ribs this time.'

'I don't know what you're talking about,' protested Max.

'You know fucking well. Some fucker shopped me. I know it was you. Now I'm under investigation. You're fucked.'

'It's nothing to do with me. You shouldn't have done what you did.'

'Only doing my duty. Can't make a tortilla without breaking eggs, can we?'

'You can't use the methods you used in Argentina here.'

'What happened in Argentina has fuck all to do with you. You're going to be sorry you ever fucked with me. You're going to have to keep looking behind you every step. One dark night . . . expect an accident.'

And with that he walked away, his anger oozing out like his fat belly over his belt.

Max continued on his way. Should he report Navarro? Would it do any good? Yes, better file something in case anything happened. He entered the Taberna, quivering both from the exertion of his walk and from the threat.

'*Hola*, Max. What the hell happened to you? You look like you need a brandy,' said Felipe, the barman.

'Oh, I just fell. Silly accident. But a brandy and a coffee would be nice.'

Max grabbed some of the papers, and sat at his favourite barrel. He'd overdone it, and was feeling tired out. Both Leila and the anti-terrorist arrests were old news now. Things were going badly in Iraq. There had been a demonstration in Madrid to bring the troops home. 'Final Act in Palestine–Israeli Negotiations,' reported one of the papers. 'There's never going to be a final act to that story,' sighed Max. He got down slowly from the raised chair at the sherry barrel, returned the papers, paid, and hobbled out of the bar.

'Take care of yourself,' called out Felipe as he left.

Max crossed the road to the taxi rank: it would be too much to climb back up to his flat. Once in his flat he felt drained. Navarro was bad news – now he'd have to keep looking over his shoulder all the time. Granada had more than its fair share of problems: drugs, underage prostitution, corruption, people-trafficking, every scam in the book – but fortunately, unlike Glasgow, it had been spared the violence. And thank God for that. There was a lot to do tomorrow. It would be wise to rest for the remainder of the day.

The next day Anita didn't arrive until after lunch. She had gone back to wearing her uniform . . . along with a diffident stiffness.

'I managed to get nearly everything done, sir,' she said.

Max felt like saying, 'The name is Max, remember,' but decided to let it pass.

'Well done. Let's begin with your report. Then we can move on to what I've discovered. But let's have a coffee first.'

'Oh. Sorry, sir . . . Max. Let me make it.'

They sat on the terrace.

'Okay. What have you got?'

'The bank was very reluctant at first. But here's a telephone number for that British family.'

'Great. I'll phone them, and see if they know anything.'

'I checked with Yasmín at the café, Al Andaluz, and she confirms all the times given us by Hassan and Javeed. But she did agree she wasn't with them all the time. Had a siesta in the kitchen. She's not sure for how long – could have been a couple of hours. When she left them they were playing chess, and when she went back in they were still playing chess. So both or just one of them could have slipped out, and she wouldn't have known.'

'Now that's interesting.'

'I didn't manage to speak to Jim Cavendish. He's away somewhere.'

'Yes. Life is just one long holiday for him.'

'I didn't manage to speak to the Diva librarian again, but I can do that later.'

'That's okay. Almost certainly nothing there.'

'I had a long conversation with one of my contacts in the Muslim community. After a lot of coaxing, she gave me the name of the married man who was meant to be keen on Leila.'

'That's really great work. And?'

'Well, I did manage to speak to him. He was very embarrassed. But said Leila had flirted a bit with him, and that was all. Don't know whether to believe him or not, so I'll pursue this one further.'

'Yes.'

'And finally, sir, I managed to get that report out of León. You know . . . the one he did on Leila's mobile. All he did was to list stuff still in the Log History, and the contacts in her address book. He said there was nothing out of the ordinary, so he didn't follow anything up. Apparently González said that was fine.'

'Christ . . . what a bunch of idiots. So they've missed anything she deleted. We need to get copies of her phone bills. Hope she's not on Pay As You Go.'

'Here's the list, sir.'

Max took the list, and glanced at it. Phone calls to Paula and a María J; calls and texts . . . Dad, Juan, Ricardo, Sul G, Jujo, ANG . . .

'Hmm. Not much there. Who's this Sul G?'

'Suleiman Grady. He's the married man, sir . . . Max . . . I spoke to. The one who said Leila just flirted with him.'

'Okay. We'll have to lean on him. He's definitely on our list now. The others . . . nothing really there. Have to check up on those we don't recognize.'

'Have done most of them, Max. María J, for example, is her hairdresser in Granada. The others . . . . I'll give you the report when I've finished going through them all.'

'Good. But is there anything else I could work on with the stuff you've got so far?'

'There's one other thing, sir.'

'Oh. What's that?'

'She seems to have had a lot of contact with Juan.'

'Let me see now. She could have been phoning to arrange when to go over to interview Paula.'

'Might have been, sir. But I think it is something we have to chase up.'

'Yes, of course. We mustn't ignore anything, however trivial it might seem. I'll speak to Juan.'

'Are you sure that's for the best, sir? I can do it.'

'No, no, I'll do that.'

'As you say, sir.'

'There may be a bit of a lead in Leila's thesis notes.'

Max summarized his findings.

'I'm sure it's fascinating, sir. But I don't really see its relevance.'

'It could be crucial. Maybe she's dug up an old scandal. I've noted down the archives where she was working. There aren't many. I suggest we visit these, talk to the librarian or archivist, find out what files she was working on and go through them.'

'But sir, we don't know what we are looking for.'

'That's true. But anything relevant should hit us in the face.'

'I'm not convinced, sir.'

The phone rang. Max went to his study to answer it. He returned a few minutes later, his face grave. 'Bugger. That was Davila: he's just had a call from González – Hassan Khan has disappeared.'

'Disappeared?'

'Yes. He told Zaida he was going out for a coffee, and never came back. That was yesterday morning. The police are treating it very seriously. They've put out an alert, saying he could be highly dangerous. They've phoned Linda, I mean Inspectora Jefe Concha. She's saying he could be on a terrorist action, and if necessary he should be shot.'

'Oh, my God. You don't believe that?'

'I don't know. Davila wants to know if we found anything that might link him to Leila's death.'

'What did you say?'

'I told him that the girl in the café, Al Andaluz, was asleep for part of the time when Hassan and Javeed claim they were in there.'

'But that doesn't mean they left the café.'

'I know, but Davila is assuming one or both of them did. It would be handy for the department if Hassan did it.'

'What should we do, Max?'

'Do? I'm fucked if I know. Sorry, Anita. Just angry at the way everyone seems to want that kid to be guilty.'

'That's okay, Max. If you're around González and León for any time words like that are par for the course. I think we should just carry on with our investigation until they pull us off the case.'

'Yes. You're right. What should we do?'

'I'll go back to Diva and find out what's happening. I'll do those interviews I missed. I'll keep you informed of what's going on.'

'Okay. I'll pursue this thesis line. And I'll try and talk to Juan.'

Max saw Anita out. He stood at the top of the stairs and watched her walk down. On the last step from which she could see him, she turned and waved.

Max went back inside his flat. It seemed empty without Anita. He phoned the operator to get the number of the archives from the Guardia Civil. He then phoned the archivist: the archives were only open 10 a.m. to 12 a.m. It was too late to go round today. Should he phone Juan now? No, best phone Paula first.

After giving a detailed description of the state of his health, and a blow-by-blow account of every visitor, Max finally managed to steer the conversation to what he wanted to know.

'By the way, *abuela*, how did you and Leila arrange your meetings?'

'Arrange our meetings? We did that after each time we met.'

'But if for some reason one of you couldn't make the meeting, what then?'

'What a strange question! We would phone each other, of course.'

'So you didn't arrange things through Juan?'

'Of course not. I'm not helpless. What's all this about?'

'Nothing really. Just curious.'

'Curious? Are you sure that knock on the head hasn't affected you? I may be old, but my mind hasn't gone.'

'I know that, *abuela*. Must go now.' And Max put the phone down hurriedly.

Paula would phone back later to complain about his behaviour. He hoped she wouldn't tell Juan. Max felt drained of all energy. He went to his terrace, and sat staring at the Alhambra hoping it would give him some insight. He just sat and stared. There was bound to be some simple, rational explanation. There were lots of reasons why Leila might phone Juan, there was nothing odd about going to a restaurant in Granada with Juan, and that sweet wrapper . . . dozens of people in Diva probably ate the same mints with the same paper. He stared and stared at the Alhambra, but answer came there none. Was there a connection he had overlooked? He must review the events calmly. Begin at the beginning, and note down everything. He went inside, and returned with a biro and notepad. A fresh notepad. Okay.

1. Juan had been out of sorts – money problems, he says. But could it have been for other reasons?
2. Juan was pale and unusually quiet at the barbecue the Sunday after Leila's death. Could he have known about her death? Unlikely. But why that behaviour?

Max paused . . . yes . . . here was that odd incident with the laundry.

3. Juan put his best white shirt along with other clothes into the washing machine when he got back from Motril. Isabel confirmed that he never did his own washing. Why would he do that?
4. Juan never mentioned a lunch with Leila in Granada until interviewed by León. Why should he mention it? No law against having lunch with Leila. But then why volunteer that he had lunch with Leila? Ricardo, the librarian, had seen them. Maybe he thought that Ricardo would mention it, and if he didn't volunteer that information he might look compromised?
5. The sweet wrapper? It's an unusual wrapping. But a lot of people could have eaten one of those sweets, and then thrown the paper into the ravine. Could have been there for ages. Probably nothing to do with Leila. But then it could be.

What does all this add up to? Bugger all . . . probably. But then?

What to do? Max sat there, his shoulders hunched, a tight band across his chest. A puff of Ventolin. He hardly noticed the sunset over the Alhambra. He nodded off briefly, but then awoke with a start. The phone was ringing. He hobbled as quickly as he could to the phone.

'Max. It's Anita. They've found Hassan Khan. He's dead, took a heavy dose of his medication and slit his wrists with a knife from Zaida's kitchen.'

'Oh Jesus. When and where?'

'Found by walkers on the the path from Pampa to Diva lying under a mulberry tree. Just an hour or so ago.'

'Oh dear.'

'León said he had a photo of Leila in his hand. On the back of the photo he had written HKMA.'

'What the hell does that mean?'

'No idea. Looks like a suicide, Max. Gonzo's in his element . . . proves Hassan killed Leila. He's sent a report to Judge Falcón wanting him to agree that the weight of the evidence against Hassan is sufficiently strong to overcome any presumption of innocence. Oh, Max,' and Anita started crying. 'I'll try and get over tomorrow. Have to go now. We're all still working at the station. González needs me to read over a press statement he's prepared to check the spelling and grammar. He's triumphant. Max, are you there?'

'Yes. I'm here, Anita. Trying to take it all in. Sorry . . . I'm still shocked. Well, at least he wasn't a terrorist. It would be great if you could make it over tomorrow. I need to talk to González again.'

'I'll try and come tomorrow, Max. And take you back to Diva.'

'Thanks. I'm missing you.' It came out without him thinking.

'I'm missing you too, Max. See you tomorrow.'

Max sat down. Hassan Khan, suicide? Could he really have killed Leila? Why the photo? It didn't look good.

I should phone Ahmed, he thought. Before he could do so his phone rang. It was Davila.

'Good news, Max. I mean . . . umm . . . sad news. González phoned.Hassan Khan has been found dead, suicide apparently, photo of Leila Mahfouz in his hand too. What a turn-up for the book. There'll be a full investigation of course. But González reckons this confirms he killed the girl. Remorse and guilt. Good work, Max, showing he could have slipped out of the café for a couple of hours. I tend to agree. Be good news for the force. Keep that bastard from Murcia off our backs.'

'Yes, sir. I heard.'

'You have, have you? Well, what do you think?'

'I wouldn't want to jump to conclusions, sir. Hassan Khan had suffered a terrible trauma in our prison, remember, and he's been mentally unbalanced since.'

'Yes. But you wouldn't commit suicide over that. Remorse and guilt seems more likely.'

'Maybe sir, but there could be other reasons for his suicide, assuming it *is* suicide.'

'Hmm. You're an odd fish, Max. Everyone I've talked to is convinced he killed himself out of guilt for killing Leila. And you're going out on a limb again.'

'I'm just trying to keep an open mind, sir.'

'We're doing that as well.'

'I'm sure you are, sir. But also what about Javeed Dharwish?'

'Javeed Dharwish? What about him? As far as I know he's back in London.'

'No, not that, sir. He was in that café with Hassan. They are alibis for each other. He . . . or both of them . . . could just as easily have slipped out and killed Leila.'

'Yes, but Dharwish hasn't killed himself with a photo of Leila in his hand. A highly symbolic photo as well – looks like blood on her hands.'

'I can't really comment, sir. I haven't seen the photo. But shouldn't we check up on Javeed Dharwish first?'

'Maybe you're right. We should at least question him. But we need a quick result. When are you back in the office?'

'Cabo Guevarra is giving me a run over to Diva tomorrow. I need to speak to Teniente González. I'm still a bit wobbly, so I thought I'd be back in the office for the start of next week.'

'Well, don't malinger too long.'

Max phoned Ahmed. There was no reply. He then phoned Anita.

There was no reply. The phone rang: it was Ahmed. He and Zaida had been to identify the body. It was definitely Hassan.

'He slit his wrists, Max. The police say the only finger-prints on the knife are his, no sign of any struggle nor any other footprints around. Tragic.'

'Will you bury him?'

'Of course. He was sick, killed himself while of unsound mind. Allah the Compassionate would want him buried with a proper funeral. I won't be able to do that today – the police have more forensics to do. So it will have to be tomor-row evening.'

Max wanted to ask whether he, Ahmed, thought Hassan had killed Leila, but this was not an appropriate moment.

'I'll try and be there for tomorrow.'

'That's kind of you. I heard you've had an accident. How are you?'

'Slipped. Much better now.'

Max put the phone down slowly. Okay. Suicide. But does that make Hassan guilty? Not a violent type. And he seemed really fond of Leila, so where's the motive? Gonzo reckons he was unstable all along. So anything could have tipped him – a quarrel? A break-up?

The phone rang. It was Anita. 'Max, I'll be over tomorrow morning, about ten. Really busy just now, so I'll fill you in then. *Chao.*'

Max went and got on with his list of outstanding tasks. He'd have to move fast. The pressure was on to declare Hassan guilty: case closed. He must get in touch with that British family and with Leila's friend, and he had to talk to Juan. Max found the piece of paper with the phone number Anita had obtained from the bank. He dialled it: no reply. He had no phone number for Shona Monroe, Leila's friend, but he did have an email address. She might be back from her trek in Nepal. He sent off a brief request to get in touch with him as soon as possible. Best not frighten her. So he added that it was something to do with her friend, Leila

Mahfouz, and asked her for her phone number: could be a shock to receive an email saying your best friend has been murdered.

Juan? Max looked at his watch. It was time for lunch. He could go to El Duende, and see if he could find out some more about that lunch Juan had with Leila. The last time he'd been there was with dad: the divorce had just gone through, and dad was moving to Barcelona. It was a sad occasion. He'd promised to keep in touch, but the phone calls had got fewer and fewer, especially on Max's part.

It would be nice to see the old git again. And Barcelona was always worth a visit.

Max hobbled into the restaurant and chose a quiet corner table. It hadn't changed much: filled with bull-fighting mementoes – photos of bullfighters, stuffed heads of bulls, bull horns, a picador's round hat, a pike pole, banderillas, the swords, and an ancient red cloak. Max smiled: grandpa and the old owner had been friends, both passionate about bullfighting. Grandpa used to bring him and Juan here as children after the bullfight in Granada. Max had never enjoyed *la corrida* – all the elaborate rituals, and then the uneven contest between the mortally wounded bull and the matador. But Juan loved it. Max got up from his table and went to look for his favourite photo, that of Manolete, el Triste, a bullfighter with a long thin face and large sad eyes, famous for replying, when asked why he never smiled, that bullfighting was too serious a business to smile. Manolete was gored to death.

Max was staring at the photo when the owner, a small, shrivelled man, came over.

'Max, a long time. How are you? And Don Bernardo, your father? And Señor Juan?'

'All fine, Pepito, all fine. Yes a long time, at least a year.'

'I miss Señor Bernardo coming in. But Juan still comes by.'

'How's *la corrida*? Still going?'

'*Sí*. But it's not the same any more. There's women in the

ring. I ask you. But what happened to you? Look like you've been in the wars.'

'Nothing much. Just slipped, that's all.'

Pepito looked at the faded photo, and sighed. 'Manolete, el Triste. One of the best. Spain doesn't produce the likes of him anymore. It's just entertainment now. But Manolete understood. It's something profound, something spiritual. Man and one of the great forces of nature.'

'So you've seen quite a bit of Juan here then?'

'Oh, now and again.'

'Was he here some weeks ago with a pretty dark-haired girl?'

'Let me see now . . . I would have been on holiday then. But Gregorio would have been here. Why don't you order, and I'll call him over. I hope Don Juan isn't . . . in any difficulty?'

'No, Pepito, I'm just trying to do my cousin a favour.'

'Of course, you can rely on our discretion. Your grandfather was a true gentleman.'

Max ordered a *rabo de toro a la Sevillana*, one of the specialities of the house. During the season it was made with the bull tails from the *corrida* in Granada. Gregorio came over. Yes, he did know Juan.

'Can you remember the last time he was here?' Max asked.

'Yes, it was about three weeks ago,' Gregorio replied. 'Don Juan was with a very pretty dark-haired girl – dark, flashing eyes. You wouldn't forget her in a hurry.'

'Did you notice anything else?'

'Not really . . . yes . . . somebody came up to them, an old friend I think, because I remember him kissing the girl on both cheeks.'

That would have been Ricardo, thought Max.

'Had Don Juan and the girl been here before?'

'Not that I remember. Now wait a minute . . . such a pretty girl . . . there was – how can I put it – a bit of gossip in the kitchen. Patricio said he had seen them at La Moraima.'

249

'Could I speak to Patricio?'

'He's here now. I'll get him.'

Gregorio returned a few minutes later with Patricio in tow. Yes, Patricio remembered the girl, a real beauty.

'You'd seen them together before, I believe?' asked Max.

'Yes. I do the odd shift at La Moraima. I'd seen them eating there the week before.'

'Are you sure?'

'Yes. She's not the sort of girl you forget.'

Max finished his meal, lost in thought. He ordered a brandy with his coffee, and then another. Juan had been less than honest. What is it the politicians now say . . . economical with the truth. It was an awkward situation. The police hoped to get the case closed: Hassan guilty of Leila's murder, probably while mind disturbed. Max would be less than popular if he threw a spanner in the works. Was Juan involved? How? It couldn't have been deliberate murder, no. But what if Juan had tried to cover up a fatal accident? There was probably a simple explanation.

Max got a taxi back to his flat. It would be wise to leave his talk with Juan until after Hassan's funeral. There might be more information – something pointing towards Hassan. Max checked his email: there was a reply from Shona Monroe, just back from Nepal. She had left a telephone number. This was going to be difficult.

Max dialled and waited; a Scottish voice answered the phone, perhaps a slight west coast accent. Max explained as gently as he could: there was a gasp of horror, then tears at the end of the line. It took a good five minutes for Max to get round to the question he needed to ask.

'Do you know anything about this man Leila had fallen in love with?'

'No. Nothing, except he was very good-looking. Leila never fell for any man unless he was gorgeous. And yes, he was married. I warned her . . . Oh . . . oh . . . sorry.'

'Just take your time.'

'Thanks . . . can I ring you back . . . I have to . . .'

Five minutes later the phone rang again. 'Sub-Inspector Romero?'

'Yes, it's me . . . can you remember anything else? Just take your time.'

'We spoke very briefly on the phone before I set off. All I got was that she was really keen.'

'Was he British, do you think?'

'British? I just assumed he was Spanish – Leila had a thing about dark eyes. No, we talked as if he was Spanish.'

'Did she say he was part of the Muslim community here?'

'No.'

'So Spanish?'

'I couldn't swear to it – it just seemed obvious he was, and nothing Leila said contradicted that.'

'Anything else you remember that might be useful?'

'No, nothing,' and Shona started crying again. 'Oh. Leila. Oh Leila. She was something special, you know.'

'I know,' Max replied.

Max then called the British family again. Still no reply. He tried again some hours later, but still no luck. He'd better rest: it would be a tiring day tomorrow. He slept fitfully. He dreamt of Juan dragging him back down to Capa in the snow, of Juan laughing when he fell out of the tree, of Juan the star centre forward in the school team, of the endless arguments with neither side willing to give ground, and then of Juan with *el abuelo* – fishing, walking, going to watch *la corrida*. What now?

Chapter 22

Decid a mis amigos
Que he muerto.

Tell my friends
That I'm dead.

Frederico García Lorca, *Desde aquí* (*From Out Here*)

Anita arrived promptly at 10.00. Max was tense after a bad night.

'Max, how are you? You look really tired. Are you sure you should go?'

'Yes, I must. I told Ahmed I would go to the funeral.'

'Really?'

'I'm just going as a friend of Ahmed's . . . I didn't ask permission.'

Anita helped him down to her car. His ribs were aching, and he had a headache. Anita looked at him. 'I'll drive slowly, and we can stop for coffee.'

Max said nothing until they were out of Granada and on the motorway to Diva.

'So what's new?'

'Nothing really, sir . . . Max. It's suicide.'

'Any doubts?'

'No. He took a near fatal dose of painkillers, then slit his wrists with a knife he took from Zaida's kitchen. There's no evidence of foul play.'

'So how are Gonzo and the gang?'

'Over the moon. Everyone's phoning in to congratulate us.'

'So what happens next?'

'Well, the evidence for Hassan either deliberately killing Leila or covering up a fatal accident is only circumstantial. No confession, no eyewitness, no forensics. But with no one else in the frame, it looks like the case will be closed once Judge Falcón has made his report and submitted it to the Juez del Juicio, and the magistrates have agreed. And you, sir, anything new?'

Max carefully detailed his findings.

'That's really awkward. But maybe there's nothing there. But Juan's not come completely clean. If he was having an affair, then he probably wouldn't want to admit it.'

'I know. But what do I . . . we . . . do now?'

'I suggest nothing, sir. We continue investigating until taken off the case. I can understand your concern. He's your best friend and cousin.'

'But they could have quarrelled, and then there could have been an accident.'

'There's no evidence for that. And the affair, if there was one, was probably over – Leila was going out with Hassan, remember.'

'That's true.'

'We'll stop here, you don't look great.'

They stopped at a roadside restaurant, went in and ordered two coffees. Max sat quietly, brooding over his coffee. Anita glanced at him, and then fell silent, respecting his need to think. She finally interrupted. 'I think it's best we wait, Max. Let's not jump to any conclusions.'

'Thanks, Anita, I've come to that conclusion. I think I'm becoming a cop after all – the honourable cop in me says I should confront Juan immediately; but the realist cop in me says he's family, a good friend, probably nothing . . . so wait and see. We'll hold back on Juan. Let's go.'

They got back in the car, and drove to Diva. The pain had

253

eased, and Max felt sufficiently calm to change the subject away from work.

'How's your sister getting on?' he asked.

Anita laughed, 'She falls in and out of love every day. I spend half my time hearing all about her broken heart, hugging her while she sobs, and then next time I phone she's over the moon, just met Mr Right, and heaven is round the corner.'

Max laughed too. 'Youth. You take it all so seriously.'

'And you, sir. You've never been married?'

'Me, married? Good heavens, no.'

'Have you noticed how cops seem to marry other cops?'

'Need someone to understand them, I suppose.'

They entered Diva, and drove straight to the police station. It was buzzing. González was in an expansive mood, his head shining with importance.

'Max, how are you? Fell off a mountain or something, I believe.'

'Something like that.'

'You've been most helpful. The information that Hassan had plenty of time to slip out of the café is invaluable. The jigsaw's all fitting into place.'

'Maybe. Any news on Javeed Dharwish and the others?'

'Oh, yes. Davila said you had suggested we should ask the British to question Javeed Dharwish.'

'Any progress?'

'No. Davila just rang. The local cops are on the case, but I don't see what good that's going to do.'

'Well, he is Hassan's alibi for the time of Leila's death.'

'Yes. But he's not going to tell us the truth, is he?'

Max needed another coffee. 'If you'll excuse me now, sir. I—'

'Of course. You've done well, Sub-Inspector. Got a result.'

Max bought a newspaper from a kiosk, and went to El Paraíso. Got a result, my arse, he thought. What about truth? The paper was full of the coming election. All the opinion polls showed it was too close to call. Any incident could tip the result either way. 'Surely the voters weren't dumb enough to let the PP back in?

Max took his mobile out of his pocket and phoned Ahmed.

'Yes. I'm here in Diva. If you have time I'd like to come round for a talk . . . Now would be convenient. Perfect. I'll be there in twenty minutes.'

Max phoned a taxi and waited, looking up at the twin-towered church that had so nearly been burnt down during the Civil War.

It took less than ten minutes to get to Ahmed's house. Max remembered the last time he was here – the death knock for Leila. And now another tragedy. Ahmed opened the door: he had aged.

'Max, come in. I heard you had an accident. How are you? Mint tea?'

'I'm fine now. Mint tea would be nice.'

Max was ushered into the study. Nothing had changed: the same photos on the wall, the same book on the little table. Everything needed a good dusting. Ahmed returned with the two mint teas.

'How are you keeping, Ahmed?'

'People have been very kind. Your *abuela*, Doña Paula, sent me a letter. She was very fond of Leila.'

'Yes.'

'And I've been busy with the campaign. It helps to keep my mind occupied.'

'That's good.'

'So . . . Max . . . how can I help you?'

'If it's okay with you, I would like to go to Hassan Khan's funeral.'

'I'd welcome that. It's this evening at eight. There won't be many there. Some think I shouldn't be giving a full funeral at all.'

'Thanks. The other thing is . . . the police are convinced Hassan killed Leila. If you feel up to it, I'd really like to talk to you about that.'

255

'Yes. You know I'll do anything I can to help.'

'Thanks. So do you think Hassan could have been responsible for Leila death?'

Ahmed rubbed the back of his hand across his eyes. 'It's all too convenient. But it doesn't feel right. I just don't see why he would have killed Leila.'

'They had a quarrel?'

'Yes. But that's not a motive.'

'I agree. He doesn't seem capable of murder, but then who knows. Can you think of anything he said which might shed some light?'

'Not really. He stayed with Zaida. We used to talk about him. He was very withdrawn, hardly said a word. He was on medication, and that left him lethargic and low. But now and again he would say some strange things.' Ahmed frowned. 'It's best you ask Zaida about that. Djins, revenge, messages from Allah, violent images . . . strange things. And then he would talk to himself, "Whisper it to the wall, Hassan. Whisper it." Followed by "Hassan Khan MA." He was ill, you know.'

'But nothing about Leila?'

'Nothing.'

'Any idea why he had that photo of Leila when he killed himself?'

'No. None. Except that he was very fond of Leila.'

'I know it's dangerous to read anything into the things someone in a delusional state says, but they usually come from somewhere.'

'Yes. But it can be from anywhere – an article in a magazine, a gesture, a childhood memory. And after what happened to him, I'm not surprised. Delusions can give you a feeling of power. So yes, there were threats . . . but don't read anything into them.'

'What sort of threats?'

'Oh, the enemies of Muhammad, Peace and Blessings be upon Him, will suffer for what they have done . . . that sort of thing.'

'What would you like me to do, Ahmed?'

'Do? In what sense?'

'Over Leila's death. The consensus seems to be that Hassan will be found responsible in some way for Leila's death ... possibly just concealing a fatal accident. But then the case would be closed, and there would be no further investigation unless some new evidence came to light.'

'I see what you mean.' Ahmed paused. 'I would like to know the truth. Nothing can bring Leila back. I'm not looking for revenge. I can forgive. Allah the Compassionate has taught me that. But yes, I would like to know the truth.'

Max stood up and embraced Ahmed.

'I'll do what I can. I'd better go now. Have to phone for a taxi.'

'I'm going into town. Let me give you a lift.'

'That is kind.'

They drove slowly into town.

'I have to go to the bank and get some bread . . . can you drop me at the lights?' said Max.

Ahmed stopped at the traffic lights, and as Max was getting out, he said, 'There's one other thing I remember Zaida said. Hassan kept repeating something like, "The Americans, the greatest djins of all, must be hurt." Means nothing, I'm sure.'

Max felt exhausted. He probably shouldn't have come. The funeral wasn't until this evening, and there was not much he could do. He should go and rest in his little *cortijo*, and close his eyes to all the weeding that needed doing. He went to the bank, bought some bread, and walked round to the taxi rank, by the church. It was a bumpy ride down the valley. It was looking parched and grey. All the wild flowers had gone; the rubbish strewn along the dry riverbank was now very obvious. Max got out at his padlocked gates, and turned awkwardly back to the taxi driver.

'Can you help me with these, please?'

'Sure, Max. Heard you'd had an accident.'

The *alberca* was filthy, a quarter full with slimy green

257

water. He'd have to get it cleaned out and filled with fresh water. The trees and plants needed watering. The oranges had long gone, apart from the few left rotting on the bare earth. He walked down the terraces to *el cortijo*. The little flower garden had been taken over by weeds already, some at least a metre high. He'd have to pay someone to look after the land. Another expense.

He pushed aside the blue, wooden beaded fly curtain, unlocked the door, and entered. He hadn't been back for weeks, and it showed: fine country dust had got over everything. He'd have to ring round and get a cleaning lady. It was stuffy inside: he opened all the windows to let in some fresh air. But it was one of those still, hot days, more likely to let in flies than fresh air. But at least there was the view of Sierra Contraviesa from his kitchen window. Fortunately there was some cold water in the fridge: he needed something to drink and then a nap before the funeral. Insects buzzed around the bedroom, but he slept.

The alarm woke him at seven prompt. He took a shower, ironed his clean white shirt, called a taxi, and walked up to the top terrace. The heavy green metal gates were too stiff for him to shut, so he closed them as best he could. Thefts were still fairly rare in this part of rural Spain, so he should be okay. The taxi tooted.

He walked along the dirt track to where the taxi was waiting, and then another bumpy ride to the mosque. He was early, and if he went inside there might be an angry confrontation. Max hung around outside the mosque, trying to look inconspicuous. A few men arrived, glanced at him curiously, and then entered. They were followed by a group of women who also looked at him with curiosity. Nobody said a word to him. When it was nearly eight Max slipped in quietly.

It was a short, simple ceremony. Nobody knew Hassan well. Everybody thought he probably had committed suicide, so the service was subdued. Four men stepped forward and lifted the coffin on to their shoulders. Max thought of the bride's lament in *Blood Wedding*,

> Ay-y-y four gallant boys
> carry death on high.

Max followed the coffin up the hill, past the ancient round church – the site of so many faiths, going back to pre-Phoenician times. Ahmed said a prayer as the body in its white shroud entered the earth. Hassan was buried close to Leila's plain headstone. At the end of prayers Ahmed turned to Leila's grave, and said in a low voice, 'Let him rest in peace near the grave of my daughter.'

Max was the only non-Muslim present, and this time he didn't step forward to throw a handful of earth on the grave. He walked back down the hill: nobody talked to him. But nobody had been hostile.

He should talk to Zaida soon, but now was not appropriate. He'd better phone Paula: she'd be sure to hear he was in Diva and would be upset if he didn't get in touch. But Max still did not want to meet Juan. It would be impossible not to say something to him. No avoiding it though. Max took out his mobile, and phoned Paula's house. Isabel answered.

'Max, how are you? Where are you?'

Max explained as briefly as he could, then asked, 'How's Paula?'

'A bit under the weather. But she's been worried about you. Hang on . . . I'll put you through to her.'

'Max, *mi querido*, where are you?'

'I'm in Diva.'

'That's wonderful. Come for dinner. Dr Muro caught five nice trout, but it's too much for us today.'

'But I don't have my car.'

'Isabel can drive over to get you. Juan's away on business.'

'But she's busy . . . I can get a taxi.'

259

'No, Isabel will come and get you. She's just ready to start cooking . . . so I can do more potatoes while she drives over.'

'That would be very nice.'

'Well, Isabel's cooking tonight, so it won't be up to the usual standard. I'm so pleased you're coming. She'll be with you in half an hour . . . No, I'm fine – old age, you know. At my age bits of you start going wrong. I feel a lot better now I know you'll be here.'

Max smiled. Isabel was actually quite a good cook, but Paula could never admit that. And at least he wouldn't have to confront Juan. Isabel arrived within the half-hour. She chatted happily about the children as she drove back along the Jola road. But when Max asked about Juan, she frowned.

'Out of sorts, I'm afraid. At least out of sorts with me. We're going through a bad patch right now, Max. I suppose . . . I know he hasn't been completely faithful, but I've learnt to ignore that.'

'Men fool around sometimes. But he's devoted to the children.'

'I don't think it's that this time. Something is getting on his nerves. He's bad-tempered with the kids, and that's very unusual.'

'I'm sorry to hear that, Isabel.'

'Let me help you out.'

Max rested on Isabel's arm, and walked slowly up the driveway to the front door. The door opened, and Paula came out wrapped in a large shawl.

'What are you doing out of bed? The doctor said you had to rest,' scolded Isabel.

'I feel better already. Max, how are you? I've been so worried about you. I asked Juan to drive me to Granada, but he said you mustn't be disturbed.'

'I'm a lot better, *abuela*. A lot better.'

'Come in, and let me hear exactly what happened. Juan says you had an accident, but I don't believe it.'

Max felt like a little boy again. Whenever he had tried to

lie to Paula to hide something, she used to brush his hair back, peer at his forehead and say, '*Sí*. I can see it now. *Mentira*, lie – written clearly on your forehead.'

Max went in with Paula holding on to his arm, and he holding on to Isabel's arm. He was hungry now. Isabel had fried the trout in butter, and there was a garlic and almond sauce for the grown-ups, mayonnaise for the children. Encarnación bounced on to Max until he had to complain that his ribs hurt. She wanted to know why he had sticking stuff on his head and why she couldn't use him as a punch-bag. She laughed when he said he had fallen.

'Silly billy, how can you fall and hurt yourself in two different places?'

Max explained how he fell on a rock, hurting his ribs, and then fell backwards, hitting his head on another rock.

'That's difficult to do. Look . . . if I fall that way, then how can I then fall another way,' she said, demonstrating the difficulty of doing just that. She had Paula's insatiable curiosity.

'Well, I just did, so there,' stated Max.

'Hmm. *Tito* Max, I think you're fibbing. *Mentiroso, mentiroso, mentiroso*,' she laughed, and skipped out to join her brother who was watching TV.

Max laughed as well. That girl will go far, he thought. She will be very pretty as well. When the meal was over, Isabel went to the kitchen to clean up, and Paula came and sat by Max. She brushed his hair back, and looked at his forehead. Max smiled and then told her what had actually happened.

'Max, it's too dangerous being in the police. There are plenty of other jobs you could do.'

'Teaching, you mean,' laughed Max. 'These days that's as dangerous as police work.' And to change the subject, he said, 'The local police think they have made some progress on finding out who killed Leila.'

'What has happened?'

'You heard about the young man who killed himself on the path from Pampa?'

261

'Yes, he was one of Leila's friends and he was arrested and treated very badly. Zaida told me that when I met her in the market.'

'Well, the local police think he killed her.'

'Could it have been an accident? I hope it was an accident.'

'*Abuela*, I don't really know.'

'What do you feel?'

'I don't really know . . . and I've probably told you too much already.'

'You need to find the truth.'

'You're looking tired, and I'm feeling tired. An early night for us both, I think.'

'You should stay here tonight, Max. The guest room's made up.'

'Thanks. I will.'

For the first time in days Max slept through the night until woken next morning by his mobile ringing. Max stretched out for it.

'*Dígame.*'

'Hi, Max . . . hope I didn't wake you.'

'Hi, Anita.'

'There's been another development. A woman has come forward . . . says she saw Hassan on the Jola road. González reckons that wraps up the case.'

'But how can the woman be sure?'

'Says she just saw the photo of Hassan in the local paper with the news of his suicide. The paper speculated about his possible involvement in Leila's death. And that jogged her memory. I think we'll be off the case in a couple of days at the most.'

'Okay. Juan's away. Can you drive me back to Granada?'

'I'll have to check, but I think so. If I don't ring, I'll be round in an hour or so. Oh – and I managed to talk to Ricardo, the librarian. Nothing . . . just a few more details on her research. I'll tell you about that later. *Chao.*'

Encarnita skipped into his bedroom.

'I've got a postcard. Look. It's from my friend Jane. She's English. She'll be back soon. They're driving all the way from England.'

'Can I see?' said Max.

Encarnita handed over the postcard. It was a picture of two bears. Max turned it over, and read aloud. 'Dear Encarnita, Be in Diva next week. Daddy and Mummy are going to drive all the way across Spain, and I will be going to school with you in Diva. See you soon. Jane. PS. How's David? Still naughty?'

Max looked at the postmark – five days ago. That's why nobody answered the phone. He'd have to return and talk to them as soon as they were back.

'Thanks, Encarnita. That's a pretty card.'

'She's my best friend. We've each got a teddy bear, and they're good friends as well.'

'That's nice.'

'Jane can speak English and Spanish.'

'You must learn more English.'

'Yes. Yes. No. No. Uncle. See I speak English. Why do you speak English as well as Spanish, *tito*?'

'My mother – your *Tía* Flora – is Scottish, and they speak English in Scotland. So I grew up speaking English and Spanish.'

There was a meow outside the door.

'That's David. He wants some milk,' said Encarnita.

'Okay. Give me a kiss first.'

Encarnita kissed him on both cheeks before running off.

Max had a shower, dressed, and went down for a late breakfast. Paula was waiting for him, looking pale and in pain.

'I'll get you breakfast, Max. Sleep well?'

'Like a log. But let me help. You don't look well.'

'I'm getting these pains in my leg. The doctor's giving me painkillers, but once they wear off the pain comes back if I try to walk or stand for too long.'

'In which case I'll get my own breakfast, and I'll bring you a coffee.'

'No, I can't have that. Men shouldn't be in a kitchen. Do you know, Juan sometimes has to cook for himself.'

Max laughed. '*Abuela*, I thought you had become a bit of a feminist.'

'It's just I don't like having a man in my kitchen. Your *abuelo* never went inside it, you know.'

'Times have changed.'

'I know, but I still like some traditions,' and with that she went into the kitchen, returning some minutes later with a tray of toast and peach jam, and two large cups of *café con leche*.

'I made this last week from our own fruit.'

'Lovely. *Abuela*, I've been thinking about that leg of yours. You must have it checked by an expert. It could be you're needing a hip replacement.'

'Dr Muro never mentioned that.'

'I know . . . which is why you should ask him to make a hospital appointment for you. I'll go with you, if you want.'

'Oh, dear. I suppose I should. I would hate it if I couldn't walk.'

There was a car hoot outside the house.

'That will be Anita,' said Max. 'I have to return to Granada.'

'So soon. Invite her in for a coffee.'

Max went out, and returned with Anita, looking shy. But within a few minutes she was telling Paula all about her sister. Max left to collect his things. When he returned Paula and Anita were in deep conversation.

'We are discussing you, Max. Anita says you don't look after yourself properly. I told her you never really did, and I was just telling her about the time you had a black eye, you remember . . . from that bully at school, and you painted both eyes, pretending to be a Red Indian.'

Anita laughed. 'We'd better go. Thanks for the coffee.'

'Come round again soon. I can tell you so much about Max. He was always in trouble as a boy, so many scrapes.'

Max and Anita both kissed Paula, and left.

'Remember, get that leg seen to,' called Max as he turned to wave goodbye.

'She's quite something,' said Anita as they left Diva on the winding road down to Granada.

'Yes, she is,' replied Max. 'Well . . . what did Ricardo say?'

'Not much. But Leila phoned about a week before her death to thank him for giving her the contacts for the Guardia Civil archive. She thought she had found something important which might throw some light on Lorca's and Antonio's deaths.'

'Did he say what?'

'No. And he never heard from her again.'

'I'll have to get into that archive and see what I can find.'

'You still think it might have something to do with her death?'

'Don't know, but worth checking. By the way I found this scrap of a sweet wrapper on the bank near where Leila was killed. Could you give it to González for me?' said Max handing over the plastic bag with the silver-coloured wrapper in it.

Anita took the bag. 'Shouldn't you have handed this in immediately, sir?'

'Yes. But I forgot. Looks like it's been around for a while.'

'Okay, sir. Oh, Max. González told me as the case is over, there's no more need to go to Granada. This will be my last trip.'

'Could you do one more thing for me: let me know when that English family return.'

'Sure.'

Max gazed out of the window as the car sped on its way to Granada. He finally broke his silence. 'I've really enjoyed working with you.'

'Me too, sir.'

No more was said until the car turned the corner on to the old Murcia road. Max coughed. 'Perhaps we could have dinner together some evening?'

'That would be nice.'

And they fell silent again. The car turned into the Albayzín before Max ventured: 'I'll ring you sometime about that dinner then?'

'Yes, do that. I'm looking forward to it.'

'We could go to El Duende. It's not all bulls' tails. They do really nice chicken.'

'El Duende sounds fine.'

Anita kissed him awkwardly on the cheek before saying goodbye.

Oh, thought Max.

Chapter 23

La nina va en el columpio
De norte al sur,
De sur al norte.

The girl on the swing
Goes from north down to south,
From south up to north.

Frederico García Lorca, *Columpio* (*On the Swing*)

After another good night's sleep, Max felt his energy beginning to return. He decided to go round to the archive of the Guardia Civil as soon as it was open. The archive was in the basement of an old building in one of the older parts of the city, El Realejo. Max walked to the Albayzín car park, cleverly concealed under a public garden. He got in his car, drove slowly down to Gran Vía, and just before Plaza Nueva, turned round the enormous statue of Isabel la Católica y Colón, giving her blessing to Christopher Columbus, into El Realejo.

The tide of building restoration had finally now reached this area. There was scaffolding everywhere as seventeenth- and eighteenth-century mansions metamorphosed into apartments and hotels. Max glanced briefly at the fresco portrait of Isabel la Católica on the façade of the Dominican church – this time with love-rat husband, King Ferdinand. Max stopped the car, and parked outside an important-looking building marked *La Guardia Civil*. A clerk finally answered the bell at reception, and agreed to contact the archivist working in the basement. Five minutes later, a youngish woman emerged, still wiping her hands on her overall.

'Sub-Inspector Romero, I'm Penélope Díaz. What can I do to help you?'

Max explained about Leila's death, and what they knew about her research.

There was a gasp of dismay. 'I didn't know. I've been away on holiday. She was such a lovely, lively girl. She was going to be a good researcher. What a waste. What an awful waste.'

'Do you know what she was looking for?' asked Max.

'August 1936, of course. She was so lucky to be here just at the right time.'

'So how did you work?'

'The archive only recently opened, and we've just started cataloguing, so the whole thing's still a real mess. It's going to take years to get it sorted. So Leila would just work through each box and list the contents. She was such a help. Oh dear . . . this is so sad.'

'Did she find anything?'

'Yes, actually . . . she thought she had struck gold. There was some good stuff . . . she was really excited.'

'So what had she come across?'

'There were some real gems . . . lists of orders to shoot people . . . material from some of the prisoners who were shot . . . last letters that were never delivered . . . poems.'

'A gold mine then.'

'Absolutely.'

'Anything on Lorca?'

'Not directly, but there was stuff on some of his friends.'

'Did she think there was anything which would add to our understanding of Lorca's last days? The question of who betrayed him?'

'Well, that would be finding the Holy Grail.'

'Her thesis notes emphasize the role of members of Acción Popular. Did she find anything on that?'

'I don't know. Unfortunately I was going on holiday, and the archive was closing for three weeks. I let her take home some boxes so she could work on them while we were shut.'

'Really?'

'I know you're not meant to. But she signed out for them, and the deal was she would catalogue the stuff for us, and return them when we reopened. I was going to call her to find out how she was getting on. Do you have the boxes?'

'No. We don't. Have you any idea where she might have taken them?'

'No. As I said, it was just before I went on holiday. I knew she was staying in Diva.'

'We've gone though all her things at her father's house, and they're not there.'

'Maybe she kept them somewhere in Granada. She sometimes stayed overnight in Granada. I know that because we went out for a meal together one night.'

'You don't know where?'

'No, afraid not.'

'Could I see the part of the building where she was working?'

'Of course.'

Max followed Penélope down a flight of dingy stairs. They came to a heavy door with large brass handles. Penélope took her keys out and opened the doors to a cavernous room. She flicked a switch. The electric bulb flickered for a while before casting a dim, yellowy light over boxes, stacked high to the ceiling.

'I think this used to be a wine cellar.'

Max looked round him. 'How did Leila know where to begin?'

'Well, things are more or less stacked by year. But that's not guaranteed. And the Civil War period is the worst of all. We need to go through the contents of each box – and half of it doesn't match the year on the label. We're a long way from computerizing any of this. 1936 is roughly over here.'

269

'It's such a jumble . . . difficult to know anything is missing,' commented Max.

'Very much so. I should have her signing-out slips somewhere here. We put it in an exercise book. Yes, here it is.'

She showed Max the book. He opened it. The only entry was in Leila's hand, '5 Boxes of 1936. 17/07/2003. Leila Mahfouz.'

'Tells us nothing,' said Max.

'Sorry . . . it was my last day. And I wanted to get away early. So I just let her take the boxes with this entry. Can't tell you any more.'

'Thanks. You've been really helpful. I'll get them back to you as soon as possible.'

Max drove to his flat: his ribs were fine. As he entered the flat, the phone rang, and he almost had to run to pick it up in time.

'González here. Just to let you know – that sweet wrapper you found at the scene of the crime matches some mints in one of Hassan's pockets. Great work.'

'Any fingerprints or anything on it?'

'No, nothing. Been in the open too long. But it's unusual. The mints are from Morocco. And there aren't many of those around. If we put everything together, the arrow of guilt points straight at young Hassan. Sending everything to Falcón today. I'm sure he will then send it on to *el Juez del Juicio*, and with a bit of luck he'll pass it on to *los magistrados*. They'll find the evidence conclusive enough to close the case.'

'Bit hasty, I think. Anything on Javeed Dharwish?'

'No. Nothing. Top brass want a result. There's not much doubt about it. We'll be having a big press conference soon. It's important you're on the top table for that one so we can officially thank the cooperation of the Granada police.'

'I'll see what can be done.'

Not much time left, thought Max. His phone rang again.

'It's Anita. Have you heard the news?'

'Yes, Gonzo phoned.'

270

'Just to let you know – the English family are back.'

'I'll be over as soon as I can.'

'Do you want me to fetch you?'

'No. I should get back to driving myself now.'

'Be careful.'

'Don't worry. I will. I'll come over this evening when it's cooled down. I'll give you a ring. *Chao*.'

Max was thirsty. He also needed something to eat. He went to the fridge. He still had some of the goodies that Juan had bought: the cured salmon looked tempting. He finished his meal, and was just about to take his siesta when the phone rang.

'Bonila here. You've heard the news, I presume.'

'*Sí*, Teniente González phoned.'

'Yes. Good work, and congratulations. Teniente González said your assistance had been invaluable. We're always pleased to help. The Teniente said you still thought he might be a bit hasty. We really do need a quick solution to this case. There's been a lot of media coverage. And it will help our force with the Navarro business. So you're our man for the press conference. Get us some glory. And emphasize the friendly cooperation between the Granada and the Diva police forces, such cooperation being the sign of the times – terrorism and all that.'

'We don't know it's connected to any terrorist plot.'

'But it could be. And we need to stress that investigation is still ongoing. Inspectora Jefe Concha phoned to emphasize that.'

I bet she did, thought Max. 'I'll do my best, sir. But I still think we should interview Javeed Dharwish first. Any news?'

'We've been in touch a number of times with our British counterparts. But for all the cooperation they give us, we might as well be talking to a brick wall.'

'We should say there might be a terrorist link.'

'We've done that already. But as long as they think they're safe, they're quite happy to let potential terrorists wander

271

the streets of London. So I don't think we can wait for them to find Javeed Dharwish.'

'I understand your point, sir. But I still think we are rushing things a bit.'

'We have to, Max. That bastard from Murcia is due next week.'

'Okay, sir. I'll go to Diva this evening, and see what help I can give.'

'That would be useful. The sooner everything is wrapped up the better from our point of view.'

Max put the phone down. If Hassan were declared responsible for Leila's death . . . well, that would certainly help Navarro.

After a long siesta, Max drove slowly over to Diva. He stopped twice for a break and a coffee. It was best not to push his luck. As he entered Diva he smiled with relief: his ribs had passed the test. He drove straight through the town, and then out along the Jola road. He stopped at a small *cortijo* with a large garden in the front. A little girl was playing on a swing, from north to south, from south to north. Max opened the gate, and walked along the gravel path. As he passed the swing, he called out, 'Hello. You must be Jane. I'm Encarnita's uncle.'

'Yes, I'm Jane. Encarnita said she had an uncle who was a policeman. Can I be of help?' she said with the stiff, formal politeness that only the English have.

'Yes. I'd like to talk to your parents.'

'Follow me. Mummy, Daddy, Encarnita's uncle wants to talk to you.'

A blonde Englishwoman appeared with gardening gloves and secateurs.

'Hi. I'm Mary,' she said extending a hand for a handshake.

'Sub-Inspector Max Romero. Encarnita's uncle. But I'm here on official police business,' said Max.

'My goodness. Official police business. I'm sure we've paid all our taxes and bills.'

272

'I'm sure you have,' laughed Max. 'No it's just a few questions about a Leila Mahfouz who was killed not far from here.'

'Leila? Dead? My goodness. I can't believe it. I'd better call my husband. Do come in.' She ushered him through the front door. 'Tom, Tom,' she called. 'Come quick. It's the police. Some dreadful news. Jane, you go and play.'

'Can't I come and listen? Leila was my friend.'

'No, you go and play in the garden. Can I get you a cup of tea, Inspector?'

'Sub-Inspector. Yes. I'd love a cuppa.'

'Oh, Tom. Have you heard? Leila Mahfouz is dead. You know, Ahmed's daughter. I'm just going to make a cup of tea. Take the Sub-Inspector into the dining room.'

Max followed Tom into the dining room, and sat in one of the armchairs. Mary returned with three cups of English tea. Max sipped his appreciatively. 'Fabulous, proper English tea.'

'Yes. We always bring some with us. You can't seem to get good tea anywhere in Spain,' said Mary.

Max looked at both of them. 'Sorry to spring this on you. It was in the English papers.'

'No, we never saw anything,' said Tom. 'I just can't believe it. Such a lovely girl. She and Jane got on well. Do you know what happened?'

Max explained what he knew. He didn't say the likely suspect had committed suicide. Instead he concluded, 'She was killed on the day you left for England. It could be close to the time you might have left. So we need to know if you saw anyone, saw anything suspicious.'

'No. Nothing. Can you remember anything, dear?' said Tom turning to his wife.

'No. It was belting down with rain, remember, when we left. But Jane was in the garden just before the rain came down. She might have seen something. I'll call her in. Jane! Come here, love.'

Jane came in, clutching a teddy bear, her face smudged with tears.

'Mummy, Mummy,' she cried, and threw herself on Mary sobbing. 'She was my friend. She made me laugh.'

'It's all right, love. Mummy's here. Encarnita's uncle would like to ask you a few questions.'

Jane dried her eyes, and turned to Max. Max smiled at her. 'I've heard a lot about you from Encarnita. What's your teddy called?'

'Max,' she replied.

'Max?'

'Yes, Encarnita called him Max because he's so soppy.'

'Hmm. Can you remember the day you left for England? In fact just before you left?'

'Yes. I was in the garden playing. And then Leila walked by. I remember it because she sang this poem.'

'Poem?'

'Well . . . silly words about me. She didn't stop, walked by.'

'Can you remember anything else?'

'No.'

'Anything at all? It could be important.'

Jane frowned with concentration. 'I went inside. Mummy kept calling me to get ready. Then I came out again. And then I saw Encarnita's car. I ran to the gate because I thought Encarnita had come to say goodbye. But the car didn't stop.'

'Encarnita's car? But she doesn't have a car. Are you sure?'

'Encarnita's mummy's car. The car her mummy drives when Encarnita comes to play.'

'Oh,' said Max, and just sat there thinking. 'But Encarnita had gone with her mother that day to the coast?'

'I know. Encarnita had come round to say goodbye the day before. But I thought she had got back, and was coming to say goodbye again.'

Max sat in deep thought. Everyone looked at him waiting. Finally he said, 'Thanks, Jane. You've been a real help. Nothing else?'

274

Jane shook her head. Max stood up, and shook hands with everyone.

He turned to leave when Tom suddenly said, 'Wait a minute . . . there is something. I remember it now. It was really bucketing with rain. And as we turned left off the Jola road for the Málaga coast road we saw this figure. Remember, dear,' he said, turning to Mary. 'We commented, odd to be out in weather like this, and no umbrella.'

'Yes. I remember now,' said Mary.

'Did you see who it was?' asked Max.

'No. It was raining so heavily I could hardly see out of the car. But I'm pretty sure it was a man.'

'Wearing?'

'Sorry. It was just a glimpse. And all we could see was a figure.'

'I saw him too, Mummy.'

'Okay. You've been most helpful. If you or Jane can remember anything else please let me know. Just ring me any time on this number.'

Max got into his car and drove to the Jola bridge. He stopped on the bridge, got out, and looked down the ravine. Could Jane have been wrong? Not likely. She would know Encarnita's car well, and it was not a common one here in Diva, an old Volkswagen Beetle.

The day Leila died, Isabel had taken the children to the beach at Nerja. Of course . . . they would have taken Juan's car for a long drive. Which meant that Juan had the Beetle for the day. So it could have been Juan in the car. Juan? Oh Christ. I'll have to talk to him now. Max took his mobile out, and phoned Anita.

'Anita, I'm in Diva. No . . . the drive over was okay . . . Look, could you do me a favour? Could you get me a copy of Juan's statement, the one he gave to León? First thing tomorrow morning will do. At my *cortijo*. You know where it is? . . . Good. *Gracias*.'

Max shut his mobile. He looked at his watch: it would be dark soon. He was in no mood to confront Juan just now. He

275

returned to the car, and drove down to his *cortijo*. He needed a puff of his inhaler. The drive over had taken more out of him than he originally thought. Tomorrow was another day, so eat, a glass of wine to relax, and then bed.

Chapter 24

Strong gongs groaning as the guns boom far . . .
Don John of Austria is going to the war.

G.K. Chesterton, *Lepanto*

Max was still in his boxers when Anita rang the bell. She smiled when he opened the door.

'Blue definitely suits you,' she said.

Max laughed. 'Put the kettle on. I'll go and get dressed. I didn't expect you quite so early.'

'No. I went in really early to photocopy León's notes. I assumed you don't want León or Gonzo to know.'

'That's right. There's stuff I should check up on. And I wouldn't want to spoil their day of glory, would I?'

Max turned, went into his tiny bedroom, and returned fully dressed. Anita was in the kitchen, waiting for the kettle to boil.

'Tea or coffee?' she called out.

'If you're having a coffee I'll have one as well.'

'Nice place. Your electric plug's wonky though.'

'I know. When I get some cash I'll rewire. Trouble is, when I start I won't know where to stop. The roof's the major problem. Lets in every drop of rain.'

'My father would have thought this was heaven. He really missed his little plot. It must be lovely here in spring.'

'It is. You must come and stay sometime.'

Anita didn't reply.

'Okay. Here's the coffee. I've got the papers in my bag,' she said. 'So what's it all about?'

Max explained about the car. 'It's probably nothing, but I thought I should double check Juan's alibi.'

Anita looked at her watch. 'Fine. Have to go. Meant to be in at nine.'

'I'll give you a ring later,' said Max.

Anita rummaged in her bag, and took out a couple of photocopies, and handed them to Max. '*Chao.*'

Max got out his notepad, began reading, and noted down the exact times and locations in Juan's testimony. When he had finished, he went to his bookcase and took out a photo album. He looked through the album until he found the most recent photo of Juan: it was one taken at a family barbecue.

Max drove through town, and then turned right to take the road down through the mountains to Motril. He felt so anxious he hardly noticed the warm sunny day, or the mountains towering above the road winding through the narrow gorge. Soon he was on the plain, where *chirimoyo*, avocado and tomato sellers lined the road to Motril. Max turned into the car park of the huge supermarket close to the disused sugar factory. He looked at his notes: Juan said he had driven to the Motril supermarket after lunch to buy things for Sunday's barbecue. He had arrived at the supermarket at around four, and left about four thirty. He had a coffee and a read of the papers for about half an hour. Then he drove back to Diva, arriving home after six. Leila died at five in the afternoon. Juan had no firm alibi except he was driving alone back to Diva.

Max entered the supermarket and found the manager. Max explained as little as possible of the background, only that he wished to talk to all the checkout girls who had been on shift that afternoon.

'The supervisor will have to juggle staff around a bit – so it could take a few minutes,' the manager said. 'You have a coffee, and I'll bring the girls to the café.'

Max walked into an open-plan café with plastic chairs and

coffee to match. He made the mistake of ordering a Danish pastry, which had been hanging around the counter for too long. He looked again at the photo of Juan, smiling next to the barbecue. The manager returned with three girls in tow.

'Sorry for the delay,' he said. 'It was difficult to rearrange things so they could get away.'

The girls sat down at the coffee table, Max showed all of them the photo of Juan. They looked at the photo carefully, and then they all shook their heads. One of the girls turned to the manager. 'It was the afternoon shift and some of the girls only work afternoons.'

'That's true,' said the manager. He turned to Max. 'If you come back at about three, I'll arrange for the afternoon shift to meet you.'

They left. Max went up to the counter to pay, and showed Juan's photo to the girl. No, she couldn't remember ever seeing him. She called over the other girls in the café. No, they had never seen him. Max was not surprised. Juan was a food and drink snob: he would never go into such a place and risk their so-called coffee. Max left: there was time to go down to the harbour, and have some nice fresh fish for lunch. He drove slowly down to the harbour, and gazed at the tankers moored on the horizon waiting to dock.

Max chose a restaurant with a view of the sea across the sands. The beaches were almost empty. Motril didn't get many tourists. After lunch, Max returned to the supermarket. He risked another plastic coffee while he waited for the manager and the checkout girls to come. He had just finished it when the manager entered with five girls this time.

'This is everyone who was on afternoon duty on the day you were asking about,' he said.

Max showed them the photo. One by one they shook their heads. The final girl stared at the photo and paused.

'I see so many people,' she said. 'I can't be sure. But I do notice the handsome ones. I'm sure it's him. He made me think of Antonio Banderas, the actor. He also made me laugh: a really silly joke, but it was funny.'

'Can you remember the time?' asked Max.

'Now . . . I started a little after three – I was late that day, my little girl wasn't well and I had to drop her off at her grandmother's. It's quiet then, and I'm pretty sure he was my first customer. So I'd say about three twenty. I wouldn't want to be more precise than that.'

Max glanced at his notes: Juan claimed he left the supermarket after four to go for a coffee.

'Thanks,' he said. 'You've been really helpful.'

If Juan didn't go for a coffee here, where would he go? Juan liked his coffee freshly ground and preferably Costa Rican. There were a couple of good cafés in Motril. He would probably go to the closest, Café Puro. Max walked into the old town and found the place he was looking for. It had jars of coffee beans from around the world on display. Max ordered an organic Costa Rican. A pretty girl brought it to him.

'Excuse me, *señorita*, but have you seen this man? He's my cousin, and I'm trying to trace him.'

'Could be,' she said. She looked at Max. 'He's a bit like you, isn't he? I remember him. He was a little flirtatious, and we had a bit of a conversation. He seemed very nice, charming really.'

'Any idea of the time?' Max asked.

'Well, I go off at four so it must have been before then. Yes, I remember we left at the same time, and he opened the door for me, and made some joke or the other.'

'Thanks,' said Max.

'I hope he's not in any trouble. He was really nice.'

'No, no. Nothing like that,' said Max.

Max got up, and left. So Juan could have left Motril about four. Max looked at his watch as he set off to drive back to Diva. He was at the scene of Leila's death in forty-five minutes. It could be done in less: Juan was a better and much faster driver than he was. Max got out of the car: he felt sick and asthmatic. He looked down the ravine, and brought up

280

the bad coffee and bits of his lunch. He wiped his face, and puffed on his inhaler.

Shit. Shit. Shit. He stood there, staring over the edge of the ravine. What the hell do I do now? Ahmed wants to know the truth. But how much is the truth going to cost? It could kill Paula. 'What if I just keep quiet? Leila's dead, Hassan's dead. What is there to gain? There's no real evidence. None.

Max drove back to *el cortijo*. He no longer wanted to stay in Diva. The anonymity of a city would be welcome: you could drown your sorrows with complete strangers in Granada. Max looked round the *cortijo*. What a mess. He'd forgotten to find someone to water the orchard and keep the weeds down. Give it all a good soak now and hope there was no serious damage done. The weeding would just have to wait. He phoned Juan on his mobile.

'No. I'm fine. Should be back at work soon . . . Where am I?' Max paused. 'I'm in Granada. Oh. You'll be here tomorrow . . . Let's have a meal together then. How about La Moraima at nine? Tomorrow at nine then.'

Max then phoned El Duende, and asked to speak to Patricio. Yes . . . he would be on duty in the Moraima tomorrow evening.

Max went into the garden, and walked up to the top terrace, then scrambled under the *alberca*. He turned and opened the valves to let the water out. It came out slowly, running along the tiny trenches that fed the water to all the trees. The earth was thirsty: it would need watering again soon. When he had finished, Max shut off the valves. The *alberca* was filthy, but he wasn't up to cleaning it out. Next trip. He returned to the *cortijo*, packed his bag, shut the windows, and carefully locked the doors. He left by the side gate, walked along the irrigation canal, brushing the laden fig tree, and then turned left to his front metal gates. He tried to pull them shut, but they were stiff, slightly buckled around the frame. His ribs began to hurt, but gritting his teeth he gave a strong pull, and the two gates came together.

He slid the bolt across, put the padlock on, and got into his car.

He arrived in Granada as night began to fall. He needed something to eat, and something strong to drink.

Max parked his car, and then walked into the centre of town. There was a maze of bars around the cathedral. He chose one at random: full of tourists. Nobody would know him there. He sat at the bar, ordered a plate of Güejar ham and a glass of brandy, Solera Lepanto Gran Reserva. The barman gently warmed the balloon-shaped glass over a candle, and then tipped in a generous measure of the brandy. Max was pleased the bar treated the brandy with the respect it deserved. He cupped the glass in both hands, swirled, sniffed, and sipped appreciatively. The warm glow went down his chest into his stomach. He asked the barman to leave the bottle of Solera Lepanto by him on the counter.

The Battle of Lepanto, he thought. Where Don Juan of Austria defeated the Ottoman navy, and stopped the Turks moving further into Europe. Don Juan of Austria. Oh Juan, Juan. Don't be involved.

Max poured himself another glass, just the right amount, the brandy not spilling when he tipped the glass horizontally. He held the glass in both hands, staring for inspiration at the amber liquid. A tourist came and sat by him at the bar.

'*Una cerveza, por favor,*' said the tourist in an unmistakable English accent.

'Where are you from?' Max asked him in English.

'Oh! You wouldn't know, a place in Yorkshire, called Pontefract, not far from Leeds.'

'I do,' said Max. 'Pontefract cakes . . . love them when I can get them. Your first trip to Granada?'

'Second. We did a day trip from the coast last year, and now we're here for a week. Going on to Almería on Friday – if I can drag Chris and Heather away from the shops.'

'So you're enjoying it?'

'Brilliant. The girls have gone to the flamenco ballet at the Alhambra theatre. *Blood Wedding*, it's called.'

'Yes – I'll be going myself next week.'

'The girls are dance-mad, so it's perfect for them. And I get a night's peace.'

'Can I buy you a drink?'

'Thanks . . . one of those small glasses of beer, please.'

'A *cervecita*?'

'Grand.'

The man from Pontefract was a Leeds supporter. He and Max gossiped about football and what to do in Granada, for the next hour. The soft, smooth brandy went down so well that Max scarcely noticed how many he was knocking back. It hit him when he stood up to go to the toilet.

'Oops – overdone it,' he said to the man from Pontefract.

'Not surprised.'

He called the barman over to ask for the bill. '*La cuenta, por favor* . . . My God. How much? It's a fortune.'

'It's one of the best brandies, eight euros a shot.'

Max paid, shook hands with the man from Pontefract. 'Have a good holiday. Make sure you get to see the monastery of Cartuja – it's amazing.'

Max zigzagged his way to the Gran Vía, and hailed a taxi. The taxi dropped him off at his flat. He climbed the stairs unsteadily, pausing now and again, finally managed to get his key in the lock, and fell on top of his bed.

He awoke the next morning with the sun streaming in through the unshuttered window.

'Ugh . . .'

Max went to the fridge, and took out a litre of water. He gulped the water down until he had to stop for breath. He stripped off his sweaty clothes, turned on the cold water in the shower, and stepped under the spray. He just stood there and let the water run over his head, and down his face until he no longer felt groggy. He returned to the kitchen, picked up his clothes and put them in the washing basket. Stark naked, he went on to the terrace and let the sun dry him until he could cope with the thought of toast. Juan had a lot of explaining to do.

For the rest of the day, Max pottered around the house. He had let it go again. As he worked though his chores he listened to some more Handel: his two favourite counter-tenors, David Daniels and Andreas Scholl. Very different styles, so difficult to choose between them, but maybe Daniels had the edge. He tried his new novel, the latest Donna Leon. Somebody should write a detective novel based in Granada, he thought. It's as dramatic a setting as Venice, and almost as corrupt. Maybe I should have a go one day.

But it was difficult to concentrate on the housework, the music or the novel. His mind kept coming back to Juan. He had never been much good at standing up to his cousin. But this time he couldn't wimp out.

At eight thirty he had another shower, combed his hair, put on his best summer jacket and walked down to the Moraima. He hadn't eaten there for a while. Max rang the bell on the ancient wooden door.

'I booked a table for two . . . the name's Romero,' he said.

'Of course, Señor Romero.'

The door creaked open.

'Can you give me a quiet table in a corner?' he asked the immaculate young woman. 'But with a view of the Alhambra.'

'I'll see what I can do,' she replied. She returned in a minute. 'This table's reserved. But you can have that one over there,' she said, pointing to the end of the covered terrace.

'That would be fine.'

'You can wait here,' she said. 'Can I get you something to drink?'

'Yes. I'll have a *fino, una manzanilla de Sanlúcar.*' Max liked the slightly salty tang of this light, dry sherry.

She returned with the pale, straw-coloured sherry. Max held it up to the moon before sipping it. 'Wish me luck,' he said to the waitress.

She smiled back at him. Max looked around: at the pictures on the wall, one of Federico García Lorca laughing with his friend, the composer, Manuel de Falla; at the Roman and Moorish artefacts. So much of Granada's history here. It was in this very house that Moraima, the wife of Boabadil, had lived when she was exiled from the court in the Alhambra.

Juan arrived late as always.

'Max. Good to see you on your feet again. How's it going?'

'Almost fully recovered. But can't rush things. What will you have?'

'What you drinking there?'

'A *fino, manzanilla de Sanlúcar* actually.'

'Ah. Okay in Sanlúcar. But not really for Granada. But a *fino* sounds nice. I'll have a *Tío Mateo*.'

They sat exchanging pleasantries until the waitress came over to say their table was ready. They went to the far corner, and ordered.

'This is on me,' said Juan. 'I know that police salary of yours doesn't stretch very far. And I'm celebrating – I've got an offer for that damn mill in Resina.'

'Great. Who is it?'

'A Granada property company . . . want to buy all five flats – and if we can sort out the taxes, I should make a decent profit. It's a relief, I can tell you. I was beginning to hit serious cash flow problems.'

'That's great,' said Max. He turned to the waitress, 'What do you recommend?'

'They're all very good, sir. The sea urchins are very fresh, collected last night. The Rota-style sea bream is good. And the ice creams are fabulous.'

'Okay,' said Max. 'I'll try that.' He looked at the menu, 'Give me the olive oil ice cream.'

'I'll have the sea urchins as well,' said Juan. 'Followed by the roast lamb with almonds and honey, and a sherry ice cream.'

The wine waiter came up, 'To drink, sir?'

'With the sea urchins . . . two more *finos*, yes? The same again, Max?' Juan scrutinized the wine list. 'Look, they've got a great red, a Syrah/Merlot, from Bodegas Señorío de Nevada. That's José Pérez Arco's vineyard. He's really come on in the last few years,' he explained to Max. 'You'd like his Green credentials: no pesticides and herbicides.'

'Sounds great,' said Max. 'On my salary I couldn't afford him, but as we're celebrating, and you're paying . . .'

The wine waiter returned with the bottles. He uncorked the red, poured a drop in Juan's glass. Juan swirled it around, sniffed, and drank slowly.

'Perfect,' he said. 'Lovely fruit aroma, blackberries and coconut.'

The waiter filled his glass, then filled Max's glass. He left, and returned with the two *finos*. The waitress arrived shortly after with the sea urchins. Juan took one look, and moaned.

'I should have guessed. Nouvelle cuisine. What the hell is that on top?'

'It looks like chocolate sauce,' said Max.

'*Por Díos*, what will they think of next? The sea urchins should be raw – just with lemon. I think all these celebrity chefs are going to ruin our healthy eating habits.'

Max laughed.

They sat and talked about food, about football, about politics.

'If the bloody Socialists get in, my taxes will go up,' said Juan. 'And they would let in thousands of these illegal immigrants from Africa. We're a Christian country, not Muslim. Culturally, we just don't mix.'

'Juan, are you really that dumb?' protested Max. 'Here we are, sitting in the house of Moraima, looking up at one of the greatest Moorish buildings in the world, surrounded by food, drink, buildings, even words, from the Moors, and you say we can't mix.'

'Hmm.'

'And of course you used their cheap labour for the mill conversion . . . and that's what's paying for our meal.'

'Okay. Okay. Always the bleeding heart liberal.'

The main courses arrived.

'At least they haven't put any artistic swirls of chocolate on these,' said Juan. 'Mine's good. How's yours?'

'Good. The bream's really fresh. I like it. I wonder if all those Yanks in Rota ever try this?'

'Doubt it, that base of theirs is a little piece of America plonked down on the Spanish coast. More wine?'

'Thanks. Did you know, there's a load of Phoenician remains there, and they won't allow our archaeologists in to dig? American territory, they claim.'

'You know what the Yanks are like. Always need to be top dogs. But it's sensible we're supporting them. Might get some money out of them,' said Juan.

The waiter from El Duende arrived with the two ice creams.

'*Hola*, Patricio,' said Max, and then to Juan he said, 'You two know each other, I believe.'

'Good evening, *señor*,' Patricio said. 'Remember me? I served you in El Duende when you were with that really pretty girl. I also served you and her here. Pretty girl.'

Juan flushed, shot a glance at Max, and hastily said, 'No I don't remember. Two brandies, Gran Duque de Alba, to follow, please.'

They ate the ice creams in silence. The friendly atmosphere, the easy banter ended. The waiter returned with the two brandies. Max looked at Juan, waiting for him to break the silence.

'All right, I did have a meal here with Leila,' he said. 'Nothing wrong with that.'

'Nothing at all, said Max. 'Only there's much more than a meal . . . isn't there?'

'What do you mean?' Juan retorted angrily. 'We happened to be in Granada at the same time. No harm in inviting her out for a meal.'

'None whatsoever. But we've checked her mobile. She seemed to have phoned you pretty frequently.'

287

'So what? She phoned me to arrange her meetings with Paula.'

'That is not what Paula told me.'

'What the hell? Have you been checking up on me?'

'Juan, I just want to know the truth.'

'The truth. The truth. What's truth?'

'I'm staying for an answer.'

'Max, what the fuck are you insinuating? That I had something to do with Leila's death? The police have got the killer, that young Muslim guy who topped himself.'

'Could be. I just want to hear your story.'

'Max, there's no story. I went out with her, that's all.'

'Not just a meal then. Went out with her?'

Juan laughed, a short, grating laugh. 'Max, you know me. Never could resist a pretty girl, and she was really pretty.'

'Yes. But you haven't told me everything, have you?'

Juan, his face perspiring, looked round the restaurant. 'I'll get the bill. I have to go now.'

'Juan, I'm not leaving you until you tell me what happened. We can talk somewhere else if you prefer?'

The waiter arrived with the bill.

'Okay. We can go to my office. It's not far, in la Calle de San Juan de Dios.'

As Juan paid, he said to the waiter, 'Could you order a taxi?'

They left in silence, and waited in silence outside for the taxi, Juan's face pale in the moonlight. Juan remained silent throughout the taxi ride. Max made no effort to talk. Juan paid the taxi, and they walked up three flights of stairs to his Granada office.

'Coffee, Max? I've got some of the real stuff.'

'Please. Black.'

They sat facing each other.

'Well, what exactly do you want to know, Max?'

'As I said, the truth about Leila and you.'

Juan looked Max straight in the eye; only his voice betrayed any tension. 'Okay. Things haven't been going too

288

well between Isabel and me lately. Then along came Leila, wanting to interview Paula. We got talking, and, well . . . we went out together a few times here in Granada.'

'Juan, come on. It's me, Max. You can be straight with me. You never just went out with a pretty girl for a talk on art and architecture.'

'Well, a bit more than that. Nothing serious.'

'Juan, we have the evidence you took her to a restaurant at least twice. I can check round the town. I just prefer you to tell me.'

Juan fell silent, and stared at the coffee stains on his carpet.

'Is this a police investigation?' he finally said.

'Not yet,' replied Max. 'Just tell me the truth.'

'The truth, the fucking truth,' yelled Juan. '*Los magistrados* are going to declare that kid guilty, close the case, and all you want is to cause problems by asking me about my affair with Leila.'

'Affair?'

'Yes, a fucking affair,' screamed Juan, his face turning red with anger.

They both stood up, and started yelling at each other.

'You stupid bastard,' Max yelled. 'You are in deep shit.'

Juan stopped yelling. 'Do you think I don't know that?' he retorted, putting his face in his hands. 'Max, I wanted to come forward, but I just couldn't. Think of the family.'

'Juan, I'm thinking of her death.'

'Death? It was nothing to do with me.'

'I've done my investigation work.'

Juan looked up at Max. 'I didn't kill her, Max. I didn't kill her. I didn't get home until after six.'

'Let's start at the beginning, shall we? So you were having an affair with Leila. For how long?'

'Had an affair, Max. I ended it. But we had been seeing each other for quite some time. But we only got together in Granada.'

'Here?'

'Here. Hotels. And a weekend in Seville. I really cared for her, Max.'

'You were going to leave Isabel? Your wife didn't understand you, I suppose.'

'Leila asked me to, Max. I wanted to. But I couldn't leave the kids. She kept asking. She said we could go and live abroad. But I couldn't. So I said we had to stop seeing each other.'

'And?'

'Oh God . . . She was furious, really lost it. It started to get nasty.'

'Okay. And the day she died?'

'The day of her death . . . I've told the police all about that.'

'I know you have Juan. And it's not the full truth. I would just like to hear the truth from you.'

Juan bit his lip, and hesitated. 'Well, as I told León . . . I drove to the Motril supermarket to get some things for the Sunday barbecue. Did that, had a coffee, then drove back, and got home after six.'

Max sighed. He was going to have to drag every last bit of information out of Juan, and the more he did so the worse it seemed for Juan. Truth will come to light; murder cannot be hidden long, he thought.

'That's what you told León. Now how about telling me what really happened. Juan, I've checked with the supermarket in Motril: I can prove you were there an hour earlier than you claim in your statement. I can prove you left Café Puro at four, and I have an eyewitness that your car was seen on the Jola road at about 4.45 p.m.'

Juan turned pale, he gulped nervously, then exploded. 'You sneaky little bastard, you little shit. You've been checking up on me, haven't you? Me, your cousin. Your best mate since we were kids. I—I—'

Juan moved towards Max, his fist clenched. Max stood still, offering no defence. Juan drew his fist back, and then let it fall by his side. Max stepped up to him, and took him in his arms.

'Juan, Juan . . . what have you done?'

290

They sat down again, facing each other.

'I'll tell you what I think happened, Juan. Correct me if I'm wrong.'

Juan nodded his head.

'You went to Motril. Yes. But you got there earlier than you said in the statement. So you finished your shopping before three thirty – the girl on the till remembers you, said you looked a bit like Antonio Banderas and you made one of your usual bad jokes. You then went to Café Puro for your coffee. The waitress says you left when she finished her shift at four . . . so you could have been on the bridge with Leila around the time she died.'

'You've made a thorough cop, after all. I never thought you would.'

'So you drove back fast to dodge the storm. But the rain came down before you got home, and you saw Leila on the bridge.'

'Yes. I did. I stopped. It was bucketing down. I wanted to talk to her again. But I didn't kill her, Max. Honest I didn't.'

'You got out of the car, and then quarrelled?'

'No. She got in the car – out of the rain. We had an awful row in the car. Then we both got out. She threatened to tell Paula, tell everyone, things she had found out from her research.'

'Her research?'

'Yes. About *el abuelo.*'

'Grandpa? Was that sufficient reason to kill her?'

'Max, I swear on Encarnita's life I didn't kill her. I got back in the car and left. When I left her, she was alone on the bridge. That's the truth.'

'I don't know whether to believe you. You haven't been exactly straight with me. What about your clothes? When I arrived at the house on Sunday, Isabel complained to me that you'd put your best white shirt in the washing machine along with all your other clothes. Is that because they had mud on them when you clambered down the ravine to see if Leila was dead?'

291

'No. They were soaked through, that's all. The rain had stopped just before I got home, and I didn't want Isabel going on and on about my sodding shirt. You know what she's like.'

'Juan, what sort of idiot do you take me for?'

'It wasn't like that, believe me. Leila begged me to go away with her. I said I couldn't. And we got out of the car into the rain.'

'And then what?'

'We both lost our tempers. She's a bloody wildcat . . . . said she'd tell Isabel everything. I could have lived with that. But then she threatened to tell Paula, and the whole bloody world, that she'd found evidence that grandpa betrayed Lorca, and shafted Antonio as well. That would have killed Paula, Max. It would have killed her.'

'Juan, I think you're telling me the truth now. But to a cop it looks bad, very bad.'

'I know. I didn't want the affair to come out. And once I delayed . . . then all the evidence pointed at me. And the more I delayed the more the arrow pointed straight at me. I was trapped.'

'And the sweet wrapper?' '

'The sweet wrapper?'

'Yes. You gave me a mint wrapped in a distinctive silver paper. I found a fragment of that paper, close to where we found Leila's body.'

'I'm fond of mints. Got a taste for them, that's all. El Café Paraíso gives them out with every coffee. Anybody could have dropped that mint paper.'

'If you didn't kill her, then who did?'

'Well, the police think it's that Muslim kid.'

'Too convenient for the police, for everyone. Where's the motive?'

'He was very keen on her. Leila told me . . . said she needed a younger man, and had a beautiful one keen on her. I assumed she was joking.'

'That's no reason to kill her.'

They fell silent, Juan anxiously looking at Max.

'Juan, I just don't know what to do.'

'What good would it do if I came forward now? Destroy the family? Kill Paula? Leila's dead. Hassan's dead. Won't do anybody any good.'

'But I'm a cop now, Juan. I don't know any more.'

'Sometimes the truth harms the good, Max.'

'I know. I know. Maybe Leila was just winding you up on grandpa?'

'Never thought of that. I've got some of her research here. She used this office to work in sometimes. I put it in the cupboard over there.'

'Have you looked at it?'

'No. I haven't. Not my scene.'

Max got up, walked to the cupboard, and opened the door. Inside were five boxes – the boxes she took from the archive.

'Could be she found something among these,' he said. 'I'll take them with me, and go through them, and then return them. I won't say where I found them at this stage. Have you got a big bin bag?'

'Should have. Let me look.'

Juan returned in a minute with a large plastic bin bag.

'You always were the historian in the family, Max. Me, I prefer to forget the past.'

'If you do that, the past will come back to haunt you,' said Max, putting the boxes in the bin bag. 'I'm exhausted.'

'Here, let me help you. I'll drive you home. My car's not far.'

Juan took the black bag, and they walked down the stairs, out of the building and round the corner to Juan's car. Juan put the bag in the back seat. Max got in beside him.

'Max, I swear to you I didn't kill her. It looks bad, I know. So bad I can't see anyone believing me if I say I'm innocent. You've got to believe me.'

'You've always had a gift for concocting stories. This time, I do believe you. But that's because I've known you all my life. Who else will believe you?'

Juan stopped the car outside Max's apartment. 'Let me carry this up for you.'

When they got to the top of the stairs, Juan said, 'What will you do?'

'Do? I don't know. For the moment, just sleep.'

Chapter 25

Max awoke early. He sat up, put the pillow up to support his back, and watched the sun stream through the half-opened shutters. He watched the light dance on the floor tiles, move across the room on to his bed, and then stroke his face before finishing its ballet on the bedroom wall. Max sang softly to himself:

> 'I Danced on a Friday
> When the Sky turned Black,
> It's hard to Dance with
> The Devil on your Back.'

And what a devil, he thought. What the hell do I do? Juan was at the scene of the crime, he had the motive, he had the opportunity, and he lied. Except he swears he didn't kill her, swears he left her alive on the bridge. Anyone but Juan, and I wouldn't believe it. Would a judge believe Juan? Unlikely. But could Juan still be lying? No, I've known Juan all my life. He's a convincing fibber, but he's never maintained a lie when it really matters.

Max went into the kitchen to make himself a cup of black coffee. He looked at the bin bag on the floor, took out the boxes of files and put them on the kitchen table. He made his coffee, and sat at the table, lost in thought. I can't do anything before Paula's birthday treat. If Juan was arrested it would kill her. There must be more evidence . . . one way or another.

Reaching that decision made Max feel a bit better. He took a shower, dressed, had a slice of toast and another coffee, and then sat down to go through the boxes of files. His task was easier than he expected: Leila had catalogued the material in each of them. He took out the papers on which she had catalogued the material, and started to read the list. His heart suddenly clenched: there, in her neat handwriting, was 'Journal of Antonio Vargas, presumed shot near Diva, August 1937.' Max took out all the material from the box corresponding to the catalogue list. And there, among piles of paper, was a small black notebook; mouldy, the cover stained with damp. Max opened it. It started with a poem. There were twenty-eight completed poems and some drawings. The second last poem was 'On the Death of Federico García Lorca'. Max read aloud in a faltering voice:

> 'The cypress and the cedar weep
> But the moon sings loudly.
> He is here. He is here.
> And the sun is pale with rage.'

The poems stopped. Then there was a letter:

Querida Madre y Paula,
    It was wonderful to see you. You are both more beautiful than ever. I am well, and in good spirits. I made my way safely to the hut, and hope to get to the coast. There are some things I should explain to you, and I may not see you for a while. I told you that Luis Rosales, the poet, came to see me on the evening of 13th August last year. It was an unexpected pleasure, as our lives had gone in such different directions. We talked about this and that, mainly our poetry. He finally told me that Federico was hiding in his family home and had asked to see me. We arranged I would go to the Rosales' house the next evening, after dark, about midnight. Luis would be waiting to let me in. Federico and I talked for over an hour. He remembered you both with affection, and wished you every happiness. He had finished another play. He told me it had started as one of his Granada comedies – *The Nuns of Granada*. But given

his circumstances he had changed direction completely, and it is now a full drama . . . *The Guns of Granada*. Art and life are very strange. It's his most political play, perhaps his only political play, he said. He hopes that one day it will be performed here in Granada, but he decided not to tell the Rosales family about this play. They had been very kind to him and he did not wish to make things more complicated for them.

I have to tell you . . . Federico was frightened something might happen to him. He asked me to give the play to Manuel de Falla, and ask him to get it out of the country. I promised to do that. We embraced, and that was the last time I saw Federico. As I was leaving he said, 'Antonio, if anything happens to me get in touch with Pablo Romero – he's a relative of the Archbishop. Nobody here would do anything if the Archbishop opposes it.'

I left. I hid the play under the floorboards of my rented room. I never managed to hand the play over to Manuel de Falla. I went to see Pablo, and told him that Federico was hiding in the house of Luis Rosales. I told him that Federico felt his life was in danger, and that if he was arrested, he wanted Pablo to go straight to the Archbishop and use his family connections to plead for his release.

Two days later, a group from Acción Popular arrested Federico. I'm sure it was not a coincidence. I saw Pablo in the street before I left Granada, just after the rumours had started that Federico had been shot. We talked briefly. I asked him if he had gone to the Archbishop. He said he had not, as the Archbishop hated Lorca and wouldn't lift a finger to help him. He claimed that just even asking the question could have compromised all of us . . . you, his own family and me. So he didn't even try. What a coward! But he thought he was being very prudent. He then had the damned cheek to ask if he could become engaged to you, my little sister. I was so angry . . . I told him that as long as I remained alive he would never marry you.

Paula, I'm sorry if you thought I was being capricious when I wrote to you and said you should not see Pablo again. I should have explained this earlier, but I did not wish to cause you further distress. Please forgive me. I underestimated your strength and firmness of mind.

A further thing you should know. Pablo went away for a few days. When I saw him again he became threatening and said, 'Watch out that you don't go the same way as Lorca. I know where you're staying.' I left my room that night, and moved out to Armilla where I laid low for months. Many people I knew disappeared. A friend warned me I was on a list of those to be arrested, and it would be dangerous if I stayed. So then I did my night walk over the mountains, and turned up at our house in the middle of the night, and spoilt your beauty sleep.

I've nearly eaten all the cakes you gave me, so I really need to get to the coast soon. The pâtisserie in Motril is no match for my mother's cakes, but the food in Morocco is meant to be very good. They have old Andalusian recipes, which the Moors brought back from Granada. I hope to spend a few months in North Africa, and come back as soon as it is safe. I will buy you both some pretty Arab silver earrings, and you will be the talk of Granada when these adventures are over. I hope Federico's play will be found. It's under the floorboards of the house on la Calle Boli, just behind el Aljibe del Peso de la Harina.

I hope this letter reaches you safely. Antonio.

Max turned the page. It was harder to read . . . as if it had been written in the dark.

Banjaron Church. They arrested me last night. I struggled and tried to escape, but they hit me with their guns. I may have a broken shoulder – it hurts so. It hurts so when I try to write. They are herding up people, mainly peasants and workers, and locking them here in the church. The priest has been offering to hear confessions. I wonder if it's the last confession. I refused. The Church hasn't lifted a finger to help any of us. I don't want to be blessed by those hypocrites. Everyone imprisoned here in the church is so brave. El Gato and Chico are here, and we have talked a lot. They are determined to try and escape to fight on. I've been trying to keep spirits up by reciting poetry. I've even got them singing. But I fear the worst. One of the young guards, a kid called Pepe, has been kind. He and Chico had been play-mates. He will try to get this book to you.

   May God help me.

This was followed by a poem.

> I have in my hand
> a mountain, an otter's skull, an ancient tool.
> This stone on this church floor
> is what remains to me of life . . .

Max rubbed his hand over his eyes and mouth. He loved his grandpa, but this . . . He went on to his beloved terrace. This . . .? He found it hard to believe. He knew there were dreadful times when neighbour killed neighbour, friend betrayed friend. But his grandpa . . .? He couldn't credit it.

Max wiped his tears away with the back of his hand, and looked up at the Alhambra. The fairy-tale palace, built by slaves, over a torture chamber. It was ever thus, he thought sadly.

He returned to Leila's cataloguing. He had almost finished when he read a catalogue item: 'Diva and District: list of those recommended for arrest'. Leila had then added to her catalogue: 'One name was added by hand, that of Antonio Vargas.' Max opened the last box. It was a mass of papers, each headed 'Republican or Republican Sympathizers', fol-lowed by lists of names. He ran his eye over the papers until he found the one headed 'Diva – Republicans to be arrested and shot'. Under that was a note, 'Use all means necessary to find the whereabouts of the following.' There then followed a list of names, all typed. At the bottom of the page, writ-ten in ink, someone had added the name of Antonio Vargas. Could it be grandpa's handwriting?

Max paused. Paula should have Antonio's notebook: she would love to see his poems again – maybe the family could get them published. The Lorca story was tough. But there was no real evidence that grandpa had betrayed Lorca – Antonio could have been completely mistaken.

Perhaps there was no need for betrayal: most biographers of Lorca just assumed it was common knowledge where Lorca was or that his sister Concha had blurted it out to the soldiers on their last visit, looking for Federico at La Huerta de San Vicente or . . . the options were endless. But Leila seemed on to something. Could Paula take it? Yes. She would be so overjoyed at getting Antonio's notebook that she might overlook the few paragraphs at the end. And they could always be explained away. Yes, give Paula the notebook. But the list of names? No.

Max carefully put the list back into the pile, then stopped. He took the list out again. It would be safer just to destroy it. He went outside again to the terrace. It's not just the Alhambra, he thought. Almost everything beautiful in this town . . . you don't want to ask too many questions unless you can cope with finding something nasty about where the money came from to build it. We burnt nearly all the Arabic manuscripts in Granada. God knows what we lost then. No. That list is part of this city's history. I have no right to destroy it.

He went inside, carefully put the list back among the papers and returned them all to the box. He looked at his watch. Time for lunch. He walked up to el Mesón el Yunque in Plaza de San Miguel Bajo, and ordered the clams. They were as good as ever, but he felt very low. He picked at his meal. And there was still Juan. A decanter of the house red might help. But the sadness didn't leave him as he walked back down past el Mirador San Nicolás, busy with hopeful young folk looking for romance in this most romantic of cities. But it's a romance full of sadness, he thought. Of what might have been rather than what is.

He awoke the next morning, thinking of Anita. After breakfast, he put the boxes back in the black bag, carted them down the stairs and into his car. He drove to the archive of the Guardia Civil, and asked for Penélope Díaz. A dusty Penélope appeared.

'Ah. Sub-Inspector Romero. What can I do for you this time?'

'I found the missing boxes. Leila had left them in a friend's office in Granada.'

'That's good. Thanks a lot.'

'I wonder if you could do me a really big favour . . . I came across the notebook kept by my *abuela*'s brother. It would mean so much to her if she could keep it. He disappeared in 1937.'

'It's not mine to give away.'

'*Mi abuela*, Paula, is eighty-three. If you could lend it, I can return it to the archives eventually.'

'Let's compromise. Give me a photocopy, and I can put a note saying the original is with the family. My husband's great uncle disappeared in the Civil War too, so I know what it all means. The lack of closure can be so hard.'

'Thanks. I appreciate that.'

She smiled at him as he handed over the black bag with the boxes. 'Do you know what happened to Leila?'

'Not yet, but I'm expecting an announcement very soon.'

'That too needs closure,' she said. 'It must be terrible for the family.'

Max returned to his flat. He must phone Ahmed soon. He was in the middle of having a bite to eat when the phone rang. It was Davila.

'Max, excellent news. Judge Falcón has considered the . . . um . . . evidence, and decided to send his file to *el Juez del Juicio*. *El Juez*, after reviewing the evidence, immediately sent the file to the magistrates. Apparently the Minister phoned the magistrates to make a quick ruling. And they have just ruled that, given the weight of the evidence taken together, Hassan Khan was probably responsible for the death of Leila Mahfouz. They can't decide between murder or . . . um . . . covering up an accident, but the case has been archived.'

'So the case is closed?'

'Yes. Bonila has ordered you off the case. So that's the job done. Good work, Max. There' s a press conference coming up in Diva. Bonila wants you there.'

'Of course, sir.'

'We've told Navarro he's certain to be reinstated. Oh – and expect a phone call from Inspectora Jefe Concha. She wants to know if you think there still might be . . . um . . . a terrorist connection. The election's very close, you know.'

'I really can't say, sir.'

'Okay then. You've done a good job, Max. It won't go unnoticed.'

Shortly after, the phone rang again. It was Linda.

'Max. How are you? Heard about your accident.'

'I'm fine now, thanks.'

'Great news about Hassan Khan. We're going to give it maximum publicity. I want to emphasize a possible terrorist connection. Got anything that might help?'

'Nothing really. I had tried to persuade González and the department to wait until we had news about Javeed Dharwish. But no joy – they're all keen to get this out as quickly as possible.'

'Sure. That's understandable. We should meet again soon. Give me a call if you're ever in Madrid. I know some great restaurants. Have to rush.'

Then González rang to confirm the time and place of the press conference in Diva. Max immediately phoned Ahmed and arranged to see him.

He carefully wrapped Antonio's notebook, its fragility a reminder of the fragility of life. He checked his best uniform – it was still clean, but could do with a press. He put the notebook and his uniform along with a clean set of clothes in the small suitcase, and went down the stairs to his car. He was not looking forward to the press conference. He would just have to bite his lip, and praise the Diva police for their brilliant detective work. He drove straight to Paula's. He got there in time for lunch. Paula was back in good form.

'Max, I've had some wonderful news. Lunch is almost ready, but I want you to be the first to know. Let's sit on the terrace.'

'Well, *abuela*. What is it then?'

'Remember I told you I'd made contact with Beatrice – you know, El Gato's daughter – and she said she might have some more information on Antonio? Well, I sent her that photo of Antonio. I didn't hear anything . . . then this morning I got an email. Chico, her uncle, was in hospital and she's only just been able to show him the photo. But he was able to tell her about Antonio, himself and El Gato . . . and Beatrice wrote it all down for me.'

'That's amazing. I've got something to tell you as well. But you first.'

'Antonio . . . didn't get away. He was shot in Banjaron in 1937. But he died well.'

'So what happened?'

'El Gato and his brother *Chico* were arrested in Banjaron, and locked up in the church there, along with Antonio and about twenty others.'

'So that's what happened to him.'

'*Sí*. Antonio kept everyone's spirits up by reciting poetry and telling stories. He made them laugh. He even got them all singing. Antonio had a little black notebook. He said it was his life in there. Chico says Antonio thought he had been betrayed.'

'Betrayed? Did he say who by?'

'No, he didn't. He said someone had also betrayed Lorca. Neither Chico nor El Gato had the faintest idea who Lorca was. Well . . . after a few days in the church, one of the guards, a young, decent kid of seventeen, warned them they were to be shot the next morning. Antonio gave the boy his notebook, and asked him to get it to his sister, Paula Vargas, in Diva.'

'Oh, gosh. That's amazing.'

'I never got it of course. Antonio had been hurt during his arrest. But he said El Gato and Chico were young and fit, and if he created a diversion they might stand a chance of getting away.'

'That was courageous of him.'

'*Verdad*, Antonio made a run for it when they came to put them all on a truck, and during the confusion Chico and El Gato managed to escape. They heard shots as they were running – Chico thought it was the soldiers shooting Antonio.'

Paula suddenly burst into tears. Max got up, and put his arms around her.

'*Está bien*,' she sobbed. 'At least I know now he's dead. He died bravely, didn't he?'

'He did,' said Max.

'That means he's probably buried in that secret grave outside Diva. I'm going to ask for permission to dig it up. Could you help me get, you know, one of those experts who can identify people from their bones? I forget what they're called.'

'Forensic anthropologist. Sure, *abuela*, sure. Now close your eyes, and let me get you my surprise.'

Max went outside and returned with the notebook, carefully wrapped. He put it on Paula's lap.

'You can open your eyes now,' he said.

'You are a rogue,' she said. 'You know how I love surprises. What's this? *Qué* . . . Max – it isn't. It is. It's Antonio's notebook. *Ay*, I can hardly believe it,' and she burst into tears again. 'Oh Antonio. It's his poems. I can't believe it.'

'You can thank Leila,' said Max. 'She found it in the police archive. The young soldier never managed to get it to you, and it ended up in the files in Granada.'

Max went over and hugged Paula again. 'I think we should try and get the poems published.'

'*Sí*. You'll stay the night, won't you. I'm so happy.'

'Of course I will, *abuela*. But let's have lunch now. I've got to go and see Ahmed soon.'

'I'll just sit here and read the poems.'

Max left, and drove to Ahmed's house. Yes. He was right not to give Paula that list of names. Over mint tea, Max told

Ahmed about the plans for the press conference, and that it looked like the case had been closed because, in the opinion of *los magistrados*, Hassan was the only person involved in Leila's death.

'I was expecting that,' Ahmed replied.

'Well, Ahmed, it seems that Leila was seeing my cousin Juan.'

'Señor Romero . . . who lives with Paula?'

'Yes, my cousin.'

'But he's married . . . and has a young family.'

'Yes. Juan finally told me about it.'

'And you think . . .?

'I don't know what to think. I know he was on the bridge with Leila shortly before . . . and they had a terrible row.'

'Oh . . . do you think . . .?'

'Juan says Leila wanted him to leave his wife and family, but he couldn't. He says they had a terrible row, but she was fine when he left. Very upset, but . . . Ahmed, what do you think I should do?'

'Do? Why ask me?'

'I didn't want to find out all this, but I wasn't sure about Hassan. I really wasn't. So I tried to do my job as a police officer, and got more than I bargained for.'

'Do you think Juan might have . . . ?'

'I don't know. He swears he didn't harm her, but I'm not convinced a court would believe him.'

'So?'

'You've met my *abuela*. She's eighty-three. It's her birthday soon. She brought Juan up after his parents died, and we've got a big family party arranged. I just want her to have a few happy days before I hand over my notes to my superior officers. I fear his arrest might kill her.'

'I see. You want to keep your concerns to yourself? You've told me now.'

'At least until after her birthday.'

'I suppose the press conference will go ahead whatever you say.'

305

'Yes.'

'And you believe Juan?'

'I do.'

'So it could still be Hassan or someone else.'

'Yes.'

Ahmed frowned, and stood up, lost in concentration. 'Max, I would like to know the truth. But give me a few days to think. I should talk to Juan.'

Max stood up, and embraced Ahmed. 'Thanks. You are very kind.'

'I am only doing what Allah the Merciful would recommend.'

'For that I am truly grateful.'

Max returned to Paula's. Fortunately Juan was staying in Granada that evening. Max sat and talked with Paula about Antonio until the evening meal was ready. Paula was tired, too tired to go through the whole notebook. Max was grateful for that: he did not want her excitement and pleasure spoilt by the last pages. After the meal, Paula went to her bed early, exhausted by the day's events. Max stayed to play games of cards with Encarnita and Leonardo. Encarnita soon got bored.

'*Tito* Max. Tell me the story again . . . about *Blood Wedding*.'

'Just a short one. I'm tired. And you must go to bed soon.'

'Only when you've finished.'

'Okay then. A long time ago, when Paula was a little girl like you, there's a farm, a bit like this.'

'Does it have a kitten like David?'

'Probably. Yes. Well . . . the people on the farms then don't have much money, and they work very hard on the land. Men are always quarrelling – over little bits of land, over water for their vegetables, and sometimes there are fights and people are killed.'

'That's very bad. We always have water for our vegetables here. Don't we?'

306

'Yes . . . There's a woman who lives alone with her son. The son's father and brother had been killed in a knife fight.'

'That's terrible, isn't it?'

'Yes. It is. The son is about to marry a girl who lives in a cave.'

'In a cave? I'd like to live in a cave. Leonardo says he knows where a cave is, and he says he will show me when I'm bigger.'

'That's good. It's time Leonardo showed you things.'

'He always says he's too busy.'

'But to return to the story. The bride is still in love with Leonardo.'

'Leonardo? Can't be, silly. That's my brother.'

'No. Another Leonardo. He's married, and has a baby son.'

'Oh.'

'The girl's a good girl, and gets up very early to make the bread and sew the clothes.'

'That's good . . . but I don't think I would like to get up so early. Why didn't they buy their bread in a shop?'

'They were a long way from shops. Well, everyone starts to prepare for the wedding. The bride has some lovely presents from the bridegroom and from his mother: she gets lacy silk stockings.'

'That's nice. Did she get presents from Leonardo too?'

'I don't know . . . but he loves her. Anyway . . . the night before the wedding, the bride runs away with Leonardo.'

'And they gallop away on his horse?'

'Yes . . . but the bridegroom finds out, and he is very angry. So he follows after them. And he catches up with them.'

'So what happens?'

'The moon appears and speaks. Then Leonardo and the bridegroom have a big fight . . . with knives. And they kill each other. The bride is very sad.'

'I'm not surprised. Does she keep the presents?'

'I don't think so. It's a tale of revenge.'

'What's that?'

'It's when somebody does something bad to you. And you decide to do something bad back.'

'Like when Leonardo pulls my hair. And then I hide his football shirt. He shouts when he can't find it.'

'Yes. Something like that. I'm tired now, young lady. And it's time for your bed. That's all for tonight.'

Max kissed Isabel and the children goodnight, and retreated to the guest bedroom. He read for a while, and then fell asleep. He woke at dawn with the cock crowing, but soon fell asleep again.

Chapter 26

Run, run,
Bring the wool,
I feel them coming
Covered with mud.

Frederico García Lorca, *Bodas de Sangre* (*Blood Wedding*)
in a version by Ted Hughes

The next morning Max put on his uniform, and went down for breakfast. Isabel was in the kitchen, washing up. 'Morning, Max. How are the ribs?'

'Better, thanks . . . had the best night's sleep for ages.'

'That's good. *La virgen María* must have been looking after you. Coffee?'

'Thanks. Where are the children?'

'Big night tomorrow, so they're getting a lie-in.'

'Where's Paula?'

'She didn't sleep much last night . . . I think she's even more excited than Encarnita. So she's sleeping in this morning. Toast?'

'Let me get it. You've enough to do without waiting on me.'

'Thanks.'

'Did Juan phone?'

'Yes. He said he'd be back this afternoon. *Santa María*, he still sounds a bit stressed.'

'Probably work.'

'I'm not sure. He'll make a lot of money on the Recina

mill conversion, so he could take it a bit easier now.' Isabel turned, and looked at Max. 'My . . . the best uniform. Important meeting?'

'Press conference – announcing *los magistrados*' ruling on Leila's death.'

'Yes, I heard about that. Everyone's saying it's that poor lad who killed himself. But if it's a press do, you can't go with your shirt looking like that! Take it off, and I'll iron it for you.'

'Thanks. It's one thing I've never learnt to do well. Are you ladies going to be suitably dressed for the performance?'

'Well, Paula will be wearing the "Persian Rose" shawl. But her good black silk was looking a bit rusty, so we found something rather similar in a tiny shop in Realejo.'

'And Encarnita?'

'I found a very pretty dress . . . ivory and violet silk . . . but Princesa Encarnita was having none of it. She insists on showing off her new *traje de Sevillanas* in true Spanish traditional style. We have a flamenco dancer . . . a red one.'

'And yourself?'

'Well, I didn't really need anything new, but Juan insisted. So I found a copper silk with an organza jacket.'

'Wow. Juan and I are going to be seriously outclassed.'

'Particularly if I don't iron your shirt. Poor Leonardo wants to wear his Seville football shirt. But Juan insists he wear a suit. Leonardo will be sulking all evening.'

'That's a bit brutal.'

'But Juan is taking him to watch the Sevilla play when the season starts.'

The Diva police station was buzzing. The media were there in force. González was strutting about, being visible and affable.

'Ah, Max. Good to see you. You know everyone. This is Roberto Cervantes from Channel TVE and Carmen Solera from *Granada Hoy*, Antonio Robinson from *Ideal,* and over there is Enrique Bardem from *El País.*'

González finally called the meeting to begin. In his best

Sunday voice, Teniente González explained the latest findings. He concluded, 'So, in light of all the evidence, and in accordance with the decision of *los magistrados*, the case has been archived. The balance of probability is that our sole suspect, Hassan Khan, was responsible for Leila Mahfouz's death. It is unclear whether it was manslaughter or deliberate murder. Señor Khan took his own life last week, so there will be no further investigation.'

Flashbulbs popped. Teniente González beamed to the crowd, and continued, 'But before I answer any questions, I would like to thank the Granada police for their cooperation, and in particular Sub-Inspector Romero whose help has been invaluable in bringing this case to a satisfactory conclusion.'

Max winced, and hoped he did not have to make a speech. It was going well for Gonzo so far. Be a promotion in it for him. Then the reporter from *El País* asked, 'Hassan Khan along with his companions had been arrested on terrorist charges. There had been some unfortunate incidents relating to those arrests, and all except Hassan Khan were eventually released without charge. Does this mean there is – was – no danger of their being in any way involved with terrorism?'

'I wouldn't go as far as that,' said González. 'But that's more the province of the Granada police. Perhaps Sub-Inspector Romero would like to comment.'

'All the suspects were released because of lack of evidence. But we are still keeping an open mind,' said Max.

'What does an open mind mean in this case?' asked the girl from *Granada Hoy*.

'Well, we are still pursuing certain discrepancies in their stories. However none of them are in Spain, and we have asked the relevant authorities in their respective countries to gather more information as well as keep them under surveillance.'

'Do you believe that or know that?' asked the *El País* reporter.

'We have no reason to doubt our allies in the war on terrorism. We are cooperating fully within the EU.'

'What information have you received from the relevant EU countries?' asked a TV interviewer.

Hell, thought Max. This is going down a tack we don't want. 'I'm sure the media appreciate that such information is highly confidential. I suggest if you want to ask any further questions you should approach the relevant officers in Madrid who are coordinating all of this. Today we should concentrate on the highly successful cooperation between the Diva Guardia Civil and the Policia Nacional in Granada. I should like to pay tribute to the painstaking and careful work of our colleagues here in Diva, and in particular, to the leadership offered by Teniente González throughout this case.'

González puffed his chest out, acknowledging the tribute. There were more questions, but finally the conference came to an end. González came up to Max. 'Thank you,' he said. 'We may have had our little difficulties, but we worked well as a team in the end. We are having a small celebration. Will you join us?'

'Thanks. But I have to get back to Granada.'

Max went round the corner to his parked car, and set off for Granada as quickly as he could. At the Suspiro del Moro his mobile rang.

'*Dígame. Sí*, Comisario Bonila. I'm on my way back to Granada right now. I'll be there in about half an hour.' Damn, he thought. This could really mess up Paula's birthday for me.

Max increased his speed, and arrived at the police car park in twenty-five minutes. He went straight to Bonila's office on the top floor. The whole top brass were there, from Bonila up to Cifuentes and General López.

'Come in, Max. I've been explaining to everyone, so I'll just summarize for you. Inspectora Jefe Concha called an hour ago. She got an email from the Anti-Terrorist Unit in London. They finally got round to doing something on Javeed Dharwish. Clearly hadn't bothered their arses until now.

But as they were unable to make contact with him, as they put it, they broke into his flat in London. The place had been cleaned out: laptop gone, phone messages cleared from the landline, nothing to identify him or link him to anything. Neighbours didn't see anything, didn't hear anything. He has literally just disappeared.'

'What?' said Max.

'Yes. But that's not the worst. Inspectora Jefe Concha requested that they take the place apart – so they took up the floorboards. And under the floorboards of his bedroom they found a diagram of Malaga Airport.'

'Malaga Airport?'

'Yes. We now all agree that Malaga Airport could be, is likely to be, the target of a terrorist attack.'

'And the others,' asked Max. 'The Moroccan guy, the Iraqi we sent back to Germany, the Algerian to France?'

'Disappeared as well.'

'Inspectora Jefe Concha is convinced they will be linking up with ETA for a planned attack.'

'ETA? I don't understand the connection. We never had any evidence of that,' said Max.

'Yes. But new evidence has come to light. One of the ETA prisoners in Bilbao confessed that ETA had made contact with Islamic terrorists for a spectacular. We are now convinced that the target is Malaga Airport.'

'Confession? Beaten out of him? Bribed out him?'

'Sub-Inspector Romero, that is enough. I understand from Inspector Jefe Davila that you have still not recovered fully from your accident. So we are asking you to be on standby here in Granada in my office. Your knowledge of English might be useful. We are all going to Malaga as soon as possible. I am leaving Inspector Jefe Felipe Chávez in charge. Report to him.'

'Yes, sir.'

Bonila turned to the others in the room. 'Gentlemen, we must go.'

They all departed, leaving a bewildered Max sitting in

313

Bonila's office. He needed a coffee fast. Had he been side-lined? Should he believe the ETA stuff? If the Brits said Javeed had disappeared, and diagrams of an airport were hidden under a floorboard . . . well, they'd no reason to make it up. It didn't look good. But the ETA connection? He should phone Martín, and find out what was going on.

Finishing his coffee, Max returned to Bonila's office. He looked around at the fake antique leather-covered desk, at the swivel high-backed chair, at the certificates on the wall, at the photos of Bonila with wife and two boys, with the mayor, with various politicians – all the insignia of a man of power but little taste. Max sat at the desk. Could this be him in twenty years? Would he want that? Was he willing to make the shabby compromises, the constant economizing with the truth to get there? He picked up the phone and dialled Martín.

'Martín? How are you? Max Romero here.'

'Fine, thanks.'

'What's going on?'

'Could be spectacular.'

'Bonila said all the guys we picked up in the raid have done a disappearing act.'

'Yep. Great, isn't it? So much for international cooperation over surveillance.'

'What do you reckon might happen?

'The smart money's on them regrouping in Spain.'

'Okay. I can accept that. But this ETA stuff?'

'*Sí*. Probably coming from Miguel Allende through Linda.'

'What a surprise.'

'Max – could you have another look at the interviews and the other material from their interrogations?'

'Okay, I'll do what I can. Immediately.'

Max called up the files from the interrogations. There was a lot to go through. He jotted down anything that struck him. It did seem a bit strange that two guys with weak credentials should have been accepted on to the course. They just didn't seem to fit. Perhaps he should chase that one up. Max retrieved a copy of the Ibn Rush'd Centre brochure from the files, and flipped through it. Yes, here it was, the names of the Governing Board. At the top was Professor William Saville, Professor of Business Ethics at the London School of Economics. There was a telephone number. Max dialled the number and waited. Finally a voice answered. 'Professor Saville speaking.'

Max explained who he was.

'Spanish police? Is there a problem?'

'I'm afraid so.'

'I hope it's not serious.'

'It could be. Has Dr Dharwish been in touch recently?'

'No, but I've been in China for the last month. I was rather expecting an email from him. A couple of students were accepted on the course at very short notice, and I was a bit concerned that they might not be the right calibre.'

'So what's your selection procedure?'

'We have the most thorough vetting of the candidates. Yes, we have a board who interviews them, and I always chair that board. This year we had a problem. Three of the successful candidates dropped out at the last minute, and the reserve list had all got fixed up with other things or couldn't be contacted.'

'So what happened?'

'Dr Dharwish said he had two good additional candidates who could go at the last minute and he'd send me their papers. I was leaving for a trip to China, so I only had time to glance at them.'

'So what did you think?'

'I wasn't very impressed, but I had to trust Javeed's judgement, or the course wouldn't run. I phoned Javeed to say I was unsure these two would make the grade. He assured me he had interviewed them himself, and they were much better candidates than their CVs and outline projects showed. So I said okay. After all it was really his show.'

'Do you know where I can find Dr Dharwish?'

315

'No. But I've only been back a few hours, and I'm expecting him to make contact soon . . . Yes, if Javeed makes contact, I'll phone you immediately. Could I know what this is all about?'

'Just something really urgent. But I can't go into details at this stage. I can contact you later when things are clearer.'

'Please. I'd be grateful. I want this project to succeed.'

'Oh, by the way,' said Max, 'could you give me the names and phone numbers of the three candidates who had to drop out?'

'I'll have to look up the files. Could take some time.'

'It's urgent.'

'Okay, I'll do it straight away.'

Max drummed his knuckles on the inlaid leather desk. It did not look good. Professor Saville rang back ten minutes later with contact phone numbers. Max hurriedly phoned the first number. A male voice, oldish, with a Manchester accent answered the phone. 'That'll be my son you want. Wait a minute, I'll get him.' Another younger Manchester voice answered. 'Yes . . . I was meant to be doing the Ibn Rush'd course. Then two days before my flight, the Director called. Said this course was cancelled . . . No, I haven't heard any more.'

Max rang the second and third numbers. It was the same story.

He hurriedly phoned Martín.

'*Gracias,*' said Martín. 'I'll pass this on. We're treating this as a potential terrorist attack, and Javeed Dharwish and the others as terrorist suspects. We've alerted all airports and points of entry into Spain with orders to arrest on sight and treat as highly dangerous. We're surrounding Malaga Airport with armed marksmen. The problem is they are probably in Spain by now, and we don't know where. Keep me posted. We have a race against time. It doesn't look good.'

Max put the phone down. He'd better go and see Inspector Jefe Chávez. He went along the corridor and knocked on the door.

'Enter,' a voice called out.

Max entered.

'Ah. Max. Good to see you. Feeling better?'

'Much better, sir.'

'What can I do for you?'

'Comisario Bonila said I should stay in his office in case anything urgent came up on the Dharwish case, and that I should report to you. Also, sir, I have arranged to take my *abuela* to *Blood Wedding* tomorrow night for her birthday with the rest of the family. Did Comisario Bonila say anything about leave being cancelled?'

'No . . . No problem with tomorrow night. In fact, leave at lunchtime. Comisario Bonila was in such a rush I don't think he thought things through. He probably forgot that you still need to rest. I'll arrange that any phone calls going to his office are diverted to me. Be useful if you could come in tomorrow morning just in case there's anything new.'

'I appreciate that, sir.'

'No problem. We don't want you to have to take six weeks off because you came back too early, do we?'

Max saluted, and left. He felt an urgent need to talk to Abbot Jorge. He phoned the abbey.

'Max, how are you? Heard you had an accident. Fell off a mountain or something?'

'Or something. But I'm fine. Can I come and see you?'

'Sure. Come over now, and stay for supper. We're not allowed many vices, so we spoil ourselves a little in good food and wine.'

'I remember. I've eaten with you,' said Max laughing.

'Ah. A few kisses on some of our holy relics and you can get a heavenly indulgence for your earthly ones. That's what I call a bargain.'

'You never change, Jorge.'

'By the way, I've had a few thoughts on that chess game you asked me to look at. I'll tell you about it when you're over.'

Max went back to his office, quickly checked the incoming

mail, and his emails. Nothing that couldn't wait. He left the building, and drove along the Sacromonte road to the *Abadía*, towering on the hill above the valley.

Jorge opened the door. 'Just in time . . . a little glass of our best *manzanilla* with some olives?'

'I could do with that.'

They sat in Jorge's study, overlooking the San Miguel fountain.

'Well,' said Jorge, settling back into his large, leather armchair. 'Tell me the whole story.'

Max began at the beginning, the rock thrown at him, his cracked ribs, bruised head, the evidence against Juan, the confrontation with Juan, the conversation with Ahmed, the so-called proof and final verdict against Hassan, the disappearance of Javeed and the others, the terrorist alert, and his general confusion.

'That's quite a tale,' said Jorge.

'It's been a busy couple of weeks. Have you had any ideas about the chess game?'

'It would require a very skilled chess player to manoeuvre another into losing in the same way. But you said Javeed played well, didn't you?'

'Wait a minute,' said Max. 'How could I have overlooked it? In the original interview Hassan said he had won that chess game. Yet up at the Ibn Rush'd Centre, Javeed said *he* won. I'm sure of that. So that blows a hole in Hassan Khan's alibi. God, I've been naive, haven't I?'

'A little too trusting perhaps, Max. But you did it for the right reasons. In such a dishonourable age, I prefer an honourable cop, even if he gets some things wrong.'

'Maybe. We have to assume Javeed and company are planning something. It's possible it was Javeed who killed Leila. Maybe Hassan said too much. It could really have been Hassan all along, and Gonzo was right. I don't know. And then there's Juan. What do I do about Juan, Jorge?'

'That's a difficult one. I would have recommended that he make a full statement to the police and trust the court

318

would believe him if he was charged. But now – sometimes the truth can be the enemy of the good. I think you did the right thing. Let's wait a little longer. Keep probing, and you might come up with something conclusive. I think it's wise to let Ahmed think about it. Maybe he doesn't want the world to know about his daughter's affair with a married man, I would go along with what he decides . . . Come, let's eat, and enjoy the good things of the Lord, be he Allah or God.'

They went down to the dining room. Jorge introduced Max to the other monks. The food was good and the wine flowed. There was a brief interlude while one of the younger monks read a passage from St John of the Cross. Max relaxed, pleased that no one questioned him about murders or terrorism, and happy that Jorge approved how he had handled the Juan dilemma.

Next morning, Max took the bus down to Gran Vía. Not a cloud in the sky. He cut through to police headquarters, stopping to admire the fountain in la Plaza de la Trinidad. Once in the office he picked up the phone to inform Martín about the chess game. He was about to phone when something struck him. What was it Hassan Khan kept chanting? Yes. 'Whisper it to the wall, Hassan. Whisper it. Hassan Khan MA.' MA – Malaga Airport, of course. He was raving about revenge. That was it, Malaga Airport. He phoned Martín. Martín was out. He asked for Linda. After a minute or two she answered the phone. Max hastily explained both the chess game, and Hassan Khan's chant.

'Max, I think you're right. We were discussing whether the drawings of the airport under Javeed's floorboards could be a deliberate decoy. He had been so careful to remove everything else – it looked suspicious. I'll alert everyone we have further evidence they're intending to hit Malaga Airport.'

'But there are other airports beginning with M – Madrid, Murcia.'

'Yes, but put the two together, the diagram plus Hassan. Also some ETA suspects have been sighted around Malaga.

It has to be Malaga. No, it all fits. But we'll keep an eye on the others as well. Martín is on his way to Malaga. I'll go and join him. *Gracias*, Max. Dinner in Madrid soon.'

Max went down the stairs, and reported to Chávez.

'Well done, Max. You have a birthday celebration for your *abuela* to attend, don't you? Can't have that spoilt in any way. I suggest you go now. I also suggest you carry your gun with you. You're known to the terrorists, and we can't take any chances.'

'Thanks, sir. Will do.'

On his way home, Max walked through the maze of streets behind the cathedral. He had spotted a suit on sale. Paula would be pleased if he turned up looking a little like Antonio and Lorca might have done on the opening night of *Blood Wedding* some seventy years ago.

He was right . . . the suit fitted perfectly.

'Would *el señor* like a shirt and tie to go with it? We have a cream silk bow tie which would be perfect.'

He normally avoided ties, but this was a special occasion. 'Let me see it,' he said. He bought the tie.

Max strolled into Plaza Nueva with his suit bag, then along el Paseo de los Tristes, and up the steep zigzag to his flat. His ribs were almost completely healed. He made himself a sandwich, had a siesta, then a shower, and dried off on the terrace. Yes, it was going to be a perfect evening.

The family had arranged to meet at the Alhambra Palace Hotel for drinks and nibbles before driving over to the Generalife Open Air Theatre. The main meal would be about midnight. Max set off about eight to the hotel.

Granada came to life as darkness was falling. Max walked up la Cuesta de los Chinos, the ancient funeral route to the Alhambra cemetery, alongside the stream that never lacked water. He continued down past the Washington Irvine Hotel, now in a sad state of disrepair, and then entered the vestibule of the Alhambra Palace Hotel. He was a little early, but he wanted to ensure everything was in order. He asked to see the manager.

'Yes, Señor Romero. Everything is as it should be. I explained to Señor Juan that we have a large group of American naval officers from Rota staying, a stag night I believe they call it. They could be a little noisy, but I have ensured that your rooms are well away from theirs. We also have a wedding reception. So we are very full. But your dining table can be either on the terrace or inside in the far corner of the dining room.'

'It's a lovely night,' said Max. 'Full moon. I think outside would be best.'

'Yes, certainly. Any special requests to Chef?'

'No, but we have children in the party. Can we order now and have our food as soon as we get back from the performance? We should be back here at midnight.'

'An excellent idea. I'll ask the waiter to bring you the menus.'

'Thank you. The rest of the family should be here soon. We'll order then.'

Max ordered a beer, and drank it on the terrace. He glanced at the two papers he had taken with him. Both carried a report on the front page that Palestine and Israel were on the verge of signing an historical peace agreement. There were riots in Gaza and the West Bank, opposing the deal.

'Would you like to order now?' asked the waiter.

'No. I'll wait until the others arrive. That's a Basque accent, isn't it?'

'Yes. I'm from Bilbao.'

'Strange language, Basque. Not related to any other, I believe.'

'Yes, that's right.'

Max sipped his beer, looking at a menu. He'd almost finished the beer when Paula, Juan, Isabel and the children arrived.

Max kissed Paula and Isabel on both cheeks, and lifted Encarnita into the air as he kissed her. Leonardo looked thoroughly scrubbed, and not happy. Juan was pale and stiff. They gave each other a quick manly hug.

They sat on the terrace, overlooking the city, the plain and the mountains in the distance. As they were ordering, Max's sister, Susanna, and his father Bernardo arrived. Paula shrieked with delight.

'You didn't expect us to miss your birthday?' said Susanna, as Paula wiped her eyes, tears of joy trickling down her cheeks.

'You rogue,' she said to Juan. 'You never told me.'

'I know,' said Juan with a big grin. 'I wanted it to be a surprise.'

'I'm so happy,' said Paula. 'All the family except Flora are here. Did you know I stayed here about ten years after it was first opened? Let me see, that must have been in 1930, and I was ten years old. It was like a picture from my book of tales of the Arabian nights.'

The Basque waiter returned. 'Everyone ready to order?'

They were. Juan turned to the waiter. 'Can you do child portions?'

'Certainly.'

' That's a Basque accent, isn't it?'

'Is it that obvious?'

'I love the way you speak Spanish so clearly. It puts us Andalusians to shame.'

The waiter laughed.

They all talked happily for the next hour. Then the Basque waiter appeared with a large bouquet of flowers and a sheaf of cards, and handed them to Paula.

'Oh, my. Flowers from Flora. How kind of her when she is so busy. Oh. And look, a card from Jaime and Miranda in Chile . . . one from Roxana and Michael in Venezuela . . . how marvellous.'

The waiter then whispered in Juan's ear. Juan stood up.

'Time to go,' he announced. 'The taxis are waiting to take us to *Blood Wedding*.'

Max took Paula by her arm and led her to the waiting taxis. Paula had an elegant walking cane with her. 'Can you manage okay?' he asked.

'I'm fine. I have an appointment with a specialist next month. But I'm not sure I want an operation at my age.'

'If it is a hip replacement you can be in and out in days. It's amazing what they can do – you can be walking around as good as new in no time.'

As they got into the taxis, Encarnita pulled Max's hand. 'Why is it called *Blood Wedding*?' she asked.

So Max told her the story again. How Lorca based his play on a newspaper article about a family feud where the daughter of one family ran away with the son of an enemy family . . . so something like this had really happened.

Chapter 27

On the golden flower,
They're bringing the dead from the river,
One dark skinned,
The other, dark skinned.
Over the golden flower
The shadow of a nightingale
Flutters and sobs.

Frederico García Lorca, *Bodas de Sangre* (*Blood Wedding*)
in a version by Ted Hughes

The happy chatter continued all the way to the entrance to the Alhambra. Max walked with his father.

'Paula's so excited, isn't she? I haven't seen her looking so well for years.'

'Yes, she is.'

'Nice suit. You should wear one more often.'

The family walked along a pathway through formal gardens to the theatre. The air was rich with the scent of clipped evergreens and rosemary. Juan herded them all to their seats, near the front.

'The best seats I could get.'

Max sat between Encarnita and Susanna.

'We must have a good gossip before I go back to London . . . this new job is really interesting,' Susanna said to Max. 'And I love the suit. Can't call you Wee Scruffy now.'

At each side of the stage was a grove of cypresses, and the full moon hung in the air. And then the spotlight lit up an old woman, sitting on a chair. A young man entered through the living trees, his boots of Spanish leather stamping the wooden stage.

'*Madre*,' he said.

The performance had begun.

Encarnita turned to Max. 'Tito Max. Why did she sing,

> "Sleep little rose,
> The horse is weeping?"
> Horses don't cry, do they?'

'It's poetry – and almost anything can happen in a poem.'

At the interval, Encarnita was bursting with questions. 'Why did . . . What was . . .' Paula, her face radiant, held her and tried to explain. But her questions didn't stop.

In Act Three, a young man, dressed as a woodcutter, his face painted white, his eyes as dark as coal, spun on to the stage suffused in a blue light. The clapping of dancers off-stage accompanied a singer's lament marking the the beat with *las palmas,* a slow flamenco that built up to a faster and faster rhythm.

> 'Tonight there'll be blood
> To warm my cheeks.'

Max felt the hairs at the back of his neck tingle.

In the final act, seven girls, moving together like a serpent's tail, stamped and spun around the stage – a Greek Chorus of Death – before Leonardo and the bridegroom fought the duel, their knives flashing in the moonlight.

Max and the family left silently at the end. Encarnita and Leonardo found a sudden burst of energy. Encarnita danced and twirled. Leonardo kicked rocks.

It was Paula who finally broke the silence.

'Oh, Max, Juan . . . that was so good. I don't know how to thank you.'

'*Abuela*, it's our pleasure,' said Juan . . . and everyone started talking at once.

As they went into the hotel Max noticed two armed Amer-

325

ican marines at the entrance. The manager was waiting for them near the terrace.

'Everything is ready,' he said. 'I've put you in the furthest corner of the terrace. Some of our American guests are . . . well . . . a little over-excited. I do hope they don't disturb you.'

'I'm sure it will be fine.'

'I feel really sorry for the wedding party. The Americans keep going through to toast the bride and groom. Fortunately the person in charge of the wedding party doesn't have a problem with it so far . . . They've got a traditional Moroccan group arriving soon when the dance band takes a break, so things should quieten down.'

The Romero family sat on the terrace, the lights of Granada beneath them, the mountains just visible in the moonlight. Encarnita skipped from mother to aunt, from father to uncle, from uncle to grandma. Leonardo sat and scowled. They had just finished the main course when Max's mobile rang.

'Max, is that you? It's Martín.'

'Wait a minute, Martín. It's very noisy here. Let me go outside.' Max walked outside to the car park. 'That's better. Can you hear me okay?'

'Yes. Fine. We're at Malaga Airport, Max. Nothing so far, but we're sure Javeed Dharwish passed though a couple of days ago. Went through the surveillance cameras, cool as you like.'

'Sounds like our man.'

'False passport of course.'

'Yes.'

'God, our security is crap. Osama himself could walk through here without any problems. I'm sure the others have got into Spain as well. I'm worried, Max. That Dharwish guy is pretty smart. The more I think of it, the more he wouldn't forget he'd left something under his floorboards. I think these guys have led us up the garden path. But Linda's convinced she's right. She's even found some ETA suspect in Malaga, so he's being trailed. Me, I think it's somewhere else. *Dios*, you must be having a real noisy party.'

A van drew up in the car park. A tall bearded man in a long djellaba got out, followed by another. The Moroccan musicians had arrived.

'That's not us,' replied Max. 'There's a bunch of American naval officers here . . .' They both spoke at once. '*Dios.*'

'Max . . . get back inside, and warn Security. I'll call the police. Keep in touch.'

Max turned towards the door. As he did so he gazed at the bearded man with the instrument case. There was something familiar about him. Max reached for the gun in his pocket.

'What the . . .'

Javeed reacted first. He sprang at Max, knocking him and his gun to the ground.

'Omar!'

They quickly overpowered Max, and bundled him inside the van.

'Tie and gag him,' ordered Javeed.

'Kill him,' urged Omar.

'No. Can't risk a shot.'

'Okay. I'll strangle the bastard.'

'No. He's police. More use to us alive than dead. Let's go.'

Max heard screams, shouts, shots. *Oh God. My family. My family.*

Suddenly the van back door burst open, and in tumbled a woman and the Moroccan, automatic weapons in their hands. The van raced through the car park, and crashed through a hedge on to an access road. Max couldn't be sure how long they travelled before the van screeched to a stop. The gag in his mouth was making his breathing difficult. He started to panic. His chest compressed by an iron band, he tried to gasp for breath. Javeed opened the van doors. 'Change vehicles,' he said. 'Fatima. Men. Well done. Let's go.'

Javeed leaned forward and removed Max's gag.

Max struggled to breathe in deeply. 'My family?' he gasped.

'Don't know. We were only after the American officers.'

'Can I kill him now?' asked Omar.

'No,' Javeed said. 'We're in the middle of nowhere. Just lock the van. Nothing gained by killing another.'

'Yes. But how many did we shoot tonight? Ten? Fifteen?'

'Yes. That was necessary. I don't want to kill unnecessarily. Allah would not approve.'

Omar scowled and took out a knife.

'Omar,' said Javeed, pointing his gun at Omar. 'I'll shoot you if I have to. Get in your car and just go.'

Omar cursed, but left.

'Asthma . . . inhaler . . . in pocket. Help me!' Max gasped.

Javeed put the inhaler to Max's mouth, and pressed it as Max breathed in deeply.

'Leila?' Max said.

'How many times do I have to tell you? Nothing to do with us.'

'But I need to know the truth.'

'I can't help you.'

'But the chess game?'

'We had to leave the café for an important meeting with Fatima. Hassan was using Fatima's laptop to finalize details of our military intervention here. He was good . . . got into the Rota Social website, and found out about the stag party here. What a gift. We had to hide that from you, and invented the chess game – using the one in *The Flanders Panel*. Unfortunately you spotted that and my mistake over who won the game.'

There was an angry blast of a car horn.

'It's war, Max. It's war. One day I hope we can meet in peace,' he said, putting the gag back in. 'I better just make sure.' And he hit Max on the head with the butt of his gun.

When Max regained consciousness he didn't know whether he'd been lying bound and gagged in the van for minutes, hours or days. He heard voices outside the van.

'What should we do, sir? The van is probably booby-trapped'

'Can we open the back, and look inside?'

'It's the door that's probably the ignition for the bomb.'

'I've sent for the bomb squad. We'd better wait for them.'

Shit. Shit. Max struggled, but the rope had been firmly tied. He heard a car arrive. More voices. One of the voices drew nearer.

'We can't risk anything. I think I'll have to set off a controlled explosion.'

With great effort he worked his way down towards the door, and lifted up his bound legs, and then let his feet fall against the door. There was some noise, but was it enough? He tried again, this time a little louder. The same voice spoke again.

'Stand back, everyone. I'm going to set a small explosion at the door.'

Max managed to find the energy to lift his legs and kick at the door.

'Hold it,' said the voice. 'There's a banging noise against the door. Can you hear me in there?'

Max tried to shout, but the gag held firm and all he managed was a gurgling noise.

'I think someone's in there,' said the voice. 'Get away from the door! I'm going to count to ten and then fire at the lock. Everyone back.'

Max felt his energy was draining fast. One last effort. He wriggled his way to the back of the van.

'. . . Eight, nine, ten.' There was a pause, a shot, and the back door of the van flew open. Max saw a uniformed officer peering inside. '*Dios*,' he exclaimed. 'There's a bloke in here in a white suit. Gagged and tied. That was a close one. Could have blown him up.'

Max felt like protesting – his suit was a pale grey: chaps in white suits look pretentious. The voice climbed in, and removed the gag, cut the rope binding his legs together, and helped Max out of the van. Max stood up, and then col-

329

lapsed to the ground. The voice cut his arms free, and Max, gasping for breath, reached into his pocket and took a quick puff of his inhaler.

'They escaped in cars,' he croaked. 'Two cars, I think. Maybe going for the morning ferries to Morocco.'

'In which case they've made it,' said the voice. 'It's noon. You look in a bad way. We'd better phone for a helicopter, and get you to hospital. Who are you, by the way?'

'Sub-Inspector Romero from the Policia Nacional here in Granada. Could you phone Inspectora Jefe Concha or Inspector Martín Sánchez of CGI immediately, and tell them Javeed Dharwish and the others are escaping by boat – probably to Morocco. Their numbers are on my mobile.'

The voice looked at him quizzically, but did as asked.

'Inspectora Jefe Concha? We have a Sub-Inspector Romero here asking to speak to you.'

'Put him on. Max – how are you? Where are you? There's been a bloody massacre. It's been chaos here.'

'I got abducted by the gang. Nearly got blown up too. I overheard Dharwish say they were getting the morning boat. Must mean the Morocco ferry. The navy could stop them.'

'They'll have landed already. Not much hope of finding them.'

'Linda, my whole family were in the hotel. Can you find out if they are okay? They are all called Romero.'

'Sure, Max.'

There was a drone, and then the buzz of a helicopter.

'Have to go now. That's the helicopter taking me to hospital.'

'Take care. Remember that meal in Madrid.'

Two men rushed out of the helicopter with a stretcher, and lifted him into it.

'My family, my family,' he moaned, before he passed out.

Max was gently awoken by a doctor. 'Good news, Inspector Romero. One member of your family was hurt, but isn't in danger. There are no other casualties by the name of Romero.'

'Thank God, thank God. Who's hurt?'

'Your cousin Juan. He's in another ward. This is the worst thing the hospital has had to cope with in years.'

'How many casualties?'

'Ten dead. More injured. There's someone waiting to see you. Do you feel strong enough to talk?'

'Yes, I do.'

'Okay. I'll tell him he can come in. Don't overdo it.'

The doctor left, and Inspector Martín Sánchez walked in.

'Max, are you all right?'

'Yes, I'll survive. What happened?'

'It was dreadful. A real massacre. They killed the marines on guard as they went in, and then started firing into the stag party. Some of the officers rushed next door into the wedding reception, and they followed them into that, firing all the time. The hotel security men managed to kill one of the terrorists. It was a massacre. The bridegroom was killed, and the bride injured. Your cousin Juan must have rushed over to help. He was wounded in the wedding reception room.'

'Juan?'

'Don't worry. I've checked with the doctors. He'll survive. Lost a lot of blood, so he's still unconscious.'

Martín leaned over Max's bed in a conspiratorial fashion. 'Problem is, we have a serious political issue right now. One of those killed was a young Basque waiter. He turns out to have ETA connections. He was arrested in Bilbao a couple of years ago on an ETA demonstration which turned nasty.'

'ETA?' said Max. 'I don't understand?'

'I know. But Allende and Linda are making the most of it. They've put out a press statement that this was a joint ETA–Islamist terrorist attack. The government has already instructed all of our embassies round the world to emphasize this. They're attacking the Socialists for opening secret negotiations with ETA. It looks bad for the Socialists with the election just due. Have you got anything we could use to counter this?'

331

All Max could think about was the family. Was Paula okay? How badly injured was Juan?

'Nothing.' he said. 'Except I don't believe for one minute ETA was involved.'

'We have to move fast. They've got this waiter story. We have to rebut it. We have to know what happened at the wedding reception.'

'Have you spoken to Juan?'

'He's still unconscious. They won't let me in. They might agree to you going in, seeing you're a relative. It's critical, Max. The election will turn on this.' Martín stared at Max, his face pleading. 'I don't want the bastards to get back in. It would be bad for Spain, bad for peace.'

Max nodded.

'*Gracias*, Max. I'll get the doctor. I'll say it will help your recovery and Juan's if you sit with him.'

Martín left, and returned with the doctor.

'You're Juan Romero's cousin?'

'Yes. We grew up together. It would help us both if I could just sit with him.'

The doctor smiled. 'I want to get the best for our public health services. Inspector Sánchez here has persuaded me this might help. You may go.'

'Thanks, doctor,' said Martín. 'Here, let me get you a dressing gown, Max. The hospital ones are not the most elegant, but they'll do.'

The doctor, Martín and Max walked along the corridor to a single room. A man lay on a bed in the room. 'I can't let you both in,' said the doctor. 'Only close family at this stage. He should be regaining consciousness at any moment now.'

'Okay, doctor,' agreed Martín. 'I'll wait outside.'

Max sat on the chair by Juan's bed. He held Juan's hand. Max dozed for a while, and was awoken by a stirring in the bed. Juan had opened his eyes. Max squeezed Juan's hand. 'Don't speak just yet. You're fine.' Max sat there for ten minutes and then went outside. An impatient Martín was waiting.

'How is he?'

'He's conscious.'

'Can he talk?'

'I'd have to ask the doctor first.'

'I'll fetch him,' and Martín pushed his corpulent frame into a run.

He returned shortly, panting. 'The doctor's on his way. This is vital. We haven't long.'

'But we don't know what Juan will say. We don't know what he saw.'

'I know. But we haven't much else to go on at the moment.'

The doctor came up to them. 'You two stay here, and I will check the patient.'

He went in. Max and Martín peered through the glass pane of the door. The doctor talked to Juan, took his blood pressure and temperature, and then came outside.

'Okay. Only the cousin can go in. Not too long, mind you.'

Max went in, and sat beside the bed. He and Juan smiled at each other.

'The family?'

'All okay.'

'Thank God. You been in the wars too?' Juan said.

'They took me hostage. But I'm okay now, and you?'

'No permanent damage, I think I was lucky.'

'Juan, do you know what happened in there?'

'I heard this shooting, and you'd just vanished. I should have known better, but I rushed over to find you. I ran into the wedding reception. Max, it was horrible – bodies, blood all over the place.'

'Did you see anything? The waiter?'

'The waiter, the poor bastard. He was really brave, threw himself on top of the bride. I saw him shot. Did he survive?'

'No, he didn't. Do you know which waiter it was?'

'Yes. It was the one serving us, you know, the Basque guy.'

'Are you sure?'

'Of course I'm sure. What's all this about? Are you sure Paula and the kids are fine?'

'They're all right. Shocked and frightened. But fine. They should be here soon to see you and me. Juan . . . are you well enough to talk to the press about what you saw?'

'You mean have my day of glory? I might as well get something out of this.'

There was a knock. The children were peering round the door, Paula and Isabel behind them.

'Juan, the gang's here. You can see them now, and then rest. I'll work on the media,' said Max.

'Okay.'

'We still don't know who killed Leila. Javeed swears it wasn't Hassan.'

'It definitely wasn't me. Thanks for believing me, Max.'

Max smiled. 'You're a lying bastard, Juan. But I think I know when you're telling the truth.'

Max went outside. Paula hobbled up to Max, and embraced him, tears running down her cheeks. 'Max. I nearly died of worry. What with both you and Juan . . .'

'I know, *abuela*. Me too.'

'How's Juan?'

'Lost a lot of blood. But no permanent damage.'

Max turned to Martín, hovering in the background. 'We're in luck. The waiter died heroically, trying to save the bride.'

'Is Juan willing to talk to the media?'

'He is. But don't tell him the background. I don't think Juan would appreciate it, helping the Socialists.'

Martín got on his phone immediately. 'Rolando. Get this out! No ETA connection. Basque waiter died to save bride. Yes. I've got evidence. Eyewitness. Yes, willing to give interviews. Get on to all the TV channels. We'll shaft that bastard Allende, right up his skinny backside. And get some demos organized.'

Max looked at Martín. 'Sometimes you seem more a politician than an anti–terrorist cop.'

'These days there's not much difference,' he replied. 'The TV and newspaper reporters should be here soon. Could they interview you first? Give Juan more time to recover.'

The interviews went well. Juan revelled in the publicity. Apparently both Max and Juan looked great on TV, and their photos in the press were dramatic. The headlines that evening created a furore. The popular media concentrated on the heroic dead waiter and the injured bride: the more serious ones emphasized the lies from the government about the ETA connection. The Socialists organized spontaneous demonstrations against the Government's manipulation of a tragic event, accusing them of trying to influence the election, which they knew they were going to lose. The government responded that there was an ETA connection, and set up a special commission to investigate.

Jorge came to see Max that evening. Max was lying on his bed in hospital watching the dramatic events unfold on TV when Jorge entered with a big grin on his face.

'Max, seeing you're spending all your time lying around, I've brought you a little something.' He unwrapped a bottle of wine, and put it on the table beside Max's bed. 'It's the best Malaga *vino dulce*. So if the nurses say you can't drink alcohol, tell them it's not alcohol, but a sweet wine and that's medicinal. You can quote me on that.'

Max laughed. 'What's happening in the outside world?'

'Well, you and Juan are stars for a start. You both looked good on TV. Cousins risk their lives . . . Those hospital pyjamas and dressing gowns are all the rage.'

Max laughed. 'Wrong colour. I'd prefer blue.'

'Looks like you've swung the election. Even my monks are voting Socialist.'

'Well, at least some good will come out of this.'

Max hoped Anita would visit. There was nothing to do but watch TV. He couldn't turn it off. There was endless coverage of the dramatic events. Max got all the newspapers:

335

the Israelis and the Americans broke off their negotiations with the Palestinians; the USA condemned the Palestinian authorities for the killings.

So you succeeded, Javeed, thought Max. You won. You pulled the plug on those negotiations. But have you won in the long run or just condemned the Palestinian people to another round of violence?

As the election results came in, Max breathed a sigh of relief. The last-minute spinning by the government made no difference. The Socialists had won an historic victory.

Max went home the next day. He went to see Juan before he left. Juan scowled at him when he entered his room.

'You lying, manipulative toad,' he yelled at him. 'You never told me anything about this ETA stuff, and I've just helped put my taxes up. I'll send you the tax bill when it comes in.'

'There's not much danger of your taxes going up.'

'But we'll have gay marriages, more women in Parliament and the Cabinet, and Christ knows what else.'

'Be good for the country, you reactionary old sod. I'm off home. I've talked to the doctor. He said you should be allowed home to rest in a week or so. I'll come round and see you before then.'

Juan smiled. 'Okay you left-wing fanatic. See you. We did well in the end, didn't we, Max? I still have to go and see Ahmed. Thanks for believing in me. You're a true friend.'

Max left. Anita hadn't been to see him. He took a taxi to his flat, and climbed the stairs slowly. He went straight to his terrace, and looked up at the Alhambra. The doorbell rang. It was Anita.

'Max, I heard you were getting out today so I thought I'd come round here to see you. You're all over the TV and papers, you know. *Dios*, those pyjamas were awful. You should have put on the blue ones, blue suits you.'

'I didn't get a choice,' said Max. 'Come in. I'm so pleased to see you.'

They sat on the terrace, blinking in the sun, as Max told his tale.

'Anita, if you're not doing anything better this evening, can I buy you a decent meal?'

'That would be nice.'

' Let me take you to Duende – I'm dying for a thick steak, and chips cooked in good olive oil. The hospital food was awful – cold chips, soggy vegetables. You'd have thought they could give you fresh fruit and yoghurt.'

'Oh, Max, I went round to Paula's before I came over. She gave me this to give you,' said Anita, handing over a small jiffy bag.

'What this?' said Max. 'A tape. I'll play it later.'

They sat watching the sun set, a fiery red over the Alhambra, until it was time to leave for the restaurant.

'Let's walk,' said Anita. 'It's such a lovely evening.'

They strolled down the Albayzín, along el Paseo de los Tristes, across Plaza Nueva, and then into a little side street off la Acera de Darro.

'Max,' said the owner of Duende. 'You're famous. I'll have to give you free meals so I can advertise you eat here.'

'You can begin with your very best steak with a bottle of your best Rioja.'

'Two steaks,' added Anita.

Max showed Anita around, pointing out Manolete, el Triste.

Towards the end of the meal, Max put his hand on Anita's. She put her other hand on top of his.

'*Gracias* for a lovely meal, Max. That's a good wine. I think I'm slightly tiddled.'

'Me too. I've hardly had a drop for days. Shall we go back to my place for the coffee? I've got a bottle of the best brandy, Solera Lepanto, courtesy of Juan.'

'Why not?'

Max, feeling a little tired, hailed a taxi. They giggled their way up the stairs.

'I'll put on the coffee if you get the brandy,' said Anita.

They settled down comfortably on Max's sofa. After the first sip of brandy, Max ran his finger lightly over Anita's cheek. She shivered slightly. He leaned forward to kiss her lightly on her mouth. She leaned back.

'Max,' she said, 'I've got something to tell you. It's just . . . I've never been out with a man. I've been out with girls . . . women. You understand what I'm trying to say, don't you?'

Max sat upright.

Anita took his hand in hers. 'Max, I'm very fond of you. You're sweet. You're different to all the other men I've met. The lads in Güejar were not exactly sensitive souls, and as for cops, forget it. Dad didn't do mum any good, and after that well . . . I just gave men a wide berth.'

Max said nothing. He didn't know what to say.

'Anita, I . . .' He looked at his watch. 'Well after midnight. It's really late. You'll have missed the last bus. You'd better stay the night. You can have my bed. I can sleep here.'

'I'm sorry. You're not angry with me, are you?'

'No. No. It's not that. I'm just taken aback, that's all. I'd better change the sheets – I haven't changed them for weeks.'

'Here, let me help.'

Once finished they went back into the living room. They sat on the sofa, some distance apart. Anita broke the silence. 'Max, I'm sorry. I need time to think about this. Can you give me some time?'

'You've got all the time in the world.'

Anita laughed. 'When I'm ready I'd gladly accept your invitation and spend a weekend in *el cortijo*.'

Max yawned.

'We're both tired,' said Anita. 'Let's go to sleep.' She kissed him gently on the mouth.

Max curled up on the sofa. He tried to sleep, but couldn't. The thought of Anita lying in his bed didn't help. Should he just go and snuggle in beside her? The thought was so tempting. But he couldn't trust himself to just cuddle. Max tossed and turned: Leila, Linda, Anita, even Penélope danced over him. He awoke after a wet dream. He went into the kitchen, and drank a cold glass of water.

He returned to his uncomfortable sofa.

What the hell, he thought. He went into the bedroom. Moonbeams filtered through the half-closed shutters, flickering across Anita's coal-black hair. He looked at her, shrugged, and climbed into bed beside her. She snuggled up against him. He put his arm around her, kissed her on her hair, murmured, 'Pleasant dreams,' and fell asleep.

When he awoke, the sun was shining through the open shutter. Anita was up and dressed.

'I've made some coffee,' she said. 'I have to fly. Seeing that pig Gonzo.' She leant over Max, and kissed him on the mouth. 'Give me time, Max. Give me time.' She then left.

Max lay staring at the sunshine. I have all the time in the world, he thought. So why not?

He wandered into the kitchen, and poured himself a cup of coffee. He remembered Paula's tape. He went to get the jiffy bag. As he took the tape out, he noticed a little note in the bag. It was from Paula.

'I know I shouldn't have done this, Max. This is Leila's last interview with me. I just didn't want you to know. So I kept it.'

Max put on the tape, not knowing quite what to expect.

Chapter 28

Paula: How are you today, Leila?

Leila: Fine, thanks. Er . . . er . . . well . . .

Paula: Cat got your tongue, *cariño*?

Leila: I've got some news for you, Paula . . . but I'm not sure you'll like it.

Paula: Is it about Antonio?

Leila: I think I've found something. It's not definite.

Paula: Don't be afraid to tell me.

Leila: I've come across some material, which might be his.

Paula: Don't stop. Let me know.

Leila: It's about your husband, Pablo.

Paula: Ah.

Leila: I think Pablo and Capitán Vicente González got hold of El Gato's land after he was shot.

Paula: That's possible. A lot of Republican property changed hands illegally after the Civil War.

Leila: That's not all.

Paula: Go on.

Leila: I think Antonio believed Pablo had a hand in betraying Lorca, and maybe . . .

Paula: Lorca?

Leila. Yes. Someone revealed where Lorca was hiding to a fascist militia group. Antonio thought it was Pablo.

Paula: Why Pablo?

Leila: He had connections to Acción Popular . . . and I think Antonio may have put two and two together and, well . . . jumped to a conclusion.

Paula: But Pablo would never have wanted anyone to harm Lorca. Never.

Leila: I'm sure you're right.

Paula: But it could explain . . . perhaps that's why Antonio stopped me seeing Pablo. *Dios mío!*

Leila: Paula, there might be something else. I . . . I . . . I've still more research to do though.

Paula: I need the truth, Leila. I have to know what really happened.

Leila: I've found things . . . and I don't understand them . . . I need a bit more time.

Paula: It's the truth that matters. We can talk another time.

Leila: How's the family?

Paula: Encarnita just passed another exam at her dancing class.

Leila: She's lovely. Juan must be so proud of her.

Paula: He is. Leila, you're very lovely yourself.

Leila: Thanks, Paula.

Paula: Juan can be so charming, can't he?

Leila: Paula!

Paula: I've seen you look at him when we're together. I may be an old woman, but I know what those looks mean. You're playing with fire.

Leila: Oh, Paula. I don't know what to do.

Paula: Don't cry, *cariño mío*.

Leila: Paula. Paula.

Paula: Turn the tape off, *querida*. Turn the tape off.

Chapter 29

'It seems a shame,' the Walrus said,
'To play them such a trick.'

Lewis Carroll, *Through the Looking Glass*

It was Sunday, and now well into September. In October, the weather would turn, and cooler breezes from the Sierra Nevada would begin to cool the smouldering heat and lift the fog of pollution over Granada. And the rains might come and fill the empty streams and rivers with water, and the ducks in the river, el Río Darro, might protest less. But there were still a couple of weeks of heat before then.

Max had promised Paula he would be over for Sunday lunch. Juan was still in hospital, so he would have to do the barbecue. He hadn't heard from Anita since that evening in el Duende. Max took two litres of water with him for the drive over to Diva. He needed it.

As he drove up the driveway to Paula's house, Encarnita skipped out to greet him, David the kitten in her arms.

'*Tito* Max! *Tito* Max . . . my friend Jane has come for lunch.'

Jane joined Encarnita as he parked the car on the driveway. Max shook hands with her formally, and in his most polite English said, 'How are you? Remember me?'

'Yes. You are the policeman who asked me questions about Leila.'

Encarnita handed David over to Jane, and threw herself into Max's arms.

'Hey,' he said. 'Careful. My ribs can still hurt.'

'Come and see what Leonardo has got,' and taking him by the hand she pulled him round to the back of the house.

'Look,' she said pointing to a hutch. 'It's a rabbit. We've called him Federico.'

'Why Federico?'

'Cause he's got big ears.'

Paula hobbled out, her arms covered in flour.

'Max, *querido*, so good to see you. Can't hug you – don't want flour all over. I've heard from the hospital. I may need a hip replacement, but not yet.'

'That's good. No point in rushing things.'

'I had invited Anita over for lunch today, but she has to deal with some crisis with her sister. She said she'd phone later.'

'Fine. But I'd better go and sort out the barbecue. Have we still got some rosemary twigs?'

'Yes. In the shed.'

Max got the barbecue going, and then went inside. Paula and Isabel were in the kitchen together, in itself a breakthrough.

'Can I wash my hands?' he asked.

'I'm just washing the salad. Can you use upstairs?' said Isabel.

At the top of the stairs Max's mobile rang.

'*Dígame.*'

'Max. It's Anita. How are you?'

'Me? I'm fine.'

'It was a lovely evening at el Duende.'

Max didn't reply.

'Sorry I couldn't make it over today.'

'Another crisis?'

'Yes. Another crisis with my sister.'

There was a pause. Neither spoke.

'Max. Are you still there?'

'Yes.'

'Max . . . Max I think I may have found something about

Leila's death, but I really don't want to talk about it over the phone. I was wondering, are you free this evening?'

'Yes. I'm thinking of spending it up in *el cortijo*. I've also got tomorrow off.'

'That must be nice. Max . . . I'm also free. Tomorrow's free as well. Could I come over and see you this evening? I need to talk to you about it privately. It's a tricky one.'

'Sure. Stay over if you like.'

'About six? See you later.'

Max washed his hands, and returned to the kitchen. Paula was there alone. 'Thanks for the tape,' he said.

'I should have given it to you earlier. But you must understand how I feel about Juan.'

'Nothing can surprise me now, *abuela*. The reference to the land deals was very interesting. Maybe that's how Gonzo got that plot by Felipe's bar.'

'Oh, that. It wouldn't surprise me.'

'Me neither.'

'Max . . . you're standing there with an empty glass. Another *cerveza*?'

'I'll get it.'

'You know that the new government is giving permission to dig up suspected Civil War graves?' I've applied for permission to dig in El Fugón.'

'Wow! Well done!'

Paula grinned . . . and hugged him. 'If we do find Antonio, I want a proper funeral.'

'Of course. He should have the best.'

'Max, do you think Abbot Jorge would conduct the funeral Mass?'

'It's not his patch, but I'm sure he would love to do it.'

'He's been a good friend to you.'

'Yes, he has.'

'Max, I really want to speak at the funeral . . . to tell everyone what happened. We must never let it happen again.'

'That could be a problem with the Archbishop – you know

344

what he's like, a real traditionalist. But I'm sure Jorge can swing something.'

The children, encouraging David to meow for titbits, dominated the meal. In the middle of lunch, Jane turned to Max.

'Did you ever find the walrus?'

'The walrus?'

'You know . . . the man I saw on the road in the rain.'

'On the road?'

'Yes. The day we left to go home to England.'

Max paused. 'No, we never did. But why walrus?'

'Beause he reminded me of the walrus in my book. I've got it here. I'll show you if you like.'

'Yes. I'd like to see it.'

She and Encarnita jumped from their chairs, and ran off to Encarnita's room. They soon returned with the book, an illustrated copy of Lewis Carroll's *The Walrus and the Carpenter*.

Max opened it. 'I still don't see . . .'

'Look, I'll show you,' said Jane. 'The best picture is here – look.' And Jane recited:

> '"The time has come," the Walrus said,
> "To talk of many things:
> Of shoes – and ships – and sealing wax –
> Of cabbages – and kings."'

Max took the book. 'I still—'

'The man I saw looked a bit like the Walrus.'

'The Walrus?'

Jane and Encarnita both laughed, and skipped out of the room giggling. Max was left staring at the Walrus.

At the end of the meal he made his apologies, and left as soon as he could. He had to get back and clean *el cortijo*. He hoped he had clean sheets in the cupboard. Also he needed to think. Had he missed something significant? What was it that Anita had found? Who was the walrus?

345

Chapter 30

Thank God. He did have clean sheets in the cupboard. Not matching, but clean. Max looked at his watch. He had an hour before Anita arrived. A quick wash of the floors, shove the dirty washing in the linen basket, tidy the books and newspapers, then stick the trash in the bin outside the side door. That should do. It only took thirty minutes to finish the tasks. Good. There were two bottles of white wine in the fridge but nothing decent to eat . . . they'd have to go out for a meal. Max looked around. The windows could do with a clean, but he hadn't time now. A few flowers would brighten the place up. He took the secateurs from the drawer and walked up to the top terrace. There were still some yellow roses blooming. He cut a few sprays, and returned to *el cortijo*. No vase. He remembered he had thrown out an empty pickle jar. It should still be in the bin. Jar retrieved, washed, and the label removed, he had a vase. Bedroom or sitting room? Best just put the roses in the sitting room. He looked at his watch again. There was still time for a quick shower.

At exactly six Anita knocked on the door. She was wearing jeans and a pink strappy T-shirt, and was carrying a shoulder bag. Max kissed her warmly on both cheeks. She responded equally warmly.

'I've got a bottle of white Don Darías in the fridge. A glass?' asked Max.

'Love one. My sister is becoming a real pain. Next time I'll just leave her to sort out her own problems.'

'Let's have the drink under the olive tree – it's cool enough now.'

Max took the bottle and two glasses. He gave Anita a bowl of olives to carry to the table under the olive tree. They sat quietly for a minute.

'Cheers,' said Max.

'Cheers,' echoed Anita.

And they clinked their glasses, smiling at each other.

'Okay,' said Max. 'What's the mystery?'

'It's probably not significant . . . but it keeps on going round and round in my head. Remember we agreed to follow up Leila's phone calls? I finally managed to get a copy of her old bills from her mobile phone company – it was a Spanish one, so it took ages for them to fax me copies. I started going through them. Well, there were two calls to a number I recognized from work. I checked my own address book . . . and it's our Teniente González.'

'González? Well?'

'González never said he knew Leila.'

'That's true.'

'I played canny on this one. When we sitting around the station chewing the cud, I casually asked if he had ever met Leila. And he said he had never met her, spoken to her or even knew who she was. What do you make of that?'

'That's interesting. Another glass, Anita?'

'Please. It's lovely here, so peaceful.'

'Yes. It's my favourite spot. So what do you make of it?'

'Don't know. But why should he deny he knew her when I have evidence Leila phoned him twice?'

'Hmm . . . we need to think this through. I'm going to get a biro.'

Max was back in a minute with notebook, biro and a bowl of almonds.

'Right. One, Leila had phoned González, but he says he'd never had any contact with her. You couldn't have got this wrong, Anita ?'

'No way. Unless someone else had borrowed or stolen Gonzo's mobile. Not likely. It's the one he uses for work.'

'Okay. So he must have a reason to hide his contact with Leila. It's not something you'd forget. It's a murder case.'

'Yes. And remember, Max – when I phoned you the day we found the body, it was because we couldn't get hold of González.'

'That's right. Gonzo turned up after we left to tell Ahmed.'

'Can you remember what he said ?'

'Yes. He'd been working on his land, and he can't get a mobile signal there . . .'

'But Gonzo's land is by Felipe's bar, and I've never had a problem with my mobile there.'

Max wrote this down in his notepad. 'Okay. Anything else?'

They looked at each other. Max poured another glass of wine.

'Max . . .' began Anita.

'I don't know, Anita. He'd been drinking that day. I remember that. He stank of booze. And he was crunching mints like a squirrel.'

'To hide the smell of the booze?'

'Probably. And . . .' Max's voice rose in excitement, 'the mints were in silver paper.' He smiled ruefully. 'I'm beginning to think that half of Diva were sucking mints in silver wrapping that day.'

'Okay . . . we jumped to conclusions with Juan, but it's still evidence,' said Anita.

'What else have we got . . . He was on edge that night, wasn't he?'

'Very. But that's pretty standard when he's been drinking. So I didn't think anything of it.'

'What else . . . He really didn't want me around,' said Max.

'But he doesn't like you anyway.'

'True. But when we were reviewing the case, he kept pushing us all to agree it was an accident.'

'Even when it was obvious – even to León – it couldn't have been a simple accident.'

Max put some more points in the notebook.

'Okay, Anita. Could it have been González?'

'What have we got?'

Max looked at his notebook. 'He denies he had any contact with Leila when we can prove he did. We don't know for sure where he was at the time of her death, and immediately after. He had silver-wrapped mints. He had been drinking . . . and we know he has a nasty temper. He pushed the accidental death hypothesis very hard, even though someone had tried to hide the body.'

'And,' added Anita, 'he tried everything to pin it on Hassan.'

'Yes, he did,' said Max. 'But . . . this wouldn't stand up in a court of law. We wouldn't even get an investigating judge to pursue it further. We don't have a motive.'

Max looked at his watch. 'Nearly eight,' he said. 'Let's finish the wine, and then wander down to Felipe's. Hey. That could be useful. That's where Gonzo left his car the night of Leila's death.'

They drank the last of the bottle.

'Whoops, better not have much more. I'd get completely tiddled, and then who knows what might happen,' laughed Anita.

'Just as well you're with a gentleman,' smiled Max.

They walked down the track to the river at the bottom of the valley, turned left and crossed over the bridge to Felipe's bar.

'*Hola*, Anita,' Felipe said, kissing her on both cheeks as they entered, 'Max, nice to see you. We got some really good *choto* in this morning. Cook's got *Choto al Ajillo a la Granadina* nearly ready to serve. You two here on business?' he asked, giving them both a sly look.

'Sort of,' said Max. 'Can you give us a corner table, away from the smoke?'

'Sure. Or you might prefer outside.'

'Yes. Outside would be nice.'

'Follow me.'

He led them to the far corner of the outside terrace, close to a climbing yellow rose.

'It will be all over town, won't it?' said Anita. 'I mean you and me here together . . . and not in uniform.'

'Yes,' replied Max. 'But we'll keep them guessing we're on police business – which we are.'

Felipe returned with the wine list.

'One of your good Riojas,' said Max without looking at the list.

Felipe returned in a minute, uncorked the bottle and poured two generous portions in their glasses.

'No more than one bottle,' said Anita. 'I have to walk back up the track.'

'Don't worry . . . I can always carry you,' laughed Max.

The young goat was a little bony, but the smooth spicy sauce, enriched with wine vinegar and the kid's liver, was, as Felipe claimed, exquisite.

Felipe came over at the end of the meal. 'Everything okay?' he asked.

'Excellent,' replied Max. 'Felipe, do you remember the night the Muslim girl, Leila, was killed?'

'Sure I do. She'd been here the night before when we had a band on. Beautiful girl, and a great dancer as well. It's not often you see one of the Muslim girls dancing away and letting themselves go. You know what that bastard González has done? Ordered me to stop having late night gigs or else he'd shut me down. Claimed some neighbours had complained, but I don't believe that. The miserable sod just doesn't like young folk having a good time.'

Max and Anita looked at each other.

'González left his car here on the Saturday, didn't he?' asked Leila.

'Yes. The fat bastard started drinking midday, and he was as pissed as a fart when I closed at four. I persuaded him not to drive. So he had to walk back to his bungalow. He was furious, but he couldn't have got the key in his ignition. The rain came down after so he would have got soaked. Serves the bastard right.'

'You said bungalow,' said Max. 'You mean his place on the Jola road?'

'Yes. He'd been on his land round the back. Kept muttering it could be worth a fortune unless someone tries to screw him. But he was definitely going back to his place on the Jola road. Needed to sleep it off.'

Max and Anita looked at each other again.

'Do you remember what time he set off?' asked Anita.

'Yes. It was before the rain came down. About ten past four, I'd say . . . I had to give one of the girls a run to the bus stop.'

'Thanks, Felipe,' said Max.

'What's all this about?' asked Felipe. 'You got the bastard who killed the girl, didn't you?'

'Yes,' replied Max. 'Just doing a bit of research on how country bars deal with customers who've come by car and had a bit to drink. Hoped I might have a bit of fun with González. But no chance.'

Anita flushed slightly.

'Felipe, I don't want this getting back to Gonzo . . .'

'*Sin problema*, Max.'

'*Gracias*, Felipe . . . lovely meal.'

Felipe left.

'Gonzo's bungalow is on the far side of the Jola bridge,' mused Anita. 'If he left here at ten past four . . . walking . . . he could easily have been on that bridge at five.'

'"It was five, exactly five in the afternoon."'

'What's that?'

'Oh, nothing. Just a line from Lorca.'

'Lorca?'

'The key thing is . . . González could have been on the bridge at the time of Leila's death.'

'Could have been. But we don't know he was.'

'No, we don't.'

351

'He'd say he was on his land here – which was why he didn't answer his mobile when we were trying to get hold of him.'

'Wait a minute,' said Max. 'The walrus.'

'The what?'

'The walrus of course – "And why the sea is boiling hot." Jane's walrus. Look,' said Max excitedly. He took out the notebook and the biro, and crudely sketched a walrus. 'Encarnita's friend, Jane, said she saw a man who looked like a walrus. Look – this is González with his bald head, droopy moustache and fat belly. See the resemblance?'

'You're right. But I still can't see a judge giving us permission to proceed. All González has to do is stick to his original story. Told Felipe he was going back to his Jola place, then saw it was about to rain, so went to his little hut close by here. The walrus thing wouldn't stand up for a second. I don't expect Jane could pick him out in an ID parade'

'I suppose not,' said Max sadly.

'And where's the motive? There isn't one.'

There was silence.

'Land,' exclaimed Max. 'Of course. Land.'

'I don't get it,' said Anita.

'Land. That's the motive. González was hoping to get his land rezoned. It would be worth a fortune if he got permission to build houses on it. As it stands it's purely agricultural land – he can't even replace his hut with a decent house.'

'Max, I bet this was El Gato's land. Gonzo's grandfather must have got his hands on it after he killed El Gato.'

'It's not worth much now. But with building permission . . .?'

'And Leila must have found out that this land used to belong to El Gato. She went through the land registry for the period with a fine-tooth comb.'

'So Leila would have phoned González to discuss it with him. That's the connection.'

'Right. If Gonzo was getting the land rezoned, he would

352

have been furious with anyone who might have threatened his deal.'

'So maybe he gets a letter from someone on Saturday morning . . . He goes into Felipe's to drown his sorrows. Felipe chucks him out of the bar, and he has to walk home. Runs into Leila on the bridge. They start arguing, and Leila ends up down the ravine. Whether he killed her deliberately or accidentally, we'll never know. But that he killed her, I'm sure.'

'Max . . . that's it. But what do we do? We could end up in real trouble,' said Anita.

'I'll keep you out of it, Anita,' said Max. 'Hell, it's really late. Let's sleep on it.'

'Sleep?'

Max paid. They set off back along the track while bats hunted overhead. Max had forgotten his torch. They missed the turning and had to follow a dry stream to get back to *el cortijo*.

'I desperately need a strong coffee,' said Anita.

'So do I. I'll put the kettle on.'

After the coffee, Anita smiled shyly at Max. 'Where's the bathroom? I'll go and get changed.'

'Over there,' said Max. 'I'll be in the bedroom.'

Max went into his small bedroom, put the pillow up, and lay down on the bed. Anita appeared in the doorway, the light from the living room illuminating her black hair.

'How do I look, Max? Do you like my nightdress?'

'You look gorgeous,' Max said. 'And the nightdress is beautiful. But you'd look even more beautiful without it.'

'Is that an order, sir?' she said.

The nightdress fell to the floor. Anita swayed towards Max.

'Any more orders, sir?'

They both awoke with the chirping of the sparrows.

Max prepared breakfast. He made sure the coffee was strong. Anita was shy, hesitant, not sure what to say. Max kissed her, leaning over the breakfast table.

353

She smiled, and kissed him back. 'We could go back to bed,' she said. 'After all, it is our day off.'

'You're right. It is our day off. We'll discuss the case further after lunch.'

Lunch was a simple affair – tortilla with aspirins. Neither could face more alcohol, so Max opened a litre bottle of cold mineral water.

'What do we do, Max?' asked Anita.

'We check up a few things this afternoon I'll go to the land registry to see if I can find anything on González' land.'

'I can walk to the Jola bridge so we get an accurate timing. I want to pick up a few things from my flat.'

'That would be good. Remember to walk slowly. He was drunk at the time.'

'No problem with that. In this heat there's no choice.'

At five they left. Before Max opened the gates, he gave Anita a lingering kiss. Max got into his car. Anita grimaced, and began to walk.

'I'll phone you later,' Max called as he waved goodbye. He drove straight to the town hall, managed to find a parking space in one of the side streets, and went down the stairs to the land registry. He requested to see *el cadastro*, the land ownership map, and then asked the filing clerk to bring him *la escritura*, the title deeds of González' plot. He skimmed back through the various owners – Gonzo, Gonzo's dad, Gonzo's grandfather . . . Capitán Vicente González . . . and then to . . .? Yes. Manuel Paz. It had belonged to El Gato. He looked at the date of change of ownership: 1947. There was a small note in the margin: 'Due to the lack of claimants by any of the deceased's family, this land has been given to Capitán Vicente González in recognition of his services to the state.' Max looked at the official stamp and signature – it was that of the grandfather of a right-wing notary family in the town.

That can't be legal, he thought. I bet they didn't put any notices in *el BOE*, the *Official State Bulletin*, or make any effort to contact El Gato's next of kin.

354

He returned *la escritura* to the filing clerk, and left. Best not be seen by González – the police building was not far from the town hall. He got in his car, and drove out to *el Camping*, ordered a beer, and sat on the terrace. He needed time to think. He was on his second beer when his mobile rang.

'Max, it's Anita. I walked slowly. He definitely could have been on the bridge. Any luck your end?'

Max explained about the title deeds.

'It's beginning to look like him,' said Anita.

'Anita,' said Max, 'I think I have to go right to the top on this one. I'll go straight to Bonila, and give him a report. I won't mention you. I also think it's best if we don't see each other until it's over.'

'Oh,' said Anita, 'I was looking forward to seeing you tonight.'

'Best not, love. I don't trust González.'

'Okay. If you think it best.'

'I'll give you a ring as soon as I'm in Granada. Big hug.'

'Big hug to you, Max.'

Max looked at his watch. Best drive over to Granada now. The drive down to Granada was relatively traffic-free. He drove round to the Albayzín car park, left his car in his allotted space, and walked down to his flat. He made himself a quick tuna salad, phoned Anita, watched some TV and went to bed early. He slept badly. How would Bonila react? He really should go to his boss, Davila, first, but Davila would certainly hum and haw, say leave it with me and do nothing.

The next morning Max went to his office, and rang Bonila's secretary to ask for an appointment. Surprisingly Bonila was free in half an hour.

'Come in,' Bonila called out when Max knocked on his door. 'Max . . . good to see you. What can I do for you?'

Max explained, his voice faltering at times. Bonila sat upright in his chair, his face stony.

Max concluded, 'I think the circumstantial evidence is very strong, sir. But I was unsure how I should continue.'

355

'Continue?' said Bonila. 'Continue on what?'

'On the case, sir.'

'What case? I see no case. The case was archived, and closed satisfactorily.'

'But this new evidence, sir?'

'I see no evidence. I see a lot of unfounded suppositions, some wild speculation, and the impugning of a good officer's reputation. It could cost you your job, you know. I think you've let a little bit of fame affect your judgement. I'm most disappointed in you, Max. I've had my doubts about your reliability, and this nonsense confirms my doubts. Moreover, you have gone behind the back of your commanding officer. You know the rules. You should have reported to him first. However, given your recent good record, I'll pretend that this conversation never happened. Do you understand me?'

'But, sir—'

'Romero, any attempt to pursue this further will be treated with the utmost seriousness. Do I make myself clear?'

'Yes, sir,' said Max. He saluted, and left the office. He needed to phone Anita. When he spoke to her, he felt like crying, but managed to hold back any tears.

'I feared this would happen,' said Anita. 'After all, it is the cops. There's nothing in it for them.'

'There is such a thing as justice,' said Max.

'Justice,' laughed Anita sardonically. 'That's only for crime novels. What are you going to do?'

'I don't know. I don't know.'

'When can I see you again, Max?'

'Not just now, but soon. I'm missing you.'

'Me too, Max. A big hug.'

'Gracias, Anita. I need it.'

Max went back inside the police station, sat at his desk, and furiously began to fill in all the forms he had left lying on his desk. He went through the motions of being a policeman for the rest of the week. But all his actions were robotic, without feeling. He phoned Anita every evening, and sometimes they talked for over an hour. He thought of phoning

Jorge, but decided it was time he grew up and solved this one for himself. He had to work Saturday, so he was unable to leave for Diva until Sunday morning. Before setting off, he phoned Ahmed. He hadn't seen Ahmed since the terrorist attack. They arranged to meet early on Sunday evening.

Chapter 31

Podrán matar al gallo que anuncia el alba,
Pero no pueden impedir que cada día el alba surja de nuevo.

They could kill the cockerel that announces the dawn
But they cannot stop the sun from rising every day.

Inscription on a memorial to Manuel Gómez Poyato,
executed outside Granada on 5th September 1936

The Sunday family meal went well. Paula and Isabel were still getting on. And Juan was still being faithful to Isabel. Max doubted it would last – Juan had a roving eye. But Isabel had learnt to live with that. Jane was over for lunch again.

At the end of the meal, Max said, 'I promised Ahmed I would call round and see him.'

'That's useful,' said Paula. 'We promised Jane's mother we'd run her home. Leonardo . . . you help Isabel with the dishes. It's time you helped out. Boys have got to learn to cope in kitchens.'

'Can I come with you?' said Encarnación.

'I could do with a run in the car myself. Why don't we all go? Encarnita and I can have an ice cream while you see Ahmed,' said Paula.

'Okay,' said Max. 'Bit harsh on Leonardo.'

'We'll bring him back some ice cream.'

Max dropped Jane off at her house, left Paula and Encarnita at la Heladería, before stopping at Ahmed's.

They embraced cordially.

'Max. Good to see you. I saw you and your cousin Juan on the television . . . Are you well?'

'Yes, thank you . . . and I read your article about the shootings. It was very perceptive.'

'It's all to do with politics, isn't it? Religion has become a part of the political struggle. Without a just political solution we'll see a lot more deaths, and Israel and America will keep bombing even more innocent civilians. What's the word they use – yes, collateral damage.'

'I agree. I don't see an end in sight.'

They talked about world events, the elections in Spain. Max told Ahmed about his last conversation with Javeed.

'So we still don't know who killed Leila then.' Ahmed bowed his head, and let the tears trickle down his cheeks. 'Allah . . . I've thought about Juan, Max. I'd be grateful if you drew a veil over Juan's relationship with Leila. It would only harm his family. It's over now. However, I would like to see Juan when he has a few minutes.'

'I'm sure he'd be pleased to talk to you.'

'I would like a memorial dedicated to Leila. She loved history, but her great passion was to be a novelist. Perhaps you and I could think of some way we might be able to encourage young Muslim writers. We don't have enough of them in the West.'

'Perhaps Juan could help you set up a scholarship of some sort.'

'I think Leila would have liked that.'

'We'll do something really good. Ahmed, you asked me to try and find the truth. I think I may have found it.'

Max then told Ahmed about all the evidence against González. Ahmed listened silently, his head bowed. When Max finished, Ahmed said, 'And what are you going to do with all that evidence, Max?'

Max then explained about his report to Bonila, and Bonila's response.

'The problem is . . . I don't think what I've got would

359

stand up in a court of law. I'm not even sure an investigating judge would let it get that far.'

'I see,' said Ahmed. 'That is a problem. But perhaps Allah's justice is already working.'

'Allah's justice?'

'Yes. It was in the paper on Friday. The autononous regional government, La Junta de Andalucia, is sending an official from Seville to investigate illegal building and illegal building permits in Diva, and has frozen all building permits until they get the situation under control.'

'Gosh.'

'Did you not say that Teniente González was expecting permission to sell his land with building consent? And was convinced he'd get it?'

'Yes.'

'Then Allah, I'm sure, will find a way to stop that. Allah's justice is wiser and more fitting than that of us mortals.'

Max paused, 'Perhaps I can be of some little assistance to Allah. I have a friend in La Junta, in the planning department. We were at Glasgow together for a while when he was doing a Master's in Planning. Let me give him a ring, and perhaps we may be able to come up with some justice.'

'Allah's ways are a mystery to man. But He always favours justice. So I am sure He will find a way.'

Max went outside and phoned his friend. After ten minutes he returned, a broad smile on his face.

'Allah's ways are indeed a mystery. But I'm sure justice will now be done. A surprise – it is my friend who is coming to Diva to sort out the scandals. We are meeting for lunch in Granada on Wednesday. My friend is a good man. He will take a particular interest in any planned rezoning of Teniente González' land. Also, I will ask Paula to contact Beatrice, el Gato's daughter. There is a good chance that she will be able to claim her father's lands.'

'That would be very fair,' replied Ahmed. 'Max, I was

going up to visit the graves. It's cooler now. I'd be honoured if you could accompany me.'

'Certainly,' said Max.

Together they climbed up to the back of town, past the little round church, the scene of so many religious conflicts, to the small plot of land with the two new graves, marked only by plain headstones.

'I will go and pray,' said Ahmed. He went to the graves, and bent his head in prayer.

Max breathed in deeply, and turned to watch the rays of the evening sun illuminate the stark beauty of the parched hillside, the silvery green olive trees contrasting with the golden brown earth. He turned back to the graves, and walked to stand beside Ahmed. Max didn't feel it was right for him to pray. Together, he and Ahmed walked back down in silence. At the bottom Ahmed turned to Max. 'Thank you, Max. I appreciate it. Ultimately, Max, *La galib ily Alah*, There is no victor but God. *Inshallah*.'

'*Inshallah*, Ahmed.'

They embraced and parted. Max phoned Anita – she would come over this evening to *el cortijo*. Max fetched Paula and Encarnita from la Heladería.

As they drove home, Encarnita suddenly said, '*Tito* Max, do you remember that play we saw?'

'*Blood Wedding*?'

'Yes. Do you remember that lady singing over the baby?

> "Sleep little rose,
> The horse is weeping."'

'Yes?'

'But horses don't cry, do they?'

'No,' said Max. 'It's poetry, using words to express emotions.'

'But if it's not true, why say it?'

'Ah. That's because our lives are stories, and we act as if those stories are true. But the truth means different things to

361

different people. So we never know which story is true. And some stories are better than others.'

'But how do you know which one is better, *Tito* Max? Which one?'

'The one which deep down inside you feel is right.'

THE END

Acknowledgements

We would like to thank our friends and relations who kindly agreed to act as a peer review group, and provided us with insights and advice, particularly Margaret Brooke, a wise and perceptive reader of detective fiction who read the first complete draft, and told us that we had pinned the murder on the wrong person. We did another draft. We spent happy hours discussing the plot with Chin and Lin Li, Chris Greensmith and Shonah McKechnie. Many thanks for all the suggestions. Very special thanks to Shonah, who had saved that crucial April 2007 draft when we managed to overwrite all our own copies of it. Jan Fairley, a former Director of the Edinburgh Book Festival, and Ewan Wilson of Waterstone's bookshop in Glasgow confirmed our hope that our manuscript was of publishable quality.

Many thanks to Krystyna Green of Constable & Robinson, who picked out the book from a pile of unsolicited manuscripts, and to Jacqueline Anne Taylor of the Language Clinic, Granada, for her painstaking final checks of the manuscript, which have both added accurate local colour and spared our blushes by weeding out mistakes. Any remaining errors are, of course, our responsibility.

We would also like to thank Val McDermid and Frederic Lindsay for a fun and instructive Arvon Foundation course at Moniack Mhor; Elizabeth Reeder, a truly inspiring teacher, and the members of her Strathclyde University Creative Writing Groups who put up with some awful earlier versions; and also Louise Welsh, Zoë Strachan and the members of the Glasgow University Creative Writing Group for early inspiration, and convincing Phil he could actually write fiction.

We are grateful to members of the Policia Nacional in Granada and the Guardia Civil in Orgiva for their advice and information on the operations of the Spanish police, and to Paco Martinez, a future judge, for his advice on Spanish judicial procedures. Our fictional police here bear very little resemblance to the real forces, which would never have employed Max Romero in the first place.